THE FINAL CRUMPET

THE FINAL CRUMPET

BY RON AND JANET BENREY

BARBOUR
PUBLISHING

The author is represented by Joyce Hart, Hartline Marketing, 123 Queenston Drive, Pittsburgh, Pennsylvania 15235.

Our mission is to publish and distribute inspirational products offering exceptional value and biblical encouragement to the masses.

ecpa Member of the
Evangelical Christian
Publishers Association

Printed in the United States of America.
5 4 3 2 1

ONE

The roaring clatter made by the earthmover astonished Nigel Owen. The "mini excavator"—a compact tractor equipped with a crablike digging arm—sounded as loud as a bulldozer inside the enclosed confines of the tea garden. Nigel felt the need to clamp his hands over his ears, but his left arm was stalwartly enfolding Flick Adams's shoulders, and she had tightly gripped his right hand between both of hers.

"I can't bear to watch this," she shouted, as the small machine began to roll along the garden's serpentine redbrick path. "I'm having second thoughts about tearing out our Assam tea plants. It's hardly fair to chop them down just because they didn't grow to full height."

Nigel didn't feel much sympathy for the two scraggly evergreen shrubs planted in the Indian Tea area of the garden, but Flick clearly did. He bent close to her ear. "Those Assams have led long and happy lives. If they could talk, they would applaud your decision to uproot them."

"Then why do I feel like a vandal?"

"Because you have focused too closely on the fate of two individual plants. Think of the big picture. We have twenty-two tea bushes in this garden. Replacing ten percent of them represents prudent husbandry of the museum's precious resources."

"Okay, so maybe I'm not a vandal. But what do you call a person who destroys history? Our predecessors planted those Assams decades ago."

"Yes, they did—for the specific purpose of educating visitors to the Royal Tunbridge Wells Tea Museum. However, these particular tea plants routinely *confuse* our current day visitors. As you have repeatedly explained to me, there are three major varieties of tea plants grown throughout the world: the *China*, the *Assam*, and the *Indo-China*. The Assam is supposed to be the tallest of the three; consequently the founders planted only two of them. But our Assams look more like bonsai miniatures. You sensibly chose to replant this corner of the tea garden with new Assam seedlings." He gave her shoulders a reassuring squeeze. "As the newly appointed managing director of the museum, I hereby certify that you are doing a wise and proper thing."

"You may be right, but you may also be wrong. While it's perfectly true that a healthy Assam plant can soar to more than sixty feet, tea growers routinely prune them back to a height of four or five feet for convenient picking of tea leaves. Our stunted bushes are really quite realistic."

Nigel squeezed Flick's shoulders again and fought the urge to laugh. How could Felicity Adams, PhD, who knew *everything* about tea, think of any tea plant growing in Kent, England—tall, short, or in-between—as being "realistic"?

The very existence of this tea garden was a tribute to the extraordinary lack of realism exercised by the museum's founders some forty-one years ago. They began by surrounding a fifth of an acre of land on the eastern corner of the museum building with a twelve-foot-high brick wall to block out chill breezes. Then they ordered a grid of iron pipes buried three feet below the surface. Two powerful pumps circulated heated water through the subterranean plumbing by day and by night, to keep the Kentish soil, and the sheltered garden itself, balmy enough to raise tropical tea plants.

Nigel gazed up at the ugly gray sky and decided that this very day provided a fine illustration of the founder's accomplishments. Outside the garden, one had to endure an icy Friday morning in mid-January, but inside the wall, one could relish springlike surroundings. He and Flick had both left their cumbersome winter trench coats upstairs, in their respective offices.

Of course, if one thought about it, there was a touch of the implausible about the whole of the Royal Tunbridge Wells Tea Museum. There it stood on Eridge Road: an imposing, four-story, Georgian-style building dedicated to the many different aspects of tea. The history of tea, the geography of tea, the economics of tea, the cultivation of tea, the processing of tea, the blending of tea, the tasting of tea, the serving of tea, the food that accompanies tea—if a topic had something to do with tea, one could probably find a relevant exhibit in the museum's galleries, library, meeting rooms, garden, or laboratories. How could sensible Brits give over such a significant institution to the veneration of a mere beverage?

Don't forget the most improbable thing of all. The transformation of his own life. He had come to Tunbridge Wells ten months earlier as the museum's acting director, a one-year-long temporary position intended to tide him over between "real" jobs. He had had every intention of returning to London, no desire at all to make a sea change in his career. And not the least notion of falling in love with the chief curator.

That had happened the previous October during a remarkable chain of events that even now seemed inexplicable. What magic had transformed a woman he disliked into a woman he loved—a woman who loved him back? And how did one explain the two bizarre side effects? Managing a tea museum abruptly seemed an utterly logical job for him, and *Royal* Tunbridge Wells—Nigel had grown fond of the prefix bestowed on the small city south of London by King Edward VII in 1909—had begun to feel like home. And so, against all odds, Nigel Owen—a lifelong Londoner, a financial whiz trained to lead major corporations with thousands of employees, a man who didn't even like tea—had gleefully accepted the trustees' invitation to become the museum's managing director.

The mini excavator's diesel engine roared even louder as it approached its prey. Nigel looked across the garden and saw Jim Sizer, an enormous smile on his bearded face, wave happily at him from the driver's seat of the rented machine. Jim, who admitted to being seventy but was undoubtedly older, served as the museum's jack-of-all-trades utility person. He had once again lived up to his reputation as a problem-solving genius by figuring out how to get the mini excavator into the tea garden. For all their ingenuity, the founders had not thought to provide a door through the brick wall. Jim had taken ten different measurements and calculated there was just enough clearance to wheel the pint-sized earthmover through the aisles of the museum's greenhouse.

Jim steered the mini excavator in line with the pair of Assam tea plants and pushed a lever that activated the hydraulically powered digging arm.

Flick shouted above the noise, "This is like witnessing an execution!"

Nigel moved behind Flick and wrapped his arms around her. "This garden party was your idea. If you don't stop shifting your mental position like the pendulum in a clock, I shall change your nickname to Tick."

She looked up at him and smiled. "You wouldn't dare."

"I'd have centuries of tradition on my side. Ask your Anglophile parents back in York, Pennsylvania—Tick and Flick are both acceptable short forms of Felicity."

Jim revved the diesel again.

"We can postpone this," she said hurriedly. "We don't have to rip out the Assam plants today."

"Need I remind you that our two-week shutdown is about to come to an end. We plan to reopen on Monday; Jim Sizer will need all of Saturday to get the restored tea garden ready for visitors."

"You're assuming that the *vultures* will finish this afternoon."

"The *appraisers* will be finished by noon—as you well know."

Nigel thought of the two teams of professional antiquities valuers—twelve experts in all—who had worked their way from floor to floor in the museum. They were a lean, sallow-faced crowd who did resemble a flock of vultures. The recent death of Dame Elspeth Hawker made it necessary for the museum to purchase the many antiquities on display that were owned by the Hawker family. The first step of the process was to value the thousands of paintings, books, maps, woodwork, and pieces of crockery that served tea, praised tea, honored tea, celebrated tea, and explained its long history. One appraisal team was hired by the Hawker family, the other by the museum; their respective findings would be averaged to establish the collection's value.

"Yikes!" Flick cried as the toothed bucket on the end of the arm tore a tea bush out of the ground. Nigel felt her shudder.

"Steady on, Dr. Adams." Nigel tightened his hug. "The worst is almost over."

Jim Sizer made a dozen more careful swipes with the bucket to knock down the other Assam tea plant and scrape away enough top soil to make a trench about seven feet long, three feet wide, and two feet deep. He finished by maneuvering the excavator close to the back wall and killing the engine.

"I finally understand the true meaning of 'blessed silence,' " Nigel said.

"What happens now?" Flick asked.

"I believe that Jim takes over with a shovel." Nigel looked over his shoulder. "Isn't that right, Conan?"

"Quite right, sir," said Conan Davies, the museum's over-sized chief of security, who today was also acting as excavation supervisor. Nigel noted that the big man was smiling; the museum's staff seemed to approve of the blossoming relationship between their director and chief curator.

Will the trustees feel differently? One of these days, we'll have to find out.

Conan went on in his gravelly voice. "We can't risk damaging the heating pipes. Jim helped to install them forty years ago. He knows the layout better than anyone else alive does. He'll dig slowly and carefully around the pipes to prepare the bed for the new tea plants." Conan cocked his head toward a flat of seedlings sitting on a table.

Nigel studied the foot-high replacement plants. They had arrived the day before on a flight from India, the gift of a tea estate in Kerala, a renowned tea-growing region in southern India. The seedlings had begun life as cuttings from established Assam plants. Flick had told him that mature tea plants were almost impossible to transplant successfully because their long taproots rarely survived the shock of a move. He and Flick had thought about cultivating cuttings in the museum's greenhouse, but she decided to make a wholly new beginning for the Assam tea plants, starting over with imported seedlings that had a proven pedigree.

Flick unwound from his embrace. She moved closer to the trench, studied it intently from a distance, and then crouched down to dribble handfuls of loose soil through her fingers. Nigel chuckled to himself. The tea tree–loving softy had given way to the hard-nosed scientist with impeccable academic and industry credentials. Her encyclopedic knowledge of tea spanned the entire life cycle—from growing tea plants, to processing and blending leaves, to brewing a good *cuppa*, to preparing and serving a classic English afternoon tea. In short, a surfeit of skills for someone only thirty-six years old. Flick had so impressed the museum's trustees that they took the radical step of appointing an American as chief curator of England's leading tea museum.

Nigel remembered his initial meeting with Flick when she came on board the previous summer—and winced. He had deemed her pompous, arrogant, dreary, and much too good-looking to be an effective curator. It had boggled his mind that a stunning brunette with big brown eyes could also be a serious scientist.

So much for the perspicacity of your first impressions—and your deep understanding of women.

"The soil feels and looks healthy," Flick said. "I wish I knew why our Assams didn't thrive."

"Well, ma'am," Conan said, "one of our security guards set up a modest betting pool that has generated many different suggestions as to the exact cause of the stunted plants. One thought is bad soil in this corner of the garden. Another is a leaky uncharted gas pipe somewhere beneath the bed. My belief is that we'll find a layer of construction rubble further down that prevented the plants' roots from reaching the proper depth. We're really quite close to the building proper; the workmen may have inadvertently buried a stack of unused bricks."

"My money is on moles," Nigel said. "I think the little blighters built a subterranean city and ate the roots as fast as the plants sent them out." He extended his hand and pulled Flick to her feet when Jim Sizer arrived with his shovel.

Nigel took a step backward to make room for the clods of earth that Jim removed from the trench at shockingly high speed. Doing all manner of odd jobs at the museum had kept the lanky septuagenarian in such vigorous shape that he steadfastly refused to retire.

"I should be so healthy at his age," Nigel murmured. In February he would be thirty-nine, a painful milestone he found difficult to contemplate.

A deep *thunk* from the trench interrupted his reverie.

"What did you hit?" Flick asked.

"Not sure, ma'am." Jim poked about with the shovel. "It may be that Mr. Davies thought right. It could be a layer of rubble, except. . ."

"Except what?"

"It's not rubble," Jim said excitedly. "This is a roof slate. Someone laid a layer of roofing tiles about three feet down."

"Well, now we know what blocked root growth."

Nigel watched Jim lever two slates loose with the tip of the shovel. He lifted them out of the way.

"Why would someone bury roofing tiles?" Nigel asked. No one answered him; Flick, Conan, and Jim had directed their complete attention to the trench.

"Do you see anything below the tiles?" Flick asked.

"Only one way to find out." Jim thrust the shovel into the earth—and immediately brought forth an ominous crunching noise.

"Blast!" Conan said. "I hope that wasn't a heating pipe."

"Oh no, sir. They go clang when you bang 'em. I can see some sort of green plastic sheeting, perhaps a tarpaulin. Whatever is there is beginning to crumble."

Nigel leaned over to look into the trench. "What do you make of that yellowish object?"

Jim used the tip of his shovel to draw back the plastic sheeting. Nigel at once recognized a discolored skull and several human bones.

Jim made a throaty moan. "Blimey! It's a skeleton!"

Nigel might have fallen face first into the trench if Conan had not grabbed his belt and tugged him away from the edge.

Flick perched against the edge of the windowsill and said, "I feel it in my bones. I don't care if you laugh at me for saying that." When she peered at Nigel, she didn't see any laughter—merely an indifferent shrug.

A few moments later, he finally spoke. "More than one detective inspector serves in Kent Police's Major Crime Unit. It's hardly likely that the plods will dispatch the only investigator in the county who has had the opportunity to yell at you."

"Want to bet?"

"Not especially." Nigel was sitting behind his desk, tilted as far backwards as his swivel chair would allow.

"Come on. You're always game for a wager. How about dinner tonight, at Thackeray's on London Road. If I'm right, you pay. . . . If you're right, I pay."

"Okay—if that's what you want to do."

"Make reservations."

He rocked forward in his chair and reached for his telephone, but stopped in midstretch. "Shouldn't we first arrange for a sitter for Cha-Cha?"

Flick looked across Nigel's office in time to see a pair of pointy ears perk up. The smiling mouth below them emitted a yodel-like yip. Cha-Cha had raised his head at the sound of his name, although the rest of him lay sprawled along the sofa, a piece of furniture he now considered his own.

Cha-Cha, a Shiba Inu, an ancient breed of dog from Japan, was compact and foxlike, with a heavy reddish coat and white puffy cheeks. He had become a ward of the museum upon the death of Elspeth Hawker. He spent alternate nights in Nigel's flat on Lime Hill Road, near the Royal Tunbridge Wells' town center, and Flick's apartment on the Pantiles' Lower Walk, opposite the three-hundred-year-old colonnaded walkway that was one of the Wells' leading attractions.

"I have custody of the hound tonight," Flick said. "We'll drop him off at my flat; it's on our way to Thackeray's."

"That's true."

"And you can withdraw the necessary funds to pay for dinner from the cash machine in the Pantiles."

Nigel sighed. "I adore scintillating small talk, my dear, and I appreciate your valiant attempts to amuse me in times of trouble; but when do we tackle the elephant standing in the corner of the room?"

Flick rolled to her feet. Nigel's melancholy mood had begun when Jim Sizer unearthed the skeleton and had grown worse as they waited in his office for the police to arrive. His enthusiastic "hail fellow, well met" demeanor had vanished, and his usually ruddy complexion looked strangely colorless compared to his reddish-blond hair. Even his tall, slender build seemed to have compressed several inches.

Let's find out what's bothering the poor dear.

"What would you like me to say, Nigel?" Flick asked. "We don't have enough information to discuss the corpse in the tea garden. For all we know, he—or she—is a two thousand-year-old Roman expatriate."

"Another nice try, but the Romans didn't wear green

plastic togas, nor did they bury their dead under modern slate roofing tiles."

She smiled. "Not to mention the bothersome detail that our tea garden, which was completely excavated when the museum was built, is inaccessible to the outside world."

"Ergo. . ."

"*Therefore*, someone who had access to the museum buried the body."

"Someone who had *after-hours* access."

"I agree," she said. "It couldn't have been a visitor. It had to be a member of the staff."

"And why would a member of the staff find himself with the embarrassing need to dispose of a corpse?"

"Probably because he or she committed murder."

"Aha!" Nigel shook his head dejectedly. "In less than two weeks, I am supposed to sign the paperwork for a thirty-two-million-pound loan to purchase the Hawker collection. The very last thing the museum needs right now is *another* well-publicized scandal casting one of us as a murderer. Imagine the tasteless reports on TV. Picture the lurid tabloid headlines. I can see our beautifully orchestrated financing deal going south." He flung his hands into the air. "*Ka-blooey!*"

Flick understood Nigel's concerns. "I've also been pondering the effects of nationwide publicity," she said.

"I hope your ruminations are more cheerful than mine."

"For starters, the murderer is not a recent 'one of us.' He can't be. A buried body needs time to decompose and leave a clean skeleton."

"Spare me the details. You enjoy forensics—I don't." After his grimace faded, he asked, "How much time?"

"At least a decade in the kind of soil we have. But because the body was wrapped in plastic, I'd say much longer."

"The museum building was completed in 1964, the garden early in 1965. Could the body have been buried that long ago?"

Flick moved behind the desk and sat on Nigel's lap. "Yep!" She pecked his cheek.

"An old grave. An old body. An ancient murder. . ."

"A murderer who probably died years ago." She kissed his cheek.

"The police will investigate. . ."

"Certainly. And reporters will write speculative stories about the corpse in our garden. And if the remains are ever identified, TV news readers will be photographed standing in front of the museum." She kissed Nigel's ear. "But we won't have a scandal."

"No fat, juicy scandal?"

"Not even a skinny, dry one." She nuzzled his neck.

"I feel better now."

"Thank goodness! You're challenging when you're gloomy. I've almost run out of feminine wiles."

Flick heard a vigorous rap on the door but couldn't react quickly enough. She was still sitting on Nigel's lap when the door swung open.

"My stars!" Conan said. "You two do get up to the strangest things. In any event, the police have arrived." He added, "A pair of old friends, in fact. Detective Inspector Marc Pennyman and Detective Constable Sally Kerr."

"I refuse to believe it!" Nigel said with a mock scowl.

"Make reservations and get money," Flick said, merrily.

"You now owe me dinner."

Nigel reached for his telephone again. Flick moved to the corner window that overlooked the tea garden and felt the usual ripple of jealousy. Her office—a mirror image of Nigel's on the other side of the top floor—delivered a magnificent view of the public car park. Flick recognized Pennyman immediately: trim, late thirties, almost bald. He was peering into the trench. Kerr stood next to him: angular, late twenties, closely cropped ash-blond hair.

"When does he want to see us?" Flick asked Conan.

"I asked. He said there's no need to disturb you now. He'll meet with you after the crime-scene examiners finish their work. He also wants to interview Jim Sizer."

"How is the plod's disposition?" Nigel said.

"Jaunty, I'd say. He looked at the remains and made a joke about this being an unusually cold case. He seems excited—like the proverbial lad in the sweet shop. Nothing like an unexplained skeleton to start one's day."

"See!" Nigel said brightly to Flick. "You're overreacting to the good DI Pennyman. He has undoubtedly forgiven all your past sins."

Flick bit her tongue. The cheerful Nigel was back—in full bloom. Now it was her turn to be dismal.

The morning passed with Nigel working on a planning document, while Flick watched the team of three crime-scene examiners attack the trench from all sides with their cameras, scraping tools, and evidence collection kits. Had the tea garden been a public location, the police would have erected a canvas screen around the "crime scene." The twelve-foot-high brick wall surrounding the garden made the screen unnecessary, leaving Flick with a bird's-eye view of the proceedings. She retrieved a pair of binoculars from the curators' laboratory and observed the examiners' painstaking efforts.

That might have been me at work.

Flick mused about the seven different courses in forensic chemistry and forensic toxicology she had taken back at the University of Michigan, when she thought seriously of becoming a scientific detective. Down below, one of the examiners begin lifting bones out of the plastic tarpaulin. Flick turned away. That was the part of the job she found difficult to handle. Her professor had been right when he blamed her squeamishness on a too-lively imagination. To be a successful crime-scene examiner, you had to mentally disconnect yourself from the painful fact that you were handling parts of a real person who had been alive before becoming a victim.

You're happier as a tea-tasting food chemist.

"Speaking of food," she murmured, "it's almost lunchtime."

"I heard that!" Nigel said from his desk. "If I have to buy you dinner, it seems only fair that you pay for lunch. When are we leaving?"

"I would have said immediately, but. . ." Flick adjusted her binoculars to full power. "Something's happening in the garden. A small crowd just formed around the trench. The skeleton and the tarp are gone, but I can see one crime-scene examiner crouched down in the hole Jim dug. Pennyman, Kerr, and the other examiners are watching her work. So are Conan Davies, Jim Sizer, and a couple of people I don't know."

"Keep it to yourself if the police just discovered another skeleton."

Flick wished that DC Kerr in particular would stand still.

Her side-to-side jockeying repeatedly blocked the view. Kerr abruptly zigged to the right, giving Flick a clear look into the trench. The crime-scene examiner was brushing dirt off a small, boxlike object.

"Boxlike, my foot!" Flick spun around. "Nigel, they found a box buried in the trench, obviously below the skeleton."

"What sort of box?"

"All I can tell from up here is that it looks rusty. Let's go to lunch via the crime scene."

Flick, with Nigel close behind, raced down the three flights of stairs to the ground floor and jogged through the World of Tea Map Room and the Duchess of Bedford Tearoom. She slowed to a walk in the greenhouse and tiptoed into the tea garden. She moved silently behind DI Pennyman, who was supporting a small pistol in midair with a ballpoint pen passed through the weapon's trigger guard.

"I've never seen a handgun like this before. Does anyone have an idea what it is?"

"I do, Inspector," Conan said. "I believe it's a Makarov automatic—the Soviet service pistol during the Cold War."

"A *Bolshie* pistol? What else is in the bloomin' box?"

Flick risked a quick glance around Pennyman and needed every smidgen of self-control she possessed to remain silent. The "bloomin' box" in question, sitting on the edge of the trench, had hundreds of brothers in the museum's basement archives. It was an antiquities storage box, made of thick steel with a heavy rubber seal under its lid, designed to provide safe, long-term protection for valuable objects not on display in the museum's galleries. The crime-scene examiner was carefully probing around inside. Jim Sizer had also recognized the box;

he was gawking at it with Frisbee-sized eyes.

Flick moved back behind Pennyman's muscular frame. It seemed safer to listen than watch.

"I can see one brass cartridge case," the examiner said, "which makes one wonder if you are holding the weapon that killed the victim. The splintered rib I found is consistent with a gunshot wound."

"No need to evaluate the evidence, Whitson," Pennyman said. "Your job today is to collect it."

"Yes, sir. The other items in the box are all of a personal nature. Eyeglasses. Wristwatch. Handkerchief. House keys. Cigarette lighter. Box of cigarettes. Fountain pen. Memo pad. And a rather elegant leather wallet—hang on. Yes, I can open it with no trouble. No credit cards. Several old English banknotes—the sort that were replaced years ago. And—hang on—a driving license that expired in 1968. *Crikey!*"

"What do you find worthy of such an exclamation, Whitson?"

"Uhh. . ." She went on, "Uhh. . ."

"We're waiting, Whitson."

"Sir, this driving license belongs to Etienne Makepeace."

Flick saw Pennyman's spine stiffen as if he'd been shocked by a stun gun. Someone said, "Wicked!" Jim Sizer said, "Streuth!" Conan Davies said, "Unbelievable!"

"Ladies and gentlemen. . ." Pennyman's voice sounded throaty. "This is now a secure investigation. All requests for information will be filtered through me."

"It may be too late, sir," Kerr said. "There was a reporter here from the *Kent and Sussex Courier*." She pointed at a heavyset man running at full speed out of the tea garden.

"You *let* a reporter look around?"

"A body buried in a garden is, well. . .*not*. . .I mean, he has reported on several routine criminal investigations and has always been perfectly well behaved. So when he arrived and asked to see the crime scene, I thought. . ."

Pennyman made an unhappy gesture. "This was supposed to be a routine case. A quiet case. An *easy* case." He pulled a mobile phone out of his jacket pocket. "I'll be back after I share our good news with the chief constable."

Flick waited for the DI to take refuge in a far corner of the tea garden; then she asked Nigel, "Who is Etienne Makepeace?"

Once again, his face looked ashen. "A well-known Brit who disappeared decades ago. Think of Judge Crater, Jimmy Hoffa, and Amelia Earhart—all wrapped in one. Makepeace vanished without a trace, in. . ."

Conan took over. "In 1966. I was only five years old, but I still remember the fuss in Scotland. Thousands of policemen across the United Kingdom searched for him."

"What was his claim to fame?" Flick asked.

"He was a BBC radio personality," Nigel said.

"And also an author and philanthropist," Conan added.

Jim chimed in. "Don't forget that Mr. Makepeace was also known as 'The Tea Sage.' He visited the tea museum several times."

"*This* museum!" Nigel howled.

"Oh yes, sir. I heard him lecture in the Grand Hall on two occasions. Very knowledgeable he was about tea." Jim chortled. "Imagine me digging up his bloomin' body." He leaned close to Flick. "And imagine the coppers finding an antiquities box full of Mr. Makepeace's clobber."

Flick met Nigel's eyes. She knew exactly what he was thinking.

Imagine the tasteless reports on TV. Picture the lurid tabloid headlines. He had been right; she had been abysmally wrong.

A mobile phone rang. "It's mine," Conan said.

He listened for a moment, then said to Nigel, "I didn't think it would happen so quickly, but an outside-broadcast van just pulled into the staff car park."

Nigel translated for Flick. "A mobile TV production studio. The first of the TV news teams has arrived." He added with a smile, "The reappearance of Etienne Makepeace seems to be a topic of some interest to the media."

Flick nodded vaguely, waiting for Nigel to say I told you so, and wondering what could be worse than a "juicy scandal." "We'll soon find out," she said to no one in particular.

TWO

"Good heavens—Stuart has torn the place apart," Nigel muttered when he saw the carnage in the Duchess of Bedford Tearoom. Stuart Battlebridge's crew had stacked the sixteen square tea tables against one wall of the museum's ground floor restaurant and arranged the sixty-four dining chairs "theatre style" in eight even rows in front of a podium that stood atop a newly installed raised platform. They had also brought in an ugly bank of floodlights that seemed bright enough to illuminate the Royal Tunbridge Wells Common.

I'll skin the man alive.

Nigel's twinge of annoyance quickly changed to a pang of remorse when he remembered that he had personally authorized the transformation. Somehow Stuart had managed to snooker him into hosting a news conference in the museum's ground floor restaurant.

You fell for his stirring sales pitch—that's how!

"The Duchess of Bedford is an *ideal* venue in which to meet the press," Stuart had said, with the delight of an explorer setting foot on an unexplored continent. "Your tearoom is friendly, accommodating, and visually exciting, yet indisputably your turf." He had done a slow pirouette, then pointed to the glass wall that gave diners a view of the museum's greenhouse. "We shall locate the podium *there.*"

Nigel had called Stuart minutes after the first outside-broadcast van appeared in the tea museum's car park. The rotund, fiftyish spin doctor—a principal in the local public relations firm of Gordon & Battlebridge—fancied himself an expert in crisis communication. He rushed to the museum from his office on Monson Road and was soon giving orders like a field marshal.

Nigel had to admit that Stuart knew how to sort out the journalists and correspondents who flocked to the museum on Friday afternoon. He cheerfully filled their requests for background information about the museum, explained that the members of the museum staff were not granting interviews today, and guided them to the police spokeswoman who had driven over from the Kent Police Headquarters in Maidstone to answer their questions.

Early on Friday evening, Stuart had managed to convince Nigel that the museum should hold a news conference and museum tour at nine o'clock on Monday morning, two hours before the museum reopened to the general public. "We'll let the weekend go by and build the media's curiosity about the museum," he had said. "They'll soon exhaust the meager information provided by the police and will start searching for other story angles. You and Dr. Adams will make a happy change from the grim police spokespeople they have dealt with so far. We have a golden opportunity to ride the surge of media interest generated by the discovery of Makepeace's body. The Royal Tunbridge Wells Tea Museum will get a million pounds' worth of free publicity."

Nigel had raised a few feeble objections. "Why should Flick and I put ourselves in the limelight? Aren't the reporters likely to ask tricky questions? Won't the police be mad at us if we speak to the press directly?"

"Fear not, Nigel." Stuart had clapped him on the shoulder. "We shall have a combination training session and dress rehearsal tomorrow afternoon. I shall personally prepare you to do battle with the ladies and gentlemen of the news media."

One more astonishment awaited Nigel when he walked into the tearoom at half past three. A makeup technician—a tall, exaggeratedly made-up blond of perhaps twenty-five—guided him to a chair, dusted his cheeks with powder, and tamed his customarily tousled hair with several well-placed squirts from a can of hair spray.

"Is this really necessary, Stuart?" Nigel hoped his voice conveyed the growing exasperation he felt.

"Absolutely!" Stuart replied. "For our training session to provide effective practice, everything must be as authentic as possible. That's why you are wearing makeup, we've set up an array of photographic lights, and you see six unfamiliar faces in the second row of chairs."

Nigel shaded his eyes. The six—all men in their twenties and thirties—were indeed unfamiliar. Two were holding little tape recorders, two were making notes on pads, and two seemed to be scowling at him.

"They are Gordon & Battlebridge staffers." Stuart chuckled. "Don't they look like working reporters?"

When Nigel replied with a grudging "uh-huh," Stuart said, "Please take your place behind the podium, alongside Felicity."

Nigel stepped up on the raised platform and whispered to her, "Don't you think this fuss is starting to get silly?"

"Actually, I'm quite impressed. Stuart clearly has everything under control."

Nigel watched Stuart sit down in the first row of chairs, next to a stocky man who looked vaguely familiar. Nigel swallowed a laugh; because the pudgy man wore a duff-colored cashmere pullover while the equally pudgy Stuart Battlebridge had on his usual Aran sweater, the pair looked remarkably like Tweedledee and Tweedledum.

And then Nigel realized with a start that the man was the local reporter who had fled from the tea garden the day before. Nigel stepped away from the podium. "Stuart, did you invite a *real* member of the press to our rehearsal?"

Stuart smiled. "Nigel, meet the man who announced the Etienne Makepeace story to the world—Philip Pellicano, of the *Kent and Sussex Courier*."

He saluted Nigel briskly with the stack of five-by-seven cards he held in his right hand. Nigel returned a feeble nod and rejoined Flick.

Stuart continued. "Philip will provide another dimension of authenticity today. There's nothing better than practicing with real questions from a real reporter—don't you agree?" He didn't wait for Nigel to answer. "In exchange for Philip's help, we've allowed him to chat with museum employees to get background information, and we promised him special access to you and Flick, if he should require it."

Nigel wondered which "we" Stuart had in mind. He had never given Gordon & Battlebridge permission to cut deals with the *Kent and Sussex Courier*.

"Shall we begin?" Stuart suddenly became as solemn as a physician preparing to conduct an unpleasant physical examination. "I trust that both of you read the briefing document that my staff assembled during the wee hours. It contains all that we could learn quickly about Etienne Makepeace."

"I scanned it this morning," Flick said. "I plan to study it this afternoon."

"Same here," Nigel said, doubting that he would ever waste time reading the document in question. It was five pages of closely typed text, filled with irrelevant biographical details of a man who died nearly four decades ago. Moreover, Nigel hadn't much liked receiving homework from Stuart Battlebridge at eight o'clock on a Saturday morning.

"Good!" Stuart said. "One detail I did not include in the briefing document is the extent of the press coverage related to the discovery of Makepeace's body. During the past eighteen hours, no fewer than thirty percent of the news stories read on British radio and television have been about Etienne Makepeace. If this does not turn out to be the story of the century, it will certainly rank as a strong candidate. I am confident that we will have a robust media turnout on Monday morning." Stuart paused to heighten the dramatic effect. "Philip, ask your first question."

The reporter consulted his cache of cards. "Mr. Owen, do you think the discovery of Etienne Makepeace's body in your garden will benefit or harm the museum in the long run?"

Nigel pondered the answer. *Benefit or harm? It's hard to say. Probably a little of both.*

"Well, I suppose there are both good and bad aspects. . ."

Honk! Nigel jumped six inches as Stuart cut him off with a blast from a palm-sized boat horn.

"*Never* respond directly to a loaded question like that," Stuart half shouted. "Any answer you give will make you sound like a mercenary businessman." He spoke to Philip. "Ask your question again, but direct it to me."

Philip simpered at Stuart. "Mr. Battlebridge, do you think the discovery of Etienne Makepeace's body in your garden will benefit or harm the museum in the long run?"

"I couldn't begin to answer that question, sir," Stuart said, his voice brimming with regret. "We simply don't think in those terms. What I can say is that everyone at the Royal Tunbridge Wells Tea Museum is delighted to have helped to resolve a national mystery that has lasted almost four decades." Stuart peered at Nigel. "Do you see how it's done?"

Nigel managed a halfhearted smile despite a strong yearning to charge down off the raised platform and punch Stuart's snoot. "Yes, Stuart. I believe I do."

Philip gazed again at his cards. "Mr. Owen, we understand that the presence of Etienne Makepeace's body below the Assam tea plants stunted their growth. Can you explain why?"

Nigel felt a grin form on his face. He'd been asked a straightforward question, and he had a ready answer. "It's quite simple, really. The roots of the plants were blocked by a layer of roofing tiles placed atop the. . ."

Honk!

Nigel caught his breath. "What's wrong now?"

"*Another* bad answer!" Stuart bellowed. "The police have not yet publicly revealed that tiles were found in the grave."

"Correct!" Philip jumped in. "In fact, DI Pennyman asked us not to mention the roofing tiles in our story."

"The police spokeswoman made the same request of the museum yesterday," Stuart said.

"Nobody told me," Nigel said.

"To the contrary. I carefully specified the two subjects to avoid in the briefing paper."

"I must have missed your instructions."

"You'll find them on the first page. In large type."

Nigel peeked at Flick, who seemed on the verge of laughing. "In that event," he said, "perhaps Dr. Adams would like the opportunity to field a question?"

Flick's smile faded and then quickly returned. "I'm game. Ask away."

"An excellent point," Stuart said, "which brings me to another important lesson I want you to learn. You're a businessman, Nigel; you don't have the proper credentials to answer questions about tea plants. You should have instantly referred the question to the chief curator." Stuart turned to Flick. "What would your response have been, Dr. Adams?"

Flick spoke confidently. "That's a very interesting question; we want to know the answer, too. When the police have completed their investigation, we intend to look into the matter."

"An excellent reply!" Stuart nodded approvingly. "Short, responsive, noncommittal—yet wholly satisfying to the questioner."

Nigel whispered, "Suck-up!"

Flick poked her finger into his ribs; no one in the audience seemed to notice.

"Ouch!"

"Do you have something to add before we move on, Nigel?" Stuart asked.

"No."

"But I do," Philip said smugly. "We should call Mr. Owen's attention to the second item on the list of forbidden subjects—specifically, the pistol found buried with the body. While the police have yet to make the information public, they have positively identified the weapon as a Soviet-made Makarov automatic, caliber 9.2 millimeters. The magazine contained seven cartridges. It can hold a maximum of eight."

"Thank you, Philip," Nigel said. "Now I know what I have to forget by Monday morning. I don't anticipate any difficulties."

Nigel watched a furrow form on Philip's brow, but before the reporter could say anything, Stuart tapped his arm with the little boat horn. "Proceed."

Philip retrieved his cards. "Another question for you, Mr. Owen. Do you have any idea *why* Mr. Makepeace was buried in the museum's tea garden?"

Nigel grinned at Philip. The man had asked a sensible question, one that deserved to be answered, one that the reporters were likely to pose on Monday morning.

The trick is to come up with a suitably hollow reply.

"I have no idea why a murderer would choose to vandalize a museum," Nigel said, "but the fact that it happened here makes me furious. We are a family museum, dedicated to helping people understand the extraordinary history of tea in Great Britain."

Nigel held his breath, waiting for Stuart to blow the ruddy horn. But Stuart set the noisemaker down. "An acceptable answer, Nigel. You seem to be getting the idea." He signaled Philip with another wave. "Carry on."

"Dr. Adams, Etienne Makepeace had an interesting nickname when he was alive—England's Tea Sage. Had you heard anything about him before his body was unearthed in the museum's tea garden?"

Flick shook her head. "Surprisingly, given his fame in England, I had not heard of Mr. Makepeace until the events of last Friday." She added, "I've learned a good deal about him since then."

"Well done, Felicity!" Stuart gushed. "A *perfect* answer."

"Show off!" Nigel hissed. Before he could move away, Flick poked her finger into his middle again. He couldn't help wincing; the spot was getting tender.

"I have a follow-up question for you, Dr. Adams," Philip said. "Please apply your newfound knowledge and give us your opinion of Etienne Makepeace's expertise. Did England's Tea Sage know his stuff?"

Nigel expected Flick to answer quickly. Instead, she hesitated—and he could sense her growing distress. But why? Philip's question seemed simple enough. After several seconds of silence, he realized that she hadn't "learned a good deal" about Makepeace at all. Her previous reply had been a fib.

"Ah. . .well. . . ," Flick finally began. "I'm not really sure, although everyone says that he knew his stuff. Uh. . .what I mean to say is that. . ."

Honk!

"In other words, Felicity, you don't have a good answer, so

32

all you can do is blither at us."

Flick sighed. "I'm afraid that's true, Stuart. I'm sorry."

He frowned. "*Sorry* doesn't cut it at a news conference. And you were ill-advised to claim knowledge you don't possess. Please remember that our objective is to get you widely quoted, to establish Dr. Felicity Adams as a nationally known expert on tea. We want the media to call you for an answer whenever a question arises about tea."

"Point taken and understood," Flick said sheepishly.

Stuart gave a forgiving grunt. "Had you taken time to *read*, rather than scan, our briefing materials, you would have stumbled on several appropriate ways to praise England's Tea Sage." Stuart opened the stapled document and began to read aloud.

"Etienne Makepeace forever reminded his audiences that he was not a professionally trained tea expert, but rather a tea lover who could be an enthusiastic advocate for tea. Because he obviously enjoyed teaching people about tea, he became known as 'the C. S. Lewis of tea.'

"Professionally trained or not, Makepeace was recognized to have an encyclopedic knowledge of tea that he displayed in the many magazine articles he wrote. . .at his many lectures across Great Britain. . .and especially in numerous appearances on many radio shows.

"Makepeace was at his best when he demystified tea and tea drinking. He didn't tolerate tea-time snobbery. He argued that sugar and milk in tea were perfectly acceptable in a good cuppa. He felt that scones served with clotted cream were too highfalutin and that it was a waste of time to cut the crusts off cucumber sandwiches. He waged a valiant battle against tea bags in favor of brewed tea and insisted that supermarket brands of tea were overpriced because the consumer paid for advertising and overly elaborate packaging—both of which did nothing to improve a cup of tea."

Stuart turned the page and kept reading.

"Makepeace was born in 1910 in Winchester, England, the only son of a fairly well-to-do family. His father, Jonathan Makepeace, was a banker. Etienne was named after his mother's father, who had emigrated from France in 1876. He had one older sister, two younger sisters. The youngest sibling, Mathilde, was born in 1922. She is still alive but suffers from Alzheimer's disease.

"As a boy, Etienne attended St. Bede's Primary School in Winchester and then the Pilgrim School, where he became a chorister for Winchester Cathedral. When his voice changed, the lad moved on to the Sherborne School in Dorset, a competent, if less well-known, public school. Makepeace proved to be a clever boots throughout his youth. He went up to Cambridge University where he read history and graduated in 1934 with a First"—Stuart glanced at Flick—"that's equivalent to 'with honors' in America. Etienne briefly attempted to follow his father into banking, but then he entered the navy in 1937. During World War II, he served as an officer with Naval Intelligence. His specialty was convoy routing in the North Atlantic."

Nigel raised his hand. "Stuart, I hope you're not proposing that we memorize the man's curriculum vitae."

"You will increase your credibility with the media if you drop a fact or two about Etienne Makepeace. Am I right, Philip?"

"Absolutely," the reporter said enthusiastically.

Nigel squinted at the lights, enjoying the kaleidoscopic patterns in his eyes, while Stuart continued to read from the document. "We didn't find anything about Makepeace's activities in the years immediately after the war. He apparently used the next decade to perfect his writing and speaking skills, and to grow his knowledge of tea. He published his first magazine article on tea in 1955, gave his first public talk in 1956, and made his first appearance on BBC Radio in 1958. His fame grew rapidly, and he soon became a beloved fixture on radio. The many photos of Makepeace published during the late fifties and early sixties show him as a handsome man who always looked in good nick—sculpted moustache, stylishly cut hair, impeccable clothing, and a dazzling smile.

"Makepeace avoided politics and controversy for most of his life. However, during the height of the Cold War, he wrote and lectured that it was unpatriotic, even traitorous, to drink tea imported from China."

Philip piped up. "More than one commentator accused him of being a fanatical, anticommunist Red-baiter. Makepeace ignored the accusations."

"As did the powers that be in Great Britain." Stuart flipped to the last page of the briefing document. "Makepeace hobnobbed with the rich and famous and was frequently seen in the company of famous royals. He was rumored to be in line for a knighthood. Shortly after he disappeared without a trace on September 29, 1966, a member of Parliament rose and said, 'Etienne Makepeace is one of the most significant Britons of the twentieth century—a man on par with any of the Beatles.'"

"A tad over the top," Philip said, "but not that far from the truth." He queried Stuart, "Can I share my bit of news?"

"Please do," Stuart said—not all that graciously, Nigel thought.

"Well, it's not widely known yet, but the police have used old dental records to positively identify the remains. It is Etienne Makepeace, without question. However, to satisfy people who prefer a more modern approach, the police are taking the extra step of conducting a DNA test. I understand they have taken a DNA sample from Etienne's surviving sister to compare with DNA extracted from the remains. It's a long process, though; we won't hear anything more for a week or two."

"Most interesting, Philip," Stuart said. "Please ask your next question."

"Mr. Owen, how have the museum's pets coped with the recent events?"

"*Our pets?*" Nigel fought to keep his voice from screeching. "Why would a reporter care two pins about our menagerie?"

"Because," Stuart said ploddingly, "many people know that Dame Elspeth Hawker arranged for the museum to care for her little family when she died. It's conceivable that an editor might decide to build a human interest story around the pets."

"What shall I say?"

"You're the exalted director of this museum. Come up with something."

Nigel gripped the podium hard enough to make it wobble. "All creatures great and small are thriving. Cha-Cha, our Shiba Inu, is in fine fettle. Lapsang and Souchong, our two British Shorthair cats, are purring. And Earl, our African Grey parrot, would be chirping joyously this very minute in the corner of

this tearoom had you not moved his vast cage into the kitchen."
Nigel looked at Flick. "Do you have anything to add?"

"Not a blooming word."

Philip chuckled. "I do believe our hosts are becoming irritable."

"Excellent!" Stuart said. "The time has come to ask the zinger."

Philip cleared his throat. "Mr. Owen, please describe the nature of your personal relationship with the chief curator."

Nigel heard Flick gasp. He glanced sideways; she was beginning to blush.

"Mr. Pellicano," Nigel said, "your question is out-of-bounds."

"Not so, Nigel," Stuart said. "Everyone in the museum knows you are. . .ah, *good friends*. We have to assume that other reporters are as clever as Philip."

Philip beamed at the compliment. "I've spoken to three different museum employees who *readily*"—he emphasized the word—"told me that you are 'romantically entwined,' to quote one of my sources."

"What of it?" Nigel said, louder than he intended to. "We're the two senior executives at this museum."

"I have a suggestion," Flick said softly. "It just dawned on me that whatever the nature of our *relationship*"—she spoke the word with a humorous lilt—"we have functioned as a team to improve the museum. Our predecessors had difficulties working together. We don't."

Nigel thought about it. More than one member of the board of trustees had told him that Nathanial Swithin, the former director, rarely agreed with the priorities set by Malcolm

Dunlevy, the former chief curator.

"Flick makes an excellent point," Nigel said. "Our friendship pays dividends to the museum. We're on the same team when problems arise, and we've solved many. We've managed to cut costs while increasing our general attendance, our tour business, our gift shop sales, and our revenues from the tearoom. At the same time, contributions to the museum are up significantly. All in all, our combined managerial performance is worthy of recognition." He smiled at her. "I think we should ask the trustees for raises."

"My advice is to not share that response with the media," Stuart said. "Work out an answer that emphasizes your genial rapport." He put the boat horn in his pocket. "You've done enough rehearsing for one day. I want you to spend the rest of the afternoon studying—*really studying*—the briefing document."

Flick gave a curt nod. Nigel said, "Aye, aye, Captain. We shall spend the remainder of today learning every useless fact and unimportant triviality about Etienne Makepeace."

"And then take tomorrow off. I want you refreshed and stress-free on Monday morning." Stuart reached into a battered leather briefcase that Nigel guessed was fifty years old. "Here. A pair of tickets for the Royal Tunbridge Wells Symphony Orchestra. Sunday afternoon at three. Just the thing to clear your minds."

"What's on the program?"

"A highly appropriate selection of pieces, Nigel. Trust me."

Nigel forced himself to return Stuart's smile. The town of Royal Tunbridge Wells had definite limits. One could find a good tea museum, several top-notch pubs, and a few restaurants that deserved one- or two-star status—but to hear a well-played symphony, one had to travel to London.

"Thank you, Stuart," said Flick. Nigel detected excitement in her voice. Without a doubt, she wanted to go to the concert.

Crikey!

"Yes, thank you, Stuart," Nigel managed to add as he pocketed the tickets. "We shall strive to enjoy our day off."

Is the rain different in England? Flick asked herself. Raindrops seemed to fall more gently here than back home in Pennsylvania and somehow had less of an ability to penetrate her Burberry. Even umbrellas gave the impression of working better in England. Perhaps Brits had perfected a more efficient umbrella-handling technique? She moved closer to Nigel and gripped his arm more tightly.

I'm glad Nigel talked me into walking to the concert.

She had hesitated when Nigel suggested that they "stroll off" the huge Sunday lunch they'd eaten at Thackeray's on London Road. It wasn't much of a hike to Assembly Hall, the home of the Royal Tunbridge Wells Symphony Orchestra—a kilometer at most—but given the chilly day and the steady sprinkle that had begun in the early afternoon, calling for a taxi had seemed a more sensible course of action.

But Nigel had persisted, and she had relented—chiefly because she'd enjoyed the other innovations that Nigel had suggested that morning.

"How about a light breakfast before church?" he had asked. "Say, coffee and biscotti?"

"Before church? Do we have time?"

"Indeed, we do. I thought we'd stay in town today and try the service at Holy Trinity with Christ Church. You know—the modern church at the top of High Street."

"Okay," she said hesitantly. For the past two months, they had attended services at St. Stephen's Church, on Pembury Road, opposite Dunorlan Park, about a mile northeast of Tunbridge Wells' town center. The vicar of St. Stephen's was Rev. William de Rudd, a member of the museum's board of trustees. Would the vicar be upset not to see them among the rest of his flock?

Nigel anticipated her foreboding. "I doubt that the good Reverend de Rudd expects us to become regulars at St. Stephen's. We're younger than most of the congregation, and we live quite a distance away. Christ Church is my neighborhood church."

Nigel had picked Flick up at her apartment in the Pantiles, the charming seventeenth-century colonnaded "shopping precinct" that had been the commercial center of Tunbridge Wells in its earliest days as a town. They had walked to the new Italian coffeehouse on the southern end of High Street and then tramped up the hill to reach Christ Church Center.

Flick liked the look of the place immediately—an in-town glass-and-brick facade that might be mistaken for a cinema. Once inside, there was no doubt about its purpose. The architect had devoted one long wall of the sanctuary to five stained glass windows: A pair of modern windows interleaved with three Victorian-era windows designed by the famous Sir Edward Burne-Jones and built in the workshop of the equally famous William Morris.

"You must be curious about the church's odd name," Nigel said. "I certainly was. Well, it seems that some thirty years ago, Holy Trinity parish merged with Christ Church parish. Voila! Holy Trinity with Christ Church."

"What on earth prompted you to do research on local churches?"

"Well. . ." Nigel smiled—somewhat reflectively, Flick thought. "When a person of my decidedly advanced age becomes a proper Christian and begins to attend church regularly, he needs to find a proper church home. I thought we might go church shopping, to use the American idiom."

Flick fought to keep her jaw from dropping.

Church shopping? Couples don't go church shopping, unless. . .

There it was again. The question that Philip Pellicano had asked the day before. The question that Flick didn't want to contemplate, much less answer.

What is your relationship with Nigel Owen? More to the point, are you prepared to trust him over the long run?

Her response during the rehearsal had temporarily sidetracked the issue. She and Nigel followed Stuart Battlebridge's instructions and worked out a simple answer of convenience: *We're good friends and committed colleagues, both devoted to the long-term success of the Royal Tunbridge Wells Tea Museum.*

It was answer enough to give to a curious reporter, but it didn't resolve the problem that she had let develop during the past eight weeks. Nigel clearly believed they had started a long-term relationship. She felt much less sure—even though they spent most of their free time together and she occasionally perched on his lap.

You also bought him a "pod" coffeemaker for Christmas.

It had seemed an innocuous enough present when she purchased it—a bright blue appliance that brewed "coffee-house-quality coffee," to echo the words on the box, by pumping boiling water through a paper pod filled with ground coffee. What better gift for a single man who enjoyed a good cup of coffee?

Nigel had been delighted when he tore off the wrapping paper. "I've wanted one of these gadgets for months," he had said. But then he smiled awkwardly. "Did you know that the stores that sell coffee pods also sell tea pods? You'll use this machine as much as I will."

Flick recalled her confused reaction. She hadn't known how to respond to the gist of Nigel's comment—the idea that they would someday share the same kitchen. In the end, she returned Nigel's smile and gave him a peck on the cheek.

The start of the service at Christ Church drove the topic from her mind; the vicar's benediction invited it back in. But then, Nigel announced his second surprise of the morning. "For obvious reasons, our Friday dinner at Thackeray's never happened. However, I am a man who pays his gambling debts promptly. Therefore, I have made us reservations for lunch today. I plan to have the foie gras starter and the roasted lamb main course."

"You'll burp through the concert."

"As will many others in the audience. Hefty Sunday dinners, served at noontime, are an age-old tradition in England. Fortunately, no one will care. After all, the orchestra is playing nothing but kitschy American music."

Flick thrust her finger at Nigel's ribs, but he sidestepped like a bullfighter and avoided the jab.

Nigel kept talking. "There's no doubt that the concert is Stuart Battlebridge's way of paying me back for not reading his blinkin' briefing document. Only a Brit set on revenge would give another Brit tickets to a program entitled 'Treats from the American Colonies.' "

This time, Flick anticipated Nigel's parry. Her finger hit home.

"Ouch." Nigel rubbed his side. "May one ask the reason for your violence?"

"You just dissed three of my favorite pieces. How can anyone not like Aaron Copland's music?"

"Oh, I grant you that 'Fanfare for the Common Man' and 'Appalachian Spring' are worth listening to, but Howard Hanson's 'Romantic' symphony is too much like movie music for my refined, old-world tastes."

"Suck it up! I intend to enjoy every note."

Now, after lunch, they strolled down London Road, Nigel's oversized umbrella vanquishing the rain. The fine mist that made it under the brolly, Flick decided, would probably moisturize her face. Well and good, as long as her complexion didn't go ruddy like his. Then they would look "a proper pair," as the English were fond of saying.

Great! You started thinking about him again. Stop it!

When they turned a corner, she gave her head a little shake and said, "I've lost my bearings. Where are we?"

"Walking east on Lime Hill Road, not far from my flat. We'll turn right once we reach Mount Pleasant Road."

They walked in silence for several minutes until Flick said, "You've become remarkably quiet—is anything wrong?"

"Not really. I've begun to feel a bit guilty about all the

work underway to get the museum ready to reopen tomorrow morning at eleven o'clock. The curators are working hard. Jim Sizer and his lads are working hard. We should be, too."

"Nonsense! Everything is under control. You and I are clearing our minds, remember?"

"I suppose so." Nigel guided Flick around a large puddle. "Are we there yet?"

"One more left turn will bring us to the Civic Centre. The time has come for you to admit that you enjoyed our walk in the rain. I can see it on your face—I know it's true."

Oh my. He's sure he can read my moods.

They climbed up the short flight of steps to Civic Way and made for Assembly Hall, a redbrick art deco building sandwiched between the Tunbridge Wells Town Hall and the police station. The letters on the marquee announced RTW SYMPHONY—SUNDAY AT 3:00 PM.

Flick cast a discreet glance at Nigel as he collapsed his umbrella and led her into the high-ceilinged lobby. What *was* she to make of him?

It's not your fault that I've made lousy choices in men throughout my life.

Flick let herself sigh. No, she was entirely responsible for committing to men who lacked commitment themselves and were all to easily attracted to other women. Men like the graduate student at the University of Michigan, the tea importer from Connecticut, and the marketing executive from Texas. They had, each in his own turn, broken her heart for the most familiar of reasons: "I'm sorry, Flick, but I've fallen in love with someone else."

Each time she had promised herself it would never

happen again. But it had—three times during a span of seven years. And because no one could tell Flick how to be sure that a man she trusted would actually be loyal in return, she decided that her safest course of action was to avoid long-term relationships.

Make me no promises, and you'll tell me no lies.

Without thinking, Flick reached for Nigel's hand and squeezed his fingers. When Nigel smiled delightedly at her, she quickly said, "Assembly Hall reminds me of an old movie palace in York, Pennsylvania. It also had a lobby that was two stories high, with marble paneling on the walls, big glass light fixtures, faux Greek decorations, gilt accents, and a flight of steps leading to the theater."

Nigel bent down and whispered in her ear, "I love it when you talk architecture."

"Stars and garters," said an amused voice behind Flick. "We meet again."

Flick felt herself stiffen. *Polly Reid. Nigel's administrative assistant.*

Flick turned and forced herself to smile. Polly went on. "You know, when I saw you in Christ Church this morning, I said to myself, 'Polly, those two look as comfortable together as an old married couple.'"

There were too many other people nearby to shout, *We're merely friends—nothing more!* Instead, Flick said, "Wow! Polly, you look spectacular today."

"And you sound completely amazed that I do," Polly replied.

"Well. . ."

When Polly began to laugh, Flick joined in quickly.

Nigel's associate was a plump, fortyish brunette, with a no-nonsense attitude and a penchant for showing up each day with quiet clothing, minimal makeup, and hair wound tight in a businesslike bun. This afternoon, she wore a dazzling red dress that deftly shaped her figure, a cascading hairdo that framed her face perfectly, and stylish makeup that would have done a supermodel proud.

"As it happens," Polly said, "I have a date, too. He's a member of the orchestra. Third violin from the end in the second row."

"You go, girl!" Flick said.

Polly crooked her thumb at Nigel. "How did you manage to get him here today? When I extended an invitation last season, he announced that he wouldn't be caught dead at a performance by an amateur orchestra."

Nigel launched a prompt defense—"That's a wee bit of an exaggeration, Polly. In fact. . ."—but Flick interrupted him.

"Aha! Now I understand your unreasonable guilt feelings and your unprovoked comments about kitschy music. You're worried that a local orchestra will play out of tune. Nigel Owen, you're a snob."

"I'm neither worried nor a snob." Nigel sniffed. "I'm properly skeptical."

"And altogether wrong," Polly said. "While there are some top-notch amateurs, the lion's share of the performers are paid musicians. Our orchestra is brilliant—you'll see."

Flick saw a bemused expression grow on Nigel's face as he watched Polly walk away. He seemed to be craning his neck so as not to lose sight of her as she passed through the double doors that led to the stalls and tiers.

"Not the Polly we see every day, huh?" Flick said cautiously.

"Not by a long shot!" He looked back at her and smiled. "But even dressed to kill, she's hardly in your league. Let's find our seats." He offered his arm. "I give you fair warning: I intend to have my arm around you for much of the concert. What better way to listen to the 'Romantic' symphony than by sitting next to an American beauty?"

Flick looked down at her clenched hands.

What am I going to do? What are we going to do?

THREE

One gentle, yodel-like woof was enough to wake Nigel on Monday morning—fifteen minutes before his alarm clock was set to ring. He raised his head and peered at Cha-Cha, who was standing expectantly in front of the wicker dog bed that Nigel had tucked between his chest of drawers and an old upholstered armchair in his bedroom.

"I'll be ready to take you out in half a tick, old chum." Nigel reluctantly pulled himself up on his elbows. "I can see that you had a good night's sleep. Alas, I didn't. In fact, I woke up twice last night and tossed and turned for more than an hour."

The little dog's big triangular eyes seemed to peer quizzically at Nigel, as if trying to understand why his master had difficulty sleeping.

"Well, if you insist on poking your snout in my business, it's this way. We will shortly be besieged by members of the British press. The confidence I felt on Saturday has oozed out of me like water from a leaky tap. I am more than a bit concerned that the future of the museum will rest on our well-chosen words. If we mess up today, misspeak, or make a bad impression, we could put both the museum and our careers at risk."

Cha-Cha tilted his head skeptically.

"Okay, I admit it. I'm worried about *me* messing up today. Flick has done this before. She has written three popular books about tea and has been on media tours. She knows how to meet the press successfully." He let himself sigh. "No wonder she did so well at the rehearsal."

Nigel glanced at the top of his chest of drawers, at the framed photograph of Flick. It was a formal pose, taken by a professional photographer soon after Flick joined the museum and sent out to the media with a news release that described her impressive background. One day soon, he would ask her for a more personal photo—one more in keeping with their blossoming relationship.

He felt himself smiling. Felicity Adams was a very special woman and, as such, required a special approach. He had decided to move slowly, to avoid the risk of spooking her with clumsy rhetoric. Before he spoke words of love to Flick, he would think long and hard about the right words to utter. A question at the news conference about their relationship would force the issue—much better if none came up. But Nigel was prepared should a foolish reporter asked a question.

"Felicity Adams and I are dear friends—and proud of it," he said aloud, testing the words.

Cha-Cha replied with a louder woof.

"I get the point—you still want to go out."

Because the level of heat in his bedroom was an uncertain thing, Nigel kept his slippers (a pair of fleecy moccasins) and his bathrobe (a venerable Scottish tartan dressing gown) at the ready at the foot of his bed. He slipped into them, cinched his belt tightly around his middle, and led Cha-Cha downstairs to the back garden.

The winter-dormant shrubs and trees placed decorously throughout the narrow walled-in plot were coated with frost that shone silvery in the illumination from the floodlight attached to the rear of the house. It had just gone six thirty and was still dark. The sun would not rise until almost eight at this time of year. Then the melting would begin. Nigel sheltered close to the back door while Cha-Cha trotted off to the rear of the garden. Chill air seeped beneath the thick plaid flannel of his robe. He tugged his belt tighter.

Nigel's flat occupied the top two stories of a four-story house on Lime Hill Road. He lived on the second and third floors while his landlords—a charming couple named Bacon and Hildegard Jenkins—lived on the ground and first floors. Nigel suspected that the Jenkinses were older than the house itself, although all three looked in sterling shape to him. Nigel's living room faced Lime Hill Road; his dining room and kitchen overlooked the back garden. The top floor contained his bedroom, an enormous bathroom, and a second, smaller bedroom that he had turned into a home office. The flat encompassed far more floor space than any apartment he had occupied in London, and Nigel had been reluctant to buy more furniture, initially assuming that his sojourn at the Royal Tunbridge Wells Tea Museum would be over in a year. When Nigel invited Flick to share a homemade dinner two weeks earlier, the first thing she said when she saw the apartment was, "My goodness, Nigel, your place is only half furnished."

That, Nigel decided, was an easily addressed problem that time and shopping would resolve. A thornier challenge was the shortage of parking spaces on Lime Hill Road. Many of the town houses on the street had been converted into small flats, and most of the renters owned cars—completely overwhelming the available curbside parking. Consequently, Nigel usually left his BMW sedan in the museum's employee car park and walked back and forth to his flat—a distance of about two kilometers. On an icy morning like this one, a brisk hike didn't seem a cheering prospect.

Nigel scanned the garden, but Cha-Cha was nowhere to be seen. He followed the dog's small footprints back and forth on the frosty grass until they passed behind a spindly fruit tree. No surprise! Cha-Cha was equipped with a plush double coat—just the thing for a cold Kentish dawn—and had gone for a quick morning sniff-around.

"Time's up, mutt!" Nigel said, in a loud whisper designed not to wake his neighbors. "I'm turning into a block of ice."

Nothing.

Nigel spoke more loudly. "Return immediately, Cha-Cha, or you'll eat dry kibble the rest of the winter."

The reddish dog suddenly appeared next to a bush not far from Nigel's feet.

"Good! The first thing you can do is help me decide what to wear at the conference."

They padded back upstairs side by side and made for Nigel's bedroom closet. Although Nigel had specifically asked, Stuart Battlebridge had provided little guidance about their clothing today. "In the past, we told our clients to dress conservatively. But those days are long over. The best advice I can give you is to look like a museum director. Dress in the sort of clothing that you would wear to a business meeting at the museum. This is a simple news conference, not a fancy dress ball."

Nigel surveyed his wardrobe and murmured, "What does a museum director look like?"

Cha-Cha gave a gentle yip and moved beneath a well-tailored black and gray herringbone tweed sport coat.

"Do you really think so?" Nigel said. "I would have chosen the safe, gray pinstripe, but perhaps you're right. My tweed coat over a white shirt and gray flannel slacks—with an elegant red tie to add a bit of color."

That was the outfit Nigel wore beneath his heavy mackintosh as he set off for the museum with Cha-Cha. The wintry sun had begun to rise when he reached the top of Mount Pleasant. A barrage of high-pitched giggles suddenly pierced the cold air like the ringing of bells, and Nigel found himself entangled in a gaggle of schoolgirls waiting for their bus. One of them began to stroke Cha-Cha.

"I didn't know you could keep a fox as a pet," the girl said.

"He's not a fox—he just looks like one."

"Well, what is he then?" the girl's friend joined in.

"A dog," Nigel said. "A Shiba Inu."

"Is that some kind of terrier?" the first girl asked.

"No. It's more like a miniature Japanese spitz."

"Does he understand Japanese then?" asked another girl who had decided to join in.

"Impeccably!" Nigel gave Cha-Cha's lead a gentle tug. He marched on, buoyed by a gale of giggly laughter. His spirits remained high until he passed the Eridge Road traffic circle and saw in the distance a fleet of outside-broadcast vans gathered in front of the museum like Visigoth war wagons lined up before the gates of Rome. And there in the middle of the muddle stood Flick, an amazed look on her face. Happily, none of the reporters milling around nearby had recognized who she was.

Nigel moved through the crowd mumbling "excuse me," Cha-Cha close on his heels. He grabbed Flick's elbow and propelled her toward the museum's side entrance. "Don't act surprised. Just keep moving. We have to get inside before someone decides that now will be a good time to start asking questions."

"Stuart was right—the media seems to be treating this like the story of the century." Her voice sounded nervous. "I almost wish we hadn't given Stuart permission to arrange a news conference; don't you agree?"

Nigel swallowed his amusement. Bit by bit, Flick was picking up English patterns of speech. Ending a statement with a polite question was a perfect example.

"I definitely agree. Stuart predicted a robust turnout, but this seems all out of proportion. We have dozens of reporters milling about a full two hours before the conference is scheduled to begin." Nigel looked back as they turned the corner. A few members of the press peered at them curiously, but none followed.

Employees used the museum's side entrance when the main entrance was locked. Nigel readied his key in case the metal and glass door was locked. It wasn't. Instead, one of the museum's burlier security guards had taken up position as a human barrier. He returned a military salute as they scooted around him into the corridor.

"Mr. Battlebridge suggested that I guard the flanks," he said.

"Good thinking!" Nigel said. "Do you know where Stuart is?"

A jovial voice made Nigel turn. "Waiting patiently for you at the Welcome Centre kiosk."

Stuart stood next to the kiosk, a big grin on his face. More surprisingly, Margo McKendrick—sitting in the kiosk—was also smiling at them. Nigel hadn't expected her to be on duty.

The marble-encased Welcome Centre kiosk sat at the intersection of the two corridors that spanned the ground floor, giving its occupant a simultaneous view of both the main and side entrances. Margo, the museum's greeter for more than thirty years, manned the kiosk when the facility was open for visitors. A security guard replaced her during "off-hours," when the exhibit halls were closed to the public but the staff was still at work in their offices and laboratories. Between mid-October and mid-April, the museum traditionally followed an abbreviated winter schedule: open 11:00 a.m. to 4:00 p.m.; closed all day Sunday and Wednesday. He and Flick had decided to lengthen the schedule—in the hope of increasing miscellaneous revenues—by henceforth opening at 10:00, but there was still no reason for Margo to be at her post at 8:00 on a Monday morning. Then he understood. . . .

She took over the kiosk so the security guard could man the side door.

Nigel stepped aside; Flick moved toward the kiosk, slipping out of her Burberry as she walked.

Crikey! She's all dressed up.

She wore a trimly cut, dark blue suit, matching blue pumps with short heels, and a pink shirt. Her only adornment was a single strand of pearls around her neck. Nigel found himself staring: There was something about simple clothing that made Flick glow. The reporters expected to interview a stodgy, stoop-shouldered scientist; instead, they would get a stunning corn-fed American beauty. They were bound to fall in love with her the way he had.

He caught up with Flick and said, "You look smashing. Absolutely brilliant."

She replied with a happy grin. "Thank you, kind sir. I've been told that I clean up nicely." She added, "What did you decide to wear today?"

He unbuttoned his mac.

"Perfect!" she said. "You're the model of a friendly, trustworthy museum director. I worried that you might wear pinstripes and look like a slick politician—or worse, a sleazy lawyer."

"Are you two ready?" Stuart asked, rubbing his hands together in obvious delight. "I may raise my fee this month for achieving such a wonderful response. The media have come in *droves*."

"I suppose I'm ready," Flick said, "although I can feel my knees shaking."

"And my mouth is getting drier by the minute," Nigel put in.

"Routine preconference butterflies," Stuart said. "Happens to everyone. Even your blooming parrot had a touch of nerves this morning. He began squawking his head off in the kitchen, so we returned him to his corner of the tearoom. That calmed him down immediately. We shall cover his cage with a tablecloth when the conference begins."

"In that event, I shall unbound the hound." Nigel unclipped Cha-Cha's lead and watched him make a beeline for the tearoom—and his morning visit with Earl.

"I have more exciting news," Stuart said grandly. "BBC Radio and BBC TV have asked for private interviews. After the news conference, Flick will escort a BBC TV reporter and his cameraperson around the museum, while Nigel has a date at the BBC Kent studios."

Nigel's heart skipped a beat. "You signed us up without asking?"

"That's why you pay me the hefty fees you so often complain about," Stuart said with a smile. "Look at the bright side—now that you have on-the-air interviews to worry about, the news conference will seem like a piece of cake." Another smile. "Are you ready for your last-minute instructions?"

"We're bursting with excitement."

"I will serve as the master of ceremonies this morning. At ten o'clock I will call the meeting to order, welcome the media, and then introduce you. I'll also be the safety valve. Specifically, I'll stop the conference and dismiss the media should I sense that their questions are getting out of hand."

"Now there's a merry thought," Flick said.

"We in public relations expect the best but prepare for the worst."

"Spout another cliché, and I shall *reduce* your fee," Nigel said.

Stuart ignored the gibe and began to count on his fingers.

"First—when you enter the tearoom, you'll find that the floor has been crisscrossed with cables. Try not to trip and fall on your face. It creates a poor initial impression.

"Second—the media will have attached several additional microphones to the podium. We will have run an audio test before you arrive, so there is no need to say *testing, one, two, three, four*—or any such hackneyed phrase.

"Third—answer only the question you're asked. Do not elaborate. Do not wax poetic. Do not spout off in the heat of the moment. In short, do not wander off into the horse latitudes, telling irrelevant tales that I will have to deny or explain later.

"Fourth—I plan to introduce you, using abridged versions of your official biographies. I shall emphasize that Nigel holds an MBA from the famed INSEAD in Fontainebleau, France, and was appointed director of the museum because of his considerable financial skills and experience. I shall likewise stress Flick's doctorate in food chemistry from the equally prestigious University of Michigan. And I shall call the media's attention to her successful books, most notably, *How to Host an English Tea*.

"Fifth—and lastly—I have provided a pad and pencil for each of you on the podium. You probably won't need them, but they're there should you want to jot something down. Don't worry about capturing the questions. I plan to record the entire proceedings."

Stuart glanced at his watch. "Ah—time to get back to the preparations. One can never take enough care up front." He began to walk away, then looked back over his shoulder. "You have well over an hour before the conference begins. Repair to the third floor, stay out of sight, do whatever it is you do. I shall call you when we need you."

When the chubby PR man had disappeared into the Duchess of Bedford Tearoom, Flick asked, "Do you Brits always make simple things so complicated?"

Nigel rolled his eyes. "I'm afraid so. Stuart is one of our most popular types—from his stiff upper lip to the self-important swagger in his walk."

Flick peered at his mouth. "What's the current state of your upper lip?"

"Quivering."

"I'm glad to hear it. Stuart's lecture has made me feel nervous enough to throw up." She began to laugh. Nigel enthusiastically joined in.

Three ceramic mugs clinking together made an odd-sounding toast, Flick thought, but mutual congratulations were definitely in order. The first news conference ever held at the museum had gone without a hitch. She and Nigel had answered twenty-odd questions—most of them harmless—and the ladies and gentlemen of the media had gone away happy.

"One can anticipate," Stuart said, "that the goodwill they demonstrated today will continue when they write their stories. With luck, we shall see a flood of cheerful articles about the Royal Tunbridge Wells Tea Museum." He raised his mug again. "You both acquitted yourselves well."

Flick was seated with Nigel and Stuart in the tearoom at a table that overlooked the tea garden. Her mug was full of Assam tea, Nigel's with strong black coffee, and Stuart's with hot cocoa. The kitchen was up and running, and, more to the point, so was the Duchess of Bedford Tearoom itself. Jim Sizer's crew had surprised everyone by striking the raised platform, rolling up the many cables, restoring the tables and chairs to their proper places, and generally returning the converted space to a proper restaurant in less than an hour. The tearoom would be ready to serve lunch—and afternoon tea—to the first group of visitors touring the museum today.

Stuart set down his mug and reached for a large yellow pad. "Now. . .in the few minutes we have before you go off to your respective interviews, I would like to review the answers you gave this morning." His mouth squeezed into a simper. "If at all possible, try to give similar answers to the BBC."

Flick saw Nigel roll his eyes again. She found it hard not to snicker at Stuart's pomposity.

"The questioning began," Stuart said, "when David Hadley of the *Kent and Sussex Courier* asked how finding the body in the garden will impact the museum. Nigel, you gave an acceptable variation of the politically correct answer we practiced at the rehearsal.

"Immediately thereafter, Brendan Baker of KM Radio asked how the museum manages to grow tea in the Kentish climate. Nigel chose to answer the question himself—and, I must admit, did an adequate job explaining the tea garden's heating system."

"Why, thank you, Stuart," Nigel said. "Your consistently faint praise is overwhelming."

"It's no more than you deserve, Nigel." Stuart turned to the next page. "At this point, there were several rather silly questions about why the museum went to the trouble of building a tea garden and what the garden accomplishes. Flick disposed of them elegantly."

"I did my best." She fluttered her eyelashes at Nigel. He stared heavenward and produced a barely audible groan.

Stuart pressed on: "The next significant question came from Janice Henderson of the *Sevenoaks Chronicle*. She asked for a description of the sequence of events that led to the discovery of the body in the tea garden. Nigel provided a straightforward chronology, beginning with the museum's decision to replace the two stunted Assam tea bushes."

"Do you think of 'straightforward' as a compliment?" Nigel asked.

Flick felt surprised that Stuart didn't take the bait. Instead, he said, "Moving right along. . .we received several surprising questions about whether or not Etienne Makepeace had an unrevealed relationship with the museum. For reasons that escape me, a few reporters seem to have concluded that Make-peace and the museum were joined at the hip during the early 1960s. You both fielded these questions quite well, describing Makepeace as nothing more than a noted tea expert who occasionally lectured at the museum."

Nigel gave a grudging nod, acknowledging Stuart's fainter praise. Stuart turned the page.

"Gillian Nash of the *Edenbridge News* asked another question we had anticipated: 'Have the authorities provided any information as to why Etienne Makepeace was buried in your tea garden?' Nigel echoed the acceptable response that he gave at the rehearsal. Unfortunately, Ms. Nash decided to press forward and ask the question again in a slightly different form. Specifically, 'Do you have any idea why a noted tea expert was murdered at the museum and buried in your tea garden?'"

"I know what you're going to say," Nigel said. "I became flustered; I hemmed and hawed."

"A perfectly natural response under the circumstances. What matters is that you recovered quickly and professionally. I especially liked the way you invited Ms. Nash to check with the police and report back to you if they provided an answer."

Flick ventured a glance Nigel's way. He was beaming at Stuart, all past slights forgiven.

"Finally," Stuart said, "David Hadley came back with an interesting follow-up question: 'Have you thought of creating an exhibit about Etienne Makepeace?'"

"I really liked my answer to that one," Nigel said, clearly expecting Stuart to concur.

Stuart, however, frowned at his yellow pad. "You responded in a way that cut off further discussion—I would have preferred a more flexible answer, and. . ."

Nigel didn't give Stuart an opportunity to finish. "The question didn't invite a wishy-washy answer. I explained that the mission of the Royal Tunbridge Wells Tea Museum is to offer exhibits that illuminate the history of tea. Consequently, because there's no connection between Mr. Makepeace's disappearance and the history of tea, the museum has no earthly reason to create an Etienne Makepeace exhibit."

"Nevertheless," Stuart said, "I would have preferred a less authoritarian answer—an answer delivered by the museum's curator, who, after all, is the executive responsible for creating new exhibits."

Flick saw Nigel peer guiltily at her; she replied with a friendly wink. She remembered feeling relieved when Nigel decided to field the question by himself. It took time and deliberation to make decisions about new exhibits. Anything she said would have been a shoot-from-the-hip answer. Nigel's forceful response proved the point.

Even so, he risked taking a shot and deserves your support.

"I thought about chiming in," she said. "I was going to add, I can't imagine why we'd want an exhibit on Etienne Makepeace, but then Earl began to squawk."

"Three cheers for the blessed bird." Stuart set his yellow pad next to his feet. "He interrupted at precisely the moment the media ran out of sensible questions. I may invite him to every news conference I organize."

Nigel turned to Flick. "Did you have any idea what the avian ruckus was all about?"

She shook her head. "That loud clucking sound Earl kept making is brand-new to me. I don't know anything about parrots—or their vocalizations."

"Whatever he was trying to say, the reporters seemed fascinated," Nigel said. "They lifted his tablecloth and forgot about the two of us."

"Earl was probably chirping, 'take my picture,'" Stuart said. "I think your bird craves attention. He seemed to be posing when the photographers cranked up their cameras. He looked like he enjoyed all those flash units going off in his face—at least until Cha-Cha arrived on the scene. That dog is a bigger show-off than the parrot."

"I wish our pets could do the BBC interview you scheduled for me." Flick emptied her mug. "I have just enough time to get myself another cuppa and run a comb through my hair before the arrival of. . ." She felt herself frowning at Stuart.

"Did you tell me the reporter's name?"

Stuart frowned back. "Now that you mention it, I don't know it."

Thirty minutes later, Flick welcomed Harry Simpson, the BBC interviewer, a tall, slightly stooped, ruddy-faced man in his late twenties. He had a thick crop of dark hair and piercing, intelligent eyes. Harry, in turn, introduced Paco, a short, swarthy cameraman who seemed barely out of his teens. Flick never learned Paco's last name.

"We haven't done a feature on the museum in decades," Harry said, as he looked around the lobby, "so everything in the place will be new to our viewers. Paco and I decided that the best way to organize our interview today is around a five-quid tour of the facility. Whenever we reach a photogenic locale, I'll ask you an appropriate question or two on-camera. Back at the studio, we'll edit the various snippets together to create an intelligible story. What do you think?"

"I love it!" Flick said. "Just promise me that you will discard all footage of my knees shaking or my voice quivering."

Harry offered his hand along with a dazzling, professional smile. "We have a deal."

Paco slung several battery packs around his neck and hefted a large digicam to his shoulder. He flipped a switch; a surprisingly small flood lamp atop the TV camera projected a beam of light that made Flick blink. "We passed a gift shop when we came in," he said. "Why don't we begin there?"

Paco wanted to photograph Flick in front of the display of tea-drinking teddy bears, while Harry's preferred backdrop was the bookcase full of tea-related novels, cookbooks, and music CDs to play during afternoon tea. Flick talked them into using the shelves that held more than two hundred kinds of loose and bagged teas produced around the world. Harry asked Flick to describe her favorite on-sale item.

"We sell all of the things our visitors need to brew and serve a perfect cuppa," she said. "Teapots, tea filters, teacups, teaspoons, tea mugs, teakettles, tea cozies—the list goes on and on. But I'm most proud of our selection of teas grown on five continents. Our visitors can take home some of the rarest teas in the world and also some of the most unusual."

"That looked perfect through the camera," Paco said.

"Ditto from my perspective," Harry said. "Where's the nervousness you promised us?"

Flick pointed to her throat. "Right here—waiting to come out if you ask me a question that I can't answer."

Paco turned to Harry. "She's confused us with a real investigative reporting team. Why not tell her the truth—that we *never* ask tough questions?"

"Well—*hardly* ever," Harry said to Flick, finishing with a big grin.

"We'll start at the rear of the ground floor, with the Duchess of Bedford Tearoom," Flick said.

"I trust the food is good," Paco said hopefully.

"I'm sure that we can get you a scone or two to munch on—in the spirit of assisting editorial research."

"I knew I was going to love this assignment."

The next hour sped by for Flick. She escorted the two BBC visitors around the museum and spoke briefly for the camera at each location.

The Tea Garden:

"Yes, the walled-in patch of land beyond the tearoom is

our tea garden. I wish that I could take you out there, but the police have asked us to keep the access doors locked."

And: "The garden is heated by subterranean hot-water pipes. On a sunny winter day, it can feel almost tropical."

And: "You'll have to ask the police whether or not our tea garden is the scene of the crime. All I can tell you is that we found Etienne Makepeace's body buried in the garden."

The World of Tea Map Room:

"The large floor-to-ceiling maps show the major tea-growing regions of the world—which are mostly in Asia. The smaller panels depict the journey tea takes from Asia to our grocery stores."

And: "Most of the antique maps on display came from the collection of Commodore Desmond Hawker—one of the great nineteenth-century tea merchants, a man who built a huge fortune importing tea to Great Britain. As you may know, the museum has undertaken to purchase the collection from the Hawker estate, following the recent death of Dame Elspeth Hawker."

The Commodore Hawker Room:

"Commodore Hawker used much of his personal fortune to establish the Hawker Foundation early in the twentieth century. The Foundation subsequently established the Royal Tunbridge Wells Tea Museum to celebrate the importance of tea in Great Britain, to honor the commodore's memory, and to house the family's many tea-related antiquities. The Commodore Hawker Room is an accurate reproduction of Desmond's business office—down to the antique fountain pens that he purchased around 1890."

The History of Tea Colonnade:

"This is the museum's most popular gallery. Visitors love the large diorama that recounts tea's long and fascinating history. Legend says that tea was first brewed as a drink nearly five thousand years ago in China. Whether or not that's true, it's indisputable that tea played a critical role in Europe's—and Britain's—economic history."

Flick watched patiently while Paco took several close-up shots of the antiquities on display in the colonnade. He seemed especially interested in the collection of formal invitations to afternoon teas issued by England's royal family during the early twentieth century. When Paco finished, she said, "Let's move to the exhibits on our second floor. . . ." Flick quickly corrected herself: "I mean one flight up, on our *first* floor."

When are you going to stop making that silly mistake?

Flick knew, but often managed to forget, that the Brits called the bottom floor of the building the "ground floor" rather than the "first floor"—a major change to the numbering scheme she had used all her life. The pattern continued: the "first floor" in England was equivalent to what Americans labeled the "second floor"—and so on, to the top of the building.

Harry Simpson smiled at her. "Another example of two peoples separated by a common language."

Flick ushered them one flight up the main staircase, where her running commentary continued.

The Tea at Sea Gallery:

"You have a good eye—that *is* a replica of the famous Indiaman, *Repulse*, which belonged to the East India Company. The Hawker Ship Model Collection includes many well-known ships involved in the tea trade."

And: "I agree—the tea clippers are among the most beautiful sailing ships ever launched. They were built long and narrow with lots of sail, in the pattern of the eighteenth-century Baltimore clippers that were noted for their speed. According to sea lore, this class of ship earned the name 'clipper' because of how fast they clipped along."

The Hawker Tea Antiquities Collection:

"I have to admit that this is my favorite gallery. The Hawker Tea Antiquities Collection includes thousands of fascinating items, including all manner of teacups, teapots, and teakettles. . .a king's ransom of gold and silver tea services. . .an impressive array of samovars. . .tea ceremony sets from Asia. . .and, my favorite among favorites, several rare pieces of locally made, wooden Tunbridge Ware, including a famous set of mosaic-covered tea caddies called 'All the Teas in China.' "

The Tea Processing Exhibit:

"This month, we're highlighting the manufacture of Chinese gunpowder tea. It's made by rolling green tea leaves into tiny pellets that resemble coarse gunpowder."

And: "Yes, this is actual tea-processing equipment, the sort you can find in use at smaller producers throughout Asia today."

Flick noticed that Harry looked at his watch. "How are we doing for time?" she asked.

"I allowed an hour for the interview—we have about twenty minutes left, and I want to leave time for a direct question or two."

"We can safely bypass the two galleries on the next floor," she said. "Our Tea in the Americas Room is more popular with visitors from across the pond than with locals, and the exhibits in our Tea and Health Gallery, though important, aren't especially camera-friendly."

And there's no point in even telling Harry about the Hawker family suite.

The museum had long provided an office for the use of the Hawker family, the institution's original benefactors. But now that the surviving Hawker heirs had no interest in the museum, the large suite could be transformed into a gallery. One of these days, she and Nigel would have to decide how to use the valuable space.

"The museum's top floor," she said, "houses our administrative offices and is off-limits to most visitors. Our offices are routine, but two locations are worth your time." Flick continued speaking as she led Harry and Paco up two flights of stairs. "The Hawker Memorial Library contains some three thousand books about the different aspects of tea. How tea is grown, how tea is processed, how tea is marketed, how tea is consumed—it's really quite amazing how many different aspects of tea one can write about. And our Conservation Laboratory has all the scientific equipment we need to study, restore, and protect the many different antiquities in our collection."

"I'll bet there's lots to photograph in your lab," Paco said.

"There certainly is—are either of you allergic to cats?"

"Cats?" Harry said. "What function do the cats perform in your laboratory?"

"If Lapsang and Souchong serve any function at all," Flick said with a shake of her head, "it's purely decorative." She pointed the way to the Conservation Laboratory.

As usual, the two cats had taken up residence on the bottom

shelves of two laboratory workstations at opposite ends of the Conservation Laboratory. One slept beneath an elaborate optical microscope, the other below a deceptively simple-looking electronic instrument called a gas chromatograph that was, Flick knew, capable of performing many kinds of sophisticated chemical analyses.

While Paco shot footage of the laboratory equipment, Harry made a beeline for the first of the cats. "This seems to be an exceedingly happy British Shorthair. Would this be Lapsang or Souchong?"

As she always did, Flick said, "Lapsang is the larger of the two," hoping she was right. In fact, she didn't have a clue which cat was which.

One day, I must properly identify them.

Harry seemed satisfied. He knelt down, scratched "Lapsang's" tummy, and finished his interview with Flick. "Lab equipment makes great scenery. Why don't you sit on the high stool in front of that colorful machine? Paco can shoot you from several angles while you talk."

Flick took her position in front of the chromatograph. "Fire when ready."

"Dr. Adams—have you given any thought to creating an exhibit about Etienne Makepeace?"

She tried not to look surprised. The question was virtually identical to one asked at the news conference by the reporter from the *Kent and Sussex Courier*.

Stuart said to give the same answers to the BBC.

Flick tried to remember exactly what Nigel had said. Something about there being no connection between the history of tea and Etienne Makepeace. Perhaps she could come up with a paraphrase. . . .

Good heavens! Nigel was wrong. And so was I.

Flick abruptly realized that they had both made a serious mistake. Keeping Etienne Makepeace out of a British tea museum would be like excluding Amelia Earhart from an American aviation museum. Equally important, millions of Brits were fascinated by his disappearance and reappearance. A good exhibit about Makepeace might draw significant numbers of new visitors to the museum.

It's a no-brainer! We need a Makepeace Gallery.

She took a deep breath and began. "What I've learned about Etienne Makepeace convinces me that he was a fascinating man—a man worthy to have his story told at the Royal Tunbridge Wells Tea Museum."

These words finished springing from her lips as the door to the Conservation Laboratory opened and Nigel stepped inside. She went on, "The focus of our museum is the history of tea. Makepeace played a small, but exciting, role in that history. His story seems worth telling via an appropriate exhibit."

Harry nodded. "I'm delighted to hear you say that, Dr. Adams. I'm sure that you and your staff will do Etienne Makepeace's memory proud. Have you given any thought to where in the museum you might place your new exhibit?"

Smack in the middle of the Hawker family suite, Flick thought. She glanced at Nigel standing in the back of the laboratory. The expression on his face had gone from happy, to bewildered, to surprised, to angry. Without saying a word, he turned and left.

Oh dear—he doesn't understand what happened.

"One more question, Dr. Adams," Harry said. "When do

you expect a Makepeace exhibit to be up and running?"

Flick worked to keep an even expression on her face despite her growing uneasiness about Nigel. She wanted to finish this interview quickly and calm him down.

"That's difficult to say. A museum can be an unpredictable environment."

Especially when Nigel Owen's feelings are hurt.

FOUR

It makes no sense at all.

Nigel retrieved a yellow pad and slammed his desk drawer shut. Why, without any warning, would Flick do an about-face on so important a subject? She had stood next to him at the news conference and endorsed his unambiguous rejection of an Etienne Makepeace exhibit. She had reaffirmed her support during their debriefing with Stuart Battlebridge. And yet, less than two hours later, she told a BBC reporter that the museum needs a Makepeace exhibit.

What could she have been thinking? And more to the point, how do I convince her to cross back to the prudent side of the road?

Nigel chose a pen and began to scrawl a list on his pad:

REASONS WHY WE SHOULDN'T CREATE A
MAKEPEACE EXHIBIT

1. *Talk of an exhibit will keep reporters poking*

around the museum—and disturbing our daily operations—long beyond the natural demise of the story.

2.   It seems likely that a former museum employee murdered Makepeace; if so, an exhibit would be in poor taste, might open an undreamed-of can of worms, and could possibly start a scandal. In the worst case, an exhibit might impact our ability to repay the enormous loan we've arranged to purchase the Hawker collection.

3.   While it is true that the chief curator is responsible for the museum's exhibits, a major new exhibit will require significant funding and thus the board of trustees' approval. The very last thing we want to do now is propose a new exhibit to the board. We need their attention focused on acquiring the Hawker collection.

4.   We have almost no information about Etienne Makepeace's next of kin. For all we know, the establishment of an exhibit might prompt whatever family he has left to sue the museum.

5.   The chief curator reports to the managing director; if she wants to propose a new exhibit, she should have spoken to me before announcing it to the press!

Nigel scratched a line through the last item. *There's no need to get snippy with Flick—she undoubtedly forgot about the realities of our situation when faced with the reporter's question. I will simply remind her of the big picture.*

He stood, walked to the window that overlooked the tea garden, and stared awhile at the small patch of grass in the center of the garden that held a green bronze sundial and a matching bronze bench. The sun had finally broken through the early morning clouds, making the odd-shaped piece of turf look warm and summery. It would become a grand vantage point for taking pictures of Makepeace's grave. Nigel felt a tremor pulse through his body as he imagined hundreds, perhaps thousands, of nosy gawkers arriving to see the place where Makepeace had been buried, undoubtedly hoping that the police had left bits and pieces of the body behind. Creating a formal display would merely encourage a host of overcurious louts to show up.

Not only is a Makepeace exhibit a terrible idea—we should probably pave over the whole ruddy garden.

Alas, that would be impossible. The museum's visitors from abroad particularly liked the tea garden. Consider the group of fifteen Japanese tourists who arrived at midmorning in a motor coach. They had made a side trip from London to visit the museum and were receiving special treatment—including a narrated tour of the galleries led by Mirabelle Hubbard, the senior docent. At noon, they dined in the Duchess of Bedford Tearoom on a gourmet lunch prepared by Alain Rousseau, the museum's renowned chef. After completing their tour, they would enjoy a typical English afternoon tea, complete with scones, fairy cakes, and savories. That's when Nigel would personally greet the group. Perhaps he would bring Cha-Cha along with him. The Japanese visitors would probably enjoy meeting an expatriate from their homeland.

"Get 'em in—and keep 'em coming back," he murmured. Flick had coined the museum's new mantra. An increasing flow of fee-paying visitors was essential to repay the new loan. "The Royal Tunbridge Wells Tea Museum is open for business."

A vigorous rapping on his door frame seized his attention. He turned, and Flick smiled at him. "We have to talk," she said brightly. "I wanted to clarify what you heard me say, and I think we should issue a follow-up statement to the media."

Nigel grunted and gestured toward the sofa. At least Flick realized that she overstepped her authority—a good job, too, because he wasn't in the mood for a fight this afternoon. He took a moment to gather his thoughts. "I suppose the thing to do is to notify the BBC that we want to correct our response to their questions."

A puzzled look flickered across Flick's face. "My notion exactly, but I don't recall that the BBC sent a reporter to our news conference. We clearly made a mistake when we rejected the idea of an Etienne Makepeace exhibit. I think we should send out a supplemental news release correcting what you said."

"You think what?" Nigel rose halfway out of his chair. "Have you lost your blooming mind? We have to correct what you told the BBC reporter." As soon as the words were spoken, he regretted shouting at Flick. Nonetheless, he matched glower for glower as she glared at him.

"You're surely not sticking with the silly statement you made this morning?" she said. "Don't you realize you were completely wrong? Etienne Makepeace, his disappearance, and his reappearance are all important aspects of the history of tea in England. Of course the man deserves an exhibit. If we reject Makepeace, we might as well ignore Thomas Lipton. . .or Desmond Hawker."

Nigel settled back into his chair with a clank. "You've changed your tune rather quickly, don't you think? What happened to I-can't-imagine-why-we'd-want-an-exhibit about the man?"

"Your feeble attempt at imitating an American accent stinks."

"High praise, indeed!"

"However, to answer your question—I realize that we both shot from the hip at the news conference. I am wise enough to admit that I blundered."

Nigel shook his head. "A Makepeace exhibit is an abysmal idea. The board won't approve it, and neither will I."

Nigel noted that Flick's eyes were shining brightly as she said, "Spoken like a true pompous prig! However, as Stuart attempted to remind you, I have the charter to create a new exhibit when I decide what is appropriate."

"I admit that you are nominally in charge. In theory, the chief curator plans new exhibits." Nigel fluttered his fingers at her. "I give you permission to dream up new exhibits to your heart's content. Keep in mind, however, that I have control of the museum's checkbook. You can't move beyond planning unless I give you the money to spend, and I will never—repeat, never—agree to an exhibit about Etienne Makepeace."

Nigel saw Flick's complexion redden as he spoke. *Too ruddy bad if she's angry; I'm getting angry, too.*

She leveled a wagging finger at him. "You don't have the authority to censor my exhibits."

"I have complete authority to act for the good of the museum." He lifted his yellow pad. "Here are the reasons we shan't be establishing a shrine to Etienne Makepeace."

Flick grabbed the pad from his hand and scanned the list. "Your first objection is nonsense," she said. "Reporters are interested in Makepeace, not us. We've gone out of our way to bring them to the museum and ride the corpse's coattails. We'll benefit from any publicity we get.

"Your second objection is equally goofy. The murder took place about forty years ago—it's ancient history. There's no way that an old killing will impact our current financial dealings. But. . ."—Flick added a dramatic pause—"a new exhibit might well improve our finances by attracting more visitors. With luck, we'll be able to pay off our thirty-two-million-pound debt in fewer than ten years.

"Your third objection proves that you don't know much about running a museum. It takes many months to plan and launch a new exhibit. I see no reason to involve the board until long after our loan has closed.

"And your fourth objection completely ignores the fact that Etienne Makepeace was a national hero. Museums don't get sued for honoring noble people—especially not by a lone, elderly sister suffering from Alzheimer's disease."

"This particular noble person got himself murdered and secretly buried under a tea bush—by an employee of the museum. What if there's a less-than-noble side to the man?"

"The fact that he was buried in our garden gives us a unique responsibility. The Royal Tunbridge Wells Tea Museum must have an exhibit that honors Etienne Makepeace. We'll tell his whole story—the bad along with the good."

"Never," Nigel said softly.

"I am getting really tired of you saying *never* to me." Flick bounded to her feet in a graceful motion, reached the door in three long strides, and slammed it with enough force to make the framed pictures shake on Nigel's thickly plastered wall.

Nigel barely had time to catch a breath before the heavy oak door flew open. Flick stormed back into the office long enough to find Cha-Cha's lead. "Come on, boy—you're staying with the *sane* manager tonight." The Shiba Inu followed Flick out of the room. She turned and slammed the door harder than before.

Nigel let himself sigh. He'd had no choice—he had acted for the good of the museum. Flick would surely understand that when she cooled down and thought about the full ramifications of an exhibit.

"On the other hand. . . ," he murmured, purposely using one of her favorite idioms. He hadn't seen Flick this mad in several months. The depth of her anger reminded him of the early days when they bickered every day—the days before he fell in love with Felicity Adams.

Perhaps a peace offering—perhaps even an apology—would be in order?

His phone rang.

Perhaps Flick had the same idea?

Nigel felt genuine disappointment when he heard a thick Scottish brogue on the other line. "It's me, sir," Conan said. "As promised, Mr. Garwood has arrived with our new toys. He asks if it would be possible for you to join us in the security office for a chin-wag."

Flip! He had forgotten his one-thirty appointment. Flick

would have to wait until he finished the museum's business.

Nigel dashed—two steps at a time—down the four flights of stairs that led from the administrative wing on the third floor to Conan Davies's security lair in the museum's dual-function basement. The eastern half of the subterranean space held the usual machinery—boilers, heaters, electrical equipment—that one expected to find in a cellar. The western half was a "basement" in name only; it had been purpose-built to store documents, artifacts, and other antiquities. And so it was dry, warm, and inviting—with a high, white ceiling, black-and-white floor tile, and plastered walls the color of vanilla ice cream. Conan and his staff of security guards had a small suite of cozy, glass-walled offices near the bottom of the staircase.

Conan was sitting behind his tan metal desk; a comparably large man—bald, suntanned, fortyish, and smiling—sat opposite the chief of security on a tan metal visitor's chair. The oversized pair made the furniture seem undersized. The smiling man leaped to his feet when Nigel stepped inside Conan's office.

"We meet at last, Mr. Owen. I am Niles Garwood. I thought it best to deliver your new security equipment in person."

"Deliver it?" Nigel said, with sufficient amazement to bring a wider grin to Garwood's mouth. "We ordered the video surveillance system only two weeks ago."

"Actually, only ten days ago," the big man said. "Our goal is to have the network up and running by the end of the week. Garwood & McHue works hard to delight our customers by exceeding their expectations." His grin melted into an expression of concern. "We've found that most museums decide to install surveillance cameras after they've been burgled. They expect us to provide protection as quickly and discreetly as possible. *Quickly* is usually the chief requirement, although our specialty is discretion."

Nigel glanced at Conan, who returned a surreptitious wink. Garwood had jumped to the conclusion that the museum was responding to the recent well-publicized theft, and subsequent return, of a priceless set of Tunbridge Ware tea caddies. In truth, the Wescott Bank had insisted on a minor physical security upgrade before agreeing to underwrite the purchase of the Hawker collection. The museum had a state-of-the-art security system that lacked only one important feature: closed-circuit TV surveillance cameras to watch over the museum's interior and exterior.

"You said you brought our cameras with you. . . ." Nigel looked around the office for a stack of cardboard boxes. He had signed Conan's purchase order for two dozen TV cameras, an associated monitoring station, and required installation services.

Garwood snorted. "They're here!" he said. "Every last one is sitting in plain view. You have to look harder."

Nigel looked left and right. Nothing in view resembled the sort of industrial TV camera he expected to see: a rectangular metal box with a lens on one end. But then he noticed an acorn-shaped gadget sitting on Conan's desk. It seemed made of black plastic and was roughly the size of a coffee mug. He reached for it.

"Well done, Mr. Owen!" Garwood clapped his hands silently in imaginary appreciation. "That's one of the twelve external cameras that will watch over the exterior of the building.

The lens inside can pan, tilt, and zoom, so each one can protect a large area. And, of course, the cameras use the latest wireless technology to transmit the images they capture to your central surveillance station." The big man made a quiet laugh. "Now, see if you can find the cameras we'll install *inside* the museum. I warn you—they are wholly camouflaged."

Nigel quickly spotted another item that seemed out of place on Conan's desk: an antique, leather-bound book. He picked it up and saw a small lens hidden in the book's spine.

"Quite right, sir!" Garwood said merrily. "We installed a wireless TV camera inside a real nineteenth-century hardback. What better disguise for the surveillance camera installed in your library?"

Nigel nodded slowly as he turned the book in his hands. Place the volume on a high shelf, and the camera would be virtually undetectable by anyone in the room.

"Keep looking," Garwood continued. "There are eleven more disguised cameras on display in this office. I'll wager you won't find them all."

Nigel peered, in turn, at every object he could see in Conan's office. His slow, methodical search eventually revealed a one-liter chemical bottle with a lens beneath its label ("that will surveil the Conservation Laboratory"); he noticed an antique teapot whose spout glittered back at him ("it will sit high on a shelf in the Tea Antiquities Collection; no one will notice that the spout was reshaped to hold a lens assembly that can take in the entire room"); and he recognized a small, wooden globe that looked out of place on a shelf above Conan's desk ("it's an inexpensive replica of an antique on display in the World of Tea Map Room; we bought it in your gift shop and installed a miniature camera inside").

"Eight more interior cameras to go," Garwood said cheerfully. "As you can see, our electronic eyes are essentially nondisruptive to your exhibits. We did our very best to keep your chief curator happy."

My chief curator! Blimey!

Nigel abruptly remembered that Flick had asked to attend the meeting with Niles Garwood. She would be furious if she discovered he had forgotten to bring her along.

Perhaps she never has to know? Perhaps she'll forget about the meeting? Perhaps the sun will rise in the west?

"Your cameras clearly represent the pinnacle of discreet surveillance," Nigel said. "I wish I had the time to finish the game, but I must get back to my other duties." He silently added, *Not to mention restoring my relationship with Felicity Adams.*

He shook Garwood's hand, wished him well, and made a mental note to have Conan prepare an easy-to-follow map of the surveillance network. He would never remember the locations—or the disguises—of the dozen tricked-up TV cameras hidden inside the building.

Nigel was huffing slightly when he reached the third floor. *Why not,* he thought, *visit Flick right now? Chances are, she's cooled down.* He made for the curators' wing.

No joy. After not finding either Flick or Cha-Cha, he asked a white-coated curator working at a large comparative microscope.

"Flick took Cha-Cha for a walk," the woman said, not looking up from her eyepiece. "She left about twenty minutes ago."

"Thank you," Nigel mumbled. Well, he was off the hook

for not bringing Flick to meet Niles Garwood—but what possible reason did she have to take a walk in midafternoon?

Feeling curiously glum, Nigel tramped to his office. He found Polly Reid placing a thick envelope in a prominent position atop his desk.

"This letter came in the morning post," she said, "but I just got around to opening it. I didn't notice the proof of delivery certificate." Polly made a little grimace. "We have a bit of a fuss concerning Cha-Cha. It seems that our dog killed a prize ferret. The owner of the deceased champion—a Mr. Bertram Holloway—is claiming significant damages."

"A ferret? When and where did Cha-Cha dispatch a ferret?"

"According to this complaint, the ferret breathed his last on the Sunday following Dame Elspeth's funeral. It happened somewhere in her vast back garden. We received Cha-Cha and the other animals the following day—a Monday. I looked it up."

Nigel yanked the letter out of its envelope and snapped, "How can the museum be responsible for something that happened before we took custody of the mutt?"

"That is a question I suggest you put to Solicitor Bleasdale, sir—especially in your present aggravated mood. I've written his private number on the back of the envelope."

"Mea culpa." Nigel held up his hands in mock surrender. "Forgive me for shooting the messenger."

Polly responded with a "forget it" wave of her hand as he dialed his telephone.

"Bleasdale here," spoke a curt voice. Nigel countered with, "Owen, ditto."

A deep sigh. "These frequent calls from the museum are becoming tedious. I shall soon consider billing you for my time."

"While you're at it, Barrington, consider the enormous fee you will earn when our loan closes and we purchase the Hawker collection from your clients."

Another deep sigh. Nigel imagined the portly solicitor wringing his hands in despair. Bleasdale did not like to be reminded of his nineteenth-century first name.

"How may I be of assistance, Nigel?" the attorney asked.

"I have here in front of me a paper that says the museum is about to be sued by a lunatic named Holloway, who seeks to recover the exorbitant cost of a prize ferret that Cha-Cha is accused of murdering the day before you delivered him to us."

"A lunatic? Not at all—Bertram Holloway is the very model of a sane and stable gentleman. He owns the estate adjacent to Lion's Peak. I believe he was on quite friendly terms with Dame Elspeth."

"You know the man?"

"Indeed. He approached me and described his distress. I, of course, referred him to you."

"Ah. Then you know that stable Mr. Holloway wants five thousand pounds compensation for a dead ferret."

"That does seem a lot of money for a small mammal, although I am really not qualified to comment."

"I urge you to get qualified—quickly. Let me remind you that Cha-Cha was in your care at the time of the alleged murder. The murdered ferret is your problem."

"The dog's caregiver at the time is wholly irrelevant," Bleasdale said calmly.

"Irrelevant? How can the museum be responsible for a dog that was not in its possession and therefore not in a position to control?"

"I shall be happy to explain. There are two significant concepts for you to consider. First, dogs of the Shiba Inu breed are well-known to be superb hunters of small animals."

"I know that, Barrington. Cha-Cha caught a squirrel in our greenhouse two months ago. He carried it to the Duchess of Bedford Tearoom so he could eat it in pleasant surroundings."

"You're aware of the fact, but likely not the legal implications. Because Shibas enjoy hunting, those who own Shibas are required to prevent them from stalking other people's small pets."

"But we didn't own Cha-Cha on the day he went ferret hunting."

"I beg to differ, Nigel. According to the terms of the contract your predecessor at the museum signed, Dame Elspeth's animals—including the dog, Cha-Cha—became wards of the museum the instant she passed away. The unfortunate killing of the ferret happened, legally speaking, on your watch. In short, the problem is yours."

"That's ridiculous."

"The law does not always make sense."

"Neither do you, Bleasdale. We didn't have the animals in our possession—you did."

"But I'm not being sued—you are."

Nigel felt himself reach a breaking point. "Bleasdale, you're a nattering dolt. Stop making inane comments and pay attention to me. . . ."

Click. The line grew quiet; then he heard the dial tone.

Barrington Bleasdale had hung up on him. Nigel stared at his phone and wondered for a fleeting minute if he should call Iona Saxby, a member of the museum's board of trustees who was also an Oxford-based solicitor of substantial repute. She would know how to resolve this problem—or at least be able to tell Nigel what to do next.

Forget it! After the miserable events of today, you don't have sufficient strength left to deal with Iona.

The invitation had come as a complete surprise. Flick's mobile phone had rung scarcely a minute after she stormed out of Nigel's office. "Dr. Adams—this is Detective Inspector Marc Pennyman. Would you have a spare moment to chat?" His voice had been friendly, nothing like the officious policeman's snarl that she associated with Pennyman.

She matched his pleasant tone. "Certainly, Detective Inspector."

"I would like to make an appointment to meet with you—preferably away from the museum, if possible early this afternoon."

"Can you tell me why?"

"I believe we may be able to help each other."

Ask a policeman a silly question and get a silly, evasive answer.

Flick doubted that pressing the point would encourage Pennyman to be more forthcoming. Her only choice was to answer yes or no and be done with it.

She glanced at her watch. A few minutes past one. The day was still young and her "to-do" list essentially complete.

This was a perfect afternoon to play hooky for a while—to give into the urge she felt to get far, far away from Nigel Owen. She also needed some time away from her desk to come up with a strategy to overcome Nigel's ludicrous objections. The more he whined "never," the more certain she felt that the museum would have an Etienne Makepeace exhibit.

"Shall we say the Pantiles at one thirty? We can meet in the Italian coffee shop just past the Swan Hotel."

"An excellent choice." Pennyman seemed to hesitate. "I have one other request—please come alone." He rang off before Flick could say that she had no intention of bringing anyone else.

The sunny, surprisingly warm afternoon immediately raised her spirits. As she guided Cha-Cha along Eridge Road, she felt like a tourist approaching the southern end of the Pantiles for the first time. Perhaps she should do a little window-shopping in the trendy boutiques and antique shops. She felt in a mood to spend some money on herself.

She spotted Pennyman as soon as she climbed the steps and reached the Pantiles. He clearly had decided that the day was warm enough for an alfresco meeting and had chosen a two-person table outside the coffee shop.

Good! Now I won't have to tie Cha-Cha to a bench near the front door.

Pennyman frowned when he saw Flick accompanied by the Shiba Inu. She straightaway realized that his request to "come alone" also embraced double-coated dogs noted for bountiful shedding. Pennyman's scowl swelled to a grimace when Cha-Cha curled up next to his chair. His hand, seemingly driven by memories of past encounters with the dog, brushed a nonexistent clump of red hair off his trousers.

"Your suit is perfectly safe, Detective Inspector," she said. "Cha-Cha doesn't appear to be shedding this week."

Pennyman grunted, then said, "I've ordered a double-shot espresso—what would you like? I doubt they make a good cuppa here."

"A simple cup of coffee would be lovely."

Flick was bursting with curiosity as Pennyman signaled the waiter and placed the order. When they were alone, she said, "What brings us here this afternoon?"

"I shan't attempt to mislead you, Dr. Adams, or otherwise take undue advantage of your willingness to cooperate with me." He paused to look around the Pantiles. Flick guessed he wanted to make certain that no one else was listening. "By any chance, have you and your colleagues considered the possibility of establishing a permanent exhibit about Etienne Makepeace?"

Flick caught her breath. Of all the questions Pennyman might have asked, she least expected this one. For some unfathomable reason, the entire world had become interested in her curatorial plans! Why would a Kent Police detective give a rip about a Makepeace exhibit at a small museum? And why would he go out of his way to arrange an unofficial inquiry?

"We've made no definite decisions yet," she said, "but I am leaning toward a modest exhibit about Makepeace's place in the history of tea in England. Now—please tell me why you care one way or the other."

"I made the assumption that to build a Makepeace exhibit from scratch, you would gather every bit of information you can learn about the man. I'd like to work with you and pool our knowledge."

Flick gave a little whistle. "Wow—I never expected to hear you say something like that."

Pennyman returned an awkward grin. "This is an unusual situation. Despite his public fame, we know very little about the private life of Etienne Makepeace. I'm hoping that your efforts will secure useful information that we don't have. Consequently, I propose a quid pro quo."

"Really?"

Pennyman nodded. "Yes, really." He paused while the waiter delivered Flick's coffee, then went on, "Although I can't disclose the particulars of an ongoing murder investigation, I can provide you with lesser-known, though public, background information on Etienne Makepeace. It should save you considerable time and effort—possibly help you launch your investigation faster."

"And in exchange, I share anything interesting that I discover about him?"

"Precisely."

Flick didn't dither. How could she lose? Pennyman's offer was an answer to a prayer she should have spoken aloud. She had planned to ask Stuart Battlebridge for his dossier on Etienne Makepeace as the starting point of her research. Now she would have an even more authoritative package of facts prepared by the fabled Kent Constabulary.

"It's a deal!" She offered her hand. Pennyman reached across the small table and shook it, then slid a hefty manila envelope in front of Flick.

"You'll find Makepeace's file inside," he said, "along with

three of my business cards. I can usually be reached at any hour of the day." He rose to his feet. "Have fun—and enjoy your coffee." He turned to leave, then paused. "I hesitate to give you advice, but we've found that a Web page is a good starting point for gathering information."

Flick smiled. "A Web page is the first item on my list of things to do."

She dove into the envelope. The biographical information matched the data in Stuart's briefing, but it was more complete. Stuart said that Etienne had earned a degree in history at Cambridge—these documents explained that his focus was first-century Rome. She recalled that Etienne had been a naval intelligence officer—she now learned that he had risen to the rank of lieutenant commander. Both briefings described his success as a "Tea Sage"—the police had gone to the trouble of cataloging the different books and articles that Makepeace had written.

But. . .neither briefing explains how Etienne Makepeace became England's Tea Sage.

Flick sat up in her chair. Where were the details of Etienne's tea education? Etienne was famous for his exhaustive knowledge of tea—how did he come by it? Nothing in the file suggested that he had ever been taught how to brew a good cuppa, much less the subtleties of different tea varieties. Neither Stuart nor the police seemed to care where his vast expertise came from.

"That's something I need to figure out," she said to her now-empty coffee cup. "But how? How do you investigate someone who died forty years earlier?"

You don't know—so why not ask an expert? Uncle Ted, for example.

It was approaching 10:00 a.m. in York, Pennsylvania—she pictured him in his office, sitting at his messy desk. She dialed the number on her mobile phone and listened to her uncle's telephone ringing more than three thousand miles away.

"Homicide. Detective Adams."

"Hi, Uncle Ted, it's Flick."

"Flick? Where are you?"

"In England, the island nation where I now reside permanently."

"Don't rub it in. Your mother complains to me about your new country once each week."

"Mother loves England; she's an Anglophile. That's where I get it from."

"Your mother—and your father, too—love *things* that are English. That's why they operate a replica eighteenth-century English inn, complete with an authentic pub, called the White Rose of York. They are also dyed-in-the-wool Pennsylvanians who will never leave the Commonwealth."

Flick ignored the implied gibe. "Well, I'm fine, and you sound fine, too."

"Did you make an intercontinental telephone call to tell me that?"

"Actually, I want to pick your brain about a corpse."

"*Another* body?"

"Relax—this corpse died way back in the sixties. His name is Etienne Makepeace."

"*Uh-huh*. The famous missing Brit they dug up in your museum's garden."

"You've heard about him?" Flick squeaked. "How?"

"Oh. . .I came across a mention or two about Makepeace

on CNN, NBC, ABC, CBS, BBC, and in *Time* magazine, *Newsweek*, the *New York Times*, the *York Daily Record*, the *York Dispatch*. . ."

"Okay, okay—I get the point. He made major news in America like he did in Britain."

"Well—*duh!*"

"Don't make a fuss—I didn't think the matter through."

"I've been wondering when you would get around to calling me." He chuckled softly, then became serious. "I take it that Makepeace was murdered."

"Shot once with a vintage Russian pistol, then buried under our tea bushes."

"Sounds like an inside job. The museum must have had a deadly docent on its staff during the sixties."

"Probably—but I'm not interested in the murder itself."

"On behalf of homicide investigators everywhere, I say thank you."

"However. . ."

"With you, there is always a 'however.'"

"I'm gathering information to create an exhibit about Makepeace at the museum."

"Complete with a pretend skeleton, I'll bet."

"Complete with the story of how Etienne Makepeace became England's Tea Sage—assuming I can find out how he managed the feat. There are troubling gaps in his biographical materials. I don't know how to fill them. Do you have any suggestions?"

"*Hmm. . .*"

"What?"

"I'm thinking."

"About?"

"About how people are likely to share information with a museum—if you ask for it. Have you asked the general public to help?"

"Not yet," Flick said, astonished that two cops an ocean apart both imagined that a modest tea museum could be a fact magnet.

"Start by setting up a Web page."

"Way ahead of you."

"Your next step is to create a telephone hotline."

"How would I get people to call it?"

"Don't you know any friendly reporters?"

"Funny you should ask. I was interviewed this morning by a BBC TV reporter."

"There you go! Ask him to mention your hotline when he airs his story. That should shake loose a few interesting tidbits."

"Tidbits aren't enough. I need big chunks of real information. I have a major exhibit to feed."

"Well, if I were trying to gather lots of details about a famous man who disappeared forty years ago, I'd try to locate the law firm who worked with his heirs."

"Why? All but one of Makepeace's heirs are dead, too."

"Famous people tend to be wealthy, and wealthy people tend to have relatives who are eager to get their hands on the money. I assume that Makepeace's kin eventually had him declared legally dead so they could collect under the terms of his will. I think English law and American law are pretty much the same—seven years after a person goes missing, a court can declare him dead. Remember the *number one* rule: Follow the money."

"I still don't get where you're going with this."

"Lawyers ask questions about people and write things down. Maybe there's an old file gathering dust in a law office that contains more of the information you're looking for?"

"I suppose it's possible. . . ."

"Talk about ungrateful! Need I remind you that you called me without any warning? You try to come up with fabulous ideas on the fly. Repeat after me: 'Uncle Ted, I owe you big-time.'"

Flick snickered. "I owe you big-time."

"I'll say you do—so tell me about your love life. Your mother reports that you have a boyfriend in England."

Flick hemmed, hawed, made excuses, and managed to end the conversation with only a cursory description of Nigel and a solemn oath to call back when she had more time to talk. She slipped the mobile phone into her purse and spoke to Cha-Cha, "I feel energized, and I'm having second thoughts about Uncle Ted's ideas. What do you say we walk back to the museum and talk to a woman about a Web site?"

Flick walked fast enough to make Cha-Cha trot along the sidewalk after her. She wanted to catch Hannah Kerrigan, the museum's new information technology guru, while she was still at her computer. Hannah worked odd hours—and often left early—so that she could take advanced computer courses at the Canterbury Christ Church University College. Flick had hired her a month earlier to enlarge and enhance the museum's Web site: www.teamuseum.org.

Hannah was a petite woman in her early twenties, with flaming red hair, large brown eyes, and a pixyish grin that made one forget she could "speak" six different computer programming languages. Flick found her in her cubicle in the Conservation Laboratory, fiddling happily with an under-construction Web page on her computer. Hannah might have been able to fiddle more productively had not Lapsang and Souchong decided to pay her a visit. The big blue cats sprawled side by side across her keyboard, covering most of the top of her workstation.

Cha-Cha eyed the felines suspiciously but sat silently at Flick's feet. She suspected that the three of them—raised together as puppy and kittens—had reached some sort of mutual accommodation. The cats probably discovered that a Shiba was a much more capable dog than his compact size suggested. Cha-Cha probably recognized that taking on a full-grown British Shorthair was not a clever idea—even for a feisty Shiba Inu.

"Wonder of wonders! Back from your walk, are you? Cha-Cha is available."

Flick twirled around. There stood Nigel, sporting a remarkably contrite expression.

"The Japanese tour group," he said. "Downstairs. Still time to show them Cha-Cha. Only if you don't object."

Flick needed several moments to interpret his fragmented request. When she finally understood, she handed him the dog lead. "I suspect that Cha-Cha will have the most fun. Our visitors will have met countless Shibas, but he hasn't met many Japanese."

"Well said! Truly astute. Will leave now. Must chat later. Many things." Nigel's eyes darted between Flick and Hannah.

He wants to apologize but not in front of Hannah.

Flick, not quite ready to let Nigel off the hook, replied with a curt nod. It was enough for Nigel—he tendered a remarkably silly smile and backed out of the laboratory, tugging Cha-Cha along the tiled floor.

"What's that about then?" Hannah asked. She craned her neck to watch Nigel leave.

"Never you mind."

"Pity. I'm always in the mood to hear a good love story."

"I bring you something even better—a brief parole from your chores as our Webmistress."

"Super! I'm having all sorts of difficulty with the JavaScript applet code for this new page."

"I have no idea what you just said, but you seem the perfect person to help me establish a telephone hotline." The obvious delight on Hannah's face increased with every word of explanation that Flick provided.

"I know just the way to do it," Hannah said. "I'll transform one of our old computers into a telephone answering system and set up different categories." She began to speak in an almost mechanical tone. "If you know anything about Etienne Makepeace's childhood, please press 1."

"That's exactly what we need, but focus the information categories on tea. I want to know how Makepeace acquired his knowledge. Did he go to school? Did he have a mentor? Was he an autodidact?"

"An auto-*what?*"

"A self-taught expert." Flick tried to perch on the edge of the workstation. Lapsang, or was it Souchong, anticipated her move and stretched to fill even more of the surface. "The next part of your assignment is to locate an especially obscure

fact related to the life and death of Etienne Makepeace."
She added, "I presume that your Internet research skills are
brilliant?"

"Totally!"

"Good—because I need to know if Makepeace was declared
legally dead by an English court, and if so, the name of the
solicitor who acted for the Makepeace family. The earliest it
could have happened was in 1973."

"Wow!" Hannah said. "That's ancient history, but I'll see
what I can find out."

"In exchange, I'll de-kitty your keyboard." Flick scooped
up the pair of cats, unceremoniously plopped them on the
floor, and watched them saunter off to the other side of the
laboratory. She sat down on the workstation.

"Lapsang and Souchong don't bother me," Hannah said.
"They keep me company because I don't pet them or make a
fuss over them."

"Sounds like cat thinking," Flick said. "One of these
days, we have to figure out which is Lapsang and which is
Souchong."

Hannah seemed bewildered. "You mean you don't know?"

"We can guess, but the only person who could tell us for
sure is dead. The cats arrived at the museum without collars
or identification tags. The only clue we have is a handful of
snapshots that the breeder took when the cats were kittens.
They were included with the paperwork Elspeth Hawker
originally gave to the museum." Flick shrugged. "Now that
the cats are grown up, their baby pictures are worthless."

"Perhaps not." Hannah leaned toward Flick as if she had a
secret to share. "What if I take new digital photos of Lapsang

and Souchong in roughly the same poses as the kitten shots? Then I could use Photoshop to compare the old images with the new. I might be able to recognize minor features that haven't changed—a fleck of color in an eye, the shape of an ear, maybe markings on a nose."

Flick threw back her head. "I love the idea! In fact, I'm furious that I didn't think of it first. It's certainly worth a try."

Hannah began to count on her fingers. "First, I'll program the computer. Second, I'll search the Internet. Third, I'll photograph the cats. Fourth, I'll compare the old and new photos."

"And fifth, you add a simple page to our current Web site that announces we'll pay ten pounds for an interesting anec-dote about Etienne Makepeace that involves tea. Acceptable anecdotes will have a minimum of two hundred fifty words."

Hannah peered up at Flick. "Do I have a deadline?"

Flick joked, "How about tomorrow at noon?"

"A piece of cake! I don't have classes this evening, and I get in early on Tuesdays. I'll probably be done by eleven in the morning."

My goodness! She's serious.

Flick wanted to laugh but managed to mumble, "*Um. . .* thank you. I appreciate your dedication. I see us working to-gether on many projects in the months ahead."

Hannah peered up at Flick with brown eyes that now seemed years older and far more calculating. "In that case, tell me what's going on with you and Mr. Owen. Did you cut him loose? Can anyone have a go at him?"

Flick heard herself gasp—and immediately felt foolish that she had overreacted. Why should a silly question from an occasionally harebrained computer techie have the power to startle her?

Because you don't want to cut Nigel loose.

Flick slid to her feet, surprised at the depth of the fondness she suddenly felt for Nigel. "I will let you know if and when anyone can have a go at Nigel. Until then—"

Hannah didn't wait for Flick to finish. "Don't get your knickers in a twist," she said with an embarrassed smile. "You can't blame a girl for asking."

FIVE

Nigel dried his face with a paper towel and glared at himself in the lavatory mirror. "Now you know what a blithering idiot sounds like. You haven't behaved so ineptly since you were fifteen. What on earth made you act the fool?"

He crumpled the towel into a wad and realized that his question had an obvious answer. There was no mystery here. *Anyone* could recognize that he was caught on the horns of a ludicrous dilemma.

One part of him wanted to apologize to Flick—and seek her forgiveness.

The other part believed that she should apologize to him—and refused to let a repentant word pass his lips.

Falling in love certainly led to surprising complications. He tried to remember if it was Keats or Browning who wrote that the course of true love never did run smooth. Either way, the words were proving painfully true. But neither he nor Flick had time in their busy lives for useless bickering. Something was bothering her about their relationship. He would have to sort the matter out as quickly as possible, for both their sakes.

Nigel stepped out of his private loo and discovered that Cha-Cha had claimed a favorite forbidden roost—dead center atop Nigel's leather-upholstered sofa. Nigel pondered chasing him off but decided the sofa was so tatty that it hardly made sense to displace the dog. Once the acquisition of the Hawker antiquities was complete, he would have an opportunity to persuade the board of trustees that the director of the Royal Tunbridge Wells Tea Museum deserved more elegant decor. His heavy and substantial wooden desk, on the verge of becoming an antique, could stay. But the various chairs in the room were long past their prime, as was the room's tea-stained Oriental carpet.

Nigel glanced at his clock. The visiting Japanese were approaching the last leg of their museum tour. In ten minutes, Mirabelle Hubbard would shepherd them into the Duchess of Bedford Tearoom. Why not intercept them in the World of Tea Map Room? It was a perfect place to say a few words before they enjoyed their cream tea and boarded the bus back to London.

Nigel had begun to frame a few appropriate remarks when his phone rang. He moved behind his desk and checked the caller ID panel: Margo McKendrick, in the Welcome Centre kiosk. He snatched up the receiver. "Hi, Margo."

"Mr. Owen, sir, you have a visitor."

Crikey. Margo had used their agreed-upon code word for "VIP alert." When she began a telephone call with "Mr.

Owen, sir," it signaled that an important person had arrived unexpectedly.

Margo went on. "Olivia Hart, from Wescott Bank, is here to see you."

Nigel struggled to put a face to the name. He had made three trips to the bank's London headquarters to work out the details of the loan package and had met eight different executives, but no Olivia Hart.

"Send her up at once," he said.

He rang off and dialed Polly Reid's telephone.

"A banker named Olivia Hart is riding the elevator to the third floor. Please steer her to my office when she arrives."

"A banker?"

"I can't figure it out either." He dropped down into his chair to think.

Had he forgotten to schedule an important meeting? His calendar was empty that afternoon—but bankers generally didn't show up unannounced.

An explanation flashed into his mind.

Of course! She's here to talk about our security system.

Nigel relaxed. Olivia Hart must be a low-level security whiz sent to evaluate Conan's new surveillance camera system. Who else but a head-in-the-clouds techie would show up without an appointment? He would pass her off as quickly as possible to Conan Davies. She'd undoubtedly have a grand time searching for disguised cameras in his office.

He heard a tap on his door.

"Enter."

The door swung open, revealing a woman stunning enough to be a supermodel. She struck Nigel as perfect in every way. To change anything—the symmetrical oval shape of her face, the sapphire blue of her piercing eyes, the enticing way she held her head—would diminish her beauty.

"Good afternoon," she said. "I am Olivia Hart."

She wore a well-tailored dark gray suit, with a miniskirt and a white silk shirt. If one kept staring at Olivia—Nigel strove hard not to—one could imagine that her flawless complexion glowed from inner illumination, rather than reflecting the light filtering through his window.

Nigel stood up and mumbled a throaty, "Hello."

Her auburn hair was styled short, allowing Nigel to glimpse two dark, shimmering spheres—each the size of a one-pound coin—that hung beneath her ears. He wondered what sort of jewels they were.

Olivia placed a business card face up on Nigel's desk. As she came close, he smelled the scent she was wearing—an exotic, flowery perfume he had never experienced before. He studied the card for several seconds, chiefly to avoid gawking at her.

> **Olivia Hart, PhD**
> **Regional Vice President**
> **Wescott Bank**
> **Maidstone, Kent**

In due course, he felt his stunned brain begin to function more or less normally.

A regional vice president? Why would Wescott Bank's regional vice president arrive unannounced for a visit? For that matter, what *was* a regional vice president? Nigel wasn't sure, but he had begun to doubt that Olivia's specialty was security.

She broke the awkward silence. "Thank you for seeing me on such short notice."

"My pleasure. Totally." He waved vaguely toward a visitor's chair. Olivia sat down and crossed her legs. They proved to be as spectacular as the rest of her.

"I'm sure you're curious about the purpose of my visit," she said.

"*Um.* . .yes, I had wondered."

"I'm eager to tell you, but it would be most useful if you invited Dr. Adams to our meeting."

"You want my chief curator to join us?"

"Her presence is essential," she replied, in a tone that left no room for disobedience. "What I have to say concerns both of you."

Nigel surrendered meekly. "I'll see if she's in." He reached for his telephone.

Olivia looked at her watch. "It's not even four o'clock on a normal workday—where else would she be but in?"

The stony edge in Olivia's voice made Nigel's stomach jitter as he dialed Flick's extension. When she answered, he spoke with an unintended rush of relief. "Ah, you're at your desk."

"And your point is?" Flick said, with obvious pique. "I've been here for most of the afternoon."

Nigel pressed the telephone tighter against his ear. Had he been alone, he might have reminded Flick about her mysterious walk with Cha-Cha that very afternoon. But since Olivia seemed attentive to his every word, he labored frantically to keep his voice calm and said, "Olivia Hart from Wescott Bank is presently in my office. She wants to chat with both of us."

"Who is Olivia Hart?"

He didn't reply, hoping that Flick would understand his silence.

"Nigel...," she said after several seconds, "are you trying to communicate that this unscheduled meeting is important?"

"*Very* important."

Flick hesitated but eventually said, "Okay. I'm on my way."

"Excellent." He added an unspoken *Bless you*.

He put down the phone and turned to Olivia. "Can I get you anything? A cup of tea, perhaps?"

"I dislike tea. Do you have any decent coffee?"

Nigel rendered up one of his warmest smiles. "Why yes, the Duchess of Bedford Tearoom serves excellent coffee. I'll have some sent up." He thought about admitting that he, too, preferred a strong cup of coffee but decided to leave well enough alone. He called Polly and asked her to arrange for tea, coffee, and biscuits.

I'll also have to forget about meeting the Japanese tourists. They would soon be drinking their afternoon tea. His gut told him that he would be coping with Olivia Hart long after the tour group left for London.

Nigel abruptly realized that Cha-Cha was nowhere to be seen. He scanned his office surreptitiously and spotted a patch of reddish hair under his sofa. The dog had run for cover when Olivia entered the room.

Amazing! That hound has a sixth sense for trouble—and troublesome people.

Flick arrived while Nigel was still pondering doggy clairvoyance. He looked up in time to see the displeasure written across her face turn to astonishment when she caught sight of their visitor. Olivia seemed perfectly content to sit still and be stared at while Flick made her way into the room. Nigel guessed that Olivia had years of experience being the center of attention.

He stood and with a gallant gesture said, "Dr. Adams, this is Ms. Hart from. . ."

Olivia cut him off. "I dislike 'Ms.' intensely, Nigel. If you insist on using formal titles at this institution, then introduce me as *Dr.* Hart. My doctorate is in economics. However, I prefer to work with clients on a first name basis." She acknowledged Flick with a perfunctory nod and extended her hand. "Please, Felicity—call me Olivia."

"Thank you. . . *Olivia*. My friends call me Flick. Welcome to our museum." Flick dropped into the empty visitor's chair on the opposite side of Nigel's desk.

Nigel saw a blaze of determination on Olivia's face as she uncrossed her legs and sat up in her chair. She was clearly getting ready to take charge. But of what? And for what reason?

"Now that we're all here," she said, "let me say that it is a pleasure to meet both of you in person. I find it difficult to get the true sense of a person from a paper dossier, no matter how complete it is."

Dossier? Nigel summoned up images of the forms he had filled out in late December. How much biographical information about senior staff had Wescott Bank requested? Not much at all, if memory served—certainly not a complete recitation of his background. He had provided little more than the brief background sketch published on the museum's Web site. It didn't include his age or even the job details one would find on a typical résumé. It hardly qualified as a dossier.

An ember of possibility burst into a flame of insight. *Had the bank done its own investigation? Perhaps even hired a private detective?* It wasn't that far-fetched an idea. If he directed Wescott Bank, he would want to be sure that the museum was well managed and likely to survive long enough to repay the loan. Why hadn't he considered the possibility earlier? There was no telling what the bank—and Olivia—had learned about him and Flick. The thought made him feel uncomfortably vulnerable.

Nigel began to squirm as Olivia settled her fantastic eyes on him. "I have a most unusual role at Wescott Bank," she said. "I serve as the bank's chief troubleshooter in Southern England. Think of me as an ambassador who speaks for our executives in London when they think it necessary to reprimand a client."

"Reprimand?" Nigel couldn't prevent his voice from climbing in pitch. "The bank sent you here to reprimand the museum?"

"I find it best to be blunt, Nigel." Olivia displayed a slight grimace. "I've been directed to read you the riot act."

Flick raised her hand. "Time out! I don't know what that means."

Olivia smiled at her. "Forgive me. It's a quaint British idiom. During the eighteenth century, the British army was occasionally called upon to quell riots among the populace. An official would give the rioters fair notice by reading aloud the Riot Act—which warned that the troops would open fire if the crowd did not disband."

Flick began to frown. "In other words, you're here to deliver an ultimatum."

Olivia shook her head theatrically. "I often have that unhappy responsibility. Today, however, I am merely bringing a serious matter to your attention. One that requires a prompt resolution."

Nigel tried not to look guilty as Olivia once again spoke to him. "The chairman of Wescott Bank is exceedingly upset that the museum hosted a news conference this morning. He fears that you have created unnecessary media interest in the link between the museum and Etienne Makepeace's death." She added, "Have you met our chairman?"

Nigel nodded. "Sir James Boyer."

"Sir James straightaway convened a meeting of his advisory council to discuss the issue. After due deliberation, he and his advisers decided that the bank will move ahead with the loan if you will promise no more extraordinary attempts to generate publicity for the next ninety days. No news conferences, no visits by media to the museum, no interviews with members of the press to talk about Etienne Makepeace. Sir James insists that the museum disconnect itself from the furor surrounding the discovery of Makepeace's body."

Nigel's mind raced to sort out the different things that Olivia's "warning" had implied. The worst of the lot was that the Grand High Pooh-Bah of Wescott Bank had come close to terminating the loan they were relying on—all because of their silly news conference.

I'll wring Stuart Battlebridge's neck for talking me into it.

Fortunately, more temperate heads at the bank had prevailed. The museum—not to mention Nigel Owen—would receive a reprieve in exchange for a promise to shun publicity for three months.

"I'll be happy to make such a commitment to Wescott Bank," Nigel said.

Olivia shifted her gaze. "And what about you, Flick? Can Sir James also count on your support?"

Flick stared at her hands a moment before she said, "I agree. No more news conferences, no more media interviews focused on Etienne Makepeace."

Nigel slapped his palm on his desktop. "We have a deal!"

"Almost," Olivia said. "There is one other condition."

"Yes?"

"Sir James requires a comprehensive explanation of how Etienne Makepeace was connected to the Royal Tunbridge Wells Tea Museum. He is not satisfied with the hazy reports presented in the news media. He wants facts, dates, and precise details."

"But. . .that's an *unreasonable* request," Nigel said. "How can we possibly gather more information than the media and the police? The events in question happened forty years ago. Where would we look? To whom would we talk?"

Flick spoke up before Olivia could answer. "The media have reported that Etienne Makepeace gave a series of lectures at the museum—what more does Sir James want to know? Perhaps you can help us understand his specific concerns."

Olivia leaned forward in her chair. "Sir James hasn't shared his thinking with me, but I can speculate that his chief concern is increased risk. Lending thirty-two million pounds to a small tea museum in Kent is a highly unusual transaction for Wescott. Most of Wescott's clientele are large manufacturing corporations. We understand how they operate; we know how to evaluate the loss potential we face. But when we deal with you, we are largely guessing. The discovery of Etienne Makepeace's body, and the ensuing media frenzy, made the calculations even more uncertain. Your news conference served as a final straw and knocked Sir James out of his comfort zone." She made a wry face. "That was an unwise thing to do scarcely two weeks before your loan was scheduled to close."

Nigel nodded gloomily. He had not thought Wescott Bank the right source of funds for precisely the reasons she had given. But Archibald Meicklejohn, the chair of the museum's trustees—a London banker himself—had insisted on Wescott, largely because he was a golfing friend of James Boyer.

A knock on the door signaled the arrival of their refreshments. Polly maneuvered a heavily laden tea cart into the office. Nigel thanked her and then played "mother." When he had appropriately distributed the coffee, tea, and Alain's famed shortbread squares, he said, "Olivia, one would hope that Sir James's contentment will be restored when he remembers that our loan will be secured by a collection of antiquities worth far more than thirty-two million pounds."

Nigel thought about taking Olivia on a quick tour of the museum. Firsthand knowledge of the Hawker collection might transform her into a more enthusiastic advocate for their cause.

"That particular argument won't impress Sir James," Olivia said, as she stirred her coffee, "because the antiquities themselves represent a major source of uncertainty." She took a sip. "Using museum exhibits as collateral for a loan is also a novel idea for us. I imagine that Sir James cringes at the thought of selling teacups and bric-a-brac to recoup our money should the museum slip into bankruptcy."

Olivia smiled at Nigel; he couldn't help grinning back. She had an enchanting smile. He caught Flick looking at him; she wasn't smiling. He immediately tried to match her pained expression.

"We will certainly try to find what Sir James *requires*"—he spoke the last word through gritted teeth—"but we are still faced with the difficult challenge of uncovering forty-year-old details."

Flick jumped in. "Nigel is talking like a sensible museum director who prefers to play his cards close to his vest and is reluctant to make promises that may be impossible to keep. However. . ."

"There is no *however*. . ." He tried to interrupt.

Flick continued. "Please tell Sir James that we're seeking the very same kind of information that he wants. We, too, need to understand why Etienne Makepeace was shot and buried on museum grounds. There's bound to be a simple explanation; most murders, after all, are fairly straightforward crimes committed by people who have down-to-earth motives." She paused for dramatic effect. "Consequently, under Nigel's direction, I've initiated a multifaceted investigation into Makepeace's relationship with the museum during its early years."

Nigel swallowed a mouthful of coffee the wrong way and began to cough. *What multifaceted investigation had Flick begun?* Certainly not one that he had "directed." Nor one that he had even heard about. The only possible explanation was that Flick had decided to lie to Olivia Hart—a course which struck him as dangerous beyond measure. Like it or not, he would have to interrupt and—*and. . .read her the riot act.*

But then he happened to glance at Olivia. She was listening

intently to Flick and nodding at every word and writing enthusiastically in a small notebook he hadn't noticed before.

Olivia raised her eyes from the notebook and beamed at Nigel. "I'm not the least bit surprised that you have the situation well in hand. A manager with your splendid credentials would surely recognize that the unfortunate discovery of Etienne Makepeace's body in your tea garden is like the proverbial five-thousand-pound elephant standing in the corner of one's drawing room. Sooner or later, the intruder becomes impossible to ignore."

"*Um. .* ." Nigel had used the same elephant metaphor himself on the day that Makepeace's body had been discovered. He delved into his mind for a suitable reply, but when none came, he settled for, "Sooner, one would think."

"And I fully understand why you would prefer to keep your inquiry a secret. It's difficult to know where such an investigation will lead."

"Very difficult, indeed," Nigel agreed.

"Still, I applaud you for choosing a proactive approach. Attempting to control one's situation makes far more sense than allowing oneself to be buffeted by a windstorm of uncertainty."

"Proactive. Yes, indeed," Nigel said. "We try our best to be proactive at all times. And prudent. We achieve both proactivity and prudence with knowledge, because knowledge is never a bad thing. Especially knowledge about Etienne Makepeace. That's why we are investigating him. To gather every bit we can."

Blimey. I'm blithering again. And Olivia Hart is making more notes.

He stopped talking.

Olivia clicked her pen shut and stood up. Nigel bounded to his feet.

"I feel certain," she said, "that Sir James will want to meet with you *before* the loan closes to hear the results of your investigation. Tentatively, shall we say *ten days* from today? I will call to confirm the time."

Nigel felt his knees go weak. What kind of "comprehensive investigation" could they accomplish in a mere ten days? He gulped back his panic and found the strength to mumble, "I look forward to meeting with Sir James."

His words earned yet another smile from Olivia—this one even warmer than its predecessors. "I am confident that he will enjoy meeting with you."

An idea popped into his mind. Why not exploit Olivia's unexpected cordiality? "Shall I accompany you downstairs? I will be able to describe several of our more impressive holdings as we travel through the museum."

"That would be lovely."

Nigel ushered Olivia toward the door. He turned and winked at Flick—a silent *thank you for saving our bacon.*

Flick didn't respond in kind. At first, she merely looked at him quizzically, but then her eyes began to narrow into an irate glare.

Nigel quickly pulled the door shut.

What have I done wrong now?

The man must be clueless!

Flick heard the oaken door close with a heavy thump

and wondered if Nigel could really be as dense as he had just behaved. How could he expect her to wink back at him *after* he had fawned like a puppy in front of Olivia Hart?

She reached for the thermal tea carafe on the tea cart. It held a superb oolong, fruity tasting and golden in color, a luscious brew that had the power to lift one's spirits. She refilled her cup and chose another of Alain Rousseau's divine shortbread squares. Flick sipped and nibbled and slowly changed her perspective. She could hardly blame Nigel for becoming discombobulated when a strikingly beautiful woman brazenly threw herself at his feet.

You would think that Nigel would be used to getting hit on by now.

She had watched local women flirt with Nigel more times than she could count. Each new occasion added to her conviction that Kentish females viewed Nigel Owen considerably differently than she did.

She saw Nigel as comfortably handsome in a particularly British way—good-looking, certainly, but not the sort of man a red-blooded American woman would label a "hunk." He was slender rather than brawny, with a ruddy complexion that looked like he had just scrubbed his face, and (let's be honest) rather large ears. Hardly the features one might observe on a movie star or a male model.

English women, on the other hand, apparently considered Nigel to be a paragon of masculinity—a man worthy of their deepest sighs, dreamiest gazes, and most candid flirtations. Curiously, it didn't seem to make any difference that he was "taken"—women who knew about Nigel and Flick's relationship would flirt with him in front of her.

Olivia Hart, for example.

Flick sipped her tea and considered the comments Olivia made. Her use of the word "dossier" was a dead giveaway. Wescott Bank had obviously filled a file with facts about the two people at the helm of the Royal Tunbridge Wells Tea Museum. Every museum employee knew that Flick and Nigel were "good friends," to use Stuart Battlebridge's label. They had not worked hard at being discreet inside or outside the building. The bank probably had a candid photograph of them holding hands in the Pantiles.

Flick helped herself to a second shortbread square and immediately regretted her lack of willpower. No wonder her clothing had begun to feel tight around the middle. She had fallen into the habit of enjoying one of Alain's treats—scones, biscuits, fairy cakes, whatever—with tea every afternoon. His shortbread was a particular favorite, a figure-destroying blend of butter, flour, vanilla, and confectioner's sugar, baked a delectable golden brown.

You have to be skinny to go head-to-head with the likes of Olivia Hart.

Flick heaved a deep sigh. How could Nigel—how could any man—resist Olivia? Besides being gorgeous, she was smart and also wealthy. Those black pearls she wore as everyday earrings were museum quality—and worth countless thousands.

"It's not fair," Flick murmured, as she poured herself a fresh cuppa.

Nigel returned twenty minutes later, a sappy grin on his rosy, comfortably handsome face.

"You're a genius!" he proclaimed, with such fervor that Flick found it impossible not to smile along with him. "You came up with magic words that quelled the savage banker. Your quick thinking—along with your total disregard of my authority as director—saved us no end of headaches. I'm proud of you." He reached out with both arms and wrapped Flick inside a mighty hug that lasted for most of a minute.

She pushed free from his embrace. "Aren't we in the middle of a quarrel?"

"A wee lover's tiff." He peered at Flick hopefully. "To my mind, it vanished as quickly as it came."

"You just mentioned your authority. . . ."

"A slip of the tongue. My authority is not worth talking about," Nigel burbled on happily. "I know when resistance is futile. I hereby grant to you in perpetuity complete curatorial decision making, including all matters pertaining to Etienne Makepeace. You decide when, where, and if we create an exhibit about him. I will support your decision without question."

"I'm in charge?"

"Completely." He put his arms around her again. "Furthermore, I owe you an apology."

"You do?"

"I behaved badly when you came into my office. I didn't give you a chance to explain why you changed your mind about the Makepeace exhibit."

"Ah."

"I also overreacted and said things I regret saying."

"Me, too." Flick gave Nigel a squeeze. "I'm sorry for not checking with you before I announced the exhibit to the BBC."

"Is all forgiven between us?"

"The whole nine yards."

"We can both speak freely?"

"*Uh*. . .sure."

Nigel's expression became serious. "Good. Then let me share the two itty-bitty anxieties I have."

Flick felt a jolt of foreboding. Was Nigel about to explain that he had just fallen out of love with her?

"Olivia Hart made a point of telling me that Sir James Boyer will cancel our loan deal if he is dissatisfied with the results of the multifaceted investigation you described to her." Nigel managed a nervous smile. "We are conducting such an investigation—right? We'll have results to present within ten days?"

Flick laughed. "The investigation is underway as we speak. Everything I told Olivia is absolutely true."

Nigel exhaled slowly. "Thank goodness! I can breathe again." He released Flick from his arms. "It also means we don't have to call an emergency meeting of the trustees."

"Yikes! I clean forgot about them."

"I didn't. Archibald Meicklejohn will be touring New Zealand for two more weeks. I didn't relish asking him to cut his vacation short."

"What do we tell the trustees who haven't left the country?"

"Nothing—yet," Nigel said. "We seem to have the situation well in hand."

"Now you sound like Olivia Hart."

Nigel shuddered. "What a horrendous woman! A modern-day dragon lady."

"I don't know her well enough to pass judgment." Flick hoped that her voice wouldn't betray her true feelings. In fact, she'd begun to dislike Olivia the moment the banker began to flirt with Nigel. Flick changed the subject. "You said you have *two* anxieties."

Nigel hesitated a moment, inhaled deeply, and spoke a flood of words: "The time has come, Flick, for me to understand what's bothering you about our relationship. I know that something is bothering you, but I can't figure out what that something is. If it's something I did or something I didn't do, please tell me. If it's something else, I need to know what else. I may sound corny, like you Americans like to say, but I've never felt this way before about anyone else. I want to tell you how I feel, but I fear that what I say may cause you even greater bother—so I am reluctant to say anything, which actually may be the root cause of the problem. Do you see what I mean?"

"Oh my!"

"Does that mean yes or no?"

"I. . .uh. . .I. . ."

"What?"

"I think I'm blithering."

"Indeed you are. I speak from considerable experience as a fellow blitherer."

Flick felt numb. For a brief moment, she considered telling Nigel about her past experiences with men, but then changed her mind.

Don't do it. Don't burden him with your silly insecurities. He'll never understand the way you feel.

She took his hand. "I've been moody because I'm trying to shed some old emotional baggage that I'm not ready to talk about. At least, not yet."

"Perhaps I can help you clean house?"

"It will soon be spotless. I need a few more days to work everything out."

"Are you sure?"

"Completely." She tugged Nigel's head down and kissed his cheek. "You know what they say—the course of true love never did run smooth."

"We'll see about that." Nigel gave her a proper kiss.

"Wow!" she said.

"By the way, was it Keats or Browning who came up with those unhappy words about true love?"

"Neither. Willy Shakespeare wrote them for *A Midsummer Night's Dream*."

"Crikey! I'm an Englishman who's forgotten my classics. See what you've done to me?" Nigel's smile faded. "A few days? You're sure?"

"A few days. I promise."

He gave a thoughtful nod. "Well, I suppose we had better make use of those days for our investigation."

"Follow me!" Flick tugged Nigel to the door. "We'll see if my associate investigator has learned anything interesting about Etienne Makepeace."

She led him out of the office, past a row of cubicles that served as offices for the curators, and into the Conservation Laboratory. As usual, Hannah Kerrigan was hunched over her computer. As usual, the two blue cats were keeping her company.

Flick approached from the front of Hannah's workstation to avoid startling the Web wizard. She rapped gently on the metal frame. Hannah looked up. Her signature grin brightened considerably when she saw Nigel standing behind Flick.

"How goes it?" Flick asked.

"Better than I'd hoped for." She began counting on her

fingers as she had earlier. "First, programming the hotline was a snap. It will be up and running tomorrow morning. Second, the Internet search took me less than an hour. I never did figure out how to access official records of the Probate Registry, but I retrieved the information you wanted from an assortment of magazine archives and a newspaper database."

Hannah looked at notes she had scribbled on several loose pieces of paper. "Makepeace went missing sometime late in September 1966. One of his sisters finally notified the police on September 29—which is now considered the official date of his disappearance. The search continued through October and November, then petered out over the next four or five months. Makepeace was declared dead by a court in London in November 1975—roughly nine years later. His three sisters were his only next of kin."

"I think one of them is still alive," Nigel said. He was, Flick decided, doing his best to honor his agreement and get involved in the investigation.

"The newspapers have been writing about the third sister since the body turned up," Hannah said. "She's in her nineties, is suffering from Alzheimer's disease, and is—to use medical jargon—'noncommunicative.' Anything she knew about Etienne Makepeace is long gone from her memory."

"Sounds like you hit a dead end." Flick said.

"Merely a momentary lay-by. I located several articles written in 1975 that mentioned a solicitor named Clive Wyatt. I did a bit of searching and discovered that he's retired now and living in a cottage in Billingshurst, West Sussex."

"Three cheers for the Internet."

Hannah nodded happily. "Naturally, I telephoned him

immediately. It turns out that Wyatt visited the museum on several occasions and is eager to meet our chief curator. In fact, I think he's put off that no one from the media called him, because he seems a man who loves to talk. I had to tell him a fib to end the phone call. He thinks I have a dicey bladder."

She unfolded two more fingers. "Third and fourth, I'll do the cats tomorrow morning. And fifth, I'm constructing the Etienne Makepeace Web page right now. Would you like to see how much progress I've made?"

Flick didn't get a chance to answer the question. Hannah spun around in her swivel chair, pressed several keys, and moved back from the computer monitor.

Uh-oh. I forgot to tell Nigel about the Web page. How will he react to another surprise?

The page had a bright blue background and was dominated by a large black-and-white photograph of Etienne Makepeace taken during the 1950s. He had been a handsome man in his prime, with well-chiseled features, a strong chin, a thick head of sandy-colored hair, and his famed sculpted moustache. The photographer had captured a boyish smile that immediately caught one's eye. The bold headline over the picture screamed, TELL US HOW THIS MAN BECAME ENGLAND'S TEA SAGE. A smaller headline below proclaimed, REWARD FOR INFORMATION.

"I haven't written the text yet. It will explain that we're offering ten pounds for interesting tea-related anecdotes about Makepeace that visitors post on our message board."

Flick held her breath while Nigel studied the under-construction page. At last, he began to smile. "It's a grand idea, nicely implemented, but may I offer a small suggestion?"

"But of course," Flick said.

"Change the headline to TELL US ALL YOU CAN ABOUT ENGLAND'S TEA SAGE. Then we're likely to get all sorts of information about Makepeace—including details of his relationship with the museum."

Flick nodded at Hannah, who immediately scribbled the new words on one of her scraps of paper.

"Does anyone know where Billingshurst is?" Flick asked.

Hannah started to answer, but surprisingly Nigel spoke first: "About thirty miles southwest of Tunbridge Wells."

"That's near enough to pay him a visit," Flick said. "Are you free tomorrow?"

Nigel started to grimace but apparently thought better of it. He settled for an uncertain shrug. "I have to check my calendar."

"Check away, but please remember that you and I will be doers, not observers, as the investigation proceeds during the next"—she paused for emphasis—"*ten days.*"

Nigel made a small groan, which seemed to encourage Hannah. "Billingshurst is absolutely precious!" she gushed. "It's a brilliant little village—one of my favorite places. My great-aunt lived there. There's a small restaurant on the high street that has romantic corner tables and does a smashing Dover sole."

Flick noted a wistful look in Hannah's eyes. The young woman was no doubt imagining Nigel sitting opposite her at one of those amorous corner tables, delicately shoveling a forkful of Dover sole into her mouth.

Forget about it, honey. That man is mine!

Six

Nigel sat in his car on the Pantiles' Lower Walk, across from the building that housed Flick's apartment, and felt exceedingly sorry for himself—even though he had miraculously found a parking spot. He didn't see the value of driving to Billingshurst, in West Sussex, to visit a retired solicitor. Nor was he sure that spending the next several hours with Flick was a wise thing to do. Most of all, he was suffering the aftereffects of a sleepless night, including a throbbing headache. He had tossed and turned until four in the morning and was now experiencing a powerful urge to recline his seat and doze off, an impulse made even stronger by the rhythmic ticking of the BMW's engine and the soothing *splooshing* of the windshield wipers in the lashing rain.

Hannah Kerrigan's mention of Billingshurst the afternoon before had shaken Nigel. He'd almost begun to blither again but had stopped himself by uttering an inane groan. Fortunately, Flick thought he was shirking work rather than trying to suppress a painful memory.

Funny—but the name "Billingshurst" had been the essential clue that made the pieces fall into place. He finally figured Flick out. Or, more to the point, he abruptly understood that Flick had accidentally figured him out.

Possibly another example of women's intuition.

Her hesitancy to declare how she felt about their relationship. . .her reluctance to discuss her "emotional baggage". . . her growing unease when they talked about their future. . .the hostile looks she cast at Olivia Hart—he now realized that all of these things pointed toward one straightforward question: Can Nigel Owen be trusted over the long run?

An interesting topic, that.

"On balance," Nigel murmured, "the answer is a resounding no."

The windshield began to steam up; he switched on the defogger and wondered how much Billingshurst had changed. He'd last been there some ten years earlier, a few months before his divorce from Sheila. She had grown up in Coneyhurst, a tiny village a few miles east of Billingshurst. Their trip today would take them past her family home. When he had told Flick about his divorce two months earlier—it was hardly a secret, after all—he hadn't shared many details about Sheila or their five-year marriage. There had seemed no reason at all to mention that Sheila hailed from Coneyhurst.

Now is unquestionably not the right time to bring Flick up-to-date about your former wife.

Nigel rarely thought about Sheila, but his restless night had dredged up a steady stream of painful memories. Chief among them was that a woman he'd thought as beautiful as

Olivia Hart had driven a wedge between Sheila and himself.

It happened shortly after Nigel won a fast-track job at a London-based insurance company. "A man with your sterling credentials and determination is destined to achieve greatness in this company," his boss had said. "We think so highly of you that we have hired an assistant to support you." Her name was Kendra. She was stunning, charming, vivacious, funny—and not above flirting with Nigel.

Truth be told, he had rather enjoyed the attentions of a beautiful single woman. They gave a married man confidence that he was still "in the game." And Kendra's flirtations seemed harmless enough. What could possibly happen during office hours in a central London office building?

Not much. But a lot more did happen during a company conference at a quiet resort in Wales.

Alas, this was not the first time that Nigel had strayed. On the day Sheila left him, she announced that he had run out of "second chances" and that she had fallen out of love with a "fidelity-challenged husband."

Now, for reasons he could not fathom, Flick was seeking an answer to the same ruddy question: Can Nigel Owen be trusted over the long run? Like it or not, one piece of the answer was his behavior at yesterday's meeting with Olivia Hart. He hadn't exactly flirted with Olivia in front of Flick, but neither had he rebuffed Olivia's flirtations.

No wonder Flick seemed mad.

What would happen if she asked the question directly? Would he lie to keep her or tell the truth and lose her? Either way was a path to disaster.

Nigel peered at the dashboard clock. Almost nine o'clock.

Their appointment with Clive Wyatt was at eleven. In theory, two hours was more than enough time to reach Billingshurst. In practice, a rainstorm like this one would slow traffic down to a crawl. They needed to get on their way.

He reached for his mobile phone but slipped it back on his belt when he heard a loud tapping on the passenger door window.

Rats! I forgot to unlock the door.

He pushed the button. The rear door flew open; Cha-Cha hurdled onto the backseat, followed by a wet umbrella that skittered into the foot well. An instant later, Flick slid into the front seat, looking damp but happy. She was wearing her Burberry, brown woolen gloves, and a rakish brown beret. A long curl had escaped from beneath the beret and lay against her cheek. Nigel decided not to worry about the effect of dog paws or sodden umbrellas on his expensive leather upholstery. He smiled at her as brightly as his headache would allow.

"What happened to the gentle English rain?" she asked breathlessly. "This is a tropical deluge."

He mumbled, "We see all manner of precipitation in Great Britain."

"Whatever. . ." She snapped her seat belt shut. "By the way, I have an excuse for being late. I made us a snack for the road." She held up a small canvas utility tote. "Coffee for you, tea for me, and biscuits for us both."

"Brilliant thinking, as always." He recalled that he hadn't eaten anything that morning. "I won't say no to a cup of your coffee and a biscuit or two."

"Onward to Billingshurst!"

"Onward, indeed," he said, without much enthusiasm.

Nigel eased the BMW out of the parking spot and quickly reviewed the trip in his mind. He would take the A26 south to Crowborough, catch the A272 west through Haywards Heath, and continue on to Billingshurst.

"I have a map," Flick said. "Where's yours?"

"I don't need one," Nigel said, without thinking.

"Really? What did you do—memorize the route?"

His heart leaped. "Something like that."

Flick rummaged in her canvas bag, apparently too engrossed to challenge his answer. "By the way, our new Etienne Makepeace Web page is online—with the headline you suggested. Hannah also e-mailed me some additional information about Clive Wyatt and Mathilde O'Shaughnessy."

"Mathilde *Who*?"

"Etienne Makepeace's surviving sister—the one who has Alzheimer's." Flick unfolded a piece of paper. "Her full name is Mathilde Makepeace O'Shaughnessy. She was born in 1911, married Kevin O'Shaughnessy in 1933, and became a widow in 1979. A tabloid reporter talked his way into her hospital ward the other day and tried to interview her—he got nowhere.

"Moving on to Clive Wyatt. . .he's in his early eighties. He joined the firm of Bradford and Smythe when he was twenty-three and worked there for the next fifty years. He retired from practice in 1995 and has since lived in quiet retirement in Billingshurst."

"Fascinating. It's amazing what one can find on the Internet." Nigel realized that he was on the verge of sounding grumpy. He took a deep breath. "Have you thought about what we're going to ask Wyatt when we see him?"

"Hannah said he liked to talk, so I thought we would let

him do so—after I explain that we intend to create an exhibit about Makepeace and want to gather all manner of information about the man, especially data about his relationship with the museum. That's the truth—well, at least part of it." She added, unexpectedly, "What do you know about Billingshurst?"

Nigel downshifted to take a sharp curve. "*Umm. . .why do you ask?*"

"Hannah described our destination as precious and brilliant. I hope Billingshurst isn't one of those cutesy towns that competes for the annual most-authentic Elizabethan high street in England prize."

"I haven't been there in years, but as I recall, it's both pretty and quaint. You should enjoy it."

That's the truth—well, at least part of it.

He caught a sideways glimpse of Flick; she seemed satisfied. With luck, she wouldn't remember his incomplete answer when the time came to explain in full the specifics of his failed marriage to Sheila. That would happen soon—if he didn't mess up their relationship first.

Nigel changed the topic back to the matter at hand. "I'm all for letting an octogenarian attorney ramble about the past today, but I'm curious about *your* grand strategy for information gathering. Frankly, I remain uncertain as to why we're driving to Billingshurst. I'm loath to admit it, but I still don't understand why Sir James Boyer wants—how did Olivia Hart put it—'a comprehensive explanation of how Etienne Makepeace was connected to the Royal Tunbridge Wells Tea Museum.' "

"Really? Yesterday, you behaved like you did."

"Yes, well, I wasn't about to act like a total dunce in front of the dragon lady." He added, "Explain it to me; I'm all yours for the next hour."

"Okay." There was a lilt in Flick's voice. She seemed happy to have an opportunity to lecture Nigel. "Pretend you are Sir James Boyer. What's your number one concern?"

"I want to be certain that the museum will have the funds to repay the thirty-two-million-pound loan over the next ten years."

"Correct! Now—you are still Sir James—where do you assume the museum will get the money to repay the loan?"

"I don't have to assume anything. When I examined the museum's accounts, I observed that there are two chief sources of incoming money. First, revenues generated by visitors. Second, gifts from wealthy contributors and foundations."

Nigel's mind unexpectedly fitted the pieces together. He let the BMW slow to a stop as he steered to the left side of the road, so he could have a proper conversation with Flick.

"Good heavens!" he went on. "Sir James fears a scandal that would impact gift-giving to the museum."

"Exactly. What if some ugly fact emerges in the years ahead and discourages wealthy people from making contributions to the museum?"

"Can you think of a good 'for example'?"

"Sure. For example, what if the founding director of the museum—your predecessor, Nathanial Swithin—became jealous of Etienne's success forty years ago, ordered one of the security guards to shoot him, and then buried the corpse in the tea garden?"

"You can't be serious!"

"Of course I'm not serious. I came up with an absurd

hypothetical example. But let's say it were true. On the one hand, curious visitors would flock to the museum to see the scene of the crime. On the other hand, we might lose the support of wealthy donors and foundations who would rather support an organization without a tainted past."

"Sir James really wants to know that the museum is not connected in a scandalous way to Makepeace's death."

"That's the bottom line."

Nigel edged out into the road and accelerated. "Okay. Presuming you're right, how do we go about proving a negative? How do we show that the museum didn't play a part in Makepeace's demise?"

"We start by finding out everything we can about Etienne Makepeace—including stuff that's not in the newspapers or police files."

"Police files? How would you know what information the police have gathered?"

Nigel heard Flick suddenly catch her breath.

"Is something wrong?" he asked.

"*Uhh*. . .I forgot to explain that Detective Inspector Pennyman is working with us. He provided an edited version of his Etienne Makepeace dossier. In return, I agreed to share any significant details we surface."

Nigel tromped on the brakes. The BMW skidded on gravel before it came to a stop on the verge alongside the road. He and Flick pitched forward against their seat belts.

"You forgot to mention that we—in fact, *you*—made a pact with the police?"

"It's hardly a *pact*. Pennyman described it as a *quid pro quo*. We're pooling our knowledge."

"You're telling me that DI Pennyman—a man who once threatened to toss you in jail—agreed to your cockeyed scheme."

"No!" Flick's voice had become even louder than Nigel's. "I'm telling you that this 'cockeyed scheme' was his idea. He came to me and proposed it."

"Blimey!" Nigel shifted to first gear. "The world has gone mad. Break out the coffee and biscuits."

Seventy minutes later found them tootling along the Billingshurst high street with Flick perusing a map of the town that she had downloaded from Multimap.com.

"I know that Wyatt lives on Daux Court, a small street not far from the station, but so far I've found a Daux Road, a Daux Avenue, and a Daux Way." Flick pronounced each Daux as "Dough."

"The locals say *Docks*, not *Dough*," Nigel said, as he maneuvered around a parked Renault van and a slow-moving Vesper motor scooter. "I believe that Daux Court is a right turn off the high street, about a quarter mile ahead."

"Got it." Flick poked the map with her index finger. "I'm impressed—you can remember a town after such a long time."

"Navigating is like riding a bicycle—one never really forgets." He chose his next words carefully. "*Um*—I should have mentioned it earlier, but the fact is, I often visited Billingshurst during the late eighties and early nineties."

Flick all but ignored Nigel's partial admission.

"Why not? It looks like a pleasant enough place to visit." She slipped the map into the door pocket. "Look—I've been thinking. Perhaps you should be the one to ask the first round of questions."

"*Me!* Why?" Nigel said.

"We need Wyatt's help, but we don't know anything about his prejudices. He could be a roaring, old-school male chauvinist who'll get insulted if a woman acts like she's in charge."

Nigel sighed. "I'll do my best—but you had better be prepared to jump in quickly when I run out of questions to ask."

"It's a deal." She pointed ahead. "There it is on the right, *Docks* Court."

Nigel had feared that parking in Billingshurst would be a challenge, but Clive Wyatt's house was set on a large plot of land and had a long concrete driveway. Nigel supposed that an estate agent would describe the house as an "early twentieth-century character cottage." His parents had owned a similar home: two stories, contrasting facing brickwork, small square-paned windows, a steeply pitched tiled roof, enclosed by a neatly trimmed privet hedge. There would almost certainly be a good-sized garden to the rear. Nigel parked the BMW in a wide spot near the top of the driveway.

When he turned off the ignition, Flick exhibited an unexpected burst of enthusiasm. He couldn't help smiling as she jumped out of the car, plowed through several puddles to reach Wyatt's front door, and earnestly worked the brass door knocker. So much for her recently expressed theories on the chauvinistic dispositions of retired British solicitors.

Nigel leaned into the rear of the car and spoke to Cha-Cha. "It's just gone eleven, old chap. You're on your own for an hour or so. Treat my genuine-leather backseat as if your life depends on it. I hope you get my meaning." He noted that the Shiba refused to dignify the threat by raising his head.

When Nigel reached the house, the front door was open and Flick was inside, shaking hands with an elderly man of medium height. Clive Wyatt was thin and seemed remarkably fit. He had alert blue eyes, a darkish complexion, and a sparse fringe of gray hair encircling his mostly bald head. He wore gray slacks, a blue dress shirt without a tie, and a green cardigan. Nigel slipped inside, behind Flick, and shut the door.

"It's good of you to see us," Flick was saying, "especially on such short notice."

"Not at all, Dr. Adams. It's quite a treat to meet you in the flesh. I read about you in the newspaper when you took up your new post at the museum—last summer, wasn't it?"

"Early in July." She put her hand on Nigel's arm. "Mr. Wyatt, this is Nigel Owen, our new director."

"My pleasure, sir." Clive seemed to become puzzled. "I've quite forgotten how a museum operates. Does the director report to the chief curator, or is it the other way around?"

"Nigel is wholly in charge," Flick said.

"Ah yes," Clive said, "that makes perfect sense." He gave a slight nod to signal his approval. "Shall we go inside and sit down?"

Nigel followed Flick, who followed Clive down a long entrance hall with a tiled floor. They passed a telephone on a high stand and an open cloak rack built beneath the staircase. Clive led them into a smallish sitting room that was bursting with old upholstered furniture. The room had a bay window, a coved ceiling, and an electric fire glowing cheerfully on the hearth of a Victorian-styled fireplace. All in all, a very *good* room, Nigel decided.

"Knowing you were coming," Clive said, "I brewed a pot

of tea. It's a rather pleasant Ceylon that I highly recommend. Would you like a cuppa?"

"Tea would be perfect," Flick said.

"Yes, perfect," Nigel echoed. It seemed patently useless to ask Wyatt for coffee.

"Sit where you like," Clive said. "I'll bring the tea."

Nigel doubted that any of the chairs or sofas would qualify as an antique. He chose a comfortable-looking winged club chair near the fireplace. Flick sat on an adjacent small sofa.

Clive returned promptly with a tray and poured three mugs of steaming tea from a gleaming round teapot that Nigel guessed was a foot in diameter.

"Where did you get that extraordinary teapot?" Flick asked. "It's one of the largest I've ever seen."

"I'm not surprised," Clive said. He sat on a straight-backed chair that didn't look especially comfortable to Nigel. "It was specially made for Bradford and Smythe. This is the teapot we used during the dark ages when the firm sponsored an official tea break every afternoon. It served the entire firm—including our charwoman. A new senior partner abandoned that civilized custom in the mid-1980s. I gave refuge to the crockery that was declared redundant." He chuckled at his pleasantry and then said to Flick, "Were you able to view the purported corpse of Etienne Makepeace?"

"Well, I saw parts of a skeleton and various personal effects," she said. "So did Nigel."

Nigel took a sip of tea: quite hearty, not at all bad. He noted that Clive—obviously a crafty old attorney—had taken control of the conversation. He leaned back, the better to enjoy the show. When, he wondered, would Flick make her move?

Clive grunted. "I presume there's no doubt that the bones in question belonged to Etienne Makepeace?"

"No. We've been told that the police used Makepeace's old dental records to identify the remains and that they plan to follow up with a DNA test. They seem quite confident."

"Pity." Clive shook his head glumly. "I've strolled through your tea garden on several occasions. It is altogether too charming a setting for the likes of Mr. Etienne Makepeace."

"*What?*" Flick lurched forward. "I mean, what makes you say that?"

"The world considers Makepeace some sort of folk hero because he was an entertaining expert on tea. But those who had the misfortune to meet the man beneath the cheerful facade found an ungrateful lout and a shameless womanizer."

"My goodness!" Flick said. "My goodness. . ."

Nigel willed himself not to laugh, not to gloat, and especially not to say, *I told you so.* He'd been right: There had been a less-noble side to England's Tea Sage.

"Let me explain—and qualify—my remarks," Clive said. "Although I never met Etienne Makepeace, I conducted a thorough investigation prior to filing the papers to have him declared legally dead. I interviewed his sisters individually—they all told identical stories, although I challenged them with the fervor of an opposing counsel.

"The three spoke with such venom about Etienne that I pondered if their assertions were a product of sibling jealousy. However, I quickly received corroborating evidence from several other people. Frankly, it was all too easy to find witnesses who would cheerfully testify that Etienne Makepeace was a scoundrel." He shook his head again. "What I heard from them quite astounded me, let me tell you. His sisters believed for many years that he was done in by a jealous husband."

No one spoke for several seconds. Nigel decided to break the silence. "I think I know the answer, but did his sisters have a reason for having him declared dead?"

"Surprisingly, their stated reasons varied," Clive said. "Mathilde wanted a semblance of *closure*, as people are fond of saying today. She hoped that a court decree would put an end to any speculation that he might show up alive one day. There were, in fact, many Etienne Makepeace 'sightings' before the court acted.

"Solène, the middle sister, felt a curious responsibility to Etienne. She believed that his soul would not rest until he was officially declared dead.

"Coralie, the oldest of the siblings, espoused a wholly mercenary position. She wanted his assets—what little there were."

"*Little?*" Nigel's mug nearly slipped through his fingers; he caught it before any tea spilled. "We've all assumed that Etienne was a wealthy man. He was regarded as a philanthropist."

Clive chortled gently. "Heavens, no, sir. Etienne Makepeace was certainly not a philanthropist. He lent his name to charitable causes—mostly to sell more of his books—but he never donated any of his own money. It simply passed through his hands too quickly. He was by all reports a profligate wastrel who spent all that he earned on wine, women, and song." He chortled again. "His sisters used more pungent labels for his expenditures. They believed that he left them everything he owned because he knew the paltry size of his estate would infuriate them."

"How did Etienne become estranged from his sisters?" Flick asked.

"I asked many times but never received a proper answer. Solène told me that as Etienne became famous he also became insufferable. Coralie claimed that Etienne had 'gone rotten,' whatever that might mean. Mathilde said nothing—other than Etienne's bad behavior was no one's business now that Etienne was about to be declared dead." He frowned at his mug of tea. "One was left with the unmistakable conclusion that Etienne did something his sisters found unforgivable."

Nigel glimpsed Flick. She seemed fully recovered from her initial surprise. She had moved to the edge of her cushion and looked eager to ask a question.

"By any chance," she said, "have you saved any of the files or notes from that period? They would be exceedingly useful if—*ah*, the museum decides to create an exhibit about Etienne Makepeace."

Clive seemed to tremble. "The very idea of such an exhibit gives one pause. Still—museums show pictures of Attila the Hun and the mosquito that carries malaria. To answer your question, no, I don't have any files or notes. . . ." He began to grin. "I have something even better. Late in 1974, I hired a private investigator to collect all that he could about Makepeace's reputation. He spent five months on the job. Because eight years had passed since Makepeace's disappearance, people were more willing to talk about the great man's foibles than they were in 1966. I used his report as the foundation of a legal brief that argued Etienne was the sort of man who was likely to be murdered. I planned to submit the brief should the judge require us to show that Etienne could have been in physical peril at the time he disappeared.

"The brief proved unnecessary. Kenneth Williams, an easy-going old judge who'd been a rabid fan of Etienne Makepeace, heard our petition. He spent hours eulogizing the man and focused solely on the straightforward fact that Makepeace hadn't been seen or heard of for nearly a decade. He seemed delighted to declare him legally dead—it enabled him to play an important role in Makepeace's life, so to speak."

"This brief of yours. . ." Flick said breathlessly. "Did you keep a copy of it?"

"Certainly." Clive's eyes twinkled as he held up an old manila envelope. "I brought the document with me when I retired. Moreover, I'll be delighted to provide it to you—for the modest price of a lifetime museum membership." He made a little chortle. "Given my advanced age, that represents a trifling investment."

Nigel glanced at Flick. She was nodding vigorously and laughing along with Clive. Nigel decided to ask the question that she seemed likely to forget.

"By any chance, Mr. Wyatt, did you learn how Etienne Makepeace became a tea expert?"

Clive's grin faded into a thoughtful frown. "I wondered about his tea-related bona fides, too. I asked everyone I interviewed, but no one could explain how he gained his extensive knowledge. Etienne's sisters told me they were surprised when he began writing articles about tea and books about tea—and absolutely astounded when he began speaking on the radio. They presumed he was self-taught. I finally concluded they must be right."

Flick joined in before Nigel could comment. "I've reached

the same conclusion. . . ." She bounced to her feet, looking like she had a thousand more details about Etienne to discuss with Clive.

Why not let her do her thing?

Nigel stood up and moved toward a window. The rain had hardened to sleet, and the sky looked an unpromising gray. *Best not to linger too long in Billingshurst before returning to the Wells.* Then again, a nice bit of Dover sole was worth a modicum of foul-weather driving.

Nigel waited for a lull in the chatter between Flick and Clive to say, "One of our museum staff talked about a restaurant on the high street noted for its first-class Dover sole. I can't imagine that she's right."

"Actually she is—in part," Clive said. "The place she had in mind is not a restaurant, but rather a pub called The Sussex Bowman. The food is generally good."

"A gastropub!" Nigel said. "I should have thought of that."

"What's a gastropub?" Flick asked.

"Combine one celebrated chef and one run-down country pub. Invent a signature dish such as Dover sole. Top with shabby but friendly decor. Voila, madam! Luncheon is served." He looked at his watch. "It's almost noon. What do you say we relocate your discussions to The Sussex Bowman and give the kitchen a try? My treat."

"With pleasure!" Clive said.

"Sounds wonderful!" Flick added.

Nigel smiled at them. The trip to Billingshurst had turned out much better than he had anticipated.

Flick wasn't surprised when she awoke at six, an hour before her alarm clock was set to ring. She had fallen asleep at eight the night before and had slept so soundly that she barely disturbed the duvet. Her bedroom was dark except for a sliver of light that poked through the gap between her curtains. She knew it was cast by a street lamp on the Lower Walk. She also knew that she would never get back to sleep that morning.

Why did we eat at that miserable pub?

Nigel's decision to have lunch at The Sussex Bowman proved to be a thoroughly bad one. They arrived at the pub to find that the "celebrated chef" had gone off on a holiday to Malta and that Dover sole was not on the menu that afternoon. They then waited more than an hour for the substitute chef to prepare a "Classic English Mixed Grill" that proved to be a disappointing platter of tough, tasteless "mystery meats."

When they were finished eating, they found that the sleet had fallen long enough and heavily enough to make the roads perilously slick. The drive back had lasted the better part of three hours, during which time the BMW had nearly skidded off the road twice. Flick had a roaring headache when they arrived in Tunbridge Wells at six. She supposed that Nigel had one, too.

He had taken her home, planted a quick good-bye kiss, and sped off with Cha-Cha because—well, he really didn't seem to have a good reason other than a general desire to be alone after a high-tension drive on bad roads, which she readily understood. She felt exactly the same way.

A pot of strong Assam tea had helped to dispel her headache.

She climbed into bed at seven but managed to stay awake—by watching a bit of the telly and reading a chapter of a mystery novel—until eight, the earliest she was willing to call it a night.

Flick levered herself out of bed and decided to use her extra hour productively. She answered three personal e-mails, paid several end-of-the-month bills she had been putting off, and vacuumed her flat—another chore she had also postponed. She had planned to make herself a proper breakfast when she finished, but as she rewound the power cord around the Hoover, she discovered that she had lost track of the time. It was nearly eight o'clock; she would have to race to get to the museum at a reasonable hour. The curating staff looked to her to establish their norms. She made it a point to be at her desk by eight thirty every morning.

Scratch breakfast—I'll grab a snack in the tearoom kitchen.

It was after nine when she marched past the Pantiles, Clive Wyatt's legal brief in her attaché case, visions of a jam-covered scone propelling her forward through the damp, gray mist. The mist became rain when she reached Eridge Road. Flick calculated that the closest entrance lay behind the museum, next to the loading dock. She jogged the last hundred yards and surprised herself by avoiding the major puddles along the way.

"Poor Dr. Adams! You got caught in the rain," said the guard on duty in the Welcome Centre kiosk.

"My fault, Ted. I thought the morning would clear up. I left my umbrella at home—purposely."

"Oh, well, one doesn't develop an Englishman's weather instincts overnight."

Flick laughed and made for the Duchess of Bedford Tearoom. She slipped out of her damp Burberry and hung it on the restaurant's coat rack.

She heard Earl before she saw him. He was squawking so purposefully at Cha-Cha that it seemed the two could communicate. Flick walked toward Earl's big cage, thinking to pay him a brief visit—until a sight she glimpsed through the corner of her eye brought her to a rapid stop.

Nigel Owen and Olivia Hart sat close together at a table, their heads almost touching, both of them laughing. There was a pot of coffee on the end table, along with a plateful of toasted and buttered crumpets. Neither Nigel nor Olivia seemed interested in eating.

"Huhh!" Flick hadn't intended to moan—but that was the sound that came out. For one brief instant, she wondered if she could turn and run before Nigel saw her.

Too late! He's looking at me.

"Flick! I searched *everywhere* for you. Olivia has brought interesting news." He patted the empty chair next to him. "Come! Join us."

She peered at Nigel as she sat down. He certainly seemed pleased enough to see her. And yet, she could see a dyspeptic look behind his brilliant smile. What was going on?

"Has Sir James changed his mind?" Flick asked.

Olivia chuckled. "He *never* changes his mind. What does vary is his level of enthusiasm. He's bubbling with anticipation about your investigation. He told me last evening that he can't wait to read your report and hear your presentation. I wanted to tell you that immediately."

Flick willed herself to nod and smile. *Especially because you now had an excuse to drive all the way from Maidstone to see Nigel.*

Olivia talked on. "However, we do have one itty-bitty change in plans."

"Which is?"

"The tentative presentation date I offered you on Monday won't work because Sir James will be in France on a business trip. We have to bring your meeting forward several days. You'll meet with Sir James next Monday, five days from today, at fifteen hundred hours—at our headquarters in London."

Five days? Ridiculous. She glanced at Nigel and straightaway understood his sour visage. He, too, realized that they could not possibly meet the bank's unworkable schedule.

Ah well. We'll have to sort that out later.

"May I have a crumpet?" Flick asked. "I haven't eaten anything this morning."

"Please do," Olivia slid the plate toward Flick. "They look too scrumptious to waste." She added conspiratorially, "I love crumpets, but I can't eat them—they go to my hips in milliseconds."

For a reckless moment, Flick considered applying them directly to Olivia's hips by pushing the plate into her lap. But she also thought that Chef Alain Rousseau's delightful crumpets were too good to waste. He somehow transformed a simple batter of flour, salt, sugar, yeast, and milk into a chewy pancake to die for. Well—"pancake" only in the sense that each blob of batter cooked on a heated grill, enclosed by a metal ring to keep the crumpet round.

Flick grabbed the largest crumpet, offered a weak smile to counter Olivia's aristocratic gaze, and took an experimental bite. When everything went right, the top of a crumpet was dotted with tiny holes that filled with melted butter. . . .

Heaven! This crumpet is perfect.

She was about to take another bite when Olivia said, "Nigel tells me that your lunch at The Sussex Bowman wasn't very good."

Yikes! Why would he tell Olivia about their trip to see Clive Wyatt? *It was our experience.* Flick wanted to glare at Nigel—instead, she gazed directly at Olivia.

"It's true that the food wasn't very good," she said, "but the *companionship* was magnificent."

Flick enjoyed seeing expressions of confusion, then annoyance, flicker across Olivia's face. A few seconds later, the banker stood up and brushed imaginary crumbs off her skirt. "Well, I had best be running along." She smiled sweetly at Nigel. "If you have any questions, don't hesitate to call my mobile phone. It's always turned on."

Flick ground her teeth. *I'll bet you're always turned on, too, honey.*

Nigel flew to his feet. "Let me get one of our large umbrellas and walk you to your car. The rain has picked up."

"That would be *lovely*," Olivia cooed.

Flick watched them leave, a knot of anger toward Nigel rising in her chest. How could he fall for such obvious manipulation? Sure—Olivia was a flirt. But Nigel had more than enough smarts to see through her coy behavior and fend her off—*if he really wanted to.* She chomped down on the remainder of her crumpet. Somehow it had lost much of its taste. She applied a liberal dollop of Alain's superb blackberry preserves.

Nigel returned faster than Flick expected him to, grinning from ear to ear. "Thank goodness that's over. She showed up on our doorstep this morning eager to talk about Sir James Boyer."

Flick made a face. "I'd have been too embarrassed to spring the schedule change in person. She must know we'll never finish our investigation *and* write a report *and* develop a presentation by then. Why didn't she send you an e-mail or call you?" She smiled at Nigel. "By the way—when do we let her know that we can't meet the new deadline?"

"*Um.* . .Olivia came in person because she wanted to explain why we *must* complete everything in five days. It seems that James Boyer's business trip is the prelude to a lengthy vacation. If we don't get his final approval next Monday, we'll have to wait three months—or begin again from scratch at another bank."

"Oh no!"

"Oh yes! We have no choice. We have to meet Sir James's impossible deadline."

Flick stared at the two remaining crumpets. She wasn't hungry anymore. Stark trepidation had overwhelmed her routine senses and emotions.

Whoa! How come Nigel doesn't feel the way I do?

"The museum is facing a genuine crisis that could ruin our careers," Flick said, "but when I arrived this morning, you and Olivia Hart were enjoying a cozy smile-in. How come?"

"Oh, that." Nigel seemed uncomfortable to hear the question. "Well, of course I had to maintain a positive front for Olivia."

"Of course."

"It makes no sense to share our worries with our bank."

"Uh-huh."

Flick watched patches of red blossom on Nigel's cheeks. "And what she had to say about Earl was rather amusing."

"Olivia spoke to you about our parrot?"

"Actually, Olivia has diagnosed Earl's loud clucking noises."

Flick managed not to scream. "And how, pray tell, did Olivia learn about the weird sounds that Earl made after our news conference?"

"Well, I suppose that I mentioned the noises when I gave her a quick tour of the museum on Monday. Our last stop was in front of Earl's cage."

"I see—and what was her *diagnosis*?"

"Olivia believes that Earl is trying to call someone."

"That's. . .*nuts*."

"I thought so, too, until Olivia explained that many African Grey parrots mimic telephone bells because they see their owners come running whenever phones ring. Other Greys will imitate the beep of a microwave oven when the timer switches off—for the same reason. It makes perfect sense when you think about it. A parrot knows that its owner responds to a specific sound—so it duplicates the sound to call its owner. A remarkably clever thing to do."

"And how did Olivia get so. . .so *knowledgeable* about parrots?"

"It seems that her aunt is one of the best-known African Grey breeders in England. Olivia told her about Earl's noisemaking. According to her aunt, once we can figure out the sound, we will be able to figure out who Earl is calling."

"Did Olivia—or her aunt—happen to reveal how to accomplish that little trick?"

"Not really." Nigel's brow furrowed. "You know, the tone of your voice suggests that you're mad at Olivia. She seems to be doing her best to help the museum."

Flick sprang out of her chair. *Were all men this dumb?*

"The museum! Do you *really* believe that Princess Perfect drove all the way from Maidstone at the crack of dawn to warn us about James Boyer's long vacation?"

"Well. . ."

"Nigel, you can't be that big of a dunce."

Flick whirled around.

"Where are you going?" Nigel called.

"To my office. To work. I have to shift our investigation into overdrive."

She heard a clatter of crockery and silverware as Nigel pushed his chair away from the table. He came up behind her.

"Look—I'm aware that Olivia Hart has been flirting with me."

"Wow!" she said, without looking back. "Let's hold another news conference."

"I've done nothing to encourage her."

"You've also done nothing to discourage her!"

Flick strode through the World of Tea Map Room and started climbing the large staircase that wove its way from the ground floor to the top floor. She surprised herself by outpacing Nigel as she took two steps at a time. He finally caught up with her on the third-floor landing. They both were huffing and puffing.

He gripped her shoulders. "We need to talk about this. Now!"

Flick broke free and looked around. They were too close

to the Conservation Laboratory for a personal discussion that might become noisy. She led Nigel to the open area that served as a foyer for the administrative side of the third floor. It was a multipurpose space that held a rank of file cabinets (solid walnut to match the wood paneling), housed the museum's copying machine (discreetly hidden behind an Oriental screen), and served as the museum's reception room (a seating area offered a sofa, two club chairs, and a coffee table).

"Okay," she said. "Talk."

"Olivia Hart is a pain in the posterior. I've let her bat her eyelashes at me because I haven't wanted to jeopardize our loan. We need Olivia on our side for the next few weeks."

"And I need to know that you're on *my* side."

"*What?*" Nigel took two steps backward. "How can you doubt that I am? I follow you around like a puppy. I blither like a fool. I defer to your judgment continuously. I apologize at the drop of a hat—about everything from my clumsy behavior to the excessive rain in Kent."

"All of that's true, Nigel, but I need to be sure that you won't hurt me. Yesterday you asked what's bothering me. Well, I have a significant problem with relationships—I choose men who run off with other women. Can I trust you not to do that to me?"

Flick watched Nigel's face metamorphose. In a split-second, his confident countenance gave way to a frightened "deer in the headlights" expression. She felt a chill that seemed to gyrate through her torso—from her stomach to her heart.

"Oh boy! I've seen that face before," she said. "Right about when I get dumped."

"Flick. . .you don't. . .wait. . .you're wrong. . . ."

"You're blithering again, so let me help you. Repeat after me: Flick, I didn't mean it to happen, but when I saw Olivia Hart, I fell head over heels in love with her."

"I'm not in love with Olivia Hart; I'm in love with. . ."

She put her hand to his mouth. "Don't say it! I won't believe it! I've seen the way you look at her. And I saw the sheer panic on your face just now."

He tried to take her hand. She pulled away.

"It's not true," he said. "You have to believe me. You need to understand *my* significant problem with relationships."

"Hey! Everyone knows that it's stupid to fall in love at work. We've just made our lives a lot simpler. We have a paltry five days to pull off a miracle—that doesn't leave any time for silly emotional turmoil."

"Flick," Nigel said softly, "you have the wrong idea about everything."

"Go. We both have work to do."

"Flick. . ."

"Please, go."

Nigel looked beaten as he walked slowly to his office.

It was only then that Flick realized the door to the Staff Office was open and that Polly Reid—standing just inside the office—had seen and heard everything. Flick felt sure that the stunned look on Polly's face mirrored her own bleak expression.

She had driven Nigel Owen out of her life.

SEVEN

I have no excuses!

Nigel swung his office door shut with a thump, retreated behind his desk, and slumped into his swivel chair. He should have been ready to answer the question he knew Flick was going to ask. Instead, he had panicked and blown their relationship apart.

It was his fault—from start to finish.

What should he have said to Flick? What *could* he have said to her? Nothing would have made much difference, because Flick had guessed right about him. She had seen the light early, before she'd invested enough of herself in their friendship to be really hurt.

Lucky her.

He loved Flick. Serious, studious, beautiful, tea-drinking Flick—a woman who'd apparently been wounded by other men. But he didn't deserve her. Not with his checkered history. As Sheila so forcefully pointed out on the day she left, Nigel had committed an unpardonable offense when he conspired with two "fast and friendly" females to wreck his first marriage.

A great irony, of course, was that women rarely flirted with the *unattached* Nigel Owen. But pair him with Flick—or in the past with Sheila—and straightaway he became an interesting prospect to unattached ladies. Even a stunner like Olivia Hart might have a go at him.

You can't blame Olivia. Neither can you change the past.

For the past ten years, he had tried to comport himself as a wholly decent chap—as a man a woman could rely on. But he had no way to undo what he had once done, no way to start over again. He knew in his heart: The past is prologue. He accepted the reality: His past deeds would haunt him forever.

That's why he'd remained a bachelor, condemned to fleeting liaisons with women who preferred a relationship du jour. He had been foolish to hope for more with Flick.

"I shall leave the museum, of course," he murmured, "and also Tunbridge Wells. This is too small a city for both of us to rattle around in. I couldn't bear knowing that Flick lived only a few streets away."

Cha-Cha raised his head and gave a little yip. Nigel noted that he didn't seem to be sporting his usual doggy grin.

"Fear not, old chap, I'll make sure that the next director lets you sleep on his aged leather sofa."

The Shiba's large brown eyes seemed to gaze forlornly at Nigel for a moment; then he laid his head atop his front paws.

"What else can I do, old boy? Flick wants assurances that I can't give her." He let himself sigh. "I wouldn't trust me."

Cha-Cha made a delicate whining sound.

"Well, if you feel that way, tell me how this tiger can change its stripes." He paused a few seconds. "Aha! You can't see a way out either."

Nigel fired up his computer and accessed the museum's current financial reports. Over the years, he had found reviewing columns of numbers a brilliantly effective way to push emotional matters from one's mind. After more than an hour spent in arithmetical contemplation, he heard a gentle tapping on the door.

Nigel felt a tremor of excitement. It had to be Flick; Polly knocked, and Conan Davies pounded. He hurtled out of his chair to let her in.

She held up a sheaf of papers. "I may have found a mother lode of information about Etienne Makepeace."

Nigel studied her face. Her eyes looked puffy—*has she been crying?*—but her expression seemed all business. *Good—she's here to talk about the investigation.* Whenever they talked about personal dealings, he seemed to dig himself a deeper hole.

She sat down on the sofa next to Cha-Cha. Nigel turned a visitor's chair around and straddled it.

"Most of these pages are a working copy of the legal brief that Clive Wyatt gave us," she said. "I put the original in our archives for safekeeping—it's a fantastic document." Nigel nodded. Flick continued, "I learned something new about Etienne Make-peace. During his heyday—the early and midsixties—the Tea Sage made his home in Cambridge, traveled weekly to London to be on the radio, and took occasional trips to Tunbridge Wells to visit the museum. He behaved badly in all three cities.

"In Cambridge, he had several smashups in local pubs over

subjects ranging from politics to football to the quality of ale on tap. In London, he skipped out on a gambling debt, which started an ongoing feud with a turf bookie who had a penchant for making people disappear. And in Tunbridge Wells, he allegedly got involved with a married woman who report-edly had an exceptionally jealous husband, a man who had previously served a jail term for 'assault occasioning actual bodily harm.'"

"Hmm. The turf bookie sounds interesting."

"Forget him—he's a dead end. Had he been responsible for Etienne's disappearance, the corpse might have been buried in Dartmoor or consigned to the North Sea, but de-finitely not planted in our tea garden. We need a suspect connected to the museum. The irate husband is a more likely candidate."

"By any chance, was he a member of the museum's staff?"

Flick shrugged. "I don't know who he is. The anecdote is unattributed. Clive stuck it in a footnote to illustrate the kind of stories his private investigator heard about Make-peace. Remember, the brief was designed to portray Etienne's reputation."

"Ah. Then the story may be a cargo of codswallop."

"That's what I thought, too." She smiled. A lovely smile, Nigel thought. "But then Hannah Kerrigan told me that folks have begun to respond to our offer of a reward for information about Etienne Makepeace. I have here part of a message on our Web site message board that was signed 'Anonymous Bystander.'" Flick read aloud from one of her pieces of paper. "'Etienne Makepeace had an eye for good-looking ladies. One evening, he made the mistake of wooing a married barmaid. Her husband, a large man noted for his jealousy, confronted the Tea Sage and threatened to kill him where he stood. Fortunately for Makepeace, the landlord was a former professional boxer and was able to restore order. Although Makepeace left in one piece, the husband swore vengeance. He announced that he intended to settle up with Makepeace in full measure, no matter how long it took.'"

"Makepeace certainly had more than his share of pub fights," Nigel said. "How do we get in touch with 'Anonymous Bystander'?"

"I left a follow-up note on the Web site message board requesting that he—or she—contact me."

"An outraged spouse. . ." Nigel made a soft whistle. "Do you think it's possible?"

"His three sisters theorized that Makepeace was murdered by a jealous husband."

"I know—but it seems such a trite explanation. Almost a cliché."

"Yeah, a cliché that explains everything we know. Etienne puts the moves on nubile barmaid. . . . Hubby waits for an opportunity to blow him away. . . . Hubby, who is somehow connected to the museum, shoots Etienne and buries him in the tea garden under a pair of stripling Assam tea trees."

"Where does *hubby* get a Russian-made pistol?"

"For all we know, hubby hails from Minsk." Nigel could hear a happy tinkle in Flick's voice. He abruptly realized that he was staring at her and that she had never looked lovelier.

Put her out of your mind. It's over.

"What's the plan?" he asked.

"We keep searching for information about Makepeace.

We amass everything that makes sense and deliver the lot to Sir James."

"Sounds reasonable."

"We also have to marshal our time. I've taken it upon myself to create a schedule for the next few days. I hope you don't mind."

"Not at all—you're leading the investigation."

"We're presenting in London next Monday. We can create our presentation on Sunday. That means all our facts must be collected by Saturday. Obviously, we'll have to work evenings and during the weekend."

"I'm game, but not this evening. Tonight is the 'clippings party' at Stuart Battlebridge's office. He wants to show off the deluge of media coverage we received during the past five days."

"I didn't forget. I had hoped I could use our investigation as an excuse not to go. I've spent more than enough time this week with Stuart Battlebridge."

"To quote Stuart, we are 'the stars' of his public relations campaign. If we don't make an appearance, he'll throw a hissy fit. Unfortunately, his audience will also include several of the museum's trustees. He's invited the lot."

"And they agreed to attend a 'clippings party'?"

"Are you joking? Stuart has laid on a buffet dinner. Our trustees would walk barefoot across burning coals for a free meal. I'll wager that at least half of them show up this evening." Nigel took a flutter and added, "The forecast calls for rain to continue all night. Shall we drive to Monson Road together? I can pick you up at your apartment."

Flick seemed at a loss. "Well, since I plan to wear high

heels. . ." She managed a timid nod. "Okay, but—"

"But nothing else has changed. I know."

Nigel hoped that Flick would disagree. When she didn't, he moved to a new topic. "Are you going to share those documents with DI Pennyman?"

"Yes—although I can't imagine that the police don't know everything we do." She smiled again. "That's probably why the police have stopped digging in our garden. They consider the jealous husband their prime suspect."

"What do we do next?"

"Something we should have done yesterday. We talk to people who worked at the museum when the Tea Sage was in residence."

Nigel unfolded himself from the chair and reached for his phone. He dialed Polly Reid's extension.

"Polly—please join us for a moment."

"Certainly, *Mr. Owen.*"

Uh-oh. A bad sign. Polly's switched to my last name.

Nigel sat on the edge of his desk and endeavored to look nonchalant as Polly opened the door, crossed the threshold, and stopped one pace inside his office. She glared briefly at Flick, then continuously at him.

"How may I be of service, *sir?*"

"We need to know which of our current employees were on staff in 1966."

"Jim Sizer, of course, and"—she paused to think—"and no one else, unless you consider Mirabelle Hubbard and Trevor Dangerfield, our volunteer docents, as current employees. Back in 1966, he was a security guard and she was secretary to Nathanial Swithin." She added, "Will that be all, *sir?*"

"Yes, thank. . ."

Polly didn't wait for Nigel to finish. She took two backward steps and pulled the door shut.

"She seems angry at us," Flick said.

Nigel grunted. "Mostly me—but I haven't a clue why."

"I do. Polly heard everything we said earlier."

"Please tell me why our quarrel would make her throw a wobbler?"

"I don't know. . . ." Flick stared thoughtfully at the closed door for several moments. "Let's track down Jim Sizer," she finally said.

They found Jim in the museum's greenhouse beyond the Duchess of Bedford Tearoom. He was leaning over a workbench, fiddling with a small petrol-powered machine that Nigel recognized as a lawn edger. Jim, visibly surprised to see them, immediately wiped his oily hands on a rag.

"Gran' morning, ma'am—and sir."

"And to you, Jim," Flick said. "We need your help."

"My pleasure, ma'am." He smiled slyly. "Does another body want digging up?"

"Heaven forbid! We're still dealing with the first one. In fact, that's why we're here. What do you remember about Etienne Makepeace?"

"What I told you the other day covers most of it. I attended two of his lectures in the Grand Hall. Both times the room was full to overflowing. Very knowledgeable Mr. Makepeace was about tea." Jim chortled. "And very debonair with the ladies, as I recall. They crowded around him during the reception after each lecture. He had them giggling in no time."

"He gave more than two lectures, didn't he?"

"Oh yes, ma'am, at least a half dozen." Jim, seemingly embarrassed, gazed at his hands. "I could have gone to the others, but, well—it's like this, ma'am. I fancy a good cup of tea as much as the next man, but all those tea facts Mr. Makepeace talked about made my head swim."

Nigel couldn't help laughing. Flick ignored his amusement and asked another question: "Jim, do you remember how often Etienne Makepeace visited the museum?"

"Well, let me see, ma'am," Jim said. "Mr. Makepeace mostly came to Tunbridge Wells by train. The museum had its own car in those days, and I fetched him from the Central Station. It had to be twice a month—maybe more often—over the course of a year."

"Really? That's more visits than I expected. What did Mr. Makepeace do at the museum when he didn't lecture?"

Jim pondered a few seconds before he answered. "Mostly he worked in our archives and hobnobbed with the bigwigs on the third floor."

"We have bigwigs?" she said.

Jim blushed. "Well, you see, ma'am, bigwigs is what the junior staff called Mrs. Mary Hawker Evans and the people from the Hawker Foundation."

Nigel laughed again. He'd never met Mary Hawker Evans—the granddaughter of Commodore Desmond Hawker had died in 1990, some fourteen years before he arrived at the museum—but he had come to know her well through the many tales and legends spawned by her eccentricities. Mary, who thought herself the biggest wig in town, would have undoubtedly relished the label. She'd worked tirelessly to encourage—many said *browbeat*—the Hawker Foundation to fund the museum. It soon became *her* project. She contributed to the building's design, oversaw its construction, and personally selected the founding staff.

"One last question, Jim," Flick said. "Do you remember Etienne Makepeace getting into a fight with anyone—either at the museum or in Tunbridge Wells?"

"A fight, ma'am?" Jim's voice had suddenly become less confident, Nigel thought. "Well, if you want the truth, Mr. Makepeace was an easy man to fight with—the sort to have many disagreements. Once or twice, I thought about booting his bum from here to the Common. I might have, too, if he had had fewer friends in high places to look after him."

Nigel wanted to ask what Jim had meant by "friends in high places," but Flick ended the impromptu interview by thanking him. Nigel added his own "thank you" and trailed Flick into the museum building. They rode the elevator to the third floor.

"An easy man to fight with. . ." Flick murmured.

"It does make one wonder how Makepeace preserved his public persona," Nigel said. "His offstage behavior seems so at odds with tea sagaciousness, to coin a felicitous phrase."

Flick's expression grew serious. "Nigel, when you think of tea, you picture little old ladies with their pinkies up in the air, serving sandwiches with the crusts cut off." She poked his chest. "You need to spend an hour in our History of Tea Colonnade. The real story of tea in England is replete with robber barons, cutthroat business practices, wars, murder, imperialism, even piracy at sea. Tea is a civilized drink built atop centuries of sometimes uncivilized behavior. Etienne the hero and Etienne the scoundrel both fit right in."

"I stand corrected," he said, as he sprinted after Flick through the third-floor reception area. "In fact, let's redecorate the Duchess of Bedford Tearoom in the style of a pirate ship."

Nigel received the reaction he'd hoped for: Flick looked back at him and stuck her tongue out.

I wish I could change my stripes.

He followed her into the Docent's Office, a small room next to the Conservation Laboratory that Nigel considered the most comfortably furnished space in the museum. The office was filled with overstuffed chairs and well-padded sofas to give the docents—all volunteers, all retirees—a cozy place to recuperate after shepherding visitors around the museum.

Flick knocked on the door. A woman's voice replied, "Come in."

Nigel worked the knob, then stepped aside to let Flick enter first. Mirabelle Hubbard and Trevor Dangerfield were sitting on opposite ends of the sofa, both reading. She, a lively, attractive widow in her midseventies. He, a tall, robust bachelor of nearly eighty who had served as a sergeant in the Royal Marines. They had met on the first day that the museum opened to the public in 1964 and had been friends ever since. Both were extremely knowledgeable about the museum's exhibits. On more than one occasion, Nigel knew, Flick had asked Mirabelle's opinion about specific antiquities on display.

"Good heavens!" Mirabelle said. "We have managerial visitors."

"That's impossible," Trevor said. "Managers never visit docents."

"Perfectly true," Nigel said. "The docent team is the one thing in this museum that functions perfectly. We wouldn't dream of mucking it up."

Trevor made a move to stand. "Please don't," Flick said. "I'll join you on the sofa."

She sat down between Mirabelle and Trevor. Nigel chose an extravagant reclining chair. He pushed backwards to raise the footrest, which sprang into position with a noisy clank.

"What can you tell us about Etienne Makepeace?" Flick said.

"Bother!" Mirabelle said. "*More* questions about the Tea Sage. We had scads yesterday from our Japanese tour group."

Trevor took over. "Who buried him in the tea garden? Why did he end up at a tea museum? Did he have a proper funeral? Why did it take so long for you to dig him up? Couldn't answer a bloomin' one, of course. Had to tell 'em to read the blinkin' newspapers."

"Actually, we're interested in what happened forty years ago. What did you think of Etienne Makepeace back then?"

Trevor frowned. "I didn't think anything about him at all because I hardly knew the chap. I shook his hand once and saw him from a distance on several other occasions. Tall fellow with lots of hair. Dressed well and walked with an air of confidence. I seem to recall that he sneered a lot. Of course, I could be wrong. These days I can barely remember where I set down my spectacles. How about you, Mirabelle? You often tell me that your memory is sharper than mine."

Mirabelle shook her head. "Etienne Makepeace is a vague blur in my mind. I was never formally introduced to him. My only connection to the Tea Sage was to type the letters sent to him by Nathanial Swithin and drop them in the post."

"How odd that you have no opinions," Flick said. "Etienne Makepeace visited the museum often during the early days. It's strange that both of you didn't come in contact with him more frequently."

Trevor glanced at Mirabelle, then shrugged. "Neither of us wishes to speak ill of the dead, but Mr. Makepeace wasn't the sort of man to spend much time with secretaries and security guards. He preferred the company of the. . .*well*. . .the. . ."

"Bigwigs?" Nigel offered.

"Exactly, Mr. Owen," Mirabelle said. "Organizations were more formal back then. Those of us who weren't bigwigs knew to keep our distance."

Nigel moved forward in his recliner; the footrest snapped downward. *It is quite amazing,* he thought, *that a man as offensive as Etienne Makepeace survived long enough to be murdered at the Royal Tunbridge Wells Tea Museum.*

I have hoisted a colossal weight off my shoulders.

Flick deftly avoided a puddle and decided that ending her awkward attachment to Nigel had been the right thing to do. She had defused an explosive relationship before anyone got hurt. Oh, there would still be painful emotions to deal with—she was quite fond of Nigel, after all—but who said they couldn't remain good friends?

Nigel gave every indication that he felt the same way. He seemed chipper, almost cheerful, as he shielded them both with an oversized umbrella. They walked side by side, but not arm in arm, along the pedestrian pathway that led from the Crescent Road Car Park to Monson Road. An observer would have rightly concluded they were two colleagues trying to avoid getting wet.

They reached Monson Road and turned right. Across the street, Flick could see the entire second floor of a narrow building brightly lit. It was the "world headquarters" of Gordon & Battlebridge, as Stuart often joked. Someone had pushed the curtains aside. Several partygoers stood near the windows, chatting. Among them, Flick recognized two of the museum's trustees.

Rats. Nigel was right. They came.

An eight-member board of trustees oversaw the museum. They were ultimately responsible for every aspect of the museum—from its operating budget to its teaching goals to the people who served as the director and chief curator. The board of trustees had hired Felicity Adams, PhD, and they had the power to fire her.

She heaved a sigh.

"What's that about?" Nigel asked.

Flick gave a disparaging wave. "I dislike after-hours office parties."

"Since when?"

"Since you told me several trustees were coming. It's a drag to act charming and erudite—and remain on your best behavior—while your feet are aching from standing around in high-heeled pumps."

He peered at her in the illumination from a streetlamp. "I don't buy it. You like to dress up, you enjoy partying with convivial people, and you know that the trustees are in awe of your tea knowledge. What's *really* bothering you?"

Flick hesitated, then said, "Well, if you must know, I'm experiencing a new round of stage fright. I won't have a good answer if the trustees ask questions about the status of the loan." She let herself smile. "Keep in mind that I'm a rotten liar."

"If a trustee asks about the loan, don't say a ruddy thing. Point to me and proclaim that Nigel Owen deals with finances, enabling you to focus your entire being on developing a new exhibit about Etienne Makepeace."

"Okay, that should get me off the hook—for a while. I'll be back in the hot seat if the trustees don't like your explanation."

"Should the question arise, I shall say that everything is progressing according to plan, and that Sir James Boyer is so fascinated with the discovery of the body that he asked us to give him a presentation about the relationship of Etienne Makepeace to the museum."

Flick pondered a moment. "That's roughly the truth."

"Exactly! There's no need for any of the trustees to know anything more about Sir James's concerns. Telling them about Olivia Hart's visit would open up Pandora's box—unnecessarily. A week from today, the matter will be resolved. If it isn't. . . well, it won't do anyone a smidgen of good to worry about the situation this evening. Am I right?"

Flick nodded as they crossed Monson Road.

"Will you get mad at me," Nigel asked, "if I say that you look smashing tonight?"

"Probably."

"In that event, I'll say nothing—even though you do."

A bronze plaque next to a glass door signaled that they had arrived at GORDON & BATTLEBRIDGE PUBLIC RELATIONS LTD. They climbed a steep flight of stairs that led to a landing decorated with a collage of covers of the many different marketing brochures that the firm had developed for its clients. The cover photos depicted steel mills, chemical plants, a smiling group of chartered accountants, high-performance bicycles, a clean room in an electronics factory, and—in the central position of honor—the exterior of the Royal Tunbridge Wells Tea Museum.

The "clippings party" took over most of the rooms in the firm's office suite. A banner hanging in the reception room read ABANDON COATS AND UMBRELLAS HERE. A large red arrow pointed to the library: THIS WAY TO THE LIBATIONS CENTER. A second arrow announced, THE MUNCHATORIUM IS LOCATED IN STUART'S OFFICE. And a large sign affixed to a pedestal read ALL GUESTS SHOULD MAKE THEIR WAY TO THE CONFERENCE ROOM FOR MIXING, MINGLING, AND ENTERTAINING.

"Good heavens!" Flick said, surprised at the crowd she saw gathered in the conference room. The firm's large conference table consisted of several smaller sections. These had been broken apart and moved against the walls to free up a large, open area that now held at least two dozen people. "Stuart must have invited the immediate world. Do you recognize any of these folks?"

"A few. Think back to our practice session with Philip Pellicano. The Gordon & Battlebridge folks who played reporters are here. As for the strangers, I suspect that Stuart sees this as a sales meeting. He wants to show off his press-agentry prowess to potential customers." He added, "You stake out the Munchatorium; I'll stow our coats and get us drinks. What would you like?"

She thought about reminding Nigel that they weren't here "together," but his enthusiastic demeanor changed her mind. *He's merely being polite. This is hardly a date.* "A tall glass of cider would be lovely, thank you."

As Flick meandered toward Stuart's office and the buffet table, the corridor became redolent with the pungent, unmistakable smell of curry. *Whoopee! Stuart chose an Indian caterer.* Flick had grown to appreciate Indian cuisine during her seven months in England. She often dined in her apartment on Indian "takeout."

"I hope they have a nice chicken tandoori," she murmured and nearly bumped into the heavily laden Marjorie Halifax.

"Felicity! How nice to see you. The buffet is fabulous. Run, don't walk—get there before all of the scrumptious lamb rogan josh is gone."

Flick had been assured by Nigel that each of the museum's trustees must meet three essential requirements: have reached fifty years old, give or take a few years. . .be extremely successful in his or her career. . .and have a fanatical love of tea.

Marjorie fit the template to perfection. Petite, blond, loud-voiced, and vivacious, she had served two terms as a councilwoman on the Tunbridge Wells Borough Council. She was widely considered an expert in Kentish tourism and had perfected a signature laugh during her tenure as a politician: a proud chuckle accompanied by a haughty toss of her head.

"You seem remarkably cheerful this evening, Marjorie," Flick said. She watched with growing hunger as Marjorie scooped up a dollop of rogan josh with a piece of naan bread, then devoured it in two quick bites. Flick's stomach rumbled as she remembered her own meager breakfast and skipped lunch.

"Absolutely!" Marjorie said. "Little Tunbridge Wells received a wealth of good publicity during the past five days—a delightful state of affairs, because The Wells needs every last line of favorable press we can get. Too many Brits still see us as the stodgiest town in Kent, full of retired colonels who write pompous letters to the *London Times* and sign them 'Disgusted from Tunbridge Wells.'"

"Our tea garden certainly proved that Tunbridge Wells can be a stiff competitor." Flick hoped that Marjorie would recognize the intended humor in her response.

Marjorie did. "I'll make no bones about it, Felicity. The town would have gained *so much* more if you'd discovered Mr. Makepeace during the summer. We'd have filled every hotel room and restaurant table. I anticipate we will see a soupçon of additional tourism as we move toward spring, but I fear the *l'affaire Makepeace* is already quieting down. All of the extra policemen seem to have returned to Maidstone. And as for reporters—well, I haven't seen one of them wandering about in days." She leaned closer to Flick. "Should you find another body, don't be so quick to make an announcement."

Marjorie added a wily wink to her trademark laugh and went off with her dinner.

Flick joined the buffet line. She looked around for Nigel and saw him—a glass of cider in each hand—chatting with Dorothy McAndrews, another trustee. They seemed thick as thieves. Dorothy held a PhD in art history and owned McAndrews Antiques, a chain of antique shops in Kent and

Sussex, but she was best known as "the-woman-on-the-telly-who-looks-like-a-Celtic-princess." Red-haired, green-eyed, and fair-complexioned, Dorothy was a regular on a BBC TV show that traveled through Great Britain appraising local antiques. This evening she wore a black crepe wool dress that hugged her like a wetsuit and had undoubtedly cost a fortune. Dorothy spotted Flick and waved. Flick returned the greeting.

Happy days. The trustees don't seem to be thinking about the loan.

Flick reached the buffet table and assembled two plates of goodies, giving ample emphasis to tandoori and rogan josh. Nigel joined her just as she finished. He liked chutney; he topped his plate with several spoonfuls of Major Gray's.

"Dorothy asked about you," Nigel said. "She thinks you look worried tonight."

"Well, *duh*!"

"I explained that you're preoccupied with gathering material for the Makepeace exhibit."

"Did she buy it?"

"Totally. In fact, she lit up at the mention of an exhibit. It seems that her antique shop in Sevenoaks has among its stock a handful of black-and-white photographs of Etienne Makepeace taken during the early 1960s."

"Pictures! We need them!"

"Whoa! Of course we need them, but we can't act frantic about it. I calmly offered to have our chief curator evaluate the historicity of the photographs in light of the other Makepeace materials we've gathered."

Flick peered at Nigel. When it finally became clear that

he wasn't going to say anything more, she blurted, "Did she agree?"

He grinned at her. "Expect to receive a package by messenger tomorrow morning."

They carried their plates to the conference room and were able to snag one of the conference table sections to use as a makeshift table.

"How many trustees are here tonight?" Flick wiped her lips with a napkin. Marjorie had been right; the rogan josh was exceptional.

"I counted four," Nigel answered.

"I've seen Marjorie and Dorothy."

"There are two more in the far corner, engaged in lively conversation."

Flick looked. "Got 'em."

On the left: Rev. William de Rudd, the vicar of St. Stephen's Church out on Pembury Road, the church she and Nigel had attended recently. The vicar was noted for his soft-spoken joviality and his steadily increasing girth. He stood as tall as Flick—five-foot-nine, one hundred seventy-five centimeters—but embodied twice her weight. She noted that his salt-and-pepper hair thinned noticeably at the crown, much like a tonsure. The vicar would soon resemble Friar Tuck.

On the right: Peter Cork, PhD, a world-renowned expert on ceramics and a professor of physical chemistry at the University of Kent in Canterbury. Peter specialized in stoneware, porcelain, and bone china—the "stuff" of teapots, teacups, and saucers. He wore thick eyeglasses and was mostly bald, pale skinned, and stoop shouldered—the perfect stereotype, Flick thought, of a horror-movie scientist about to reanimate a dead monster.

Nigel chuckled. "The two of them are having a grand time boring each other. I overheard the vicar explaining to Peter that the word 'ceramics' derives from *keramos*, the Greek word for 'pottery.' "

Unexpectedly, he frowned. "Polly Reid is here, too. She gave me a sour look and sped off when I tried to say hello."

"Oh dear. We have to find out what's pulled her chain."

A spoon clinking against a glass caught Flick's attention. The chattering in the room faded to silence. A movie screen descended from its ceiling-mounted shell. Stuart Battlebridge stepped in front of the screen as the lights dimmed. One of Stuart's associates pushed keys on a laptop computer connected to an electronic projector and started the "show"—a PowerPoint presentation that detailed the media's coverage of the discovery of Etienne Makepeace.

Stuart offered a running commentary of the various video clips, audio sound bites, and newspaper articles. Flick thought several of his observations over the top:

"Imagine a drum roll as we relive those exciting moments when our lovely tea museum became the object of the world's fancy."

And: "The historic discovery at our beloved institution has resolved one of the twentieth century's greatest mysteries."

And: "People on five continents now know that Tunbridge Wells is the home to a center of excellence of tea scholarship."

Flick found the next segment especially entertaining. Stuart had edited together a collage of TV news reports in several different languages—each of them using the museum building as a backdrop for a reporter's "talking head." As

Stuart opined, "Many of the Commonwealth nations cared about Etienne Makepeace and sent news crews to cover the story of his reappearance."

Flick's and Nigel's faces suddenly filled the screen. *Rats! Stuart filmed the news conference.* Flick had quietly dreaded the possibility—she disliked watching videos of herself. This time she had good reason. Her makeup at the conference had been overdone. Her hair appeared too curly. Her clothing made her look fat. Her voice sounded shrill. And she seemed utterly goofy compared to Nigel, who was easy to watch and projected a solid image of charm and competency.

To make matters worse, Stuart had added an orchestral treatment of *Tea for Two* to the soundtrack. The music would get softer when people were talking and louder when she or Nigel was thinking about an answer. Besides being corny, it called attention to her inability to think quickly on her feet.

"The camera loves you, Dr. Adams."

Flick twirled to her right. Dorothy McAndrews had moved next to her.

"It does?" Flick said, not making any attempt to hide her astonishment.

"You're what we call camera-friendly in the telly trade. You come across as skilled, intelligent, confident, and friendly—a woman in charge of the situation."

"Really?" Flick thought back to the news conference. At the time, she hadn't felt in charge of anything.

Dorothy patted her shoulder. "Hey! You're our chief curator, which puts you in charge of everything that makes our museum worth visiting. I can't wait to see your Etienne Makepeace exhibit."

Flick glanced at Nigel. He was studying the screen intently, a half smile on his lips, silently nodding to himself. What did he think of her performance? He must have sensed her looking at him because he unexpectedly smiled at her and made a "thumbs-up" sign. Perhaps Stuart's video deserved a higher grade than she had given it.

The lights came back on. Flick noticed a gleam in Stuart's eye as he surveyed the conference room.

No! Don't do it!

"Ladies and Gentlemen. I give you the stars of tonight's media fest." He made a sweeping gesture toward them. "Nigel Owen and Dr. Felicity Adams."

Flick made a mental note to murder Stuart Battlebridge as a cloud of clapping partygoers promptly surrounded them. There were the four trustees. . .and Stuart himself. . .and well-wishers who proved to be staff members, associates, and interns working for Gordon & Battlebridge. . .and, as Nigel had guessed, potential clients from companies in Kent and West Sussex.

Many had questions about Etienne Makepeace. Flick soon found herself separated from Nigel, describing—and rehashing—the events that had led to the discovery of the body. She endured the mini-inquisitions for twenty minutes and then escaped to the ladies loo. Once inside, she used her mobile phone to call Nigel's mobile phone.

"I want out of this party," she said. "Can we leave now?"

"Where are you hiding?" He laughed when she told him. "I'll meet you next to the coat rack."

Flick made her way to the reception room and retrieved her Burberry. She had finished doing up her belt when Polly

Reid stepped in front of her. Polly was holding an empty plastic tumbler and seemed to be unsteady on her pins.

"What a waste!" she hissed at Flick.

Polly began to rock back and forth; the plastic tumbler slipped out of her hand. Flick moved forward to steady her, but Nigel arrived first and grabbed Polly's elbow. She leaned against him and recovered her balance.

Polly looked up at Nigel. She stood on tiptoes and tried to whisper in Nigel's ear, but her voice was loud enough for Flick to hear. "How stupid can you be, Nigel? Don't you listen on Sunday? Didn't you learn anything in church?"

She abruptly dropped her head against Nigel's shoulder. He put his arm around her waist to support her. "I'll drive her home in her car," he said to Flick, "then return in a taxi."

"Do you want me to come along with you?"

"Easier said than done. Polly drives a two-seat Mazda MX-5."

"Oops. I'll hold down the fort."

"My thoughts exactly." He gave a resigned sigh. "Help me find her coat."

Flick watched Nigel guide Polly toward the stairs. She heard Nigel ask, "Okay, Polly, where did you park your Mazda?" She saw Polly point in the general direction of the Crescent Road Car Park.

A voice behind Flick spoke: "You seem to have lost your squire, Dr. Adams. I shall be honored to provide alternative transportation."

She turned. "Thank you, Vicar, but Nigel will be back shortly. Polly is somewhat under the weather."

"I suspected as much. On two separate occasions this

evening she encouraged me to provide Nigel with a lecture on St. Paul's second letter to the Corinthians. When I asked why, she urged that I watch the two of you closely and be ready to act when necessary."

Flick hadn't read Second Corinthians recently. She thought about asking the vicar what relevant points the epistle made, but decided that would invite a midweek sermon she was not in the mood to hear. Flick went instead to the "Libations Center" and filled a paper cup with tea. She sat near the bottom of the staircase and waited for Nigel. He returned in less than twenty minutes.

"Don't even think of going upstairs," she said with a smile, "unless you want to hear a discourse on Second Corinthians. Vicar de Rudd is on the verge of creating one—especially for you."

"Good heavens! Why?"

"It was Polly's idea." Flick went on. "How is she?"

"Green. I don't know what she drank tonight, but it didn't go well with Indian food. The wind blowing in her face as I drove her home seemed to help. She's also blooming embarrassed."

"Did she explain what's bugging her?"

"I asked, but she waved the question away. She promised to 'tell us all' when she's feeling better."

Flick pulled her Burberry tight around her as they left the building. It had stopped raining, but the temperature had fallen. Her raincoat's thin wool lining didn't do much to stop the damp chill from making her shiver. "This is the kind of night that makes me wish I had a fireplace in my apartment," she said.

The day before, they would have walked arm in arm. Tonight, Flick let Nigel walk a half pace ahead as they crossed Monson Road. Even the sounds of their leather soles striking the macadam lacked harmony, she thought.

When they reached the Crescent Road Car Park, Flick remembered that the elevators stopped running at six thirty. *Ouch.* She'd been on her feet for nearly three hours, and her shoes had begun to pinch. Now she would have to climb four flights of stairs to the rooftop parking area to reach Nigel's BMW. Every parking stall on the lower floors had been full when they arrived.

Don't think about it. Just do it.

It seemed colder and windier on the roof, but the night-time view of Tunbridge Wells was excellent. Nigel had parked near the northern end. Flick paused a moment to scan the rooftops and pick out landmarks she recognized. She quickly found the floodlit, castlelike spire of St. John's Church and the oddly configured roof of the Royal Victoria Place shopping center.

Nigel beeped the passenger-side door open.

Flick sank gratefully into the soft leather seat. She slipped her left shoe off and wiggled circulation back into her toes. Nigel climbed into the driver's seat and turned the ignition. The engine growled to life and settled to a purr. Flick fastened her seat belt. "I'll have you home in a jiffy," Nigel said, as he put the BMW in gear and began to back out of the parking space.

Flick heard another engine roar. Nigel hit the brakes hard. She twisted in her seat and looked out the rear window. A dark green minivan—that's how Flick would describe a similar

American vehicle—had pulled directly behind the BMW. Its windshield and side windows were tinted; she couldn't see the driver's face.

"What's going on?" she said and immediately regretted posing a foolish question.

Nigel seemed not to consider the question silly. "Some idiot in a Ford Transit van has me blocked in."

He tooted the horn. The van didn't move.

He honked his horn. *No joy.*

He pushed the button to open his window. "Please move your vehicle. . . ."

Nigel's words were suddenly overwhelmed by a crisply accented male voice that boomed at them from a small loudspeaker that seemed stuck to the van's roof.

"It would be best, Mr. Owen," said the man, "for you and Dr. Adams to stop seeking additional information about Etienne Makepeace."

Flick felt a stab of fear. Nigel yanked his door open. "Who are you?"

The loudspeaker crackled. "Raking up the past can be dangerous work—especially when it serves no purpose. Let sleeping dogs lie."

"I said. . .who are you?"

"Etienne Makepeace disappeared because he made the mistake of wooing a married barmaid whose husband exacted vengeance. You don't need trivial details or names of specific people. So why continue stirring the pot and asking more questions? It can only lead to unnecessary pain and discomfort for you. And disappointment at the museum."

"I don't react well to threats." Nigel said—boldly, Flick thought.

"We assumed as much, Mr. Owen. Let me assure you that we make *promises*—not threats. To prove the point, we've arranged a modest demonstration of our capacity to influence the future of the museum. Pay close attention to what transpires tomorrow morning." The voice paused. "I've said all that I need to say, except for one obvious caveat. Do not attempt to follow this vehicle or engage in any other heroic acts. We prefer that no grievous harm come to either of you."

As quickly as it appeared, the van roared away leaving Nigel and Flick staring at a cloud of blue diesel exhaust. Flick tried to read the number plate, but it had been obscured, perhaps with a coating of mud.

"I'd better call the police." Nigel reached for his mobile phone.

"And tell them what?" Flick said, surprised at the calm she felt.

"That a man in a green Ford Transit van threatened us."

"Okay—then what do we say to the reporters who come calling? Or to Olivia Hart when Sir James Boyer reads the stories they write?"

"Flip! You're right, of course, we can't get the police involved." Nigel returned the mobile phone to his belt. "Still, I'd love to know who that rotter is—and better yet, have an opportunity to sort him out good and proper, as my dad likes to say."

"I don't know his real name," Flick said, "but from the way he spoke, I'm fairly certain we just met 'Anonymous Bystander.'"

EIGHT

Halfway along Castle Road, in the heart of the Tunbridge Wells Common, Nigel regretted his decision to walk to the museum that Thursday morning. He had chosen not to drive because—returning from the "clippings party" the night before—he had found a legal parking space directly beneath his flat. This was such a rare occurrence that Nigel elected to take advantage of his annual street-parking permit. Upon leaving his building, he had ignored the chill, damp wind that defied his mackintosh and guided Cha-Cha westward on Lime Hill Road.

Nigel often walked to work; he had two favorite routes. The shortest—an easy two-kilometer hike—followed London Road past the back of the Pantiles. The longer, more scenic route—the one that Cha-Cha liked best—took them along Castle Road through the Common.

Perhaps it was the clammy mist that hovered close to the ground, or possibly the occasional icy spots that made the

178

path treacherous, but the Common seemed unusually desolate that morning. Nigel had seen only one jogger and no other pedestrians. Each step made him feel more exposed, more vulnerable to a host of unknown dangers lurking behind trees. He began to wish for the secure feeling of slamming the car door and pushing the LOCK button.

Of course you're uneasy. What happened in the car park would make anyone edgy.

Remarkably, he hadn't felt any fear when the man in the green Ford Transit van demanded that they stop seeking additional information about Etienne Makepeace. The voice had been loud and the words moderately threatening, but there had been something artificial about the bizarre confrontation. At the time, it had struck Nigel as vaguely theatrical— more pretense than genuine.

But later, as he drove home after dropping Flick at her apartment, he'd had second thoughts. What if the man in the van had been armed? Or what if he had decided to ram Nigel when he "boldly"—or perhaps foolishly—stepped out of the BMW?

Nigel shivered, unsure if it was the wintry air or a stray frisson of anxiety.

At least he had a fine cup of coffee to sustain him. He had brewed a triple shot—three individual pods—of French Roast blend to fill his stainless steel travel mug. Nigel stopped, pushed open the top slide, and took several sips.

Nigel looked around the Common. There was no one in the immediate vicinity. He let Cha-Cha off his lead; the Shiba raced off behind a tree.

The van itself had been an unremarkable Ford Transit,

dark green, diesel powered—not new, but not exceptionally old. There must be thousands of similar vehicles in service across England. The only distinguishing feature had been the small loudspeaker temporarily affixed to the roof by what Nigel had recognized as a magnetic antenna mount. The driver had undoubtedly removed the loudspeaker minutes after leaving the car park. Flick had tried to read the number plate but couldn't. Nigel sighed. Even if he or Flick had opted to notify the police, the plods could never have located the van.

It had been Flick who recognized that the man in the van spoke the same antique phrase—Etienne Makepeace "made the mistake of wooing a married barmaid"—that had appeared in the Web site submission signed by "Anonymous Bystander."

"He clearly did it on purpose to identify himself," Flick had said, as they traveled to her apartment. "And since no one under sixty says 'wooing' any more, we have to assume that he's a contemporary of Makepeace."

"I agree," Nigel had replied. "But why would 'Anonymous Bystander' give us information via our Web site and then demand that we halt our investigation? Does that make any sense to you?"

"Not much—unless 'Anonymous Bystander' is the jealous husband who shot Makepeace. Maybe he's trying to control what we find out, because he's worried about being discovered forty years after the murder?"

Nigel had shaken his head. "I repeat the question I just asked: Why would a guilty party respond to our request for information in the first place?"

In the end, neither Nigel nor Flick had a sensible

explanation for the bizarre episode in the Crescent Road Car Park. They'd sat in the BMW, in front of Flick's apartment, for nearly a half hour trying to figure out what "Anonymous Bystander" had meant by a "modest demonstration of our capacity to influence the future of the museum." That seemed the oddest threat—or promise—of all.

"We'll see what today brings," Nigel murmured.

Cha-Cha emerged from behind a bush. Nigel reattached the lead.

"We're going to have an interesting morning, Cha-Cha," he said, "as we wait for the other shoe to drop. I'm counting on you to be our watchdog."

The Shiba gave a yodel-like bark, trotted to the end of his lead, and tugged Nigel toward the intersection of Castle Road and London Road.

Ten minutes later, Nigel and Cha-Cha reached the roundabout on Eridge Road. Nigel saw two small lorries parked in front of the museum that belonged, he presumed, to Garwood & McHue. As he neared the front door, he counted three workmen in nondescript uniforms working outside the building. Two of them were standing on ladders that reached beyond the first floor. They were installing two of the small acorn-shaped TV cameras—one above the museum's front door surround, the other alongside decorative stonework on the edge of the building. The black plastic gizmos seemed to blend well with the trim; once in place, they would be almost invisible.

Nigel felt Cha-Cha increase the pull on his lead as they approached the side entrance. The dog clearly anticipated his early morning visit with Earl in the Duchess of Bedford

Tearoom. Nigel unfastened the lead and let Cha-Cha run ahead.

Maybe I should visit the tearoom, too.

He knew that Flick often ate a light breakfast before she went upstairs. It might be a perfect opportunity to reopen the discussion about their relationship. She had sent mixed signals the evening before. Her words proclaimed that they were no longer a twosome, but her demeanor suggested that she hadn't fully made up her mind. There might still be hope.

Actually, I feel a bit peckish myself.

When Nigel arrived in the tearoom, Flick was in her favorite corner, saying hello to Cha-Cha, who had conveniently placed his head in her lap. Nigel approached and stopped next to an empty chair. "May I join you?" He glimpsed the table. "Good heavens! You're drinking coffee. A whole potful."

She looked up. Her face appeared tired.

"I had a rotten night," she said, "without much sleep. I kept seeing green Ford vans and waking up." She gestured toward the chair. "How about you?"

"I slept splendidly. My imagination switched on as I walked through the Common. I began to feel especially defenseless—a not at all pleasant sensation, I assure you."

"We decided not to call the cops last night, but I think we should tell Detective Inspector Pennyman what happened."

"Ah. The arrangement."

She nodded. "It might be significant that we've been. . . *warned.* I imagine that's the right word. We can ask him to keep the encounter quiet."

Nigel spotted a stack of mugs on an adjacent table. He borrowed one and filled it.

"Have a scone, too," Flick said. "They go great with coffee—I'm not very hungry this morning."

"I believe I will. . . ," he began to say, but was interrupted by Earl who began to make his loud clucking sound. "Flip! I wish he'd stop doing that."

"Tell me about it!" She put her hands over her ears. "Shut up, Earl—it's too early, and I'm too tired."

Nigel felt Cha-Cha slide past his leg as the Shiba disentangled himself from Flick. He ambled off toward Earl's cage.

"A brilliant idea, old chum! Do your best to silence the fowl. If necessary, you have my permission to eat the blooming bird."

Nigel broke a scone in half and dropped a spoonful of blackberry preserves on the piece he had targeted. In the distance, the clucking tapered off.

"I agree we should tell Pennyman about the green van," he said. "We also have to inform Conan Davies on the off chance that 'Anonymous Bystander' has the ability to cause physical damage to the museum."

Flick returned a sheepish grin. "I hope you don't mind, but it's done. I called Conan at two thirty this morning. He assured me that I'd done the right thing to wake him up." She went on. "He would like to see both of us this morning—I quote—'at our earliest convenience.'"

"I don't mind. In fact, I feel better already. It's a great comfort to have Conan in our corner."

She beamed at Nigel. "I agree."

Nigel felt his heart flutter. This was the Felicity Adams he had fallen in love with—and still loved. Did the warmth of her smile indicate that she still felt the same way? Perhaps she was ready to reconsider her hasty dismissal?

Not bloomin' likely—because it's your fault.

Nigel abruptly remembered that he was the primary cause of their split. Nothing had changed in his life. He still couldn't assure Flick that she could trust him without question. He turned away before Flick could see the unhappiness that he knew must have darkened his face while she was smiling.

Nigel was saved from the awkwardness of explaining his strange maneuver by the fortuitous arrival of Giselle Logan, the hostess of the Duchess of Bedford Tearoom.

"Excuse me, Dr. Adams. May I have a moment? I need some advice."

Giselle—whose father was German, her mother from Singapore—had inherited the best genes from both parents. She was a slender brunette with striking Eurasian features, a fascinating voice, and talent for precise organization. She held an honors degree in hospitality management and would, Nigel felt sure, soon outgrow her humble job at the Royal Tunbridge Wells Tea Museum. Until that happened, however, he intended to make maximum use of her skills and talents. And so, he gave her the further responsibility of managing the museum's growing business of hosting academic conferences. She worked closely with Flick to coordinate the use of the museum's facilities. The museum offered an ideal setting for one- or two-day conferences of, say, twenty to thirty scholars. In past years, the museum had accommodated three or four academic conferences a year; Nigel wanted to increase the number to three a month.

"Certainly, Giselle," Flick said. "Fire away."

"Well. . .I feel rather bewildered by what occurred this morning. Thirty minutes ago, I received a call from Professor Garrett at the University of Kent. He informed me the Kent Chapter of the Society of Elizabethan Fiction has decided to cancel next month's conference. They were scheduled for the first week in February."

"Did he give you a reason?"

"An odd one. He said that the chapter chose the tea museum on the assumption that the tea garden would be available for their use. However, he has received information that the police intend to keep the garden off-limits indefinitely."

"From who?" Flick stiffened, as if she'd received a personal insult. "We haven't been told when the police will get their paraphernalia out of the garden, but I can't imagine they will still be here in February." She suddenly shrugged. "On the other hand, my assumption may be wishful thinking. I guess we just have to smile and accept the cancellation as one more cost of discovering Makepeace's body in our tea garden."

"That may not be necessary." Giselle held up a piece of paper. "What is most peculiar is that ten minutes after the professor called, I received this e-mail message from someone named 'Anonymous Bystander.' "

"*What?*" Nigel bounded out of his chair and nearly tore the message from her hand. He set the document on the table so that both he and Flick could read it.

To: Giselle Logan (Royal Tunbridge Wells Tea Museum)
From: Anonymous Bystander
Subject: Modest Demonstration

Our modest demonstration is complete.

Because we don't want to cause needless injury to the museum, we point out that Professor Garrett is an easy fellow to sway. We suggest you make him a promise that should the tea garden not be available during the conference, you will reduce the cost of the meeting by fifteen percent.

Please be assured you have our best wishes for the museum's continued success!

Nigel dropped back into in his chair. "Well, now we know what the man in the van meant by his 'capacity to influence the future of the museum.' He seems to have the ability to injure our business."

"Are you acquainted with this person who calls himself 'Anonymous Bystander'?" Her voice and her face both expressed the puzzlement she felt.

"We met him last night," Flick said. "Well—*almost* met him."

Before Giselle could ask a clarifying question, Nigel said to her, "We don't know who he is—only that he represents a real threat to the museum. Nonetheless, I suggest that you follow the advice in his e-mail message. Call Professor Garrett, explain that we have every confidence that our garden will be open to visitors by February, and throw in the promise of a discount, should we be wrong."

Giselle paused a moment. "Yes, a discount seems appropriate under the circumstances," she finally said, "but not fifteen percent. That would cut too deeply into our profits. He ordered a plain afternoon tea with scones for his group. I will offer a free upgrade to our deluxe cream tea and negotiate from there."

Nigel started to laugh, swallowed hard, and managed to produce a sound that resembled a weedy cough. Giselle Logan would go far. He envisioned her at the helm of a London hotel in a few years, or possibly overseeing a posh club.

"Press on, Giselle," he said. Then to Flick, "Let's go see Conan Davies."

As Nigel expected, they located Conan in his basement office. He was fiddling with the controls of a computer monitor and seemed in high spirits—no worse for the wear for receiving Flick's early morning telephone call.

"Good morning, ma'am. Sir." Conan gave them each a crisp military salute and waved toward the visitor's chair on either side of his desk. "Three of our new surveillance cameras are operational, and a fourth will be on-line within the hour. The 'Anonymous Bystander' will find it difficult to sneak up on us today."

Nigel looked at the screen. Three small images showed the visitors' car park, the area surrounding the front door, and the interior of the Commodore Hawker Room, on the ground floor. "Regrettably," he said, "our nameless interloper has already come and gone."

"*No!*"

Nigel marveled—as he often did—that Conan could transform "no" into a three-syllable word. For some mysterious reason, Conan's Scottish brogue usually sounded thicker in the morning.

"Conan, you are au courant with what happened to us in the car park last evening—correct?" The big man nodded; Nigel went on. "There are four other things you need to know. First, the chief curator and I are under significant pressure

187

to complete—in record time—a detailed investigation into Etienne Makepeace's connection to this museum. Second, although you may find it hard to believe, Detective Inspector Pennyman of the Kent Constabulary has volunteered to assist us with *our* inquiries. Third, the initial stages of our investigation uncovered some rather unpleasant information about England's Tea Sage. And fourth, we learned this morning that 'Anonymous Bystander' poses a credible threat to the museum." Nigel took a deep breath. "Sit back, and we will tell you a convoluted story."

Twenty minutes later, Conan Davies said, "Let me summarize the relevant details, sir. A jealous husband—a man somehow linked to the museum—may well have murdered Etienne Makepeace for good reasons. We need to move ahead with our investigation to satisfy Wescott Bank, but a man using the alias 'Anonymous Bystander' has warned us to let sleeping dogs lie. Consequently, we are between a rock and a hard place, because both parties have the power to inflict harm upon us."

"Well done!" Nigel said. "Your précis demonstrates Scottish thrift at its finest."

Conan seemed to blush at the compliment. He cleared his throat and said, "I believe you are absolutely right in your decision to explain the circumstances to DI Pennyman. He seems a forthright fellow—I trust his judgment. We definitely want the first incident to be on record should there be a second."

"Now there's a comforting thought." Nigel unclipped his mobile phone from his belt. "Does anyone know Pennyman's telephone number?"

"I have his card," Flick offered.

"Good." Nigel handed the mobile to Flick. "He's your friend and confidante."

Flick sighed. "You're right, of course." She pushed the buttons.

Nigel struggled to make sense of the side of the conversation he could hear:

"Detective Inspector Pennyman, please."

"I see. Can you tell me where he is?"

"Okay. Then when will he be back?"

"Ah. Then how can I reach him?"

"No. There isn't anyone else with whom I would like to speak. I need to talk to DI Pennyman."

"I understand he's unavailable. Do you have a mobile phone number?"

"Well, I'm sorry, too."

Flick ended the call. She made a face and uttered in what Nigel thought to be a wholly credible accent from the south of England: "DI Pennyman been called away although I can't say to where. Nor can I tell you when he will return. And no way will I give you his mobile number."

"Odd for him to be out of pocket," Nigel said. "I presumed he was actively involved in the Makepeace murder investigation."

"He was definitely involved when we spoke on Monday afternoon," Flick said.

"He still might be, ma'am," Conan said. "Mr. Makepeace traveled throughout England. Perhaps DI Pennyman's inquiries took him to another city."

"Good point," Nigel said. "If so, that puts a full stop to any notion of cooperating with the peelers—at least until

Pennyman returns to Tunbridge Wells."

"Not necessarily, sir," Conan said. "What about that police-woman who accompanied him on all his visits to the museum?"

"Detective Constable Sally Kerr," Flick said. "I could try her."

"Do it!" Nigel turned to Conan. "We'll use your speaker-phone. Then we can listen to two people talking."

Flick pulled her chair closer to a starfish-shaped telephone atop Conan's desk and dialed the main number she found listed on Pennyman's card.

"Kent Police."

"Detective Constable Kerr, please."

"Putting you through."

"DC Kerr speaking. Good morning."

"Detective, this is Felicity Adams, from the Royal Tun-bridge Wells Tea Museum. I have been. . .*ah*, cooperating with DI Pennyman."

"Yes, ma'am. The detective inspector has told me of his arrangement with you."

"Well, there's something I'd like to report. A curious confrontation in a car park."

"Does it pertain to Etienne Makepeace's death?"

"It seems closely related."

"In that event, tell me." She added, "DI Pennyman has asked me to relay any new developments in the case to him."

"Ah, then you know where he is."

The policewoman seemed to waver. "I expect I can share his location with you," she said, after a brief interval. "The detective inspector is in Scotland, pursuing a lead related to a possible suspect."

Nigel flashed a "thumbs-up" sign at Conan. The chief

of security responded by raising his arms in victory—and accidentally produced a clanking noise with his chair. Flick held a finger up in front of her lips. Nigel winced; DC Kerr could hear any sounds they made.

Kerr went on, "I can't say any more. Now, tell me about your confrontation."

"Last night, Mr. Owen and I attended an office party on Monson Road in Tunbridge Wells. At approximately ten fifteen, a man driving a green Ford Transit van accosted us. He demanded that we stop seeking additional information about Etienne Makepeace and warned us to 'let sleeping dogs lie.' We're confident that he is the same man who submitted an anecdote about Makepeace to our Web site. He signed his name as 'Anonymous Bystander.' "

"Did you report the incident to the local police?"

"No. We don't want to create any more public hoopla that will bring reporters to the museum. In fact, we don't want the details of what happened known by anyone other than you and DI Pennyman."

"Well, your report is rather sketchy, but I'll pass it on to the detective inspector."

"Please also tell him that two sources have told us Etienne Makepeace was threatened by a jealous husband not long before he disappeared."

Nigel heard a distinct change in the tone of Kerr's voice. "*Uh*. . .very interesting. . .*uh*, who provided that tidbit of information?" Nigel could also hear a pencil scratching frenetically; Detective Constable Kerr had begun to take copious notes.

"Our first source was the solicitor who represented Makepeace's heirs in the court proceedings that declared him legally dead. Our second was 'Anonymous Bystander.'"

"Most interesting. Did either provide a name for the. . . *alleged* wronged spouse?"

"No. The full extent of our information is that Makepeace made inappropriate advances toward a barmaid at a local pub and that her husband intervened."

"Fancy that. Astonishing." DC Kerr took several breaths. "This 'Anonymous Bystander' of yours seems to have a rather vivid imagination. I can't imagine who he is and where he learned. . .I mean, *what* would cause him to act in such a curious manner."

Nigel glanced at Flick. Her pleased expression told him that she, too, had recognized DC Kerr's late-blooming evasiveness The policewoman was trying hard not to reveal the obvious: The police, too, knew about the legendary jealous husband. More to the point, they clearly considered the legend a serious possibility.

"Would you like me to prepare a written summary for DI Pennyman?" Flick asked.

"Why, yes—if you wouldn't mind. I feel sure he'll be interested in everything you have to report. Thank you for your call."

DC Kerr rang off.

"She didn't give you a chance to say good-bye," Nigel said.

"Or the opportunity to ask her where to send the 'written summary,'" Flick said. "So—what do you think?"

Nigel smiled. "The same thing you do. The police are trying to identify the man who threatened Makepeace in the pub. The detective constable was rattled to find out that we knew about him—and she can't wait to contact Pennyman and share the news."

"Hello, hello!" Conan pointed to the surveillance camera monitor. "What have we here?" He pulled his keyboard close and tapped a few keys. A single image filled the monitor screen. A title along the bottom read, OVERVIEW: ERIDGE ROAD ENTRANCE.

Nigel peered at the screen. "What we have is a young man, in his early twenties I estimate, standing at our front door. Probably a museum visitor who doesn't know our winter opening hours."

"You could be right, sir," Conan said.

"I hear a 'but' coming."

"Well, our new cameras may give us more information before we have to decide." He pressed other keys; the image changed to WIDEVIEW: ERIDGE ROAD—LOOKING TOWARD NORTH.

Nigel squinted. "Is that a motorbike resting against the NO PARKING sign?"

"Indeed it is." Conan used the computer mouse to adjust the focus. "If I were a betting man, I'd wager the young man is a local messenger who chose to ignore the large sign out front that clearly explains all deliveries should be made to the service entrance at the rear of the building."

Nigel and Flick said, "Dorothy McAndrews's photographs!" in perfect synchronism.

"I'll be right back," she said excitedly.

Nigel watched through the office's glass wall as Flick sprinted out of view, up the staircase. When he looked back at Conan, he found him smiling.

"A fine lass she is, sir. You're a lucky man."

"Undeservedly lucky." Nigel quickly changed the subject. "I can see how these new cameras will improve our security."

Conan grinned. "Not by half you haven't, sir. Capturing a simple image is child's play. We look forward to showing you all the spiffy things a modern surveillance system can do."

Nigel groaned to himself. He might have to sit through *another* round of science fair demonstrations by Conan Davies and Niles Garwood.

❧

Flick felt unsure if she should tip the messenger who handed her an oversize manila envelope. He looked older in person, closer to thirty, and much scruffier than he seemed in the surveillance image. He helped Flick make a decision when he leered, then winked, at her. She said, "Thank you," and let the big front door swing shut in his face.

She tore open the envelope's sealed flap as she trotted down the stairs to the basement, and then paused outside Conan's office to slide four large black-and-white prints—sandwiched between two pieces of stiff cardboard—out of the envelope. The photographer who had made the prints knew how to adjust the process chemistry to achieve rich blacks, clean whites, and a wide range of gray tones. Even the photographic paper was a high-quality archival grade.

The first showed Etienne Makepeace lecturing to a standing-room-only crowd in the museum's Grand Hall. Flick concluded from his big smile, enthusiastic gestures, and confident stance that he delighted in public speaking.

The second photo, obviously taken in the Pantiles, caught

a brightly smiling Makepeace talking with a well-endowed blond in front of the Swan Hotel. The woman wore a tight sweater, an even tighter miniskirt, and a pair of white knee-high boots—a somewhat inappropriate outfit, Flick thought, for a woman who must be at least forty years old.

The third and fourth photographs both showed Etienne Makepeace sitting on a wooden bench in what looked like a waiting room. Above and to the right of him was a large wall clock. In one photo, the clock read 11:14, and in the other, 11:22. The two photos—taken from the same vantage point— seemed identical. Flick could find only one significant differ- ence: The earlier shot had captured another man sitting on the opposite end of the bench, an open newspaper covering most of his face.

"Will they help our investigation?" Nigel asked.

"You tell me." Flick lined the photos up along the edge of Conan's desk and stood back.

"Crikey! Do you think that the woman in Photo Number Two could be the errant wife in question?"

"I had the same thought," Flick said. "I suppose it's possible. Forty-plus years is a long time, but we should be able to locate people in Tunbridge Wells who can identify her from her photograph."

Nigel peered at the other photos. "Photo Number One could become a centerpiece of a Makepeace exhibit—but I can't make sense of Numbers Three and Four."

"Same here. Why would anyone waste film to photograph Makepeace doing nothing?"

"I believe I know the answer, ma'am," Conan said. "Observe that no one is actually looking toward the camera in any of the pictures. And note that the photographer has carefully scribed dates in the bottom margins."

What dates?

She looked again. *Rats! Conan was right.* The photographer had written the dates with pen and ink in a tiny hand. They ranged from 5 September 1966 to 8 September 1966.

Conan went on, "These seem to be high-quality surveillance photos, probably taken surreptitiously with a concealed Leica or Rolleiflex. A good photographer seems to have been following Mr. Makepeace around Tunbridge Wells not long before he disappeared."

"Crikey!" Nigel said. "How would surveillance snaps find their way to an antique store? Do you suppose. . ." He shook the large manila envelope that Flick had stood against Conan's in-basket. A square of paper fell out. "I thought as much. Dorothy included a note with the photos." He read aloud:

My dearest Felicity,

Please do evaluate the "historicity"—did I spell it right?—of the enclosed photographs. One of my shop managers purchased the set at a church jumble sale, twenty years ago, for ten or twenty pence. She recognized Etienne Makepeace and thought that photos of him, especially photos this odd, might interest a specialized collector. Alas, no such collector ever darkened our door. About ten years ago, we filed the photos away in a cabinet full of celebrity photographs at my Sevenoaks store. I saw them back then but pretty much forgot about them. Do you think they have any value?

Best wishes, Dorothy

Flick saw Nigel's eyebrows merge together as he frowned. "I still don't understand," he said. "How did the photos end up at a church?"

"You see, sir," Conan said, "it happens more than we security folk would like to admit, but one can guess that the photographer made an extra set of prints for himself, as a kind of keepsake. I doubt he surveilled many celebrities, so not surprisingly he wanted a souvenir of his assignment. . . ."

Ting.

Flick immediately recognized the pleasant, though considerably muffled, sound of the 10:00 a.m. chime. It had rung in the Welcome Centre kiosk to announce that the museum was open for visitors. Thursdays often brought busloads of London-based tourists. The building would soon be full of friendly sounds: laughter, chatting, footsteps on the marble stairs, the occasional child's shriek.

"You were saying, Conan," Nigel said.

"Yes. I suggested that the photographer made himself an extra set of pictures. If we also imagine that he died twenty years ago. . ."

"Now I get it!" Nigel tapped his forehead with the heel of his palm. "His wife cleaned out his office and donated everything that looked salable to her local church, for its next jumble sale."

"Precisely, sir." Conan added, "It's quite possible that there are other photographs to be found in Tunbridge Wells, and perhaps other artifacts about Mr. Makepeace that we can. . ."

"Guys!" Flick interrupted. "The museum is open, and we're toddling down a rabbit trail. Remember what our problem du jour is. I don't see anything in the photos that'll help us defend ourselves against 'Anonymous Bystander.' "

"Quite right, ma'am," Conan said, a touch of pink on his cheeks. Nigel merely returned a guilty smile.

"How do we resolve our dilemma of being between a rock and a hard place?"

"If I may offer an observation," Conan said. "We have no choice but to satisfy Wescott Bank; therefore, our only possible solution is to increase our guard and continue the investigation in such a way that is invisible to anyone outside the museum."

"Well said. How do we walk that tightrope?"

"We begin," Nigel said, "by killing our Makepeace Web page and withdrawing our reward for more information."

Flick nodded. " 'Anonymous Bystander' contributed information. He's bound to keep watching our Web site to see what we do. I'll ask Hannah Kerrigan to remove the page."

"It might be wiser," Conan said softly, "to have Hannah remove the content and label the page 'under construction.' We want 'Anonymous Bystander' to keep checking on us. Every time he accesses our Web site, we log the Internet address he's using. Right now, his address is one of many, but if he repeatedly 'hits' our site—well, we could get lucky and identify him."

"Make it so," Nigel said.

"One idea down—many ideas to conceive," Flick said.

Conan suddenly smiled. "Well, hello, Mirabelle—we hardly ever see you down in the dungeon."

Flick looked over her shoulder. The docent stood in the doorway of Conan's office, clearly angry.

"You wouldn't see me down here today," Mirabelle said,

"hadn't I felt an urgent need to get away from a rather obnoxious visitor who insisted. . .no, *demanded* that I bring his card to Dr. Adams, *immediately*." She held up a business card by one corner, as if its surface dripped with slime.

Flick moved to Mirabelle's side. "What's the man's name?"

"Martin Maltby."

Flick took the business card. The card stock seemed costly, and the printing felt engraved, but the card contained only two items of information: Maltby's name and a Kent telephone number. She turned the card over. Three neatly written lines proclaimed, "I have essential information about Etienne Makepeace."

"Can you describe him?" she said.

"Medium height, thin, with gray hair and pale brown eyes. Well-dressed in blue slacks and a tweed jacket. A gentleman in appearance if not in his manner."

"His age?"

"Younger than I. Perhaps seventy."

Flick experienced a prickle of fear. Was Maltby the "Anonymous Bystander"? He was certainly old enough to have been involved in Etienne Makepeace's murder.

"Where is the safest place for Dr. Adams to meet with an elderly gentleman of uncertain character?" Nigel asked Conan.

"You read my mind," she said.

"The Commodore Hawker Room, without question." Conan tickled the keyboard. The interior of the Commodore's restored office appeared on the surveillance monitor screen. "Not only can we watch his every move, there are two security guards only a few steps away should he become. . . *threatening*."

"There will probably be other visitors in the room," Nigel said, "and I can make it up the stairs in fifteen seconds flat, if necessary." His abrupt earnestness surprised Flick. He seemed more anxious than she felt. Once again, his concern demonstrated that he cared for her. And once again, she wondered if she was wrong to demand an actual promise from him. Didn't his actions speak louder than his words?

That's wishful thinking. The kind that got you into trouble before.

Flick took Mirabelle's hand. "Force yourself to smile at Mr. Maltby," she said. "Show him to the Commodore Hawker Room and say that I'll join him in five minutes."

Flick moved nearer to the computer monitor and—with Nigel and Conan at her side—watched the interior of the Commodore Hawker Room. Three or four museum visitors poked their heads into the exhibit area and looked around, but none stayed. A few minutes later, Mirabelle led Martin Maltby into the heart of the room. He seemed fascinated, as many visitors were, by the large oil portrait of Commander Hawker hanging on the wall.

"It's a pity we can't hear what's going on, too," Nigel said.

"Begging to differ with you, sir," Conan said. "Our disguised cameras are equipped with highly sensitive microphones. We can listen to everything that's said." He touched another key. Mirabelle's voice streamed out of a speaker above the monitor: "Quite true, sir. Commander Hawker was one of a kind." She continued, "Make yourself comfortable, Mr. Maltby. Dr. Adams will join you in a few minutes."

Flick and the others gazed at the monitor until Nigel broke the silence. "Does anyone recognize Maltby?" he asked. "I don't."

"Me neither," she said. "He looks more elegant to me than dangerous."

"I agree, ma'am." Conan zoomed the camera to get a close-up of the man's face. "My surmise is Mr. Maltby is a retired military officer or possibly a former government official. A man used to getting his own way."

"Well—there's only one way to find out what he wants from us." Flick took a slow, deep breath to strengthen her resolve. "Onward and upward."

Martin Maltby was sitting on a padded visitors' bench opposite the commodore's massive oak bookcase when Flick entered the Commodore Hawker Room. He stood up and offered his hand. "Dr. Adams—we meet at last."

Flick shook his hand. She noted that Maltby had the kind of classic British accent that most radio announcers would envy.

Maltby continued. "I've enjoyed reading your books on tea. It goes without question that I own all three. My only criticism is that you seem to favor black and green teas at the expense of white tea."

"I take it that you prefer white tea?"

"Indeed. I began drinking white tea because I sought a brew with less caffeine—but now I fancy the subtle sweet flavor. White tea is so much more elegant than green tea, which, I'm afraid to say, makes me think that I'm drinking grass soup." He laughed softly to himself.

"We have a gallery on the first floor devoted to tea processing that includes an exhibit about white tea. Have you seen it?"

"It would be a total waste of my time. I am fully aware that white tea is made by picking the leaf buds before they have opened and had an opportunity to turn green."

"Yes, well—you wanted to talk to me about Etienne Makepeace?"

"A recent broadcast on the BBC reported that you plan to create an exhibit about Etienne Makepeace. You said—I paraphrase here—that you want to tell his story to the world. Moreover, you have been seeking information about Makepeace. Am I correct?"

Flick hesitated. Should she find out what Maltby knew about the Tea Sage? Or should she follow their new strategy and deny that the museum had an interest in Etienne Makepeace?

Maltby pressed: "I asked you a *simple* question, Dr. Adams."

"In fact, Mr. Maltby, you asked me *two* questions." Flick fought to control the wave of annoyance that Maltby had generated by his snide comment. "We may create a Makepeace exhibit in the future, but we are no longer seeking information about him in the present."

"That seems an odd decision. Nonetheless, you need to know what I have to say." Maltby didn't give Flick a chance to object. "Etienne Makepeace was a fake and a fraud. He knew little about tea and cared less. I speak from profound personal experience because everything that Makepeace said or published under his name was written by me and another ghostwriter named Rupert Perry."

Flick tried not to reveal the confusion she felt. "You say that Makepeace's writings were ghostwritten?"

"Every bloody jot and tittle." The soft laugh again. "I thought that would pique your interest."

"Do you have. . .*proof* of your accusations?"

"Why else would I bother coming here today?" Maltby reached into his breast pocket and brought out a folded document. "Here is a carbon copy of a manuscript that was published in the April 1959 issue of *Town and Country* magazine. Forgive the occasional error; the man who prepared the draft typed it by hand on an old Imperial Model 55 typewriter. For your convenience, I have also attached a photocopy of the article as it appeared in the magazine. You will see that they are identical."

Flick scanned the carbon copy quickly: a six-page draft on the virtues of different teas grown in Ceylon. The color of the typed characters, their slightly blurred appearance, looked right for a carbon copy. The paper was a thin "onion skin," the kind often used for copies in the days before every office had a photocopying machine.

Maltby seemed to read her mind. "This is a museum. I suspect you have equipment that will enable you to verify the age of the document and its authenticity."

Flick nodded. "By itself, of course, a single authentic manuscript doesn't prove much. It could have come from anywhere."

"Do you take me for a dunce? Rupert Perry and I can provide copies of *dozens* of other draft manuscripts. We wrote Makepeace's articles, books, speeches, clever ad-libs—*everything*. We earned a pittance for our work; Makepeace took the credit and became an international celebrity."

Flick fought to maintain her composure. "May I keep this carbon copy?" she asked evenly.

Maltby replied with a sarcastic grimace. "And the photocopy of the article, too. Why else would I have given them to you?"

Flick could feel her expression tighten into a scowl.

Maltby lifted his hands in an impromptu stop signal. "I perceive that my forthright manner has caused you considerable irritation. I warned Rupert Perry that that would be the case; I urged him to come instead of me, because he is charming, personable, likeable—all the things that I am not. But Rupert preferred not to travel from London to Tunbridge Wells. And so, I came instead." He sighed. "You will have to go to him to obtain the rest of our evidence."

"I have no intention of traveling to London, Mr. Maltby."

"Nonsense. I'm confident that you'll make the trip."

"And why is that?"

"Chiefly because you are ethical, curious, and loath to perpetrate a historical catastrophe in this museum." His sudden smile conveyed a hint of sadness. "I can read the doubts on your face. You've studied Etienne Makepeace enough to suspect that he falsified much of his public persona. Consequently, you've become skeptical of the adulation heaped on him, and you want to uncover the full extent of his deception—and possibly the motive for his death. Rupert Perry can give you the information you seek. He lived through chapters of the story that I can merely present to you as hearsay."

"I'll think about it. I make no promises."

Maltby reached into a side pocket. "This mobile phone is for you. Use it to contact Rupert Perry and arrange a meeting. He is awaiting your call."

Flick took the palm-sized device. "I have my own mobile phone."

"Undoubtedly. However, we prepaid for one hundred

minutes of service on that telephone and programmed Rupert's number into the memory. Press 5 when you are ready to talk to him."

"Why not just give me his phone number?"

Maltby repeated his soft laugh. "In fact, Rupert is a man who values his solitude. He can be somewhat obsessive about guarding his privacy and rarely provides his personal phone number. You will talk to him on an identical mobile device. Both were acquired using. . .shall we say, names of convenience. It's a simple precaution to ensure that he is in control of all communications. Should you try to contact him using another telephone, he will not answer—and you will have squandered your only opportunity to learn the complete truth about Etienne Makepeace."

"As I said—I'll think about it."

"Naturally, you will contact Rupert Perry at a time you deem most appropriate. However, I urge you not to delay. He can be unpredictable when slighted. It would be foolish to ignore such a gift, freely given. No one knows more about Makepeace than Rupert Perry."

"I'll see you out, Mr. Maltby," Flick said.

"That's hardly necessary, Dr. Adams. You should return to the important work of this museum." He gave a friendly wave, then turned to leave. "Ta-ta."

She waited in the Commodore Hawker Room until Nigel poked his head around the door frame. "Maltby's gone," he said. "He climbed into a red Peugeot 607 sedan and drove off toward Tunbridge Wells." Nigel looked through a window that overlooked Eridge Road. He seemed to be trying to catch a glimpse of Maltby's car.

"Who do you suppose he is?" Nigel asked.

"Evidently a ghostwriter of some sort."

"Perhaps, although Conan thinks he wore a disguise."

"Impossible! I was standing next to him—nothing about Maltby seemed unnatural."

"Well, it seems that our new surveillance camera reached a different conclusion."

Flick did a slow pirouette. "Where is the new camera? I know it's somewhere over in the corner, but I don't see anything out of place."

Nigel pointed to a jeweled pewter stein on a shelf. "Notice there are now three steins on display, where before there were only two."

"Nifty."

Flick looked down at the carbon copy in one hand and the mobile telephone in the other. "What's on your agenda this afternoon?"

"Ah. You think we should go to London."

"You heard Maltby. Rupert Perry is a font of information about Etienne Makepeace—probably the only one left. I don't think we have a choice."

NINE

Nigel followed Conan back to his office and peered over the chief of security's shoulder while he examined the mobile phone. "It's a cheap, refurbished, off-brand telephone, sir," Conan said, "with limited features—the kind sold for thirty pounds or so for those who choose pay-as-you-go mobile service."

Nigel picked the phone up. As Maltby had promised, a single number had been programmed into its memory and assigned to speed dial 5.

"You don't suppose we can lift Maltby's fingerprints from the surface, do you?" Nigel asked.

Conan smiled. "The only fingerprints anyone would find on that phone belong to Dr. Adams, and perhaps one or two from you, sir. She held it tightly in her palm when Maltby gave it to her, and you have a healthy grip on it right now."

"Good heavens!" Nigel dropped the phone on Conan's desk as if it had delivered an electric shock to his hand.

"Have we destroyed evidence?"

"Not really. I can't imagine what we would do with a set of Maltby's dabs. We don't have access to the National Fingerprint Database. And even if we did, who's to say that Maltby's prints are currently on file."

Nigel grunted. He sat down in a chair next to Conan's desk and considered the image of Maltby that filled the surveillance camera computer monitor. There was something strange about the man's appearance. His eyes perhaps, or possibly his mouth. Conan had mentioned a disguise but hadn't explained what he meant.

"Pennies for your thoughts."

Nigel looked up. Flick had quietly slipped into Conan's office.

Nigel shrugged. "I wasn't thinking about anything worth repeating."

"How about you, Conan?" she asked.

"Well, ma'am, I was musing that the more we learn about Etienne Makepeace, the less likable a chap he becomes. We've been told that he was an easy person to fight with. . .an ungrateful lout. . .a shameless womanizer. . .and lastly a fake and a fraud. He was estranged from his kith and kin, reviled by those who knew him, and eventually murdered by someone who apparently did the nation a good turn. One would expect a bit of good to surface sooner or later—after all, we Britons once considered the man a national treasure—but we've heard nothing save bad about him. It's a pity to discover that a revered icon is really the nastiest of men."

Flick nodded. "I've been thinking about that, too. Etienne Makepeace died a hero, but he might have been unmasked as a villain any day back then had he not been murdered. He had too many blemishes to keep covered indefinitely." Nigel could see a touch of sadness on her face. "I can understand Makepeace being less than likable and difficult to get along with—many geniuses are. But Maltby brought us evidence that England's Tea Sage took credit for other people's work. That's an unforgivable sin for a man in his position." She sighed. "I asked one of my curators to examine Maltby's document. I fear it will prove to be genuine."

"Would you like a fresh cuppa, ma'am?" Conan asked.

Flick spotted the teapot atop his bookcase and pounced. She filled a cup and then browsed the other items on offer. "Yum! Crawford's Garibaldi biscuits. They're hard to get in the United States, but my parents often serve them at the White Rose of York."

Nigel found himself thinking of his former wife, Sheila. She liked Garibaldi biscuits, too, although many of their friends insisted they didn't go well with tea. Flat, rectangular, stuffed with currants, and baked with a shiny glazed surface, they were more like miniature fruitcakes than traditional English tea biscuits.

Apparently, Cha-Cha also liked Garibaldis. He had curled up on the rug in front of Conan's desk, pretending to snooze. His tail began to wag when he saw her break one of the biscuits in half. She tossed a nibble, which he deftly caught in midair.

Conan cleared his throat. "Mr. Maltby couldn't have arrived at a more opportune time. He has provided a superb test subject for our new surveillance system." The big man pulled his keyboard closer to the edge of his desk and touched several keys.

"Here he is in the visitors' car park, walking toward our building. His Peugeot is the third car on the left."

Conan's fingers zipped along the keyboard.

"Here he is again when he entered the Commodore Hawker Room with Mirabelle Hubbard."

More finger tapping.

"Finally, here is Mr. Maltby departing. As you can see, he turned right upon leaving the visitors' car park."

"I can almost make out the car's number plate," Nigel said.

"No need to strain your eyes, sir"—he tapped more keys— "we can easily freeze and enlarge the image of the plate."

"Amazing."

"Do you see the small red sticker on the boot lid?"

"Blimey! The Peugeot is a hired car."

"Indeed, sir. Should it become necessary, I'll call in a favor from a policeman friend of mine and try to ascertain who signed the rental agreement. I doubt, however, that we would learn anything useful; Maltby obviously knows how to cover his tracks." Conan paused, then said, "Now let me replay the first two of these sequences side by side. Do you observe any significant differences?"

Nigel peered at the screen as "Martin Maltby in the Car Park" and "Martin Maltby in the Commodore Hawker Room" walked in adjacent image windows.

"He has a definite air of bravado about him in the car park," he said, "but a much more halting walk inside the building."

"I believe that's part of his disguise," Conan said.

"You talked about a disguise earlier. What do you have in mind?"

"If I may defer your question until later, sir—what else do

you perceive about the gentleman?"

"Well, I'd say he's looking for something in the Commodore Hawker Room. He seems to be searching methodically."

"My thoughts exactly," Flick said. "What do you suppose he's looking for?"

"Surveillance cameras, ma'am," Conan said. "Maltby is a rather sophisticated operator. He guessed that he might be photographed and tried to take appropriate precautions." The big man laughed. "Of course, so did we. I don't believe that he ever located our hidden camera." Conan tapped the keyboard and continued talking. "Here are two outwardly identical close-up images of Maltby's face."

Nigel looked. There was nothing "outwardly identical" about the photos. They seemed perfectly matched in every respect.

"The image on the left," Conan said, "is an untouched frame caught by the camera. I have the ability to manipulate the image on the right by applying various filters. This is possible because our new surveillance cameras capture light across a broad spectrum of colors." He laughed again. "It's all very technical, of course, but as Mr. Garwood pointed out, all one needs to understand is how to press the right keys. *Voila!*"

"What did you do?" Flick asked. "The image on the right looks. . .*pasty*."

"I applied a bit of infrared filtering, ma'am. It highlights anything artificial applied to the subject's skin. I believe that the blotchy patches on his cheeks are theatrical makeup and the darker region on his nose some sort of prosthesis to change its shape."

Nigel felt Flick poke his arm. "This is truly weird," she

said. "I didn't spot anything out of the ordinary."

"Note also the blotchy appearance of his hair on top of his head," Conan said. "I believe he is wearing a high-quality hairpiece. Mr. Maltby is likely bald in real life."

"Now that you mention it. . . ," Flick groaned softly. "His hair did look rather thick for a man his age."

"Finally, his lips are protruding more than the usual distance. He may have placed another prosthesis in his mouth to change the shape of his face. A tweak here, a push there can really alter a person's appearance. In fact, I'd wager a Scottish supper that you wouldn't recognize Maltby if he walked past you on High Street without his makeup."

Nigel studied the pair of images. "Assuming you're right, Conan, where does one acquire the skills to achieve such a remarkable change?"

"I've been pondering that very question, sir. I can think of two possibilities: Maltby was trained as an actor—or a spy."

"Well, whichever he is, we have to assume that 'Martin Maltby' is a fictitious name."

"Undoubtedly false, sir."

"What about Rupert Perry?" Nigel asked.

Conan grinned. "As my father might have said, the name Rupert Perry also lacks the *ring* of authenticity." He trilled the word "ring," adding two or three extra syllables.

Flick's mobile phone beeped. She listened for a several seconds and then said, "Thanks. I thought so, too."

"The document?" Nigel said.

Flick nodded. "Maltby may be counterfeit, but the carbon copy he gave us is almost certainly the genuine article—the pun is intended."

"Right! Maltby's a fake, Perry's a fake, the document is real—so what do we do next?"

"I'll call Rupert Perry and arrange a meeting. If he has more old manuscripts to give us, I want them. They represent an extraordinary window into the life and times of Etienne Makepeace."

"Absolutely not," Nigel said. "We can't possibly take the risk of sending you off alone to meet a man whom we know doesn't exist."

"I won't be alone. You're coming with me—remember?"

Nigel turned to Conan. "What do you think?"

"Well, sir, granted that we face an extraordinary amount of uncertainty, I advise you to let this inning play out. The man who calls himself Martin Maltby has gone to a good deal of trouble to organize a meeting in London between us and Rupert Perry. I admit that I'm curious as to his intentions."

Nigel realized he had lost the battle. "Very well then, I'll arrange the schedule. Fire up the prepaid mobile phone."

He pressed the SEND button and put the phone to his ear. "It's ringing."

"Rupert Perry here. To whom am I speaking?"

"Nigel Owen."

"Satisfactory—although I expected Dr. Adams to call. Is she there with you?"

"Yes."

"Good. She must attend any meeting we arrange."

"Why is that?"

"She is a scientist; you are a bureaucrat—she creates exhibits; you don't. Have I made myself clear?"

"Perfectly."

Nigel tried to place Perry's accent. He recognized it as European, rather than English, but he couldn't pinpoint a country. It struck him as a curious blend of German and Polish, with a bit of Scandinavian thrown in.

"Are you prepared to come to London this afternoon? A prompt meeting will serve both our interests."

The notion of an immediate meeting caught Nigel off guard. "You want to meet *today*?"

Nigel glanced at Flick. She nodded vigorously and mouthed, "Set up a meeting as soon as possible."

"Very well then, we are prepared to meet with you later this afternoon. We can drive to London or take the train."

"Go by train." Nigel heard papers shuffling. "I have a current South Eastern Train timetable in front of me. Listen carefully. Take the 13:11 from Tunbridge Wells, Route Code 22. It arrives at Charing Cross Station at 14:03. Go directly from the train to the Left-Luggage Office just outside the glass doors at the main station entrance. Be patient. I will contact you when I consider it safe to do so. We will meander through the station's inner concourse and complete our business in ample time for you to return on the 16:15 train. You'll be back in Tunbridge Wells by 17:09."

Nigel realized he'd forgotten to ask a crucial question. "How will we recognize you?"

"That shan't be a problem. I will recognize you." He hesitated and then said, "Needless to say, I shall expect the two of you to come alone. I am familiar with all of the security personnel at your museum, including Mr. Davies. Should I see any unexpected faces in the station concourse, I will not approach you."

The line went dead.

"My, that was fun," Nigel said. He repeated all that Rupert Perry had said.

Conan whistled softly. "I must say, Etienne Makepeace has interesting friends. Messrs. Maltby and Perry must have researched the museum, possibly paid us a visit whilst sporting other disguises." He frowned. "I would offer to accompany you. . . ."

"He'd spot you immediately," Flick said. "We can't take the chance."

"Well, ma'am, one must always consider the possibility that Perry will have his friends along to watch his back."

"Even so, there's no need for you to tag along," Nigel said. "Charing Cross is a highly public place. We'll be fine."

Had he spoken too rashly? Nigel thought about the odd conversation throughout the rest of the morning. He'd tried to work on a revised staff handbook that would clearly set forth the conditions of service and explain the museum's policies and procedures affecting different employees. The old employee handbook had been prepared during the late 1980s and was hopelessly out-of-date. His progress had been slow because his mind often jumped back to Makepeace, then Maltby, then Perry. Nigel could picture both Makepeace and Maltby, but not Perry—and that made him question whether he'd been reckless to agree to a meeting, even in a highly public place.

He ate an early lunch with Flick in the Duchess of Bedford Tearoom. At 12:15, they walked from the museum to Flick's apartment in the Pantiles. Neither he nor she had much to say; even Cha-Cha seemed subdued and in a mood to behave. They'd decided that Flick would take over custody of the Shiba early that day and that the dog would spend the afternoon in her flat.

Nigel waited outside Flick's building when they reached the Lower Walk. The few minutes alone with his thoughts made him realize that the events of the past week had conspired to create the malaise he felt. The discovery of Makepeace's body, the bank's threat to the museum, the incident in the car park, the mysterious Messrs. Maltby and Perry, and, most of all, the loss of Flick—weighed heavily on his mind. Not even a vacation somewhere warm and sunny would improve his outlook.

Nothing will change until the problems are solved.

She emerged at 12:35 dressed in tan wool slacks, a plum-colored cashmere sweater, a dark leather car coat, and comfortable-looking brown pumps—a sensible outfit, he thought, for a train trip to London. He had worn a blue blazer over khaki slacks that day. The plumy tones in his tie perfectly balanced the comparable hues in Flick's sweater; they would look like a color-coordinated couple. Had she chosen her outfit on purpose—or had it been a happy accident?

"The pooch has plenty of food and water," she said. "He seemed delighted to curl up on my sofa."

"Cha-Cha has a sixth, seventh, and eighth sense. He knows precisely when discretion is the better part of valor."

They walked to Tunbridge Wells Central Station. Nigel bought two return tickets to Charing Cross Station, and they went to the northern-bound platform. The silver and white train—actually four identical carriages with bright yellow doors—emerged from the short tunnel at the southern end of the station promptly at 1:09 p.m. for its scheduled two-minute stop in Royal Tunbridge Wells.

Nigel looked at the sleek 375-class carriages and realized that he missed the classic English trains he had ridden for three-quarters of his life. The new, self-propelled cars lacked character, he thought, and had sterile interiors: London Underground carriage meets low-fare airliner. He guided Flick aboard the train and to a pair of forward-facing, gray upholstered seats.

"Window or aisle?" he said.

"Definitely the window. I love train rides to London. There's so much to see along the way."

Nigel began to relax once the train left the station. The new carriages were at least more comfortable than the railcars of his youth. He felt calmed by the restful rocking of the carriage and the muffled rumble of wheels rolling on rails. With luck, the Makepeace mess would soon be over. But what of his tattered relationship with Felicity Adams? Hadn't he also committed a sin that she would consider unforgivable?

He risked a quick sideways look. Flick was indeed watching, with unalloyed interest, the Kentish countryside slip by. Nigel leaned back against the headrest and closed his eyes.

He felt fingers squeezing his hand. Flick's voice tugged at him. "Wake up, Nigel."

He blinked. "How long was I asleep?"

"Nearly an hour. We're crossing the Thames River."

He looked out the window. The train was on the Hungerford Bridge. They were seconds away from arriving at Charing Cross Station.

Flick jabbed his chest. "I just noticed—you're wearing a tie clip."

"You aren't supposed to notice."

"I wouldn't have, except I've never seen you wear one. If I owned a tie clip set with a diamond, I'd show it off every day."

"It belongs to Conan. The ersatz diamond is the lens of yet another surveillance camera. The power pack and recorder are clipped to my knickers and are blooming uncomfortable. I agreed to wear them solely because Conan insists that we need a photograph of Rupert Perry."

"How do you turn the camera on?" She held up her hand. "On second thought, don't tell me. I don't want to know."

"Then I'll talk about something else." They stepped onto the platform. "Have you ever seen a photo of Charing Cross Station taken from the other bank of the Thames?"

"Yep. A big office building sits on top of it."

Nigel smiled. "In Britspeak, we say 'office block.' It's an odd-looking structure that some say is supposed to resemble an ocean liner. Whether or not you agree, it covers part of the station's platforms. We're beneath it right now."

"I guess that's why the ceilings are so low in here. I'd feel claustrophobic if it weren't for those enormous light fixtures."

"The office block opened in 1992. The tenants are a firm that specializes in international accounting and consulting. I wanted to work upstairs the very first time I saw the rebuilt station."

Perhaps I will work here when I move back to London.

He drove the thought from his head. "At the risk of sounding like a tour guide," he said, "do you know where the name 'Charing Cross' comes from?"

"Rats! I thought I did, but now I can't remember."

"I'll give you a hint. King Edward I and Eleanor of Castile."

"Keep hinting."

"When she died in Nottinghamshire, Edward built a cross at every place the funeral cortege stopped on the way to Westminster Abbey. Charing Cross was the final stop before Westminster."

"I remember now. All distances from London are measured from the Eleanor Cross, which stands upstairs in the station's forecourt."

"Your strong finish earns you partial credit."

Nigel let Flick precede him into the station concourse. She stopped for a few seconds and looked around. "Now *this* is what a famous train station should look like," she said.

"When the station was rebuilt, the original nineteenth-century cast iron and steel framework was restored and repainted. The thousands of glass panels in the roof are new, too." Nigel added, "Left-Luggage is over there, to the left."

He could sense—and understand—Flick's growing tension as they crossed the spacious concourse and walked past hundreds of people. They didn't have a clue what "Rupert Perry" looked like, other than he was probably in his seventies. He might be another master of disguise. Perhaps he would appear as a woman.

Nigel spotted several people standing near Left-Luggage. A woman in her fifties, he guessed, reading a map of the Underground. A thirtyish couple with a little girl crying at their side. Three male teenagers, all wearing backpacks, who gestured in a way that suggested they were French. Two women of a certain age whose similar outfits suggested they were traveling together. But no elderly males.

"What do you think?" Flick asked.

"I think that we appear confident and wait."

"How long?"

"Well, I have the mobile phone Martin Maltby gave us in my pocket. What do you say I call Rupert Perry if he doesn't show in fifteen minutes?"

"It sounds like a plan."

Nigel regretted that he hadn't brought along something to read. Waiting for Perry would be difficult enough; looking confident all the while might be impossible.

Be gone from my life, Etienne Makepeace—and every nutter who knew you.

🕱

Rupert Perry telephoned them first.

Flick caught her breath when the mobile phone rang. They had been standing silently for nearly ten minutes, and her mind had wandered to thoughts of whether Nigel and Olivia Hart had a future together.

Nigel yanked the device out of his mackintosh's side pocket as if it were about to explode. He bent sideways so that both he and Flick could listen to the small speaker.

"You follow instructions well," Perry said.

"Where are you?" Nigel replied.

"Watching the two of you from a convenient vantage point, much like I've done for nearly ninety minutes. In fact, I rode up with you on the train from Tunbridge Wells."

"We didn't see you."

"Then I didn't want you to, but now is different. Come, buy a burger for me, and we'll have a friendly conversation."

He abruptly rang off.

"That's the second time today that Rupert Perry has hung up on me. I'm beginning to take offense."

Flick decided not to remind Nigel that Perry wanted to see her, not him. "What did he mean by 'buy a burger for me'?"

"There's a Burger King on the other side of the concourse, near the passage to Track 1. I suppose it's his sly and fly way of saying that we should meet him there."

"Why toy with us? He seems to enjoy cloak-and-dagger games."

"Why indeed?" Nigel seemed pensive. "He may have inadvertently given us a piece of interesting information. I didn't see anyone over forty-five board the train at the Wells. If he did accompany us, he must have got on in Wadhurst. We've assumed that Perry lives in London, because that's what Maltby suggested. Do you suppose that Perry might actually live near Tunbridge Wells?"

"I haven't the vaguest." Flick peeked at her watch. She wondered how long they could keep Perry waiting.

"And then there's the question of Perry's slightly off accent. It's mostly Oxbridge, but with peculiar overtones I don't recognize."

"Thank you, Henry Higgins, for your lucid analysis."

"I'm serious. I can't get a bead on the man."

"Maybe he was educated outside of England?"

"That's one possibility, I suppose." He stared off into the distance. "However, I attended graduate school in France, and I don't recall hearing an accent like his before."

"*Um.* . .shouldn't we beat feet over to Burger King?"

"Let the twit cool his heels like we did."

Flick forced herself to speak calmly. "Nigel, we can play tit for tat *after* we've spoken with Perry. We don't want the *twit* to get away."

"Oh, very well. Give me a moment to activate the surveillance camera I'm wearing."

He surreptitiously slid his thumb beneath his tie. Flick heard a muted *click*.

"That's it?" she asked.

"That's it. I can feel my knickers humming. Lead the way."

Flick scanned faces as she walked toward the big BURGER KING sign. She soon picked out a lone male, perhaps seventy years old, standing to the left side of the restaurant. He appeared to be watching her intently. As Flick moved closer, the man began to beam.

I'll bet you're Rupert Perry.

He looked the quintessential English country squire. Medium height. Solid physique. Strong hands and arms. Hair and eyebrows that mixed brown and white in even proportions. A full round face with rosy cheeks that seemed to glow. And what would such a man wear, she asked herself. Exactly what Perry had on today: a heavy Harris Tweed sport coat, with leather elbow patches, baggy wool slacks, and a schoolmaster's leather satchel hung on his left shoulder.

A character right out of a Thomas Hardy novel.

He extended his hand. "Good afternoon, Dr. Adams. Thank you for coming."

Flick hid her surprise. His voice had sounded thin and reedy through the inexpensive mobile phone, but she heard a hearty resonance now that they were face-to-face. Rupert Perry would have made a first-rate radio announcer.

"We found your invitation too compelling to pass up, Mr. Perry. Your colleague left a fascinating. . .*calling card* with us."

"The article draft? Yes, I suppose it came as an unpleasant shock to see irrefutable evidence of Etienne Makepeace's duplicity." Perry chuckled. "And yet, I'm astonished that someone as young as you even recognizes a carbon copy. Surely the only typewriters you've seen have been in museums."

When Flick smiled at the compliment, she heard a firm "ahem" next to her. *Oops, I forgot about Nigel.* She took a step backwards. "Mr. Perry, I'd like you to meet Nigel Owen, the director of the Royal Tunbridge Wells Tea Museum."

"I'm quite familiar with Mr. Owen—we became acquainted over the telephone." Flick noted that they didn't exchange handshakes. Perry didn't seem to like Nigel any more than Nigel liked Perry.

"You don't really want a burger, do you?" Nigel asked.

"Of course not. But perhaps you are hungry?" Perry gestured toward the Burger King. "Dr. Adams and I can chat while you eat."

Nigel glared at Perry. "No, thank you. We've both eaten."

"Well then," he said, "let us explore the inner concourse. Window-shopping is an excellent reason for three friends to talk together without attracting undue attention. To achieve the most natural appearance, one should occasionally point to the goodies on display. It also helps to be a greedy person; true window-shoppers wear delightfully covetous expressions."

Perry offered his right arm to Flick. She took it, leaving Nigel a half pace behind. He seemed displeased but also willing to let the "inning play out."

"When we go our separate ways," Perry said to Flick, "you

will leave with my leather satchel. Inside, you will find many fascinating items packed in four separate envelopes. The first envelope contains seven issues of a long-defunct Russian-language magazine that was published in the old Soviet Union between 1949 and 1970. Its rather boring name in English is *Journal of the Peoples' Tea Manufactory*. Do you know the publication, Dr. Adams?"

"No."

He shrugged. "Only a handful of Westerners have seen it. The seven issues you will soon possess date back to the early 1950s. Do you read Russian, Dr. Adams?"

"A smattering of technical Russian, no more."

"Then I urge you to have the magazines translated into English. A tea expert such as yourself will find the content quite interesting. There are essays on the history of tea. . .monographs on the correct way to brew tea. . .medical treatises on the health benefits of tea. . .botanic discourses on different tea varieties. . . articles about various tea-processing technologies. . .all written by obscure experts in the Soviet Union.

"The second envelope contains photocopies of fifteen articles allegedly written by Etienne Makepeace. They appeared in several different English magazines between 1955 and 1958. When you compare the English articles and the earlier Russian articles, you will find that their content and substance are virtually identical."

Flick leaned closer to Perry. "Are you telling me that Etienne Makepeace systematically plagiarized from a Russian tea magazine?"

"I find your question painfully ironic, Dr. Adams. The brutal truth is that Etienne Makepeace didn't have sufficient skills to be a proper plagiarist. He didn't speak or read Russian. Consequently, he hired me to translate the articles into English. I speak Russian fluently; I learned it from my mother, an expatriate Muscovite. In fact, Russian was my primary language until I was almost seven. That's when my *veddy, veddy* British father insisted that I learn to speak the King's English properly."

Flick glanced at Nigel. He returned a quick nod. They had solved the mystery of Perry's "slightly off" accent.

"How did Etienne find you?" she asked.

"Through a mutual friend at Cambridge University. I read history, too, some twenty years later than Etienne did. Coincidentally, my favorite senior lecturer in medieval history had been Etienne's housemate during their student days." He broke into a grin. "I was perennially short of money in those days. I saw the chance to work for Etienne as a godsend. One does imprudent things at the age of nineteen years."

Flick decided to bring Perry back from his reminiscences. "What's in the third envelope?"

"An agricultural textbook from the late 1930s. Also in Russian. It has a surprisingly simple title—*Tchai*."

"The Russian word for 'tea.' "

Perry nodded. "I translated the book for Etienne in 1954. He adapted the content for his first book on tea—the one that established him as a tea expert."

"We have a copy in our library."

"I thought as much. Compare Etienne's book with a translation of *Tchai*. You'll discover that the volumes are virtually identical."

"What do you mean that he 'adapted' the Russian book?"

"That's a term that Etienne often used. He believed that

the act of paying for the translation from Russian to English represented a sufficient adaptation to make the material his."

"The idea is. . .*ludicrous.*"

"I agree, but you must realize that Etienne was never the sharpest knife in the drawer. He bumbled along largely on his good looks and personality. He could be unreservedly charming when he chose to be."

Flick glanced at Nigel again. He seemed spellbound by Perry's revelations and no longer angry at the supposedly cavalier treatment he'd suffered. Nigel had taken to darting back and forth—walking first next to Flick, then next to Perry—to escape the background noise in Charing Cross Station and hear everything that she and Perry said.

It's time to find an oasis for this caravan.

"Walking around the concourse is getting somewhat tedious for me, Mr. Perry," she said. "Do you suppose we might choose a place to sit down?"

"There's an Italian coffee shop scarcely fifty feet away. Will that suffice? I don't know if they serve tea."

"Oh, I'm getting to like Italian coffee."

You'd better. These days there seem to be more Italian coffee shops in England than tea shops.

"In that case, *avanti.*"

Flick found a small table in the shop's eat-in area, close to a window that overlooked the station concourse. They would still be in a "public" area. Nigel went off to buy refreshments—almost joyfully, Flick thought—and returned with three cups of *caffè americano* and three blueberry muffins.

"*Grazie mille,*" Perry said.

"*Prego,*" Nigel replied. Then, "*Mangiare.*"

Flick and the others sipped in silence until Nigel said, "Tell us about the fourth envelope."

"It contains drafts of a dozen of Etienne's radio scripts and speeches."

"I presume you wrote them, too."

"Not entirely." Perry's eyes sparkled. He sat back in his chair and laid his hands in his lap. "You see, I continued translating for Etienne after I finished my degree at Cambridge. In time, the inevitable happened."

Flick and Nigel asked, "What happened?" in unison.

"I became a tea expert in my own right, of course. I no longer needed old Russian publications and textbooks as my sources. I began to ghostwrite Etienne's articles directly, so to speak. The draft that Martin Maltby gave you is one of mine. I also wrote Etienne's other books."

"What was Maltby's role in this. . .*deception*?" Flick asked.

"He didn't tell you? Pity! Martin is not a people person, but he is a superb speechwriter. I brought him into our little circle when Etienne began to receive invitations to speak. I provided the details about tea, while Martin wrote all of Etienne's speeches and his radio scripts and his museum lectures—down to the last bon mot. Martin is truly responsible for transforming Etienne Makepeace into England's 'Tea Sage.' "

"I have a question," Flick said. "Why tell us this now?"

Perry heaved a deep sigh. "Maltby and I did what we did when we were young and hungry. We had no regrets back then, but now—forty years later—it galls us to think that Etienne Makepeace will have his reputation restored. What pains us most is the idea that a museum of your caliber plans to honor the fool with an exhibit. We simply can't let that happen. Martin and I have reached our golden years. This is a final gesture—a way to make amends. We're willing to pay the price of making our past sins known so that the world will finally learn the truth about Etienne Makepeace."

"When Etienne Makepeace disappeared, what did you think happened to him?"

Perry smiled. "Oh, we assumed the absolute worst—that he'd been murdered by one of the many husbands Etienne had cuckolded over the years." His smile faded. "That was Etienne's hobby. He sought out married women, because he had no interest in long-term relationships of any kind."

Perry pushed back his chair and stood. He slipped the schoolmaster's satchel off his shoulder and handed it to Nigel. "Etienne Makepeace was a nasty piece of work, Dr. Adams. You will ultimately decide whether or not to create an exhibit that honors him. Martin Maltby and I understand that. All we can do is offer up evidence that reveals his true character."

"We might have more questions. . . ."

"Use the mobile phone. Leave a message if I don't answer immediately." He gave a curt bow and picked up his cup of coffee. "Until we meet again."

Perry left the coffee shop quickly. Flick watched him disappear into the crowd of people walking through the concourse.

"Did you believe him?" Nigel asked.

"Yes."

"Me, too. He may have a phony name, but what he said had the 'ring of authenticity.' "

"You do a good Scottish accent." She added, "Where can we find a Russian translator?"

"You want to double-check?"

"We have a saying back in Pennsylvania—trust everyone, but cut the cards."

Nigel grunted. "A wise philosophy—especially with someone who may be wearing a sophisticated disguise. Which reminds me. . ."

Nigel used his thumb to switch off the tie-clip camera. *Click.* He murmured a few words too quietly for Flick to make sense of them.

"Pardon," she said.

"I was thinking about one of my favorite sayings, a quotation from Shakespeare they taught us in business school. 'Things without remedy should be without regard; what is done, is done.' It's from *Macbeth*." He winked at her. "And this time I'm utterly certain about the source."

She nodded, not sure where Nigel intended to go.

"The idea," he went on, "is that it's foolish to live in the past. We can't change what happened—and what's done is done."

"Sounds right to me."

"Except you and I are all wrapped up in the past this week. Things that happened years ago came to life again with the power to change our future. What's done is *not* done." He shook his head. "It seems that Willy Shakespeare was wrong."

Flick looked away from Nigel, toward the bustling concourse.

Is he talking about the museum or about us?

TEN

Nigel gazed out the window at the syrupy, gray fog that had wrapped itself around Tunbridge Wells. He decided that the mist looked thicker and darker viewed from the former Hawker family suite. No surprise, really. The suite was on the second floor of the museum, directly beneath his office, and thus closer to the ground.

"Any idea when this pea-souper might lift?" he said to Conan Davies, who was completing the finicky task of affixing a strip of double-sided sticky tape the length of the long wall opposite the window.

"I don't doubt the fog will be long gone before we open at ten, sir."

"One hopes so. Fridays are usually among our busiest days. Today is especially promising, because we have another large tour group coming down from London this morning."

Conan grunted—rather indifferently, Nigel thought. The

chief of security had focused all his attention on keeping the sticky tape at a uniform height of sixty inches and parallel to the floor. He clearly wasn't bothered by the potential impact on the museum should a party of twenty-five Czech tourists decide to cancel. Nigel sighed. He and Flick were probably the only employees of the Royal Tunbridge Wells Tea Museum who fretted about revenues.

The rest of the staff were in for a rude awakening. For the next ten years, the museum would have to scramble to repay the loan from Wescott Bank—assuming, of course, that the results of Flick's accelerated investigation satisfied Sir James Boyer.

Think positively. We're going to get the loan.

Thirty-two million pounds! A princely sum for a small institution. To be repaid, with interest, at approximately four million pounds per year. More than three hundred thousand pounds per month. And no longer could they rely on the largesse of the Hawker family or the generosity of the well-heeled Hawker Foundation.

We're on our own—like most other museums.

Nigel shuddered. Like other museums, they'd be required to hold fund-raising campaigns, sell annual memberships, host academic conferences—generate revenues through all possible means. Every pence became significant. Thus, they couldn't afford to lose even one tour group that might spend money in the Duchess of Bedford Tearoom and the museum's gift shop.

None of this tumult would be necessary if genetics hadn't let the Hawker family down.

Nigel surveyed the nearly empty Hawker family suite.

Every item of decent furniture used by Mary Hawker Evans and later by Dame Elspeth Hawker had been distributed among the curating staff, leaving three uncomfortable wooden chairs, a battered metal table, and a lumpy upholstered wing chair that no one wanted. Flick had claimed the Oriental carpets for her office. He had commandeered the pictures on the walls. The now-bleak office testified to the start of a new era—the surviving Hawker heirs had all but disconnected the Hawker family from the museum.

Nigel presumed that Harriet Hawker Peckham and Alfred Hawker would be the last generation of Hawkers, since they were childless and well into middle age. The two siblings, both scrawny, had limp handshakes, weak eyes, narrow noses, and mousy hair on the verge of going gray. What they lacked in charm, they amply made up for in avarice and stinginess. With luck, Nigel thought, he would have to see them only once more: when the museum consummated the deal to purchase the Hawker collection of antiquities. After that, should the younger Hawkers ever ask for accommodations at the museum, he would scrounge a morsel of space for them—in a basement storeroom.

Ah well. No use crying over spoiled Hawkers.

"How does this arrangement strike you, sir?" Conan asked.

Nigel looked at the back wall. Conan had hung two groupings of photographs—a total of thirteen in all—on the strip of sticky tape. It had been his suggestion to create an "Incident Room," as he called it, in the now-vacant office. "A place to display the evidence," he'd said, "where we can meet and discuss our conclusions."

Nigel moved closer. The leftward grouping included nine photographs of Etienne Makepeace, four of which were the surveillance shots borrowed from Dorothy McAndrews. The rightward grouping consisted of paired images of Martin Maltby and Rupert Perry, one "normal" and one "filtered" to reveal the disguises they had worn. Nigel felt a surge of pride. "His" pics of Rupert Perry were sharp and perfectly centered; they provided clear evidence that Perry had camouflaged himself with a wig, contact lenses, and facial makeup.

"Conan, you have a fine eye for wall decor," Nigel said.

"Why, thank you, sir." The tall Scot smiled jubilantly. "There's plenty of room left on the wall for Dr. Adams to post the documents she's collected." He appraised his handiwork once again and gave what Nigel took to be a satisfied nod. "Well, I'd best get back to my office and read more instruction manuals. Our network of surveillance cameras will be fully operational by the end of the day. My lads and I have to learn how to use all the gadgets and thingummies."

Nigel perused the photographs after Conan left. Did any of them count as "evidence"? And would it make an iota of difference if every piece of paper they'd collected during the week were hanging alongside? All the so-called facts about Etienne Makepeace they'd gathered told them nothing new about his relationship to the museum.

He felt Cha-Cha thump against his leg. A moment later, Flick bounded into the room and said, "I've had a brainstorm."

"We can certainly use one."

"Look at this image."

"It's a life-size picture of a cat. One of ours, I suppose." He made a vague gesture toward the wall. "Flick, we have to talk about our investigation."

"And so we shall—*after* I tell you what I did. I turned

Hannah Kerrigan loose on Maltby and Perry."

"I haven't a clue what you just said."

"This image didn't come from a camera. Hannah made it—with Photoshop."

She lifted the photograph as high as her chin; Nigel looked at it. "I repeat," he said. "It's a picture of a cat. Plush blue fur, big orange eyes—a British Shorthair."

"Exactly. Except Hannah created it from a photo taken a couple of years ago. She used her retouching skills to transform a kitten into a full-grown cat."

Nigel gave up trying to make sense of the muddle. "Okay. And your point is?"

"I've asked her to do the same thing with Maltby and Perry."

"Turn them into cats?"

"No, silly! Use Photoshop to peel away their disguises. She thinks it's possible. She learned how to use the program to retouch photographs. You know—soften wrinkles, eradicate age spots, lift sagging muscles." Flick pointed at the pairs of photographs taped to the wall. "I gave Hannah copies of the Maltby and Perry surveillance images. She'll try to eliminate their wigs, wipe the makeup off their faces, and remove any prosthetic devices."

"To what effect?"

"We'll know what the *real* Maltby and Perry look like. We may be able to identify who they are and then figure out why they wore disguises and used phony names."

"And what happens, pray tell, if we do identify them?"

"We'll be a giant step closer to understanding this mess."

Nigel dropped into the wing chair. *Crikey. She hasn't twigged to the depth of the crisis we face.*

"Flick, assuming that you're able to identify Maltby and Perry. . ." he said calmly. "So what?"

She moved closer to him. An astonished glower had replaced her now-vanished smile. "*So what?* I can't believe you said that. Martin Maltby and Rupert Perry were contemporaries of Etienne Makepeace. They knew him. They're living links to a man who died forty years ago. For all we know, they're the *only* people still alive who can answer our questions about Makepeace."

"Or. . .they could be two barmy eccentrics who enjoy dressing up in toupees and makeup."

"You heard Rupert Perry's story. You said you believed him."

Nigel sighed. "Granted. . .I believe his long-winded tale about ghostwriting tea articles. But he said nothing to suggest that he or Martin Maltby have any knowledge about Makepeace's relationship to this museum."

"Well, I have no doubts that they do."

"What makes you so certain?"

"Call it a hunch, a gut feeling."

"Well, at least you reached your conclusion without tarot cards or a crystal ball."

Nigel regretted his words immediately; he hadn't meant to ridicule Flick. Fortunately, Flick seemed more exasperated than annoyed. "What's with you this morning?" she asked. "You don't usually show up for work in a melancholy mood."

"I'm not melancholy—I'm on edge. We have fewer than three days to satisfy Sir James Boyer's demands for information. I fear that we won't be able to do it."

"Three days is plenty of time to flesh out our understanding of how Etienne Makepeace was connected to the museum."

"You seem to have forgotten that you promised Olivia Hart the earth. Lord knows what you had in mind, but you assured her that we'd be able to explain *why* Etienne Makepeace was shot in the museum and buried in our tea garden. Sir James expects to get the impossible because you said we would deliver it—in person, no less."

"I didn't hear you argue with me."

"Too true. Your promises sounded brilliant at the time. I was happy to hear them. It's a pity we can't fulfill the commitments you made."

"Who says we can't? We know the motive behind Makepeace's murder."

"Spare me the nebulous jealous-husband theory. I don't believe it, and I doubt that Sir James will, either. We have no names, we have no dates, and we have no *facts* to support our conjectures." He waited for Flick to respond; when she didn't, he went on. "We can't even explain how 'Mr. Jealous Husband' gained access to our tea garden. Candidly, it's difficult to accept that anyone connected to this museum back then was married to a wanton barmaid."

"That's a rather pretentious thing to say."

"Pardon my pretensions. I'm up to my snoot in a wretched mess."

"A mess of your own making."

Nigel leaped out of the chair. *"I beg your pardon!"* He saw, out of the corner of his eye, Cha-Cha leap for the only available refuge in the room: The Shiba dove under the wing chair Nigel had just vacated. "Need I remind you that the Wescott loan was in the bag until Sir James Boyer learned about our ill-conceived news conference? I admit that I let Stuart Battlebridge lead me down the garden lane, but I recall that you thought talking to the media was a grand idea."

"Baloney!" Flick underlined her expletive by raising her right index finger in a triumphant gesture. "This *mess*, as you call it, began when you wimped out and let Archibald Meicklejohn dictate the bank we had to use. You had the opportunity to exert your leadership, to act like a genuine museum director. Instead, you caved. And now we're stuck with the wishy-washy Wescott Bank—not to mention James Boyer and his Kentish henchwoman, Olivia Hart."

"Balderdash! No one in this blooming building acknowledges my leadership. Let's not forget how *you* publicly announced—on your own authority and against my well-reasoned judgment—that you intended to establish a Makepeace exhibit at this museum. And look what's happened—the subject of *your* new exhibit turns out to be a cad and a fraud."

Flick let out a mighty groan. "Etienne Makepeace was England's Tea Sage, you ninny, and this is a tea museum. We have a responsibility to tell his story—even if it turns out that he took advantage of the queen and stole the crown jewels."

Nigel walked to the window and saw Flick's reflection. She had moved to the opposite corner. She stood straight as a stanchion, arms crossed, glaring at him.

Your posturing has no effect on me, Dr. Adams. I am the aggrieved party this morning, thank you very much.

He looked out at the fog. Conan had been right; most of the mist had burned off, and it hadn't yet gone nine fifteen. The busload of tourists from London would probably arrive on time. He decided to return to his office.

When he turned to leave, he saw Polly Reid standing in the doorway, holding an unfolded newspaper. She seemed hesitant to speak.

"Yes, Polly," he said. He hoped that his voice had returned to its normal volume after his brief shouting match with Flick.

"I didn't want to disturb you, sir; however, I expect you'll want to see the latest issue of the *Kent and Sussex Courier* immediately." Nigel noted that she spoke more crisply and carefully than usual. "A small news report on page 9 alleges that we are being sued because a dog in our possession killed a prizewinning ferret."

"Oh, mercy me!" He snatched the newspaper out of her hands and began to read it. The article implied that the museum harbored a "killer dog" that gleefully murdered small mammals. "How on earth did the local rag get hold of this cheerful piece of news?" Nigel abruptly looked up. "Consider that a rhetorical question, Polly. The only possible source is Bertram Holloway, owner of the deceased ferret."

"Actually, there's a bit of a problem with Mr. Holloway. If he exists, I can't find him. I did learn, however, that none of the homes surrounding the Hawker family estate are owned by a Bertram Holloway."

"What made you check?"

"Well, sir, the very notion of a tame ferret making its way into the Hawkers' back garden in time to be eaten by Cha-Cha doesn't ring true. Lion's Peak is one of the largest holdings in Tunbridge Wells. A hundred acres of deep woods surround the grounds, and it's my understanding that pet ferrets do not survive long in the wild. Moreover, I remember Dame Elspeth talking about fencing in her garden to keep the rabbits away from the many expensive Dutch bulbs she planted. I fancy that a rabbit-proof fence would also deter the occasional roaming ferret."

"Quite possibly it would. . . ." He glanced inside the newspaper again, and then wished he hadn't. A second look at the brief news article merely increased his annoyance. "But that raises another problem. If Bertram Holloway is the figment of someone's imagination, who sent us the letter threatening a lawsuit?"

"I thought about that, too, sir. Upon reflection, the letter we received appears to be written by someone who has a solid grasp of legal terminology."

"You don't suppose. . . ," Nigel started to say before a terrible thought gelled in his mind. "Barrington Bleasdale!" He spit the name out like a curse. "But why would our least-favorite solicitor send us a sham letter and then notify the *Courier*?"

From her vantage point in the corner, Flick said, "Probably because most men are pinheads."

"Lo, a trained scientist speaks." This time, Nigel intentionally filled his voice with sarcasm. "I'm thrilled by your rational explanation that so neatly encompasses all the facts of our situation." He ended by intoning, *"Most men are pinheads."*

"Yeah, and I'm thrilled by. . ."

Woomph!

The thunderous noise made Nigel flinch. He realized that Polly had yanked the door to the room shut with all the force she could muster.

"When the pair of you bicker—as you so often do these

days—please have the courtesy to fight behind closed doors where others can't overhear your immature drivel." She glared first at Nigel and then at Flick. "I hoped we could avoid this summit meeting, but you two have made it inevitable. I'm going to dispense some serious advice to both of you, and I fully expect you to sack me when I finish. Now, sit down. *There.*" She pointed toward two of the wooden chairs.

Nigel sat down as ordered. He caught a glimpse of Flick. She looked ashen-faced. He felt sure that his face had gone just as pale.

Polly towered over them like a schoolteacher lecturing two errant pupils. "Since Wednesday afternoon, the junior staff of this museum have wondered why Nigel Owen and Felicity Adams—two of the cleverest people in Tunbridge Wells—have become complete ignoramuses. Your relationship is the topic of all the watercooler chatter in the building. As it happens, I know the answer—but because I refuse to participate in gossip, I've kept what I know to myself."

Nigel heard himself blither. "Very wise. . .chatter unfortunate. . .must put an end to silly rumors. . ."

Another dose of Polly's withering glare silenced him instantly.

"On Wednesday, I couldn't help overhearing Felicity admit that she has a significant problem with relationships." She aimed her scowl at Flick. "To be blunt about it, you spoke loudly enough on the third floor to ensure that most of Tunbridge Wells heard about your predicament."

Polly wagged her finger at Nigel. "Felicity explained to you that she has a propensity for choosing men who run off with other women. She asked you a simple question: Can she trust you not to do that to her?" She added, "What was your answer?"

"Uh. . .well. . ."

"Precisely! You dithered, which obviously caught her off guard. That's why she misinterpreted your answer."

"*What* answer?" Flick asked.

Polly traversed her wagging finger toward Flick. "You expected Nigel to say what every man you've ever known would have said—*Have no fear, my dear; I am as faithful as Santa Claus.*"

"Well. . ."

"When he didn't lie to you, you panicked."

"Well. . ."

"Hold that thought."

Nigel squirmed as Polly redirected her finger at him.

"Felicity presumed that she had already lost you to Olivia Hart. And why not? Olivia is a looker. Shallow as a puddle, but extraordinarily good-looking."

"I didn't give Olivia Hart a second peep," he said.

"Pull the other one, Nigel," Polly said with a mocking frown. "I've seen you go goofy when she's around. Stunning gals do that to men. Olivia would make any wife or girlfriend worry."

He decided not to argue. What would he achieve? Better to sit quietly and let Polly get whatever was bothering her out of her system. And as for giving her the chop—well, she was much too valuable an assistant to dismiss, especially at this juncture of the museum's history.

"Nigel," Polly resumed, "what do you suppose happened last May when the new acting director, namely you, arrived at the museum?"

He thought for a moment, then answered warily, "I don't get your meaning."

"What happened, Nigel, is that the four single women who work in this building immediately became curious about you. Now, because this is a museum, the people who work here are skilled in research." She smiled. "Can you see where I'm going with this?"

"They researched *me*?"

"We learned all that we could about you—down to the marginally useful fact that you have type B-positive blood."

"Good heavens!"

"I know—an appalling invasion of your privacy. But there it is." She thrust her face toward his nose. "Do you know what we did with the information we gathered?"

He felt a chill zip down his spine as he blithered, "*Uh...*no."

"We treated you like a racehorse running at Royal Ascot. We analyzed your form and estimated your handicap and concluded that Nigel Owen doesn't have the staying power to go the distance with a woman. A fine fellow for a brief flutter, Nigel is, but not a sound bet for the long haul."

"Blimey!" He stared at Flick. "I suppose that's what you think about me."

Polly answered before Flick could respond. "Of course she doesn't! Flick loves you. However, that's what you think about yourself. Am I right?"

Nigel didn't want to continue Polly's interrogation, but something he could see in Flick's eyes urged him to go on. *In for a penny, in for a pound.* He paused a few seconds to choose his words.

"Unfortunately...Flick...in the past, I have not been the

sort of man a woman could rely on."

"Quite true," Polly said. "That being the case, why did you melt down when she put a direct question to you?"

Nigel kept looking at Flick. "You asked me to make a promise that I knew I might not be able to keep." He heaved a sigh. "I love you too much to tell you a lie."

He felt Polly touch his arm. He looked up at her. "All very noble of you, I'm sure," she said, "but there's a serious flaw in your logic. You've based your self-doubts on past behavior that took place—*when?*—ten years ago."

Nigel nodded grimly. "What happened in one's past is usually the best predictor of the future."

"No, it isn't. Not for you—not since you became a Christian." Her voice filled with a kind of exhilaration that Nigel had not heard from her before. " 'Therefore, if anyone is in Christ, he is a new creation; the old has gone, the new has come! All this is from God, who reconciled us to himself through Christ.' Paul wrote that in his second letter to the Corinthians. Chapter 5, verses 17 and 18."

"I hardly think that Paul had my romantic life in mind when he wrote. . ."

"Dish the glib retorts." She held a hand up to his lips. "Think about Paul's words. Focus on what scripture is trying to tell you." She moved even closer to him. "You've been changed, Nigel. That's what Jesus does to people. But you don't yet appreciate what's happened to you. The old Nigel was powerless to resist when a woman like Olivia Hart began to flirt with him. The new Nigel, supercharged by the Holy Spirit, has the capacity not to be a weak-kneed twit." She put her hands on his shoulders. "You can make Felicity a promise and really hope to keep it. You're still capable of sin, but now you're also able to *not* sin."

"*But.* . .but why don't I feel that way, Polly?"

"Because the penny has yet to drop that God worked a dramatic change to your nature. Your brain remains cluttered with rubbish. Leftover guilt. Surplus shame. Superfluous self-doubt." She leaned forward, kissed Nigel's forehead, and patted the top of his head. "Declare the lot redundant. Let Jesus be your dustman. Ask Him to cart the muck away. He'll do a brilliant job. And as for you, Felicity. . ."

Nigel heard Flick catch her breath. *Perfectly understandable— it's her turn to be skewered.*

"What?" she said softly.

"My advice to you," Polly replied, "is to wait a day or two, then ask Nigel your question again—if you still require an answer."

"*Um.* . .yes, I shall," Flick said, and followed this by a little laugh of obvious relief.

Polly moved to the door and opened it. "Hang in there, both of you. And please figure out what to do about Barrington Bleasdale. This whole business with Cha-Cha is quite disturbing." She hesitated. "By the way, am I sacked?"

Nigel managed a shake of his head. He felt too drained to do anything else.

"Smashing!" Polly said as she left.

❧

Flick tapped gently on Nigel's door and wondered if an hour had been enough "post-Polly" recovery time. Poor Nigel had seemed shell-shocked when she left him sitting in their makeshift "Incident Room." She wished she could leave him alone longer, but they couldn't afford to give up a whole day—not with such little time left before the bank's deadline.

"Come in," spoke a faint voice from deep inside the office.

The office was dark when she stepped inside. Nigel had drawn the curtains, pulled down the shades, and switched off the lights. He lay stretched out on his couch, his arms crossed.

"Why are you lying in the shadows?" she asked.

"The better to contemplate a move to the hills of Afghanistan. I imagine that the daily life there will be less challenging than in Tunbridge Wells. I'll also be able to find a lower-stress job. Perhaps defusing land mines."

"Next question. How do you feel?"

"Foolish."

"The same as me."

"Ah. Polly was right about you, too?"

"Yeah. I should have understood what your dithering meant. I've been a nincompoop."

"True."

She uttered a stage snicker. "Isn't it lovely when we both can agree about important things?"

"What time is it?"

"Eleven twenty."

"I take it you want me up and about."

"I've been thinking—don't make any snide comments—that we've ignored one promising lead in our investigation. Jim Sizer, Mirabelle Hubbard, and Trevor Dangerfield told us that Etienne Makepeace hobnobbed with the bigwigs at the museum, including the people from the Hawker

Foundation. We need to converse with a former bigwig about Makepeace."

"How do we accomplish that? Mary Hawker Evans is dead and so is the man who was chief curator throughout the '60s. I can't even remember his name. Nathanial Swithin, my predecessor, was around back then, but he's currently relaxing on a beach in Majorca. Although I might enjoy a jaunt to Palma, we don't have sufficient spare time to make the trip. Besides, we must assume that he's driven all memories of this flipping institution out of his head. I definitely plan to do so when I relocate to Afghanistan. Lastly, we won't get a whit of cooperation out of the Hawker Foundation. As you well know, Jeremy Strain, the current managing director, is not a fan of the Royal Tunbridge Wells Tea Museum."

"As it happens, Nathanial Swithin is back in England. I just spoke with him on the telephone. He's expecting us at two this afternoon. He still lives in Tunbridge Wells, on Broadwater Down. Close enough to walk."

"Goody."

Flick raised the shade on the window opposite Nigel's sofa.

"Zounds! You are a cruel, cruel woman!" He turned over and buried his face in the leather upholstery.

"As you would see if you looked, the fog is completely gone, and there are large chunks of blue sky punching through the clouds. A stroll through Tunbridge Wells will do wonders for your dismal disposition."

"I may never leave this sofa."

"That will be awkward." She raised another shade. "Hannah Kerrigan is dropping by at eleven thirty to show us her retouched pictures of Rupert Perry and Martin Maltby."

"Fie on thee, woman."

"Oh. I put the mug of coffee I brought you on your desk."

"Coffee! Bless you." He extended his hand.

"Nope. If you want it, you get it."

"I withdraw my blessing."

Flick did her best not to laugh when Nigel slid off the sofa and stumbled to his desk. She continued to work her way around the office raising shades and switching on lights. The ambience—and Nigel, too—were largely restored when Hannah arrived and placed two large photos on his desk. "Here's my best guess of what one will find under the wigs and the makeup."

"Conan was right," Flick said. "The undisguised Martin Maltby looks remarkably different."

"Quite distinguished, actually," Hannah said. "A proper English gentleman, now that his nose is the right size and his lips don't protrude."

Flick examined the photograph. The man in the image looked somewhat older than the Martin Maltby she had spoken with, chiefly because Hannah had given him a mostly bald pate, with a sparse fringe of hair around his head.

Hannah went on. "I found Mr. Perry more of a challenge, because I believe that he has a poor complexion beneath his makeup. He's more leathery-faced than rosy-cheeked, with the sort of skin that spent lots of time exposed to tropical sunshine. And, as you can see, I supposed that his head was totally shaven under his wig."

"You do great work!" Flick said. "I'll tape these pictures to our 'wall of fame.'"

"I figured you would." Hannah gave Flick a small envelope. "I also made a set of smaller prints, in case you want to carry the images around with you."

Flick peered at Nigel. He had studied both pictures intently but hadn't said a thing.

"So, what do you think?" she asked.

"I'm greatly impressed. I didn't think it could be done, but these images seem mostly right to me." Nigel added, "Now all we need are their real names."

Flick winked at Hannah. Perhaps another attagirl from the chief curator would counteract the somewhat faint praise offered by the director? The museum's Webmistress didn't notice; her wistful gaze had been riveted on Nigel all the while.

Tough luck, kid. You had your chance, but he's soon going to be taken again. By me!

Nigel's telephone rang. Flick glanced at the caller ID panel.

"Speak of the devil! It's Barrington Bleasdale."

She cordially, but firmly, shooed Hannah out of Nigel's office while he answered the phone. He held the receiver away from his ear. Flick moved close enough to hear both ends of the conversation.

"Good morning, Mr. Owen." Bleasdale's voice oozed with synthetic compassion. "I just read the unfortunate article in the *Kent and Sussex Courier.*"

Flick found it difficult not to laugh. *You probably proofread the piece, too, before they ran it.*

He went on, "It's a nasty business—the awkward sort of publicity that puts you on the defensive with the public.

One can hypothesize that mothers will hesitate bringing their children to a museum that is home to a destructive and dangerous animal."

"Thank you for caring. . .*Barrington*." Nigel said evenly. "And thank you for calling."

Flick imagined tying the current issue of the *Courier* around a brick and tossing it through Bleasdale's window. *Probably not a good idea.*

"In point of fact," Barrington said, "I called today for a reason. I am the bearer of good tidings who can show you the silver lining in the cloud now hanging over the museum."

Flick looked at Nigel; they both shrugged. Flick mouthed, "I have no idea what he's talking about—do you?"

"Go on," Nigel said.

"The Hawker heirs have instructed me to tell you that they are willing to ignore the agreement that Elspeth made with the museum. They are willing to have Elspeth's animals returned to the bosom of the Hawker family."

Flick came close to shouting, "What?" at the telephone but was able to control her zeal. Nigel grabbed a pencil and wrote on a pad of paper, "*I smell a rat.*"

Flick snatched the pencil from Nigel's hand and scrawled, "*Me, too! They've never been interested in the pets—even when Elspeth was alive!*"

Her dealings with the Hawker heirs had been limited, but she couldn't imagine that they cared two pins about Cha-Cha, Lapsang, Souchong, and Earl. Harriet and Alfred's sudden concern about the little menagerie made no sense at all.

Bleasdale droned on, "Now for the good news. Harriett and Alfred have agreed to assume whatever liability you face for the death of the unfortunate ferret. They have asked me to offer the claimant an equitable settlement—all in the spirit of neighborliness."

"The claimant? That would be Bertram Holloway?"

"He's really a fine fellow, despite his misplaced affection for ferrets."

"Then you know him?"

"I've met him on one or two occasions, at Hawker family gatherings."

"Yes, well, you've given us much to think about, Counselor. When do you need an answer?"

"As quickly as possible. It's always wise to strike when the iron is hot. One never knows when the Hawker heirs will change their minds." Bleasdale lowered his voice to a conspiratorial whisper. "Just between you and me, they can be difficult clients at times."

"I'm more than a little curious," Nigel said, "why Harriet and Alfred would want the pets returned?"

"Well, it seems that Harriet misses the cats while Alfred had become attached to the dog and the bird."

"An affair of the heart?"

"Exactly. The Hawker heirs are highly affectionate people."

"Quite." Nigel rang off.

"That last bit about Harriet and Alfred missing the pets. . . ," Flick said. "Balderdash!" She smiled at Nigel. "Did I say that right?"

"Perfectly. I can't imagine why they would want Elspeth's pets back. . ."

"I can. We've never thought about it, but they're worth a good deal of money."

Nigel seemed to stiffen. "You're right, of course. I should have realized earlier. Bleasdale wrote the letter and placed the news item—they're all part of a grand scheme to encourage us to return the pets so the Hawkers can sell them. I wish we could repay the swine in his own currency."

"Perhaps we can." Flick giggled. "I have a weird idea. Where's the anonymous mobile phone that Martin Maltby gave us."

Nigel tugged open a desk drawer. "Right here. What else do you need?"

"The telephone number for Lion's Peak."

"Half a mo." He looked it up on his computer. Flick pressed the keys.

"Alfred Hawker here," said a bored, nasal voice.

Yippy. The least savvy of the siblings answered the phone.

Flick began speaking in her most accomplished English accent. "Yes, Mr. Hawker. This is, *ah*...Mrs. Lenora Fielding." Flick wondered why a name she had last spoken twenty-five years ago popped into her head. Then she remembered: Lenora, a childhood friend, was the best twelve-year-old liar that York, Pennsylvania, had ever produced. Flick went on, "I live in Sevenoaks, Kent. I have been told that you have a pair of show-quality British Shorthair cats for sale."

A pause, then "May I ask who told you that?"

"A friend of a friend in Tunbridge Wells. I promised I would not reveal her name."

Another pause. "Well, it is true that we expect to have two British Shorthairs available for purchase within a few days. Both have extraordinary pedigrees."

"Have you set a price yet?"

"As you undoubtedly know, Mrs. Fielding, show-quality British Shorthairs are difficult to acquire. We plan to have an informal auction, with the initial bids beginning at two thousand pounds each."

"That seems an eminently fair approach. How does one place a bid?"

"Our solicitor, Barrington Bleasdale, is handling all of the details. Call him for instructions."

"That's 'Bleasdale' with a B?"

"Quite. Be sure to let him know you are interested in the cats. Should you be interested, we are also disposing of a fine-quality African Grey parrot and a pedigreed dog of the Shiba Inu breed."

Flick cringed at the word *disposing*. "Most interesting. Can I trouble you for your solicitor's telephone number?"

She heard Alfred sigh. "Directory Enquiries can provide more assistance than I can in that direction. I rarely call the gentleman myself. I believe that Mr. Bleasdale has an office in Tunbridge Wells."

She pushed the END button and repeated all that Alfred had said to her.

"It's all about money," she added. "Somehow Harriet and Alfred found out that Elspeth had exquisite taste in pets. They must be kicking themselves for insisting that the museum take them in after she died."

"How much money are we talking about?" Nigel asked.

"Two British Shorthairs, one Grey parrot, and a Shiba Inu. I suppose their total value could reach ten thousand pounds."

"*Hmm.* Perhaps we're being too hasty? Ten thousand quid is a lot of lolly. Do you think we could hold our own auction?"

"Over *your* dead body."

"I take your point. What's next?"

"Well, now that we know we've guessed right, we ruin Bleasdale's day." Flick switched to Nigel's telephone and pressed REDIAL.

Bleasdale answered on the second ring. *He must have caller ID, too,* Flick thought.

"Mr. Owen—I presume you're calling because the museum has reached a decision about the animals?"

"Mr. Bleasdale, this is Felicity Adams. Mr. Owen referred the matter of Dame Elspeth Hawker's pets to my attention. And you're right—we have made a decision."

"Really?" His cheerful voice immediately began to sound suspicious. "When can I pick the creatures up?"

"*Never,* Mr. Bleasdale. While we appreciate the Hawkers' kind offer, we feel we must keep the animals after all. We feel morally committed to care for them in perpetuity. As you yourself pointed out to Mr. Owen, the museum and Dame Elspeth entered into an ironclad agreement to adopt her pets after her death."

She could envision wheels in the solicitor's head spinning as he tried to think of something profound to say. All he managed in the end was a feeble, "*Uh. . .*Mr. Owen seems to have misunderstood my earlier comments. An ironclad agreement? Certainly not. The contract was nothing more than an expression of Dame Elspeth's. . .*wishes* that her animals have a good home."

"That's exactly what we've given them at the museum."

"I'm sure you mean well, but do you really think a museum is the right place to house cats and dogs?"

"They seem quite happy here. The four of them are thriving."

"Possibly. But you still have to deal with the threatened lawsuit. Legal fees could be substantial, not to mention the impact of negative publicity."

"We also hope to reach a settlement with Bertram Holloway."

"A settlement. . ."

"But we've had some difficulty locating the gentleman."

"You've tried to find him?"

"Oh yes, but he seems to have left Tunbridge Wells." She raised her voice a notch. "I wouldn't be surprised if we *never* hear from him again."

"*Uh*. . .that's utterly possible."

"I fear that Alfred and Harriet will be disappointed by our decision. I'm sure they value the animals highly."

"Yes. Quite highly."

"Please assure them that they're welcome to visit the museum whenever they would like to see their loyal friends."

Flick waited for Bleasdale's reply. When none came, she hung up the telephone.

"Well done, Dr. Adams!" Nigel said. "You've cheered me up to no end."

And you me, Mr. Owen.

She sensed that he felt a tad reluctant to hug her—so she hugged him.

ELEVEN

"Did you bring any breadcrumbs?" Nigel asked. "We'd better leave a trail so we can find our way home."

To his delight, Flick stuck her tongue out at him. A promising sign that their relationship was on the mend.

"Our route from the museum to Nathanial Swithin's house is really quite simple," she said. "We make nothing but right turns. Right on Eridge Road. . .right on Neville Terrace. . .right on Linden Park Road. . .right on Montacute Road. . .right on Frant Road. . .and right on Broadwater Down, which—although it makes little sense—is actually the name of the road that runs through Broadwater Down, a neighborhood that some have nicknamed 'Millionaire's Row.' Coming back, we make six left turns."

"Got it," Nigel said. "Still, a breadcrumb or two would be welcome. I didn't eat much of a lunch."

"Here." Flick handed him a packet of potato crisps.

"Where did these come from?"

"Polly gave them to me. She guessed you would be peckish about now."

"Good heavens! Am I that predictable?"

"No. *She's* that smart." Flick added a satisfied toss of her head. "I intend to sign up for 'How to Decipher Nigel Owen' lessons with her."

Nigel found himself enjoying the hike. The sun was sufficiently strong to make topcoats unnecessary; they both wore heavy pullovers. Flick had swapped her pumps for trainers; they could both walk with quick, long strides.

He had lost track of the right turns when they arrived at Nathanial Swithin's home, an elaborately trimmed, redbrick Tudor that had apparently served as the model for countless baked gingerbread houses. The large dwelling was partially hidden behind a hedge of sprawling rhododendron bushes that were asleep for the winter.

"What a fabulous house," Flick said.

"I have it on good authority," he said, "that the late Mrs. Swithin didn't lack for the odd bob or two."

"Which door do we use? The one in the center and the one toward the end are both the same size."

While Nigel was trying to decide, the door closer to the side of the house swung open. Nathanial Swithin stepped outside—a broad grin on his face—and waved.

"He's been waiting for us to arrive," Flick said. "He even seems eager to talk to us."

"Did you tell him what we've come to talk about?"

"No—not really."

"Let's see how eager he is when he learns the truth."

When Nigel had first met Swithin the previous summer, he'd been amazed to learn that the former director had recently turned seventy. Nathanial looked at least ten years younger. He was nearly as tall as Nigel, with a wiry build, sharp features, thick, mostly dark hair, and what seemed a reasonably healthy suntan. His only concession to age was the pair of thick eyeglasses he wore. They made his eyes appear oddly small.

Nigel was well aware of Nathanial Swithin's legendary reputation at the Royal Tunbridge Wells Tea Museum. He had served as director for forty years—beginning on the museum's first day of operation—and was widely credited with being the driving force behind the excellent reputation for scholarship and research that the institution enjoyed today. Nigel had lost count of the number of people who reminded him that he had "an enormous pair of shoes to fill."

Nigel suddenly saw, out of the corner of his eye, a black-and-tan blur whiz past Swithin and race toward him. Nigel made a quick sidestep, but the agile blur compensated. An instant later, two paws landed solidly on Nigel's thigh. He looked down at a small, square-faced dog, about the same size as Cha-Cha, who seemed delighted to make his acquaintance.

"Taffy!" Swithin shouted.

The dog immediately reversed course and raced back to its master's side.

"Forgive her her trespasses, Nigel," Swithin said. "Being a terrier, Taffy is not the best behaved of hounds, but she is friendly and has a good heart."

"Taffy is. . . ?" Flick asked.

"A Welsh terrier, of course. I don't believe it's legal in Great Britain to name any other sort of dog 'Taffy.'" Swithin took time to scratch her back before he asked, "How goes life at the Royal Tunbridge Wells Tea Museum?"

"We've been. . .*busy*," Nigel said.

"I can well imagine. You've had a thrilling few months. The unexpected death of Dame Elspeth, a surprise upheaval on the board of trustees, the need to acquire the Hawker antiquities, the astonishing disinterment of Etienne Makepeace—that's far more excitement than I experienced during my entire career at the museum. In truth, I feel guilty that I escaped to the Balearic Islands before any of these problems arose." He smiled at Flick. "I'm delighted that you telephoned this morning. I'm ready to help you in any way I can. And one other thing—now that I'm retired, everyone calls me Nate."

"And all of my friends call me Flick."

"Speaking of the Balearics," Nigel said, "I thought you planned to spend the entire winter in Majorca."

"I've settled into a schedule of convenience. Three weeks toasting in the glorious Spanish sun, one week back in Tunbridge Wells to be rained on. The best of both worlds, so to speak. I plan to fly back to Majorca on Monday morning." He made a face. "Of course, I picked a terrible week to be back in Kent. When I arrived home last Saturday morning, I found my answering machine full of messages from reporters who wanted my reaction to the unearthing of Etienne Makepeace. Most of my would-be inquisitors reminded me that Etienne had been buried on my watch. Naturally, I didn't return any of their calls. One of the joys of retirement is that I am no longer required to bow and scrape in front of nosy journalists." He saluted Nigel. "That joy now belongs to you."

"Thank you for nothing, I'm sure."

Nate beckoned. "Come. I've lit the fire in the sitting room and prepared large mugs of my world-famous hot cocoa." Flick walked beside Nate; Nigel and a reasonably well-behaved Taffy brought up the rear.

The sitting room had tall leaded windows that looked out on an expansive rectangle of lawn. In the distance, Nigel could see Broadwater Down. The Regency-style furniture looked comfortable, genuine, and expensive. Most of the pieces were probably real antiques. The Oriental rugs on the floor appeared properly threadbare, and the draperies suitably sumptuous. The only twentieth-century item in the room was the portrait hanging over the fireplace. Nigel presumed that the young woman smiling prettily at him was Nate's late wife and that her picture had been painted in the 1950s.

Flick sat on a well-padded sofa. Nigel chose the armchair closest to the fire and cupped his hands to catch the warmth of the flame. "Lovely. I rarely get to enjoy a real fire."

Nate distributed mugs of cocoa and sat down beside Flick. "So. . .what sort of advice do you want from me, Flick? This morning, you explained that you were having difficulty deciding whether or not to create an exhibit about Etienne Makepeace."

Nigel sat back in his chair. The touch of skepticism he heard in Nate's voice suggested that the former director—his mind as nimble as ever—hadn't been fooled by Flick's quickly fabricated cover story. *Let's see how this discussion unfolds.* He sipped his cocoa gingerly and felt pleased to discover that it was home brewed, not store-bought. It tasted thick, strong, and delicious.

Flick charged ahead. "Indeed," she said. "Reaching a decision, and sticking with it, has proved to be more complex than we expected. At first, we decided not to create an exhibit. Our thinking was quite straightforward. The chief mission of the museum is to illuminate the history of tea, and we saw no direct connection between Etienne Makepeace's disappearance—and reappearance—and the history of tea."

Nate nodded. "That seems a sensible position to take."

Flick continued. "But then we realized that Makepeace held a unique position in Great Britain. He emerged as England's Tea Sage. He became a celebrity on the radio. He lectured from time to time at the museum. How then can we possibly ignore him in our exhibit galleries?"

Nate nodded again. "I can imagine several of our. . .I mean, *your* trustees making the very same point."

"Well, toward the middle of the week, we received new information about Etienne Makepeace that raised our level of confusion. A highly reliable source assured us that Makepeace had been a thoroughly miserable human being."

Nate chuckled. "I always described Makepeace as a *bounder*. It's an archaic term, I agree, but an apt one. I prefer not to use profanity."

"Then it's true?"

"Utterly. I'd be hard-pressed to name a more unpleasant man within my acquaintance. Etienne Makepeace was cursed with an ego that stretched from Brighton to Lands End. If that were not challenge enough, he *also* displayed an overwhelming sense of indifference to people around him. He thought himself the center of the universe.

"Makepeace merely annoyed men by his pretentiousness and posturing, but women were forced to fend off his unwelcome overtures. He seemed to lack any sense of appropriate office-place behavior. I suspect that every woman employed at the museum had to deal with his. . .*propositions* at one time or another. Not even my secretary was immune from his heavy-handed advances. Today, of course, Makepeace would be charged with sexual harassment and, at the very least, be drummed out of the museum's employ—but back then, we didn't have the Sex Discrimination Act and similar legal protections."

Flick frowned. "Does a man like that deserve an exhibit at our museum?"

Nate replied with a small shrug. "Oh, I suspect that many of the men esteemed by the museum had similarly defective characters. Desmond Hawker himself was widely acknowledged to be an unprincipled scoundrel during the first half of his life. And doubtless, the ranks of Britain's successful tea merchants are amply stocked with men who are ruthless, disagreeable, spiteful, immoral. . .take your pick of vile attributes. Despite their natures—or perhaps because of them—they played vital roles in the history of tea. As you noted earlier, their successes—rather than their failures—earned them places of honor in your exhibit galleries."

Flick set her cocoa mug down on a mahogany side table. "Etienne Makepeace may fall into a different category. We're well aware of the way he treated women. Moreover, we've heard that the police are leaning toward the theory that an irate husband seeking revenge shot Etienne. But two days ago, we received credible information that he was a fraud—a tea sage who, despite his sterling reputation, knew nothing about tea. We now have compelling evidence that his books, his articles, his lectures, his radio scripts were either plagiarized from foreign sources or ghostwritten for him. I won't create an exhibit that honors a complete sham."

Without saying a word, Nate stood up and walked to a window. Nigel noted that he seemed suddenly pale.

"Forty years is a long time. . . ." He turned around slowly and faced Flick. "You asked for my advice about an exhibit. Well, here it is—*don't* create one. The most sensible thing you can do is to forget Etienne Makepeace. Stop asking questions about him. Discard the information you've gathered. Replant the hole in the garden. Expunge Makepeace from the museum's pantheon of tea heroes."

Nigel decided to jump in. "We can't do that, Nate."

Nate's shoulders sagged. "You haven't told me the whole story, have you?"

"No."

"I thought as much. It stretched credulity that you needed my wisdom to make a routine operational decision."

"Our problem is somewhat more complicated than deciding whether or not to launch a new exhibit," Nigel said. "The bank we chose to fund the acquisition of the Hawker collection is having cold feet. The chairman wants to understand Etienne Makepeace's relationship to the museum before he gives us the money. He also wants to know why Makepeace was buried in our tea garden."

"Find another banker."

"We could—but he or she would ask precisely the same questions. Frankly, we want to know the answers, too."

"Why would you suppose that I can provide them?" Nate moved close to the sofa but didn't sit down.

"Because we know that Etienne often spent time with the 'bigwigs' on the third floor of the museum, including

Mary Hawker Evans and representatives of the Hawker Foundation. I assume that the director of the museum sat in at those meetings."

"You assume wrong." Nate sighed. "I rarely attended the meetings you have in mind. The 'bigwigs,' to use your label for them, usually deemed my presence unnecessary. Consequently, I know very little about what went on." He added, "Although, I have my suspicions."

"Every item of information we get fills in another piece of the puzzle," Flick said.

Nate abruptly raised his voice. "You speak as if you are asking me to merely break a minor confidence, young lady. To tell you what I know about Etienne Makepeace, I'll have to violate British law."

"What law?" Flick asked breathlessly.

"The Official Secrets Act. I was required to sign my life away in 1965."

The room fell silent. Nigel, not wanting to look at Nate, stared into his half-full mug of cocoa and wondered if the former director had lost his mind. *The Official Secrets Act? What possible connection could there be between tea and state secrets?*

A few moments later, Nate began to laugh. He retook his seat on the sofa next to Flick. "Please excuse my outburst of sanctimonious twaddle. You have a right to know the truth of our early days. Furthermore, I acknowledge that I've wanted to tell the story for decades. I've even fantasized about publishing my memoirs and revealing *all*, as the tabloids often say. I sincerely doubt that Her Majesty's government will toss me in prison for ignoring a forty-year-old vow. No—what holds me back today is my reluctance to harm the museum."

Nigel glanced at Flick. She wisely had decided to say nothing and let Nate feel his own way forward, at his own pace.

Nate heaved a deeper sigh. "Both of you are too young to remember the Cold War—the *real* Cold War of the 1960s, when people truly feared that a minor conflict would escalate into a full-scale nuclear war between East and West. Keep in mind that the Cuban Missile Crisis took place during the same October when workmen were laying the brick walls of the Royal Tunbridge Wells Tea Museum."

Nigel took another sip of cocoa. Where was his predecessor taking them with his odd history lesson?

"You see," Nate went on, "many in Britain at the time had a strong sense that we were all at risk, that we were all soldiers in the battle against Communism. Many of us felt that we had a role to play in containing the expansion of the Soviet Union."

Nigel couldn't stop himself from saying, "Nate, does the 'many of us' you refer to encompass the staff of a small tea museum in Tunbridge Wells—or the Royal Fusiliers on duty in the Fulda Pass?"

Nate hesitated long enough for Nigel to wonder if he had accidentally insulted the elderly man. At last, Nate went on, "The former, of course, Nigel. The handful of us at the museum who knew the details thought of ourselves as being at the front line in the battle against the Soviets."

"Details? Nate—*what* details?"

"It's difficult. . . ." He took a deep breath and began again. "I suppose it's best to be direct and succinct. In 1965, the British Secret Intelligence Service, MI6, conscripted the tea museum. MI6 used the museum to 'credential' several intelligence agents who then had legitimate tea-related reasons to visit China and the Soviet Union."

Flick sat up straight. "Our little tea museum served as a cover for Cold War spying?"

"In so many words, yes," Nate said. "I believe that we provided bona fides for five agents over an eighteen-month period. Their names were on our staff lists, and their research activities were described in our annual report. They even had telephone extensions and mailboxes to make them seem authentic, should anyone check."

"But that's outrageous!" she said. "Didn't anyone complain? File a lawsuit? Write to their congress. . .I mean, member of Parliament?"

"My, my, Flick—you really don't grasp what the sixties were like. The Hawker Foundation actively supported and cooperated with the scheme, as did Mary Hawker Evans. I had no choice in the matter, other than the unacceptable option of resigning my post in protest. But I also admit that I felt no particular outrage at what the museum was doing. The Soviets spied on us; we spied on them." He gave a feeble laugh. "My role was especially easy. I simply looked the other way on occasion—and signed a few false letters of introduction."

Nigel locked eyes with Flick and sensed her struggle to cope with the anger she clearly felt. The scientist inside had many more questions to ask Nathanial Swithin.

"Getting back to Etienne Makepeace. . . ," she said, "how did he fit into the 'scheme,' as you call it?"

Nate prefaced his answer with a grudging nod. "Makepeace's relationship with the museum started soon after we began to cooperate with MI6. One day, I found a letter from him in my in-box offering to deliver a trial lecture. Naturally, we accepted. Within two months, he had become a frequent visitor. He lectured, he attended the meetings you asked about, and he often browsed through our archives."

"And he routinely harassed the women at the museum," Flick said glumly.

"I won't deny that our affiliation with Makepeace was, in many ways, a pact with the devil. Makepeace was an obnoxious fellow to have around, but we were a newly established museum, struggling to build a clientele. Makepeace's lectures brought people in and boosted our reputation as a center of learning about tea. He regularly talked us up on the BBC. Whenever he lectured, reporters would flock to the Grand Hall, then write glowing stories that ran in newspapers across England." Nate offered a tentative smile. "We needed the good, so we tolerated the bad."

She shook her head with determination. "You should have given him the boot. Then he'd have been buried somewhere else."

Nate peered at Flick—quizzically, Nigel thought. "I didn't have the authority to discharge Etienne Makepeace. I thought you understood—he worked for MI6."

Flick's face became a mask of amazement. "Etienne Makepeace was a Cold War spy. . .a *spook*?"

"Without a doubt." Nate's expression grew serious. "Makepeace never explained himself to me, but anyone with open eyes could see he was linked to the intelligence support the museum provided the government. He rubbed shoulders with the bigwigs; he routinely attended their Wednesday afternoon

266

closed-door meetings; and when he disappeared, our association with MI6 came to an abrupt end."

"A moment, Nate," Nigel said. "What do you mean by 'Wednesday afternoon' meetings?"

"During our early years, the museum remained closed to the public every Wednesday—even during the busy summer season. The off day in the middle of the week gave the staff time to fine-tune new exhibits and do behind-the-scenes work. The meetings involving MI6 always took place on Wednesdays."

"This. . .is. . .incredible," Flick said quietly, to no one in particular. She seemed to be staring at the fire. "It changes everything."

Nate frowned. "I fear that I've placed a significant burden upon you. The government still considers the museum's link with MI6 a secret. You know the truth, but you can't do much with it—certainly not present the details in an exhibit. And as for your banker. . .well, I doubt he'd believe a word of my story. It seems incredibly fanciful, and I can provide no solid evidence that Etienne Makepeace was a. . .*ghost?* I've forgotten the term you used."

Flick half smiled. "Spook."

"Ah, yes. Spook."

Nigel glanced at his watch. Two forty-five. The conversation had reached an obvious low point. The time had come to offer Nathanial Swithin their good-byes.

"Thank you, Nate," he said cordially. "You've been of great assistance to us today."

"Spectacularly helpful indeed." Flick tried to match his cheerful tone, but Nigel could hear considerable disappointment in her voice. He should probably feel the same way;

they'd have little to offer Sir James Boyer come Monday. Well, when Wescott Bank reneged on their loan, they would have to find a more visionary institution. They would have lots of help from Barrington Bleasdale, whose clients expected the sale to go through quickly. It was a terrible prospect—an enormous challenge for everyone involved—but somehow getting Flick back made it seem unimportant. And there was something else, too. God, the super dustman, could also be a brilliant problem solver. He and Flick might have been a lot further along had they turned this problem over to God, too.

"May I ask one more favor of you?" Flick said to Nate.

"But of course."

She dug into her handbag. "I have two photographs that I'd like you to look at." She handed him the small prints of the retouched images of Martin Maltby and Rupert Perry. "Do you recognize either of these men?"

Nate studied the photos. "I don't know this fellow." He handed Perry's picture to Flick but kept staring at Maltby. "This chap looks familiar. I'm sure that I've talked with him at the museum when we were both substantially younger. I can't remember precisely when, although I have a vague notion that he had something to do with the Hawker Foundation." He stared some more. "That being the case. . .I do know one person who might be able to put a name to the face. In fact, I should have thought of Gwen earlier."

"Gwen who?" Flick asked.

Nate returned Maltby's photo. "Gwen Sturgis, the Hawker Foundation's official archivist. She's a delightful woman who possesses the finest memory I've ever encountered. Gwen can put most computers to shame. The Foundation will suffer mightily when she retires next year." He punctuated his pronouncement with a curt nod. "If Gwen ever encountered this man, she will remember the time, place, and name. Moreover, she oversees rooms full of ancient documents, photographs, and miscellany. Perhaps she can find a nugget buried deep within that will help assuage your banker's curiosity."

"Unhappily," Nigel said, "we are persona non grata at the Hawker Foundation. Jeremy Strain, the current director, decided that a mere museum is not worthy of the foundation's financial support. I've memorized the statement he made on BBC TV when he took the helm of the foundation: 'The function of *my* foundation is to do measurable good in the world and not to teach the Tunbridge Wells gentry how to brew a cup of English Breakfast tea.'"

Nate chuckled. "I'm well aware of Jeremy's snobbishness, and so is Gwen Sturgis. She works for the man. However, he is a theoretical stumbling block rather than an actual obstacle. As is often said, the left hand needn't know what the right hand is doing—especially if I invite Gwen down from London for a Saturday in Tunbridge Wells."

"We'll provide lunch," Nigel said.

"Good! I'm in the mood to sup on posh victuals," Nate said with a sniff.

"Please call Gwen," Flick said. "Find out if she's available."

Much to Nigel's surprise, Nate averted his eyes. "Oh, Gwen will be available. I had planned to ride the train to London tomorrow and spend a quiet day with her. We'll simply reverse our travel plans, as we often do."

Nigel choked back a laugh. Flick also appeared to be doing her best to hold a straight face. Evidently, Nathanial

Swithin returned to England every fourth week to enjoy more than the rain.

"Where shall we meet?" Nigel asked.

"At the museum, of course," Nate answered. "If the South Eastern Train operates on time tomorrow, she'll arrive at ten forty. We'll be there a few minutes before eleven."

"Nearly eleven it is." Nigel peeked sideways at Flick. Her earlier gloom had largely dispelled. Nigel understood; Gwen Sturgis represented a new hope for the investigation. Curiously, he felt the same way.

Nigel and Flick followed Nate out of the sitting room. "I'll walk with you as far as Frant Road," he said. Taffy appeared magically at Nate's side the instant he picked up her lead. When he opened the door, Taffy raced behind a rhododendron bush.

"Where did that infernal animal go?" Nathanial walked into the yard and made a clucking noise with his tongue.

Nigel looked at Flick in time to hear her say, "That's the crazy noise Earl makes."

"You don't suppose?"

"I *do* suppose." She threw up her hands. "Olivia Hart was right, darn it. Earl is trying to call Cha-Cha. The silly parrot is obviously repeating the sound that Dame Elspeth made when she called him."

"So how do we fix the bird?"

"It should be simple."

"How simple?"

"All we have to do is retrain him to use a more. . .*convenient* signal."

"Do you have such a signal in mind?"

"I'm thinking."

Nigel grinned. "Please keep me informed should you make any progress." He escorted Flick to the bottom of the long, macadam driveway, where Nate was waiting with Taffy securely attached to her lead. The three set off together on Broadwater Down.

"I thought I was out of questions," Flick said to Nate, "but I have one left. In your experience, how. . .ah, *exuberant* is the British Secret Intelligence Service in protecting their secrets?"

Nigel needed a moment to grasp the import of Flick's indirect inquiry. Could MI6 be responsible for the frightening episode in the Crescent Road Car Park and the subsequent "temporary cancellation" of the academic conference?

Nigel was not surprised when Nate answered the question from his perspective. "If by 'exuberant,' " he said, "you're suggesting that MI6 might tap my telephones or follow me around the streets of Palma—well, I see those as rather far-fetched possibilities. Nonetheless, I would rather not get on their bad side. To that end, I trust you'll be discreet with the details I've shared with you."

Nigel exchanged a concerned glance with Flick. Had they managed to get on MI6's "bad side"? Perhaps British Intelligence still considered Etienne Makepeace's "double life" a state secret worth protecting? He and Flick had been advised—in a most threatening way—to stop seeking additional information about Etienne Makepeace and to let sleeping dogs lie. They'd been expressly cautioned that raking up the past could be dangerous.

Precisely the sort of warning one can picture MI6 delivering late one night in an empty car park.

Nigel shook Nate's hand, Flick gave him a hug, and they turned left on Frant Road.

When they were out of Nate's earshot, Flick said, "Before you ask me 'what do I think,' I want to go on record that I have no flaming idea about anything. I am entirely confused. Every time I think I've figured out what might be happening, something else turns up and knocks me for a loop."

"For example?"

"For example," she said, "what kind of dingbat secret agent dabbles in sexual harassment? In other words, why would the Brits hire a spy who blatantly calls attention to himself by chasing married women and picking fights in pubs?"

"An excellent 'for example.' I have one, too."

"Carry on."

"For example," he said, "what kind of British spy during the Cold War hires a ghostwriter to plagiarize Russian-language tea journals? American, even Indian, magazines I might understand—but *Soviet* journals? The Bolshies must have known what he was doing."

"I agree. It was more calling attention to himself, and that makes no sense at all."

Nigel took her hand in his. "This is fun. We may have invented a new party game. Nonsensical facts about the weird life and death of Etienne Makepeace—the spy who loved tea."

"You've just come up with another game," she said excitedly. "Potential names when they make a movie about Etienne Makepeace, tea sage and spy. My choice is 'The Man with the Golden Oolong.'"

"I offer 'You Only Dunk Twice.'"

She stopped walking while she thought. "Drat. All I can

think of is 'Dr. Nose,' nose being the technical term that tea tasters use for the aroma of tea."

"I quickly counter with 'On Her Majesty's Secret Tea Service.' I believe that's sufficient for a win."

"Who says?"

Nigel looked around. The large trees overhanging the sidewalk offered a modicum of privacy, even during the winter. He pulled Flick toward him and kissed her. He observed that she did not protest or pull away; instead, she kissed him back.

Afterwards, she looked up at him. "Polly Reid said not to ask you my question for a few days, but I'm yearning to know the answer." She took a breath, then asked, "Can I trust you not to run off with another woman?"

"Completely. Fully. Unconditionally. Utterly. Exhaustively. In all respects. In every circumstance. Without reservation. Did I say utterly?"

"You did."

"I've never been good with adverbs."

"I wouldn't say that. You seem to be doing fine."

"Oh—I just thought of three more. Categorically. Thoroughly. Veritably."

"Veritably?"

"Consider it a British idiom."

She smiled. "I suppose that's enough. I stand convinced that I can rely on you."

"In that event. . ."

Nigel kissed her again.

"That was nice," she said. "What's more, I just had another brainstorm. About Etienne Makepeace."

"While I was kissing you?"

"Consider yourself an inspirational person." She unwrapped herself from his arms. They began to walk north on Frant Road. "I think all the puzzle pieces fit together if Makepeace was a British secret agent killed by the other side."

"Your brainstorm asserts that he was shot by the KGB?"

"That explains the mysterious Soviet pistol."

"Okay. But why would the nefarious KGB then decide to stash Makepeace's body in the museum's tea garden?"

"As an object lesson for MI6, of course! The Soviets figured out that the museum was being used as a cover for British agents. They probably assumed that Makepeace's body would be found immediately."

"But if they wanted his corpse discovered quickly, why do such a thorough job of restoring the ground around the two Assam bushes. They did such expert work that the museum's gardening crew never noticed the soil had been disturbed."

"Well. . ."

"And why cover the body with slate tiles? Someone expended a significant effort to lug the tiles into the tea garden from outside the museum."

"Uh. . ."

"And why bury the pistol and all of Makepeace's personal effects in an antiquities storage box planted under his body?"

"This is too easy for you," she said.

"And why bother burying him in the first place? If one wanted to deliver an object lesson to MI6, wouldn't it be best just to prop the corpse up in the museum's Welcome Centre kiosk?"

"Rats! I'm back to 'I have no flaming idea about anything.'"

Nigel thought about kissing Flick once again when his mind noted a new background noise on Frant Road. He realized it was the sound of an engine. Curiously, the sound kept growing louder—loud enough, in fact, to capture his attention. He looked up from Flick's face in time to see a dark green minivan, driving half on the road, half on the sidewalk, roaring toward them.

Nigel wrapped an arm around Flick and leaped sideways. He felt the bare branches of a thick bush scratch his exposed skin as the van whooshed past only inches away from Flick's back.

"Oh my!" Her voice sounded husky. "Did someone just try to kill us?"

He nodded. "Someone driving a green Ford Transit mini-van. The same van, I think, we saw the other evening."

"Stop thinking. Just hold me tight."

"Indeed, I will," he said. He decided that he should also stop talking.

# TWELVE

Flick rolled over and found herself face-to-face (so to speak) with Cha-Cha's furry hindquarters. Although still half asleep, she distinctly remembered that Nigel had custody of the pooch on Friday night. How did the dog end up in her bed? And then she remembered—she wasn't in her bed. The afternoon before, Conan Davies had insisted that both she and Nigel relocate to the museum "until we sort out this 'Anonymous Bystander' chap of yours."

At first, they both had been reluctant, but Conan refused to compromise. "The two of you in one place will be easier to watch over," he had said. "Furthermore, now that our surveillance camera network is working, the museum is a very safe place to be." He had rolled the "r" in very. "One of my lads will be on duty all night." Conan had escorted them to their apartments, and each had packed the essentials for a night or two away from home.

Flick wondered what time it was. She lifted her head

and was able to glimpse the illuminated clock on her desk. Six forty-five a.m. She'd slept for more than seven hours. *All things considered, pretty good for spending the night on an old sofa.* Conan had offered to set up a camp cot in her office; the museum had a good supply on hand, although Conan could not explain why. "It may have had something to do with civil defense, ma'am, or perhaps an old health and safety regulation. For whatever reason, we have ten cots and a dozen blankets stored on a shelf in the basement."

"I'll take one of your blankets," she had replied, "but I'll sack out on my sofa."

Flick sat up, stretched, and recalled that her satisfactory night had been prefaced by a highly enjoyable evening. She and Nigel had prepared a light supper in the tearoom's kitchen—tomato soup and grilled cheese sandwiches, as she'd suggested—and then spent several hours enjoying the club-like atmosphere of the Commodore Hawker Room. They'd broken many of the museum's daytime rules by moving aside the crowd-control stanchions and ropes, sitting in the commodore's personal club chairs, and snacking on grapes, Stilton cheese, and Jacobs Jaffa Cakes biscuits. They read more than they talked, but when they did talk, neither brought up the near-hit-and-run attack on Frant Road.

Flick abruptly remembered something else. They had allowed Cha-Cha to choose with whom he wanted to spend the night. She'd been pleased when he trotted off to her office.

"However, old chum," Flick said to the Shiba Inu, "you clearly ignored our understanding. You were supposed to curl up on my newly acquired Oriental rug. The sofa's not big enough for both of us."

She shambled to her feet, switched on the room lights, and heaped unspoken praise on the nameless architectural hero who had decided to install a bathroom, with a real shower, in both the director's and chief curator's offices. Less than thirty minutes later, she was dressed for the day in a colorful knit blouse, wool slacks, black leather jacket, and matching leather boots.

"Thank you for being so patient," she said to Cha-Cha. "Because you chose me last night, the least I can do is take you *walkies* this morning."

The security guard on duty in the Welcome Centre kiosk provided simple directions: "Stay where I can see you on the surveillance TV monitor. The various grassy areas on the sides and the back of the building are okay, but don't cross Eridge Road."

"Did you hear that, Cha-Cha," she said. "We can't go to the Common today."

Cha-Cha seemed to understand. He sniffed his way through the allowable terrain with commendable speediness. They were back in scarcely ten minutes. As she had hoped, she found Nigel and Conan having breakfast in the Duchess of Bedford Tearoom.

"I was just explaining to the director, ma'am," Conan said, "that I asked the guard who went off duty at four yesterday to make a side trip on his way home and examine the. . .*scene* of your unhappy experience. Fortunately, the tire marks on the sidewalk were still evident."

Nigel made a chagrined grimace. "It seems that we over-estimated the danger we faced."

Conan nodded. "The van's left-side wheels definitely

climbed on the sidewalk, ma'am—but most of the van remained in the street. It was a frightening sight, I'm sure, and not without risk; but if one is a good driver, that sort of exhibition can be performed without undue peril to the pedestrians involved. I wager that the perpetrator had fiddled with the van's muffler to increase the engine noise. That will make the vehicle seem closer than it really is."

"So you don't think that the driver intended to harm us?"

"More likely, ma'am, he wanted to deliver a second message advising you and the director to stop digging into the life of Etienne Makepeace."

"The question lurking in the background, needless to say," Nigel said, "is who sent the message?"

"I vote for MI6," Flick said. "If it's really true that Etienne Makepeace worked for them forty years ago, perhaps they don't want the fact known today."

"Even assuming that's so, ma'am, chasing you into the bushes strikes me as heavy-handed for MI6 in the twenty-first century. A van is a foolish means of communication—you might have panicked, jumped the other way, and been killed. And there's always the possibility that the odd police car might have been cruising nearby. No, a van threatening to run people down smacks of vintage melodrama and ancient spy novels."

"How do you suppose 'Anonymous Bystander' knew where to find us?" Nigel asked.

"I presume that you were followed yesterday when you left the museum. Did you notice any suspicious persons or vehicles?"

"In truth, Conan, we had our minds on other things."

Flick bit her tongue. Nigel often displayed a magnificent

sense of British understatement. On the way to Nathanial Swithin's home, they'd been recovering from Polly Reid's lecture; on the way back, they'd been sorting out Swithin's revelations and the implications of a kiss. Going or coming, neither of them would have noticed a volcano erupt on the Broadwater Down.

After breakfast, Flick returned to her office and began to think about the kind of presentation they could prepare for Wescott Bank. It was all very tricky. What facts would satisfy Sir James Boyer, and what details would scare him off? Would he be outraged to learn that the museum had served as a "cover" for MI6? Or would he be delighted to know that Etienne Makepeace apparently served as a frontline Cold Warrior?

Flick found these questions irritating as well as difficult to answer. She happily set them aside when Hannah Kerrigan came into her office toting a sheaf of photographs.

"You got stuck working on a lovely Saturday, too, I see," Flick said.

"I wanted to finish the cat analysis and also catch up on the new Web page. The mountain of photo retouching I did this week threw my schedule off."

"Ah—did you figure out which cat is Lapsang and which is Souchong?"

Hannah shook her head forlornly. "It can't be done," she said. "At least, not by me."

"It can't?"

She spread more than twenty pictures of British Shorthairs across the top of Flick's desk.

"I tried all the tricks in the Photoshop manual," Hannah

said, "plus a few that I invented for the occasion. I studied my new cat photographs in every conceivable way. I manipulated the images until Lapsang and Souchong resembled dogs. And you know what—the two are lost in an irreversible muddle, thanks to whoever mislabeled their kitten pictures."

"Dame Elspeth Hawker," Flick said with a sigh. "She meant well, but her eyesight was not the best."

"What do we do now?" Hannah giggled. "Don't say 'ask the cats,' because I already tried that."

"We make a command decision that the past shall not be allowed to impact the future. Henceforth, the larger cat is Lapsang and the smaller is Souchong. And thus it shall be forever. The chief curator of the Royal Tunbridge Wells Tea Museum has spoken."

"Do you think people will mind?"

"No one will mind, because no one will know. Your study is *our* little secret."

"Imagine that! I'm only twenty-two and already part of a high-level conspiracy designed to mislead the public." Hannah gathered up the photographs. "Do you want to tell the cats about their permanent names, or shall I?"

"Consider that your next assignment."

"I knew this would be a fun place to work," Hannah said as she left.

Flick was pondering a return to the difficult questions when her mobile phone rang. *Crikey. . .it's in my handbag across the room.* She got hold of it at the start of the fifth ring—an instant before her voice mail would have answered the call.

"Good morning, Dr. Adams, it's me," a familiar voice said.

"DI Pennyman! Are you still in Scotland?"

"No. I'm back in Kent." He went on immediately, "Have you had any further contact from 'Anonymous Bystander'?"

Flick hesitated before she finally said, "Yes. A childish threat. The green Ford Transit minivan sped past us with his left-side wheels on the curb and forced us into the bushes."

"You seem reluctant to describe the encounter."

"I am reluctant. We don't want any further awkward publicity. Any suggestion that the museum is the target of threats could seriously affect our future. The bank that will fund our purchase of the Hawker antiquities is exceptionally risk-averse."

There's no need to tell him we're lying low in the museum.

Pennyman's tone became sharper. "Some might describe a motor vehicle operated that way as attempted murder. It's a serious crime."

"We don't think he meant to kill us."

"Ah. Then what did he mean to accomplish?"

"He wants us to stop poking around in Makepeace's past. We're required to let sleeping dogs lie."

"If memory serves, that was the content of the message you received in the Crescent Road Car Park."

"Yup. Except yesterday's message was more pointed."

"The implication is that you ignored his first warning."

Flick paused again. She needed a few seconds to find the right words. "Some rather unusual information about Etienne Makepeace has come to our attention—by that, I mean it was brought to our attention. We are fairly confident that Makepeace was a fraud who did not write most of the things he took credit for."

"Extraordinary! Makepeace displays the unpleasant

characteristics of a dead fish too long in the sun. The closer one gets, the worse he smells." He added, "What does 'fairly confident' mean?"

"We have a stack of journals and magazines, published during the 1950s, that were plagiarized by Makepeace. They are virtually identical to the works he supposedly authored."

"In short, you found the smoking gun, as you Americans are fond of saying."

"I'm afraid so." Flick's mind raced. Should she tell Pennyman about the possible MI6 connection? Not yet, she decided. Not until they had additional confirmation, and certainly not without Nathanial Swithin's permission.

"Do you suppose that any of his ethical lapses as England's Tea Sage could be linked to Makepeace's murder?" Pennyman asked.

"It's hard to see how. I'm still a fan of the jealous husband hypothesis."

Pennyman made a soft groan. "You and most of the police establishment of the United Kingdom. To use your words, the authorities are *fairly confident* that Makepeace's killer has been identified." His voice sharpened again. "You must not repeat what I'm about to tell you to anyone. Agreed?"

"Agreed."

"The putative jealous husband is a man named Hugh Doyle. Well, that was his name before he relocated from Tunbridge Wells to Glasgow in 1966. Once in Scotland, he became Hubert Daugherty and led a quiet, modestly success-ful life as a greengrocer. He died in 1995."

"I take it he wasn't a grocer in Wells."

"In fact, Hugh made his living as a villain who specialized

in truck hijacking and smuggling. Along the way, he may have murdered three people."

"My goodness. What connection would a man like that have with our tea museum?"

"Now that's an interesting question—I asked the very same thing. It seems that Doyle had a day job. When the pickings from crime were off, he worked as a bricklayer. He was part of the crew who built your building and also the brick wall that surrounds the tea garden."

"I get it. Doyle obviously knew his way around the museum. When he shot Makepeace, he was able to break in and dispose of the body."

"So goes the theory."

"Does Doyle have a barmaid wife?"

"Indubitably. Clara Doyle died in 1998. However, in 1966 she was a fortyish, well-built blond who worked as a barmaid at The Horse and Garter, a small pub on the London Road that was demolished decades ago. We have evidence that Makepeace often frequented the pub, and we have a photograph that shows him chatting up Clara in the Pantiles."

Flick gave little cough to mask the surprise she felt. That must be the same photo—one of the four provided by Dorothy McAndrews—that was taped to the wall of their Incident Room.

"You seem reluctant to accept the story," she said.

"I become suspicious when comprehensive solutions to forty-year-old mysteries fall into my lap. Of course, I'm a voice in the wilderness. My masters love Hugh Doyle as the prime suspect. He seems to answer every thorny question we skeptics raise."

"Let me raise one. Where would Hugh Doyle have acquired a Russian pistol?"

"From a shipment of smuggled arms and ammunition that Hugh Doyle, wearing his criminal hat, helped transport from France to England. The conjecture goes that he skimmed a few weapons off the top for himself before the arms left England for Central America." He sighed. "It's possible, I suppose."

"Why is Hugh Doyle still a secret?"

"The circumstantial evidence against Doyle is obviously quite strong, but we still lack compelling proof that links him directly to the murder. A large task force of investigators is searching for the missing pieces. Given the notoriety of this murder, there's great reluctance in the higher ranks to name the killer until we've built an ironclad case against him."

"I shan't say a word, without your okay."

Pennyman grunted. "By the by, where are you today? I had planned to visit you at your flat, but obviously you weren't there when I called."

"I'm at the museum." She hid another gust of surprise by sounding cheerful. "Saturday is a busy day for us. I often spend the day here."

"You must leave for work deucedly early. I phoned you at seven fifteen this morning."

"Yes, well, we're working very hard to prepare for the acquisition of the Hawker antiquities," Flick said. In a way, it was perfectly true. "The best way to contact me is to call my mobile phone. It's always switched on."

She rang off.

Note for future reference: Don't talk to a smart, skeptical cop when you don't plan to tell him the whole truth.

Flick left her office at a quarter to eleven and walked downstairs to the ground floor, and then through the Duchess of Bedford Tearoom to the museum's greenhouse. It was likely that Nate would use the rear door—the door closest to the staff car park—because he would know that the front and side "public" entrances were closed until eleven. She found that Nigel had had the same idea.

"I thought someone should welcome them to the museum," he said. "They're honored guests, after all—our former director and a senior staff member from the Hawker Foundation."

"We seem to think alike."

"Definitely a promising sign."

"I agree." She moved closer to him and lowered her voice. "I had an interesting chat with DI Pennyman. I can tell you some of what he said, but not the nitty-gritty details." She gave a little shrug. "He swore me to secrecy."

"Hmm. You know, of course, that I will strive to get even with you. Just you wait until I know something that you don't."

"I can't imagine that ever happening."

"*Ooh*. Cheeky monkey!"

Flick saw his hand move toward her, but she couldn't twist aside in time. Nigel tickled her ribs; she began to laugh. She was still laughing—and dodging Nigel's fingers—when she noted, out of the corner of her eye, that Nathanial Swithin and a tall, gray-haired woman were walking toward them.

Flick said the first thing that entered her mind: "Oh my, Nathanial—I'm so sorry. We never act this way when the museum is open to the public."

"It might increase attendance if you did," he said with a

smile, "although I grant that the trustees are likely to object."

The gray-haired woman chimed in. "This is hardly fair. Where is *my* dashing young man? I want to be chased around the museum, too."

Nigel offered a courtly bow. "Fear not, ma'am, I'm here to serve. Would you like a head start?"

"That won't be necessary. I intend to let you catch me." She extended her hand. "Hello, Nigel, I'm Gwen Sturgis." And then to Flick. "Nate warned me that I'm not to call you Felicity. I promptly explained to him that because my obnoxious cousin called herself"—she began to spell—"F-L-I-C-K, I have stricken the nickname from my vocabulary. I do hope you will understand."

Flick knew straightaway that she would like Gwen Sturgis. She was an unusually tall woman, probably four inches taller than herself, Flick estimated. She was in her midsixties, quite attractive, with a small, upturned nose, a lovely complexion, and short, fashionably cut gray hair. She wore a well-tailored tweed skirt of mixed somber hues, a tan cashmere sweater, a hiker's mountain jacket, and—most surprising of all—a compact backpack. Flick glanced at Gwen's shoes: good-quality leather walking boots. She was clearly a hale and hardy woman who enjoyed traveling on foot. Flick conjured up an image of her tramping across the Scottish Highlands.

"Let's go up to my office," Nigel said. "I've asked the tearoom to prepare a cart of refreshments for us."

Flick had talked briefly with Nigel after breakfast about the wisest way to interview Gwen. "You take the lead again," he had said. "That strategy worked superbly with Nathanial, so why not with his 'bird.'" Flick had chuckled at Nigel's use of the somewhat-dated British term for girlfriend, but it seemed to fit Gwen. Her long-legged walk, the graceful way she moved, both appeared birdlike.

Flick led the way to the museum's compact service elevator. They rode up to the third floor smiling at each other and found the tea cart waiting for them alongside Nigel's desk. He dispensed the tea and coffee; Flick served scones and crumpets.

"It hasn't changed much," Nate said, as he surveyed the office. "Perhaps you can talk the trustees into newer furniture. I never could." He turned toward Gwen. "Lay claim to the sofa—it provides the only really comfortable seating in the room."

Gwen slipped out of her backpack and sat down; Nate sat next to her. Flick and Nigel positioned visitors' chairs opposite the sofa.

Flick noted that Gwen smiled affectionately at Nate, who then patted her hand. Flick felt sure that Nate had told Gwen all that had been discussed the day before.

"I thought we'd begin with the obvious question," Flick said to Gwen. "What do you remember about Etienne Makepeace?"

"A lot, actually," Gwen replied. "Etienne visited the Hawker Foundation on three occasions that I know of. Contrary to other people's experiences, he always behaved as a perfect gentleman—at least, he did when he was near me. I'd been informed, of course, of his unsavory side. Mary Hawker Evans loathed Makepeace. She told me that we had to tolerate him for the national good."

"Do you recall why he visited the Foundation?"

"He attended planning meetings with 'our friends from

the government.' That's how Mary Hawker Evans described people from the security services."

"MI6?"

"I suppose so, although she never discussed their affiliation with me. Everything that I know, I learned by typing Mrs. Evans's correspondence. I should explain—as the most junior staff member at the Foundation, it fell to me to serve as her secretary on the days she visited the Hawker Foundation."

Flick saw Nate roll his eyes. "I had to make my secretary available to her whenever Mary Hawker Evans showed up at the museum. She could be a highly demanding woman."

"But also quite sensible," Gwen said. "Mrs. Evans demanded that stringent guidelines be established to define how the people from the security services would go about their work. For example, she insisted that any 'clandestine use' of the museum's facilities take place after hours, when there were no visitors present."

"Consequently," Nate said, "the 'bigwigs' held closed-door meetings on Wednesday, when the museum was closed to the public. I recall now that we scheduled many of Makepeace's tea lectures for Tuesday evenings, so that he could attend the meetings the next day."

"I'm confused," Flick said. "Who arrived first at the museum, Etienne Makepeace or MI6?"

"As I recall," Nate replied, "they arrived more or less simultaneously." He looked at Gwen. "Am I right?"

She nodded. "They also departed at the same time. When Makepeace vanished, the visits from MI6 people stopped. In my mind, Etienne Makepeace and 'our friends from the government' are inseparable."

Flick realized that she had frowned unintentionally when Gwen added, "Does that surprise you?"

"In a way it does. I still have great difficulty imagining Makepeace as an agent for MI6. He seems an extremely indiscreet person—hardly the sort of man anyone would send on a covert mission."

Gwen laughed. "I had similar concerns about the Tea Sage, until I stopped picturing him as a tea-drinking James Bond. Consider that Makepeace's stature as an internationally renowned tea expert enabled him to travel to the Soviet Union and China at a time when most other Westerners were excluded. He could attend conferences, visit trade fairs, tour tea plantations, meet tea importers and exporters—do all sorts of things of potential value to MI6."

"Like serve as a surreptitious courier?" Flick asked.

"That sort of thing, exactly. The same is true of the agents who were 'credentialed' by the museum. As far as I know, they were all obscure academics and midlevel business people. Their apparent affiliation with the museum gave them a legitimate reason to travel behind the Iron Curtain.

"I can recall one special day when Mary Hawker Evans was in an ebullient mood. She seemed like one of those characters in a movie musical who bursts into song while walking down the sidewalk. She was full of good news and had to tell someone. So she told me more than she ought to have. One of the agents credentialed by the museum apparently played a central role in a spectacular intelligence success. He was part of a team that acquired detailed photographs of a closed Soviet 'nuclear city'—one of those places in the middle of the steppes whose name includes both words and numbers." Gwen's face brightened. "She said that one success made all the tumult with Etienne Makepeace worthwhile."

"And then Makepeace simply up and disappeared," Flick said.

Gwen made a vague gesture. "All of England seemed to hold its breath when its Tea Sage went missing. Speculating about what had happened to him became a national pastime. At least one of the London tabloids alleged that Makepeace had been abducted by aliens."

"I recall rather liking that suggestion," Nate said. "It struck me as an especially fitting way to bring down the curtain on a man of Etienne Makepeace's character." He smirked slyly. "Although becoming sustenance for a pair of sickly tea bushes fits nearly as well."

Gwen slapped his knee. "That's not funny, Nathanial. Many, many people throughout England admired, and even loved, Etienne Makepeace for the many good things he accomplished." She spoke to Flick. "Which reminds me. . ." She retrieved her backpack. "I liberated several items of Makepeace memorabilia from our archives." She unzipped the flap and reached inside. "I have a set of twelve handouts that summarize what he spoke about at his lectures. . .nine glowing reviews of his various lectures clipped from the *Kent and Sussex Courier*. . .and an autographed copy of *The Comprehensive Compendium to Tea Varieties*, probably his most popular book."

Flick glanced at Nate. His expression had become decidedly self-conscious. And so it should be. For reasons of his own, he had chosen not to warn Gwen that Makepeace might be a fraud and a plagiarist. Flick wondered what those reasons might be.

I'll bet he doesn't want to shatter Gwen's illusions. Along with much of Great Britain, she still thinks of Etienne Makepeace as England's Tea Sage.

"Moving to the other side of the Makepeace coin…," Gwen said. "I also have three letters sent to the director of the Royal Tunbridge Wells Tea Museum by female employees, complaining about Makepeace's boorish and inappropriate behavior. The authors include the clerk in the gift shop, Nate's secretary, and the curator responsible for the preservation of paper artifacts and antiquities."

"Aha! I wondered what happened to those letters," Nate said. "They vanished from my files without explanation."

"Mary Hawker Evans. . .*transferred* them to the Foundation's archives shortly before Makepeace disappeared," Gwen said. "I believe she intended to document his transgressions at the museum, but when Makepeace disappeared, the need went away." She handed the stack of materials to Flick. "You'll find these things useful should you go forward with an exhibit about Makepeace."

"We can keep these items?"

"Oh yes. They're safer here than at the Foundation. If Jeremy Strain found them in my archives, he'd order them destroyed."

Flick looked at Nigel and gave a tiny nod—their signal for him to bring out the retouched images of Martin Maltby and Rupert Perry. She handed them to Gwen.

"Do you recognize either of these men, Gwen?" Flick asked. "I know it won't be easy, because these images are not true photographs; they are our best guesses of what the men look like today."

Gwen stood and moved to the window. She looked first at one, then the other, for what seemed an eternity to Flick.

"Yes," Gwen said. She tapped the image of Martin Maltby, as had Nate the day before. "I met this man—many years ago."

"What did I tell you?" Nate said proudly. "The best memory in London."

"Do you remember his name?" Flick asked, increasingly doubtful that Gwen could dredge up a name heard "many years ago."

Gwen seemed to anticipate Flick's thoughts. "My head works in a rather strange way," she said. "I get little glimmers of recall—feelings, really—that propel me forward, until, *bang*, the full memory suddenly bursts open like a flower." She tapped Maltby's face. "Now this chap makes me think of the late King George VI, Queen Elizabeth's father."

"That's the king who replaced the fellow who abdicated, right?" Flick said.

"Indeed," Nigel said. "George VI followed Edward VIII, who reigned only a year."

Gwen spun to face them. "The penny dropped! Everyone at the Hawker Foundation called this man Bertie. He had the same *nickname* as George VI."

Flick noticed Nigel looking at her expectantly. "Nope, I'm not going to ask you how Bertie can be a nickname for George. I am aware that he grew up as 'Prince Albert.'"

"Well done!"

"You betcha!"

Gwen had turned back toward the window. Flick could see her reflection in the glass. She'd closed her eyes; not a muscle on her face moved. And then she finally spoke. "His full name can be a tongue twister. Bertrand Bartholomew. He was one of the government men who came to the Foundation." She gave the print to Flick. "This picture doesn't do him justice. Bertie was an exceptionally handsome man back then. He had a charming voice, as well."

"Yes—I remember him now," Nate said. "He was one of the MI6 chappies. He came to the museum several times for those hush-hush, closed-door meetings."

"Crikey! Martin Maltby is from MI6," Nigel said.

"Oh, I'm sure he retired years ago," Nate said. "He's older than I."

"I'm still befuddled." Nigel sighed. "A *former* MI6 operative dons a harebrained disguise, knocks on our door, and offers us a barrowful of disparaging information about Etienne Makepeace —the very same Etienne Makepeace who once was in the employ of MI6. Can anyone suggest why?"

Nigel didn't wait for anyone to answer. "I freely admit that what I know about the Cold War can be written on the back of a postage stamp. But I can't believe it was fought by knaves and lunatics. There must be a rational explanation for every crazy happenstance we've experienced this past week." He shook his head sadly. "The museum director will now step down from his soapbox."

Flick raised her hand. "I vote that the museum director bring the name 'Bertrand Bartholomew' to the attention of Conan Davies, who has eagerly sought the true identity of Martin Maltby."

Nigel sprang from his chair. "My mind is mush this morning. Here I am complaining when we've actually made spectacular progress, thanks to Gwen's memory."

"I'll tag along with you," Nate said. "Conan is one of my favorite people."

"What would you like to do now?" Flick asked Gwen, when Nigel and Nate had left.

"I'd love to see Makepeace's grave in the tea garden."

"Easily done. Step over to the window on the far wall of Nigel's office. The gravesite is still a designated crime scene, and the police have placed barrier screens around the area, but you can see the corner of the improvised grave from up here."

Gwen moved to the window. "Yes, I see it. Most interesting. But rather odd."

"Odd. In what way?"

"Nate told me that an irate husband might have done the deed. I can certainly understand a man committing a crime of passion—or an act of revenge—but when I look at your tea garden, I can't imagine the selfsame husband going to the trouble of burying the corpse beneath a tea tree." She looked back at Flick. "You may laugh at me for saying this, but this sort of spontaneous funeral seems much too complicated to have been thought up by a man. Are there any female suspects?"

"None that I've heard of." Flick wondered if the police also considered Clara Doyle a suspect. Then she realized that it would have taken a person much stronger than Clara to break into the museum, lug the body into the tea garden, dig a grave, and then replant two tea bushes over the corpse. No, a large man must have disposed of Etienne Makepeace.

Gwen abruptly changed tack. "Let me have another look

at the second photograph."

"Are you feeling an unexpected 'glimpse of recall'?"

"Merely a little tickle. But it might mean something."

Flick sat next to Gwen on the sofa while she studied the retouched image of Rupert Perry. Nigel's office was quiet enough for Flick to hear Gwen breathing and the gentle tick of the antique coach clock that reposed on a shelf above their heads.

Gwen finally spoke. "The tickle has become a gentle throb. I'm confident that I've seen this face before, probably at least twenty years ago. But the completely bald head seems wrong. More than that—I think it's confusing me."

"We can fix it," Flick said. "Follow me."

Flick guided Gwen to Hannah Kerrigan's cubicle in the Conservation Laboratory. Not unexpectedly, a British Short-hair cat lay sprawled across Hannah's workstation. That would be the next mystery to solve: Why did the museum's cats enjoy the company of the museum's Webmistress?

"Hannah, meet Gwen," she said. "Gwen and I come bearing a challenge. Can you please fire up Photoshop again?"

"Sure. What game am I playing this morning?"

Flick pushed the cat aside—it seemed large enough to be Lapsang—and dropped the print of Rupert Perry on the workstation. "We need an image of this man that's twenty years younger, with hair."

"In other words, you want me to use Photoshop like the plods use their identikits."

"Can you do it?"

"I'll have a go. The age part is easy—I'll use the 'healing brush' to soften his wrinkles and firm up his skin. But the gent's hair may turn out rather scrappy, because I'm not much of an illustrator."

Flick and Gwen watched Hannah manipulate Perry's face on the monitor. His wrinkles faded, areas of sagging skin disappeared. "Gracious," Gwen said, "I wish I had a 'healing brush' in my cosmetic bag."

"That's about a fifty-year-old face, isn't it, Dr. Adams?" Hannah looked up at Flick and smiled.

"Watch it, kid," Flick replied. "I'm not sure, either."

"Regrettably, I am," Gwen said. "The face is perfect. Now all we need is his hair."

"What sort of *do* would you like him to have?" Hannah asked.

"Well, my glimmer is rather hazy on that point. I'd say he had hair, but not a lot of it."

"Okay. I'll start with a short haircut. What color hair would you like?"

"Goodness, I have no idea."

Flick jumped in. "He's fifty, after all. Give him steel gray hair."

Hannah went to work. After five minutes, she said, "That's as good as it gets, ladies."

Flick studied the screen. Perry's new head of hair looked more like a gray cap than a collection of real tresses, but at least he was no longer completely bald.

"The glimmer is getting stronger," Gwen said. "I know I've seen that face before. But I can't think where. Can you tell me anything more about him? Even a trivial fact might jumpstart my memory."

"All I know is what he told me, which is probably not

true. He claims that his mother was Russian and his father was British."

Gwen gazed at the photograph and began to smile. "You're right; that isn't true. His family circumstances are the other way around. His mother is British, and his father is Russian. I've never met him in person, but I remember seeing two TV shows about him in the late eighties. And, of course, several news broadcasts on the telly. He was a high-ranking defector from the Soviet Union, an officer in the KGB, I believe. The sort of person you read about in a John Le Carré novel."

"Do you remember his name?"

"I think it ends with a 'kov.' "

Flick laughed. "That narrows it down to about one hundred million Russians."

Gwen shut her eyes and began to rock back and forth. "Nick. . .Nicky. . .Nicolas. . .*Nikolai*, that's it. Nikolai *Something*-kov."

Flick wanted to shake Gwen's hand, pat her back, give her an attaboy—do *something* to encourage her. But Flick knew that anything she did would merely interrupt her concentration. Hannah, too, clearly understood the need to be silent. She seemed amazed at Gwen's single-minded focus on a tiny fragment of the past.

Gwen's eyes popped open. "His name is Nikolai Melnikov. His nickname, of course, is 'Kolya.' "

"Brilliant," Hannah said, with great sincerity.

"You're amazing." Flick gave Gwen a hug. "How can we ever repay the intensity of the thinking you've done for us?"

"Nathanial mentioned that a posh lunch is on offer."

"We dine at one. Alain Rousseau, our chef, is worth a

special trip, as the guidebooks say, but even one of his spectacular lunches seems too little a reward for doing the near impossible. I fear we've taken advantage of your kindness."

"To the contrary. I enjoy delving into the past, although I rarely get as juicy an opportunity to do so at the Hawker Foundation."

Flick couldn't help staring at Gwen. *Will I ever* enjoy *delving into the past?* she wondered. The rummaging that she and Nigel had done in their own pasts had led to heartache and near disaster. They had stirred up old mistakes, moldering sins, and failed relationships—if anything, she now feared looking backwards.

Polly Reid had urged Nigel to invite "Jesus, the Dustman" into his life, to remove the old and dangerous rubble. Flick smiled at the metaphor. It had struck her as faintly irreverent at the time, but now she realized that she needed Him to "cart the muck away" as much as Nigel did. She was also a new creation. Where Nigel had the power not to sin, she would have the power not to doubt. She found that an exceptionally comforting thought.

"Let's find Nathanial and Nigel," Flick said. "I'll bet they're in our ad hoc Incident Room with Conan, swapping manly tea-museum war stories."

Flick offered her arm; Gwen took it. They descended one flight of stairs to the second floor; they walked past four visitors browsing in the Tea and Health Gallery and another three perusing the Tea in the Americas Room.

"Isn't this the Hawker family suite?" Gwen asked.

"Not anymore." Flick used her key to unlock the door. She stood in the doorway and announced, "Gwen performed a second bit of magic. She remembered who Rupert Perry really is."

Three male voices simultaneously shouted, "Who?"

Flick gestured toward Gwen like a jackpot presenter on a telly game show. Gwen acknowledged the salute with a regal wave of her hand. She stepped into the room and said, "He's Nikolai Melnikov, nickname *Kolya*, a Russian defector who came to England in the mid-1980s." She added, "Oh, yes, he's a former KGB officer."

Flick moved aside as Conan stormed out of the suite, an exceedingly determined look on his face. She, Nigel, Gwen, and Nathanial followed him downstairs—albeit at a slower pace—and made their way to the Duchess of Bedford Tearoom.

Flick had just finished an extraordinary lobster salad when she saw Conan maneuver around other diners to reach their table in the corner. The big man crouched down next to Nigel.

"Well, sir," he said, "we needed mere minutes to ascertain that Kolya Melnikov owns a farm down the road in Frant, scarcely three kilometers away from Broadwater Down. I immediately sent one of my lads over to have a look-see. Well, imagine his surprise when he discovered there were two vehicles parked in the driveway. One is an elderly Mercedes sedan. He copied down the number plate and telephoned me. I quickly confirmed, through one of my law-enforcement acquaintances who shall remain nameless, that it belongs to a Mr. Bertrand Bartholomew, current residence in Brighton."

"We found Bertie," Nigel said.

"What about the second vehicle?" Flick asked.

"That's the most interesting part, ma'am." Conan smiled.

"It seems that Mr. Nikolai Melnikov of Frant, East Sussex, is the proud owner of a dark green Ford Transit minivan."

"We found the van," Nigel said.

"This is unbelievable!" she said.

"Indeed, ma'am. It's unusual, to say the least, to see two former enemies—an MI6 operative and a KGB officer—working so closely together."

"That's not what I have in mind. What's really incredible is that Nigel and I have had the wind blown up three or four times by a pair of retired geezers."

Flick heard Nate and Gwen begin to laugh, but she didn't join in. She'd just realized who killed Etienne Makepeace.

Thirteen

Nigel leaned back in his chair and put the question to Conan, "Do you agree with Felicity? Do we have to sort things out ourselves?"

"Aye, sir," the big Scot said, with a nod. "I don't see as we have a choice—not if the museum is going to provide the bank with a satisfactory explanation on Monday. It seems like the police are perfectly content with their prime suspect and their theory of the crime. We would need time to convince them to look elsewhere, far more time than we have available." Conan slammed his right hand into his left palm. "I vote to visit the two scoundrels as quickly as possible."

Nigel looked at Flick. "Don't we run the risk of a downside if we act alone and go charging ahead without the police?"

"I never suggested that we 'charge ahead' without DI Pennyman," she said. "We'll involve him when the time is right."

"Which will be. . ."

"When we have the information we need from Bertie and Kolya. We won't make any real progress until we understand what was really going on at the museum in 1965 and 1966."

"Of course, this whole scheme presumes that your deductions are correct."

"Can you think of another way to explain the facts we know?"

Nigel sighed. "No. I wish the police were right; I wish the bloomin' jealous husband, whomever he might be, had had the gumption to shoot Etienne Makepeace. But I can't argue with your conclusions."

"Nor can I," Conan said, "although I am concerned about the holes we have to patch to make your theory hang together. Where did the Russian pistol come from, for example? The police will certainly want to know. And it would be nice if we could tell the coppers which of the two actually shot Makepeace."

Flick nodded. "We need answers to several questions—that's the number one challenge we face. But once we get them from Bertie and Kolya, the other pieces will fall into place."

"And if we don't get them, your entire scheme crumbles." Nigel tried not to sound as pessimistic as he felt. "What happens if Bertie and Kolya decide to keep mum? What if they deny everything and tell us to get lost? When you get right down to it, they gain no benefit by working together with us. And our threats don't have especially sharp teeth. We can't prove anything. All we really can pin on them is a lame practical joke."

"And your point is? You began this discussion by asking if

we have to sort things out by ourselves. What do you think?"

He sighed again. "That both of you are right. We have no other choice. It's obvious who shot Makepeace. We have to visit the farm and confront Bertie and Kolya. We have to try to push them over the edge. It may not work, but we don't have any other alternatives."

He wished for a moment that Nathanial and Gwen had stayed. They had offered to help, but it had seemed better at the time to let them go off for their weekend in Tunbridge Wells while he, Flick, and Conan decided what to do next.

At least we won't have anyone else to blame. The ball is squarely in our court.

He turned to Conan. "You've sent men to watch the odd couple?"

"Two of my largest lads, sir. They'll have no trouble keeping Bertie and Kolya at home should they decide to depart."

"Both of them are former spies; do you suppose there's a chance that they might be armed?"

"I doubt it, sir. Bertie and Kolya were chiefly bureaucrats in their respective agencies. They controlled agents in the field— they aren't the sorts who do the messy work themselves."

"I hope you're right."

"Give me the directions once more."

"Take the A267 toward Frant, then swing left on to Wadhurst Road. A few hundred yards along, make another left turn on a narrow lane that has a thick hedgerow growing on either side. You'll see a little sign that says Briar Wood Farm."

"And you'll be. . ."

"A few minutes behind you, sir, in the museum's van."

Nigel nodded. It had been Flick who suggested that the

later arrival of Conan might help convince Nikolai Melnikov and Bertrand Bartholomew to cooperate. Well, it was worth a try. He hadn't come up with a better plan.

Neither he nor Flick was especially talkative on the walk from his office to the staff car park. "I hope your scheme works," he said as he clicked open the doors to his BMW. "Our careers are toast if it doesn't."

"Look at the bright side," Flick said, a mischievous smile on her lips. "The very worst that happens is that you and I get to move to London. Perhaps we can apply to MI6 for jobs? In all likelihood, they've forgotten their past unfortunate experiences with tea people."

"Very droll."

Nigel put the car in gear. They drove in silence, not even commenting when they passed the spot on Frant Road where Melnikov's green van had forced them into the bushes.

"Ah. Frant Road is the A267," Flick finally said.

"Watch for Wadhurst Road."

"That must be it on the left."

"Got it."

"And there's the sign at the entrance to the lane."

"The lane is not much wider than my car."

"Briar Wood Farm seems the only residence served by the lane, so the odds of meeting someone coming the other way are pretty slim."

"Granted, but the odds of these blooming hedgerows scratching my paint are quite high."

Nigel drove at a leisurely pace down the lane, endeavoring to keep the BMW in the center. At last, the hedgerows came to an abrupt end.

"Good heavens," Flick said. "I expected an ugly farmhouse. Kolya lives in a fairy-tale cottage."

Nigel let out a soft whistle. Ahead, a long gravel driveway led to a wooden bridge that crossed a small stream, then continued on to a collection of buildings that included several sheds, a barn, and a farmhouse that did look like something out of a fairy tale—or more likely one of the ceramic village collections sold in Tunbridge Wells's gift shops. It had a thatched roof, a mixture of whitewashed wood and stone walls, and small windows tucked in unusual places. Nigel guessed the main part of the house had been built at least four hundred years ago, and that all manner of additional rooms and extensions had been tacked on over the years.

"I'll wager there's not a level floor or plumb wall in the whole structure," he said.

"And I'll wager that Nikolai Melnikov didn't buy Briar Wood Farm with the wages of a humble Soviet bureaucrat."

"An interesting observation. I'd say you're right."

Nigel drove across the small wooden bridge and stopped next to two large trees that stood as sentinels on either side of the driveway. They exited the BMW without slamming the doors and walked slowly toward the house.

"This is unquestionably not a working farm," Flick said. "I don't see any utility vehicles, and there's not a cow or chicken in sight. I doubt there are any in the barn; it looks more decorative than real."

"One should hardly expect live chickens this close to Tunbridge Wells in this day and age. A horse perhaps—that can add to the ambience of a proper gentleman's farm." He couldn't help raising his voice. "And there's the ruddy Ford

Transit van. How would you feel about slashing its tires?"

"Maybe later." She added, "Where do you suppose Conan's men are hiding?"

"Somewhere close to the house—I hope."

"I can see movement inside the living room, behind the curtains," he said. "This is your plan—do you have any last-minute advice?"

"Yes. Next time, please don't listen to my ideas."

"You're having second thoughts?"

"And third and fourth and fifth."

"It's too late to retreat. I just saw a curtain flutter; someone has seen us."

Nigel moved ahead of Flick to the front door. He lifted the heavy brass doorknocker and brought it down twice. He heard the thud reverberate through the old house, then the sound of shoes walking on a planked floor.

Nigel stepped backwards as the door swung inwards. He immediately recognized Nikolai Melnikov from the retouched image prepared by Hannah Kerrigan. She'd gotten the key points right: His head was shaven and his complexion leathery. Amazingly, Kolya in the flesh bore little resemblance to "Rupert Perry," a sign of the man's great skills at disguise.

"Yes?" The retired KGB officer offered a weak smile. "How can I help you? I presume that you've lost your way."

Nigel noticed a muscle twitch in Kolya's jaw, but otherwise he gave no hint that he recognized them.

Flick pushed past Nigel into the house. "Playing dumb won't work, Kolya, my boy. We know who you are, and you know who you are."

That's my Flick. Strong. Confident. Invincible.

What was left of Kolya's smile vanished. "Stand still. Make no further attempt to enter my home." He called to the next room. "Bertie, your attention is required. We have a lunatic female on our doorstep."

Nigel could hear definite vestiges of a Russian accent in Kolya's speech, which probably meant that he was feeling stress. *Good.*

Nigel moved alongside Flick into an Elizabethan version of a great room, although this particular example could easily have been mistaken for a Danish modern furniture showroom. Every piece in the room looked to be made of teak. The upholstery seemed a festival of strong primary colors. All in all, Nigel decided, an interior that had absolutely nothing in common with the exterior.

One can probably say the same thing about Kolya himself.

Nigel looked to his right as Bertrand Bartholomew entered the room. Because he hadn't seen "Martin Maltby" in person, he couldn't say how effective his disguise had been. But once again, Hannah's rendering had been remarkably on-target.

"These people claim to know who we are," Kolya said to Bertie.

"That's hardly a matter worth bragging about. We've both been on the telly, and we make no secret of our identities." He pointed to Kolya. "His name is Melnikov; my name is Bartholomew. He lives here; I live in Brighton. He used to work for the Soviet government; I used to work for Her Majesty's government."

Flick pressed on. "In fact you both have two names. Mr. Bartholomew, you sometimes call yourself Martin Maltby; and Mr. Melnikov, your occasional alias is Rupert Perry."

Bertie made a face. "I truly have no idea what you're talking about, young lady."

Flick smiled. "Wow! That sounded *utterly* sincere. It's tough to look another person in the eye and tell a barefaced lie. Is that a trick they taught you in spy school?"

"I think it's time for you to be on your way," Kolya said.

Flick reached into a manila envelope. "Okay, but before I go, let me show you Exhibit 1. I have here a photograph of Martin Maltby taken two days ago at the Royal Tunbridge Wells Tea Museum." She let the picture slip between her fingers. It fell like a leaf at Bertie's feet. She reached into the envelope again. "Here's the very same picture after a skilled digital retoucher removed the wig, nose prosthesis, mouth prosthesis, and makeup you wore. Isn't it amazing? It's *you*." She let the second picture flutter down to his feet.

Bertie shook his head. "You are mad."

"Do you think so?" Flick smiled prettily, then dropped before and after images of "Rupert Perry" face up on the floor.

Nigel took a quick glance at Bertie and Kolya. Their self-assured expressions had faded considerably. Kolya in particular had a despondent look on his face. Nigel began to relax. With each passing minute, the two retired spies seemed more and more like two old gents living out their retirements in the bucolic English countryside.

But just because they're harmless doesn't mean they will tell us anything.

"Shall we sit down and talk about it?" Flick asked.

"Talk about what?" Bertie said. His voice had lost much of its previous confidence.

"About the quid pro quo we're going to arrange. You are going to tell us your secrets, and we are going to pledge to keep them secret."

"What *secrets* do you have in mind?" Kolya asked.

"The ones we haven't figured out already that pertain to our chief topic of interest. Specifically, gentlemen, we are trying to understand Etienne Makepeace's relationship with the Royal Tunbridge Wells Tea Museum. We are convinced that you can illuminate this topic for us and answer many of our pressing questions." Flick put her hand on the back of a teakwood rocking chair. "I'm sure that we'll be more comfortable if we sit down; we're going to be here for quite a while."

"We know nothing about Etienne Makepeace other than what we've seen on the telly," Bertie said.

"We certainly have no secrets about the man," Kolya added.

"What a pity," Flick said. "If that's true, we won't be able to help each other."

"What do you mean, *help each other*?" Kolya said. "First you talk about secrets, now you talk about help. You make no sense."

"Ah. Then let me explain. You were going to help us by telling us secrets. We were going to help you by keeping you out of prison."

"We have nothing more to talk about," Kolya said. "You have no right to threaten us. Leave my house."

"Nigel, can you see if Conan has finished his examination of the green minivan?"

Bertie dashed to a front window. "*What* examination?"

Nigel moved to the front door and opened it. He made a showy wave and shouted, "Conan, how goes it?"

"I'm all finished, sir," said a disembodied voice from outside. A moment later, Conan walked through the door. "There's no doubt, it's the very same van. They made no attempt to camouflage it. We've got them trussed up like pheasants in a butcher's window. They'll go down for common assault at a minimum, more likely attempted murder."

"Who is he? And what is he talking about?"

"Oh no," Flick said, "now you're being silly. You certainly know that Conan Davies is chief of security at the museum."

"Good afternoon, gents," Conan said, "it's a pleasure to make your acquaintance after taking so many photographs of you." Conan turned a Danish modern chair around to face them and sat down.

"I've been eager to ask you a question," he said. "What game are you playing at? I can't figure it out. Why would you commit felonies in public places when you know that you'll be photographed doing the evil deeds? You're not stupid men; that much I'm sure of. But yet, you threaten these people in a car park and then attempt to run them down on Frant Road, in broad daylight."

Conan shook his head sadly. "There are only two possible answers that I've been able to come up with. The first is that you think I'm a fool and that I don't know how to watch over the people I'm hired to protect. I agree, of course, that I *might* be a fool who doesn't make use of the latest surveillance technologies. If this is what you think, you've made a serious mistake. I have high-resolution telly movies of everything you've done."

Nigel caught a glimpse of Kolya's face. His brow was sweating, and there was a definite look of panic in his eyes.

Conan went on. "My second answer is worse than the first. It's that you gentlemen are locked in some sort of mental time warp, in which dismal condition you honestly believe that the spying tradecraft you learned during the 1950s and 1960s can still be used during the first decade of the twenty-first century."

He lifted his hands in an inquiring gesture. "Is it possible that you believe a disguise composed of a wig, some theatrical makeup, and a simple facial prosthesis can defeat a modern, multispectral surveillance camera and digital image correction? If so, you're too much of a danger to yourselves to be allowed out on your own. I suggest, for your own safety, you hire a guardian to watch over you."

Nigel held his breath. Flick and Conan had played their trump cards. If Bertie and Kolya refused to cooperate now—well, the good guys would have to slink away.

Nikolai Melnikov smiled. "If we're going to have a chat, I'd best prepare some tea for Felicity and coffee, I suppose, for Nigel. Conan—what would you like?"

"Tea is perfect, sir."

"Kolya, what are you doing?" Bertie growled.

Kolya smiled. "I'm being hospitable. That's really the sort of person I am."

"They're bluffing."

"I think not, Bertie. You can see the pictures they brought. We needed hours to build those disguises; their camera saw through them in seconds." He heaved a deep sigh. "The world has changed. We are decades behind the times, my friend."

Nigel glanced at Flick. The expression on her face hadn't changed. *Good.* The slightest hint of gloating or self-satisfaction might cause Kolya to reverse course. Their "win" seemed exceptionally fragile; one could almost sense the brittle atmosphere in the room.

Bertie shrugged. "I don't suppose it makes much difference, although I really wanted that knighthood. All the section heads I worked with have found their way to the *honors list*—and most of them are younger than I."

"You know that I wish you well, Bertie; many late-age knighthoods are announced each year. But you also know how I feel. Becoming a knight is nothing but a decadent, bourgeois remnant of the failed English class system. The so-called honor is not worthy of you, my friend."

"You're saying that merely to cheer me up."

"True—but my efforts should prove that I care about you." He added, "Now, what would you like to drink?"

"Do you have any Ovaltine left?"

"For you, always."

Flick chimed in. "Kolya, would you like me to help in the kitchen?"

"That would be most welcome, Felicity."

Nigel exchanged stares with Conan. He could guess what his security chief was thinking. When had their carefully orchestrated interrogation session become a tea party?

Flick placed one of the heavily laden trays on a low table near the great room's large hearth, then stepped aside so Kolya could put his tray down. She surveyed the arrangements. The refreshments were in easy reach of five Danish armchairs

Nigel and Conan had arrayed around the table: She, Nigel, and Conan would sit on one side, Kolya and Bertie on the other. Flick took her seat; the four men quickly followed.

"May I ask a preliminary question?" Bertie said.

"Of course," she answered.

"You talked about establishing a quid pro quo earlier. Why were you prepared to keep our secrets secret?"

"Because the pair of you worked so diligently to send us messages, we presume that you have a sound reason for wanting to discourage an exhibit about Etienne Makepeace."

Flick glanced at Bertie. He seemed wholly satisfied with her explanation. She made a show of stirring her cup of tea. There was no need to tell them that she had thought of the phrase because DI Pennyman had offered her a reciprocal arrangement a few days earlier. Besides, "quid pro quo" had such a charming ring to it.

The room grew quiet. Flick realized that everyone was looking at her expectantly. *Showtime.* She took a deep breath and began.

"Let's start with the secrets we know, shall we? The first of these is that Etienne Makepeace worked for MI6. He was a British intelligence agent."

Bertie made a soft groaning sound; Kolya began to chuckle.

"It is perfectly true," the Russian said, "that Makepeace *appeared* to work for MI6. In fact, he was on *my* payroll. First and foremost, England's Tea Sage was a Soviet spy. His code name was *Chai*." His chuckle became a deep, rumbling laugh.

Flick heard Nigel cough and Conan huff. She herself uttered a slight squeak of surprise.

"Crikey!" Nigel exclaimed. "Are you saying that Etienne Makepeace was a double agent?"

Bertie grimaced. "The man turned out to be perfidy personified. Of course, we had no idea at the time."

"By 'we,'" Flick said, "you mean MI6."

Bertie nodded. "The Secret Intelligence Service. I was a section head during the 1960s. Who could have guessed that Makepeace was working for the Russkies? A shame, really, he was a perfect match after I organized the. . .*activities* at the tea museum."

"That was your idea?"

"Indeed it was." Bertie nodded again. "A grand idea, too, until Makepeace betrayed us. All of the credentialed agents were known to the KGB before they left England."

"I heard that one of them scored an intelligence coup."

Bertie rolled his eyes. "Ah, yes. The so-called Soviet nuclear city. . ."

Kolya jumped in. "We took many of those pictures in the back alleys of Birmingham and Leeds."

"He's joking, of course."

"Okay. The back alleys of Minsk and Pinsk." Kolya laughed again. "Now you understand why MI6 had Makepeace killed. When they learned he was a double agent loyal to us, they panicked. The Brits didn't want another spy scandal just three years after the defection of Kim Philby to the Soviet Union. So 'MI6 done him in,' as my cleaning lady might say, then disposed of the inconvenient corpse in your museum's tea garden." He bent his fingers into the shape of a pistol. "Bang! *Good-bye, Mr. Makepeace.*"

"We did no such thing," Bertie countered. "This is a

civilized country. We would have arrested Makepeace—given him a show trial—embarrassed the Russians. It's now clear to me that the KGB *eliminated* him."

"Think, Bertie! Use your British noggin. Why would we kill one of our most effective operatives?"

"Probably because Makepeace was as mad as a March hare. He'd gone round the bend, become too unstable to rely on."

"*Tufta!*" Kolya made a dismissive gesture. "Nonsense! I keep telling you, but you don't believe me. We were *delighted* when Etienne began to pinch ladies' bottoms and make a fool of himself. We hoped that his actions would embarrass MI6."

Bertie spoke to Flick. "In recent days, this has become a point of significant disagreement between us. As you can see, we have agreed to disagree."

Flick fought to maintain what she hoped was a non-committal expression. On top of her surprise to learn that Etienne Makepeace had betrayed Britain during the Cold War, she also realized that neither Bertie nor Kolya understood how—and why—Makepeace had died. How they would react, she wondered, when they learned the truth?

"When did the Soviets 'turn' Mr. Makepeace?" she asked. "I believe that's the correct term."

Bertie offered another sorrowful groan.

Kolya smiled. "The Brits *never* turned Etienne Makepeace. I created him. He was my idea. A spy designed to penetrate the British gentry. What better person than an expert on tea? He soon became our pipeline to Britain's upper crust. He went to parties, met influential people, and picked up many tidbits, useful intelligence. An amazing success, if I say so myself." He lifted his hand, palms outward. "Alas, he became far more famous than I intended him to—and the worst aspects of his personality emerged."

Kolya went on. "It was also my idea to have Makepeace offer himself to MI6 as a potential agent. Naturally, they clutched him to their collective bosom. The rest, as they say, is history. Once welcomed to the museum, he had the run of the place. He spent time with the chief curator, so he was able to learn who was doing real research and who wasn't—and he even used your library to find obscure tea publications to plagiarize."

"And one day Makepeace vanished," Flick said.

Bertie nodded. His voice became somber. "It was during the massive national search for Etienne Makepeace that we discovered his link to the KGB. We realized at once that he had betrayed us. Of course, I terminated every project that he'd touched. I immediately severed MI6's relationship with the Royal Tunbridge Wells Tea Museum."

"We thought it happened the other way around," Kolya said. "We assumed that Makepeace disappeared after the Brits learned he was really a KGB agent."

Flick peered first at Bertie, then at Kolya. "I presume you used to be enemies during the Cold War."

"Deadly enemies," Bertie said.

"Without doubt," Kolya agreed.

Flick noted that they looked affectionately at each other.

"And yet, you've become friends. How did that happen?"

Kolya led off. "We bumped into one another about ten years ago. Literally. In a car park in Tunbridge Wells. I pulled out of a parking spot and dented Bertie's fender. We recognized each other and exchanged small talk."

Bertie took over. "We discovered that we lived a short drive apart, we began to meet socially, and we soon became good friends."

"And why not?" Kolya finished up. "We're two over-the-hill Cold Warriors with much in common." Another laugh. "What's more, we can talk to each other without worrying about the Official Secrets Act. I know all his secrets; he knows some of mine."

Flick was about to ask another question when Nigel, who had been quietly sipping his coffee, found his voice. "The discovery of Makepeace's body seems to have caught both of you by surprise."

"I was astounded," Bertie said. "For many years, I believed that Etienne had disappeared into the USSR after his triumph at the museum—much like Kim Philby. But when you discovered his body, I realized that the KGB had assassinated him."

Kolya snorted. "I have explained to you a thousand times, we did nothing of the sort." He added. "If we had, his body *never* would have been found."

"I posed my question awkwardly," Nigel said. "What I meant to ask is, why were you both upset by the discovery of Makepeace's remains?"

Flick felt startled by the coincidence. This was the precise question she had planned to ask Bertie and Kolya.

"I would have thought the answer is obvious," Bertie said. "The sudden reappearance of Etienne Makepeace turned a spotlight on things that neither of us wanted England to remember."

"Such as?" Nigel prompted.

Bertie sighed. "What would the reaction be should the

general public learn that members of Her Majesty's Secret Intelligence Service had conscripted the Royal Tunbridge Wells Tea Museum to support spying on the Soviet Union?"

Flick answered first. "Outrage."

"*Outrage. . . ,*" Bertie echoed, softly. "People today don't understand the challenges we faced during the Cold War. At my stage of life, the very last thing I need is to become a lightning rod for public indignation, or more likely a scapegoat. I'd be pilloried, blamed for everything—for turning England's Tea Sage into a spy, for causing his disappearance, even for failing to tell his kin what I knew at the time he disappeared."

"No doubt Bertie is right," Kolya said. "You Brits are remarkably touchy about things that happened long ago. I've come to enjoy my comfortable 'English squire' lifestyle; I have friends throughout the neighborhood. But I doubt that my neighbors would remain cordial should they learn about my role as a Soviet spymaster in Britain. I, too, would be blamed for helping to destroy one of England's national heroes."

Kolya went on. "There is also another minor matter. . . ." Flick saw him begin to blush. "I fell in love with Tunbridge Wells when I was overseeing Makepeace. It is so conservative, capitalistic, *English*. Naturally, it was the first town I thought of when MI6 asked me where I wanted to live after I defected. Fortunately, I had. . .*accumulated* some personal funds in a Caribbean bank which enabled me to purchase Briar Wood Farm."

Flick managed to stifle her laugh. Koyla had undoubtedly stolen from the KGB for years. He, too, did not want a 'spotlight' illuminating the things he had done during the 1960s. She couldn't stop herself from saying, " 'Things without remedy should be without regard; what is done, is done.' "

"Exactly! I wish the English would see 'the Scottish play' performed more often."

Flick retook control of the conversation. "How did you attempt to dim the spotlight that Etienne Makepeace's reappearance had turned on?"

"I thought we were quite clever, actually," Bertie's voice bubbled with pride. "I conceived our plan. It had two distinct objectives." He held up this thumb. "Our first goal was to provide the police—and the media—with a credible explanation for Makepeace's death that had absolutely *nothing* to do with the MI6 or the KGB. I concluded that the obvious solution was to offer the authorities a jealous husband." He gave a self-satisfied nod. "We understand that the police and the media have taken quite a fancy to the case we've built."

Flick gazed at the floor. *Well, most of the police are happy with the jealous-husband theory.*

"If I may ask a question, sir," Conan said. "How did you invent a jealous husband?"

"We didn't need to," Bertie said. "We had at our disposal a genuine husband that Etienne Makepeace had made jealous. His name was Hugh Doyle."

Flick cringed to hear Doyle's name. *Oh well, I didn't break my word.* She hoped that DI Pennyman would believe her.

Bertie continued. "Hugh Doyle was a bricklayer, a workman who actually helped to build your museum. In his off hours, he provided muscle for a local hoodlum and took part in a hijacking or two." He glanced at Kolya. "That's right, isn't it?"

Kolya nodded. "I was forced to learn more than I wanted to about Hugh Doyle to get him off Etienne's back. The man was an authentic villain."

Flick let herself smile. Pennyman had said the same thing about Doyle.

Kolya kept speaking. "Doyle had a wife, a tarty barmaid who worked at a now-defunct pub in Tunbridge Wells. I forget the name. . . ."

"The Horse and Garter," Bertie offered.

"Thank you, The Horse and Garter. The least-pleasant pub in Tunbridge Wells. Providentially, it was demolished years ago." He frowned, seemingly plagued with an unpleasant memory. "In any event, Etienne chanced to stop in at The Horse and Garter. He met Clara, and nature took its course."

"Is that when Doyle threatened Makepeace?" Nigel asked. "We received information that a jealous husband had confronted Makepeace in a pub. . . ." Nigel blinked. "Whoops! I forgot that *you* sent the message. You're 'Anonymous Bystander.'"

Kolya offered an apologetic shrug. "To answer your question, the confrontation came later. Hugh Doyle was a practical villain. He knew that Etienne was fairly well-off and saw this as an opportunity to make a few bob. He hired a private investigator to follow Makepeace and Clara around—an investigator who was an excellent surveillance photographer." Kolya laughed. "I'll tell you how good he was. He took photos of a secret meeting between Makepeace and me in a bus station waiting room. Even I didn't know he was there. Fortunately, my face is hidden by a newspaper."

Flick laughed along with Kolya. *Well, that explains the other photos taped to our wall.*

Kolya made a fist as a gesture of emphasis. "Armed with

his set of compromising photographs, Hugh Doyle attempted to extract money from Makepeace—who, being a spendthrift, had very little available. That's when the yelling began and Hugh threatened to kill Makepeace."

"But Doyle didn't kill Makepeace?" Nigel asked.

Koyla shook his head. "I sent a bag of banknotes to Hugh Doyle to buy him off. The money was delivered by two KGB thugs who suggested that Doyle give them the photographs and leave town immediately."

"He moved to Scotland and became a greengrocer," Flick said.

"So I heard. My money clearly benefited the British economy."

"He also changed his name."

"I'm not surprised. I chose two exceedingly large thugs."

No one seemed in the mood to speak for several moments. Bertie broke the silence. "So much for our campaign to confuse the police and the media. Frankly, we never doubted our success with them. We considered our greatest challenge to be the Royal Tunbridge Wells Tea Museum."

"That baffles me," Flick said. "Why would you care if we gathered information about Makepeace through our Web site or created an exhibit about him?"

"Why did we care?" Bertie said. "Look around this room. You've found us—the police have not."

"Only because you threatened us."

He exhaled slowly. "*We* felt threatened first. We knew that your exhibits, your research programs, your academic conferences would set the stage for *endless* digging into Etienne Makepeace's life by hundreds of people. You would make it impossible for Makepeace to be forgotten. Sooner or later—probably sooner—everything we wanted to keep secret would be known."

He held up his thumb and index finger. "Our second objective was to encourage you to abandon the research you'd begun in preparation for an exhibit."

"That's where you made a mistake. Our research, as you call it, is a short-term investigation to keep our bank happy. We haven't decided what to do about an exhibit."

"Oh dear."

"You didn't have to frighten us in the car park or attack us on Frant Road or try to cancel our upcoming academic conference."

"You're right, of course. Three egregious mistakes. Endless apologies. But please understand, we would never have hurt anyone. We sought to apply mild coercion and threats—just enough to discombobulate you, to make you rethink your plans."

"You certainly did that."

"Our chief strategy was to tell you the absolute truth about Etienne Makepeace. We presumed that once you understood he was a fraud, a plagiarist, and a harasser of women, you would lose interest in creating an exhibit about him."

Flick nodded. "You may have accomplished that, too."

Conan raised his hand. "I have a question about Mr. Makepeace. Reputedly, he was a very bright person. He earned a First at Cambridge, after all. And yet—look at the way he behaved. How do you square these two opposing facts?"

Kolya nodded. Flick guessed that his faint smile conveyed a hint of sadness. "I knew Etienne Makepeace for almost ten years and could never explain Etienne's inconsistencies. He was bright, but also incredibly lazy. Competent when he wanted to be, but otherwise sloppy. Sensible about many things, but an absurdly foolish *babnik* when it came to women."

"One might say, *fatally* foolish," Flick said. "That's what got him killed."

"It's certainly a possibility," Kolya said. "But we'll never know for sure."

"Not so," Nigel said. "We *do* know for sure."

He smiled at Flick. "Congratulations, my dear—I'm convinced. There can't be any other explanation. Not even MI6 or the KGB."

Bertie leaned across the low table toward Flick. "You know who shot Etienne Makepeace?"

Flick nodded.

Kolya said, *"Obaldet!"*

Flick looked at her watch. Four thirty. *Too late on a Saturday afternoon to sort things out.*

"Be at the museum tomorrow at one," she said. "We'll meet in the tea garden. That's where the story began, and that's where it will end."

FOURTEEN

At twelve forty-five on Sunday afternoon, Nigel pushed the remains of his roast beef sandwich aside, sipped instant coffee he had prepared in his office, and scanned his checklist one more time:

Security guard stationed at front entrance to admit "participants."
Other security guards at rear and side entrance to discourage "unanticipated departures."
Round table (to accommodate eight people) set up in tea garden, with large umbrella if necessary.
Eight chairs.
Tea, coffee, and snacks for eight (set up on side table).
Memory-jogging item (as suggested by Flick).
All necessary "participants" invited (and invitations accepted).
Check weather forecast; provide guest umbrellas if rain likely.

Everything was ready; he had toured the tea garden and

verified that the items on the checklist had in fact been completed. The weather had cooperated admirably; they would enjoy a springlike afternoon in the tea garden, with sufficient clouds passing overhead to make a sun umbrella unnecessary.

All was well, yet Nigel felt anxious. He wasn't surprised; he often experienced a touch of stage fright before chairing important meetings.

Flick and he had returned to his office after their Saturday visit to Briar Wood Farm. She had been adamant about today. "You are the director of the Royal Tunbridge Wells Tea Museum," she had said. "He works for you, and so does she. You are duty bound to lead the meeting tomorrow. It will also look less suspicious if you issue the invitations."

"Will they come?"

"Why not? They both live nearby—and you aren't asking for much. Merely a few minutes of their time after church on a Sunday afternoon to talk about the future of the museum. They won't know until they get here that we really plan to talk about the past."

"I suppose. . . ."

Flick had moved behind his desk and perched on his lap. "What's really bothering you?"

"I hate all this uncertainty. Once again, we're organizing a meeting that could fizzle like a dud firework should the principal participants decide to clam up. We were lucky today—but tomorrow could be a gold-plated disaster."

She had pecked his cheek. "Well, I'll let you brood about tomorrow on your own."

"Oh? And what will you be doing while I grind my teeth to mere nubs?"

"I'll begin to assemble our presentation to Wescott Bank."

"Our plan was to do that on Sunday."

"I thought I'd get a head start. We don't have any time to waste."

"I concur fully."

He had kissed her, and once again, she had kissed him back.

Nigel looked at his checklist again. The one item he had not written down—on the off chance that Flick would happen across the list—was, "Say an appropriate prayer before the meeting."

Nigel wished that he had better skills at ad hoc praying. He found it difficult to frame a coherent prayer on the fly. Even now, all he could think of was a rather tepid petition: *Heavenly Father, we are relying on You to take charge of our meeting today, to guide our actions every step of the way, to sort out truth from lies, to ensure that everything turns out according to Your plan.*

Nigel had no difficulty speaking extemporaneously to his colleagues—why then did he feel awkward talking with God? Probably, he decided, because he wasn't fully comfortable turning his problems over to God. He wanted to remain in control, to snatch his problems back and solve them himself. Well, that would be something to work on in the months ahead.

That morning, Flick and he had once again attended Holy Trinity with Christ Church in Tunbridge Wells. He'd seen a bumper sticker on the car in the adjacent parking space. "God is God, and you are *not*."

I certainly hope so, because I can use Your help today, even though I'm not at all especially good at asking for it.

The alarm on his desk clock began to beep. Five minutes before one.

Nigel walked down three flights of stairs, through the World of Tea Map Room, through the Duchess of Bedford Tea Room, through the greenhouse, and into the tea garden. The stage fright hadn't left him, but it seemed less menacing now that the meeting was about to begin. One of his old colleagues, an expert public speaker, had explained, "The trick with stage fright is to get the butterflies in your stomach to fly in formation. Then they'll help you give a better performance."

Nigel made a mental note: *Send a letter of commendation to Jim Sizer.* He had been a good sport that day. Without asking for an explanation, he'd cheerfully reported for work early on a Sunday morning and set up a large, round table and eight chairs in the Chinese Teas exhibit area across the garden from Makepeace's grave. Jim had cleverly placed the refreshments table athwart the garden's winding redbrick walkway, putting it only a few steps away from where everyone would be seated.

Nigel spotted a small thermal carafe. More out of habit than need, he pumped a cup of black coffee for himself, then sat down next to Flick. She was chatting animatedly with Kolya about this year's forecast crop of Darjeeling tea. Across the table, DI Pennyman and Bertie were complaining to each other about soaring tax rates in Kent. Conan, sitting next to Bertie, waited for Nigel to get comfortable, then said, "Big day, sir. I'll be delighted to see quit of this muddle, won't you?"

"Indeed, I will," he said, just as Mirabelle Hubbard and Trevor Dangerfield walked into the tea garden.

"Good afternoon, sir," she said. "I hope we're not late."

"You're right on time, Mirabelle. Please join us."

Nigel smiled as brightly as he could. Mirabelle smiled back, but Trevor—seeing three men he didn't know sitting at the table—clearly sensed something was wrong. He stopped a few paces away and said, "Pardon, sir, you did say that this meeting was to talk about the future of our docent program. . . ."

"In a way, it is. Let me introduce you to our guests. This gentleman next to Dr. Adams is Nikolai Melnikov, formerly with the Soviet KGB. That is Bertrand Bartholomew, late of Her Majesty's Secret Intelligence Service, and to his left is Detective Inspector Marc Pennyman of the Kent Police."

Nigel heard both Mirabelle and Trevor gasp at the mention of Pennyman's name. The wind seemed to leave their sails simultaneously, and they dropped limply into the two empty seats at the table.

"What is this about?" Trevor croaked. His voice had aged a decade in seconds.

Nigel looked at Mirabelle and said softly, "Mirabelle, during the month of September 1966, you had an altercation with Etienne Makepeace that eventually led to his death. Can you tell us about it?"

Trevor put his hand atop Mirabelle's. "That won't be necessary, sir; there's no need to trouble Mirabelle. I killed Mr. Makepeace by myself. She had nothing to do with the crime in question."

Nigel nodded. He'd expected Trevor to be chivalrous. He had even worked out a strategy to respond.

"I see. Can you tell me why you killed him, Trevor?"

"Because Mr. Makepeace was a bad man, sir. He treated us all badly. He deserved to die."

"That being the case, you decided to shoot him?"

"Well, sir, it was a toss-up between knife and gun—they taught me how to use both in the Royal Marines—but the pistol won. Less personal, if you take my meaning."

Pennyman abruptly spoke up. "So, Mr. Dangerfield, you shot Makepeace with an old service pistol you had somehow acquired."

"Yes, sir, a Browning 9-millimeter automatic. I'd kept it after I was demobbed from the marines. It's long gone now, but I had it then—kept it in my locker at the museum. I used the weapon to shoot Mr. Makepeace."

"Amazing. How did you accomplish such an unusual feat of small arms ballistics?"

"Accomplish *what*, sir?"

"You apparently fired a 9.2-millimeter Makarov round through a pistol chambered for the 9-millimeter Parabellum cartridge. I merely wondered how you did it."

"Well. . ." Trevor stared at the table, his face suddenly bright red.

"It's no good, Trevor," Mirabelle said. "We have to tell them the truth." She sighed. "They seem to have figured it out, anyway." She looked at Nigel. "You asked about an 'altercation' with Mr. Makepeace—there were actually several, sir."

"We suspected as much, Mirabelle. We knew that Makepeace had revealed his swinish nature to female employees throughout the museum. According to Nathanial Swithin, not even his secretary was immune from Makepeace's advances.

That's why we were a bit surprised when you told us that Etienne Makepeace was a vague blur in your mind and that you'd never been formally introduced to him."

Nigel winked at Flick. She had been the one to recognize the inconsistency. He hoped she wouldn't mind his use of "we"; they were, after all, in this together.

Nigel reached into the inside pocket of his jacket. "With your permission, Mirabelle, I would like to read a letter that you wrote to Nathanial Swithin on 13 September 1966. That was a Tuesday, by the way."

A look of astonishment crossed the elderly woman's face. "My letter? From back then?"

"Indeed. May I read it to everyone?"

"If you wish, sir. I'm not ashamed of what I wrote."

"To the contrary. You should be proud of yourself." Nigel smoothed the letter flat on the table, cleared his throat, and began. "Dear Mr. Swithin—it pains me to write like this to you, but I need your assistance in ending the intolerable and inappropriate behavior of Mr. Etienne Makepeace toward me during his Wednesday visits to the museum.

"This has gone on for three successive Wednesdays and has disturbed me greatly. I have explained to Mr. Makepeace over and over again that I am a married woman and have no interest in his repeated advances. He keeps insisting, however, that he much prefers 'married birds.'

"Tomorrow will be the fourth Wednesday since he began bothering me. I am quite concerned that he will attempt to follow me around the museum and accost me should he find me alone. I ask that you give your immediate attention to this matter.

"Yours faithfully, Mrs. Mirabelle Hubbard."

Nigel let the letter fall onto the table.

"Did Mr. Swithin solve the problem for you on Wednesday, 14 September?"

"No, sir." Mirabelle averted her eyes. "He never came in to work that day. We heard later that he went to London for a meeting at the Hawker Foundation."

"Were your fears realized? Did Etienne Makepeace accost you?"

Mirabelle nodded. "Late in the afternoon, sir. I was in the tearoom when Mr. Makepeace appeared out of nowhere. I made a mistake; instead of running toward the museum, I fled into the greenhouse."

"I best take over now, sir," Trevor said. "There's no reason to make Mirabelle talk about. . .what happened."

"An excellent idea, Trevor. Carry on."

"I was in the Welcome Centre kiosk when I heard a scream from the greenhouse. It took me perhaps ten seconds to get there. When I arrived, I saw that Mr. Makepeace had cornered Mirabelle and had shoved her down on one of the potting benches. He kept saying, 'Why are you fussing? All I want is a bit of crumpet.'

"I pulled him away from Mirabelle and poked him in the solar plexus—rather hard. As you would expect, he fell to his knees. He puffed and wheezed and struggled to catch his breath for the better part of a minute. He would have recovered more quickly, but the whole time on his knees, he kept cursing me for all he was worth.

"Well, sir, I thought the worst was over, but then he took a small, black pistol out of his pocket and pointed it at me. I knew what to do, of course. My Royal Marines training took over, almost without my thinking about it. I brought my left arm sideways in a parrying blow and knocked the gun out of his hand. I watched it skitter along the concrete floor and come to rest underneath one of the workbenches.

"Well, Mr. Makepeace was a good fighter, too. When he observed that I had taken my eyes off him, he gave me a push that sent me reeling. He immediately leaped for the pistol; I saw his fingers brush against it. I knew that I had to stop him before he could aim the gun at me. I had no doubt that he intended to shoot.

"I struggled to my feet and tackled him as hard as I could. The gun was now between us—he gripping it in his right hand, my left hand pushing it back toward him. The gun suddenly went off, and he dropped like a stone." Trevor gave a smile of relief. "That's the whole story. The God's honest truth."

The tea garden went silent. All Nigel could hear was a gentle rush of breeze through the leaves of the evergreen tea trees arrayed behind him. Bertie was the first to speak.

"I'm sorry I doubted you, Kolya. It's clear to me that the KGB did not eliminate Etienne Makepeace."

"And I you, Bertie. I plan to rethink my views of MI6."

Pennyman made a face. "If you gentlemen are through reliving the Cold War, I have a relevant question or two." He stared hard at Bertie, then at Kolya. "As I understand the situation back in 1966—and I'm largely dependent on Dr. Adams for my knowledge—Etienne Makepeace worked. . . *simultaneously* for both the British and Soviet governments. However, it seems that his primary allegiance was toward the

Soviet intelligence establishment. Is that a factual summary?"

"Unfortunately so," Bertie said.

Kolya made a soft grunt that Nigel took as a polite, non-boasting yes.

Pennyman went on. "The small, black pistol that we found buried beneath Makepeace's remains is a Markarov automatic of Soviet manufacture. We have yet to establish as an unquestionable fact that it is the very same small, black pistol described by Mr. Dangerfield—but let's make the logical assumption that Makepeace was walking the streets of Tunbridge Wells in 1966 in possession of a loaded Soviet firearm." He stared again at Kolya. "Why would you give a man like Etienne Makepeace a lethal weapon?"

Kolya held up his hands, palms open, in a gesture of conciliation. "Naturally, it was not my decision. Early in 1966, Makepeace attended a training session in Eastern Europe for intelligence officers. He returned with the pistol. He was proud of the weapon and seemed to enjoy having it with him. I advised him that carrying an illegal handgun in Great Britain added a foolish, incalculable risk to everything he did, but alas he didn't believe me."

Pennyman shook his head heavily, then turned to Trevor. "The events you just described, Mr. Dangerfield, might well represent a case of justifiable homicide under British law." He glanced at Flick. "What you Americans label self-defense." Then back to Trevor: "You apparently came to Mrs. Hubbard's aid valiantly, at considerable risk to yourself. Why didn't you call the Kent Constabulary immediately and report what happened?"

"That was my doing, sir," Mirabelle said. "Mr. Makepeace

was famous—England's Tea Sage—and he had a good name. I felt that no one would have believed that he attacked me. I was good-looking back then, and like the other ladies at the museum, I wore a miniskirt. Everyone would have said that I led him on. I insisted that we not call the police."

Trevor added, "I buried his pistol with him—inside a protective box I took from the museum's archives—with the idea it might help us prove our innocence, should we ever be charged with a crime." He sat up tall in his chair. "On that subject, sir, will we be charged with a crime?"

"You ought to be. You inconvenienced tens of thousands of people. Your decision to bury Makepeace set in motion a nationwide search that lasted months and created a mystery that endured for forty years." He let air flutter though his lips. "However. . .finish your story. Etienne Makepeace is lying in front of you. What did you do next?"

"Well, sir. . ." Nigel noticed that Trevor looked skyward and his eyes lost focus. He seemed to be pushing himself deeper into the distant past. "The very first thing I did was to ascertain that he was dead. There was no doubt about that at all. Next, we verified that we were alone in the museum. I remember feeling worried that someone nearby might have heard the shot and called the police—but no police ever knocked on the door.

"Mirabelle and I talked for quite a while about what to do, and then we decided to bury him in the tea garden. We had all the tools we needed in the greenhouse, of course, and I found an extra tarpaulin in the storeroom next to the greenhouse to wrap around the body. We didn't have a coffin, but Mirabelle came up with the idea of covering him with roofing tiles. There were several stacks out back that the construction company hadn't carted away after they finished the building.

Mirabelle chimed in. "That was another mistake I made. If I'd been less concerned about giving the man a proper burial, those two Assam tea trees would have been half as tall as the museum by now."

Nigel bit back a smile. *And the world would still be searching for Etienne Makepeace.*

Trevor went on. "It was easy to clean up the blood in the greenhouse—we rinsed the floor with a hose. Actually, our biggest challenge was Mirabelle's husband. She wanted to help me, but he expected her home after work. We came up with a clever solution. Mirabelle went home, and then I called with an 'emergency request' to come back. She was able to spend two hours helping me dig the grave.

"It took me most of the night to restore the ground around the tea trees. I had to risk leaving the lights on while I worked. Very frightening, it was. But no one came by."

Pennyman nodded. "One last question. It's surprising to me that no one realized that Etienne Makepeace went missing on September 14. Did you do anything to cover up his disappearance?"

"No. We were lucky. He intended to take the train back to London later that afternoon. We didn't say anything. No one ever asked us about him."

"Do you have anything to add, Mrs. Hubbard?"

Mirabelle sighed. "No. You have the whole story."

Flick reached across the table and patted Mirabelle's hand. "Did you ever figure out what Makepeace meant when he called you a 'crumpet'?"

"Oh, ma'am. . ." Mirabelle began to blush.

Nigel couldn't help laughing. He noted that the other men around the table were also chuckling or sniggering. He decided to explain. "*Crumpet* is a term that Brits often use to describe objects of their desire. For example, when I look at you, I am tempted to say, "Felicity Adams is the thinking man's crumpet.""

Once again, the other men at the table—even DI Pennyman—reacted with bursts of, "Hear! Hear!" and "Indeed!" and "Well said, Nigel!"

"I get the idea," Flick said, as she threw a crumpled piece of paper at him.

Mirabelle, though, seemed lost in thought. She finally said, "Mr. Makepeace kept saying, 'All I want is crumpet.' " She sniffed. "I guess I was his final crumpet."

Flick looked at the seven other people sitting around the table and decided that the most interesting person in sight was DI Pennyman. His face seemed unusually animated; his eyes darted back and forth, his fingers drummed on the tabletop. What, Flick wondered, would he decide to do?

Surprisingly, he abruptly leaned back in his chair and said, "Does anyone have any advice for me?"

Kolya answered immediately. "Let sleeping dogs lie. Hugh Doyle killed Etienne Makepeace."

Flick smiled at the expatriate Russian. *At least he's consistent in his use of clichés.*

"You think so?" Pennyman said.

"During my youth," Kolya said, "I was a policeman for eight years. I achieved a rank not far from yours. I can say with some certainty that your superiors will not be pleased if you take Hugh Doyle away from them."

Pennyman nodded. "We might say he's a classic villain."

"Without doubt, a smuggler, a hijacker, an extortionist, and a murderer. An evildoer *worthy* of Etienne Makepeace."

"Was Doyle really an extortionist? We didn't know that."

"The police will have more evidence by. . .*say* Wednesday."

"Doyle did threaten Etienne Makepeace."

"Noisily. In public."

"And he did flee to Scotland."

"Why would anyone relocate up there unless it was to escape prosecution?"

"An excellent point."

"All in all, Hugh Doyle is easily understood. An evil man who overreacted when his good wife succumbed to the obvious charms of England's Tea Sage. The 1960s, after all, were a *flexible* time in England. Infidelity was common—one can forgive Etienne for sinning in that manner. And one can feel sorry that he ran afoul of Hugh Doyle."

"On the other hand, Trevor Dangerfield and Mirabelle Hubbard have confessed to—to. . .*something*."

"Indeed, they have." Kolya gestured with his index finger. "Two elderly people with questionable memories. Have they a scrap of proof of their outrageous claims? No. It's their feeble word against a significant quantity of documentary evidence that two public-spirited citizens have provided to the authorities."

"Another excellent point." Pennyman turned to Trevor. "Mr. Dangerfield, exactly how old are you?"

"I turned seventy-nine last month, sir."

"Amazing. You look much younger. How's your memory?"

He began to grin. "Well, now that you and Mr. Melnikov mention it, I don't suppose it's all that good. In the Royal Marines, I spent a good deal of time near weapons that made lots of noise."

"What about Mrs. Hubbard?"

"She's only seventy-four but has been known to have her senior moments."

Pennyman nodded. "Thank you, Mrs. Hubbard and Mr. Dangerfield, for your most interesting input. You've definitely assisted my inquiries. I will, of course, take everything you've told me under advisement, but I would note that the present course of our investigation seems to be propelling us in a significantly different direction."

"Praise God" said Mirabelle.

"Praise God, indeed," murmured Flick.

Thirty minutes later, the group sitting around the table had dwindled to a "precious few"—Flick thought—of Nigel, Kolya, Bertie, and herself.

" 'It is a tale told by an idiot,' " she murmured, " 'full of sound and fury, signifying nothing.' "

"More Shakespeare?" Nigel said.

"More *Macbeth*."

"You sound in a gloomy mood," Bertie said.

"I *am* in a gloomy mood. We don't have much to tell our bank tomorrow." She looked at Nigel. "Do you think Sir James will be satisfied with what we can share about Hugh Doyle? It really doesn't talk to Etienne Makepeace's relationship to the museum."

Kolya smiled. "If it's more evidence you require, I may be able to provide. . ."

Bertie suddenly silenced Kolya by grabbing his arm. Flick stared at Bertie. His face was glowing.

"Sir James *who?*" he uttered through anger-tightened lips.

"*Uh.* . .Sir James Boyer, the chairman of Wescott Bank."

"Boyer is an insufferable twit! I know, because he used to report to me at MI6 when this whole tea museum business transpired." Bertie made a low-pitched growl. "The twit was on last year's *honors list.*"

"Whoa, whoa. . . ," Flick said. "Boyer knows what happened at the Royal Tunbridge Wells Tea Museum?"

"Of course. He frequently attended those closed-door meetings that have caused you so much fascination."

Nigel joined in. "Then why would he demand that we conduct an investigation into Etienne Makepeace's relationship to the museum? We have to demonstrate that we are a low-risk lender—otherwise Sir James—will not close on the loan we've arranged to finance our acquisition of the Hawker collection."

"James Boyer is as worried about the past as I am—for most of the same reasons. He doesn't want to be linked in any way to Etienne Makepeace or the museum." Bertie frowned. "I'll wager he's looking for an excuse to terminate his business dealings with you."

"Now it all makes sense," Flick said. "That's why he gave us an impossible deadline and impossible demands. He's counting on us to fail. He wants to pull our plug."

"Flip! We've jumped through all those hoops for. . . *nothing!*"

"I wouldn't say that," Bertie said. "Those hoops led you to us. I know how to deal with little Jimmy Boyer."

"You do?" Nigel said.

"One need only point out to him that the breakdown at this point of your loan arrangement will attract the interest of the newspapers."

"True," Flick said. "Especially when we publish a news release explaining what happened."

"You will, of course, have to hold another news conference."

"Indeed, we will," Nigel said.

"At which conference, you will introduce the reporters to Mr. Bertrand Bartholomew and Nikolai Melnikov—the very same gentlemen who became fast friends during the investigation demanded by Wescott Bank. They will explain *why* Sir James felt concerned enough about the distant past to stop a project of promise for the future."

"And you think that will do it?" Flick asked.

"His mind will change as quickly as the weather over Lands End." Bertie suddenly shook his head. "You know, delivering a message like that to James Boyer is simply too much fun to miss. Kolya and I will accompany you tomorrow."

"In that event, we should prepare ourselves," Kolya said. "Perhaps a small disguise that makes you appear somewhat deranged—and thus more dangerous."

"What an extraordinary idea."

As Kolya and Bertie left, Nigel bent close to Flick's ear. "I'm a bit worried about Bertie's plan."

"Why?"

"It may damage my relationship with Olivia Hart."

Flick drove her elbow into Nigel's ribs.

"*Oof.* I was only joking. I promise—I'll never flirt with another woman."

"You had better not. I know how to plant a corpse under a tea bush so that the tree will thrive!"

POSTSCRIPT

Words on a tent card placed on every table in the Duchess of Bedford Tearoom:

- Patrons are advised not to be startled should Earl (the Grey Parrot) begin to trill "Un Bel Di," the famous aria from Giacomo Puccini's renowned opera, *Madame Butterfly*, in the style of Daniela Dessi. The "performance" is merely Earl's creative way of inviting his friend and companion, Cha-Cha, for a visit.
- Cha-Cha is the small, fox-like dog you may see strolling through the exhibits and galleries of the Royal Tunbridge Wells Tea Museum. He's a Shiba Inu and *does* believe he owns the museum.

The following articles—all written by reporter Philip Pellicano—appeared in the *Kent and Sussex Courier* shortly after the events described on the previous pages:

MAKEPEACE DISAPPEARANCE MYSTERY SOLVED

The Kent Police have apparently concluded that Etienne Makepeace, England's renowned "Tea Sage," disappeared some forty years ago because he was shot by a jealous husband in a fit of rage and buried in the garden of the Royal Tunbridge Wells Tea Museum by the same man. A spokesman for the

Kent Police confirmed that they investigated a potential suspect who lived in Tunbridge Wells at the time and is now deceased. They declined to provide the man's name or other biographical details, but our own investigation indicates that the man in question is Hugh Doyle, a bricklayer by trade. He was the husband of Clara Doyle, who worked as a barmaid at The Horse and Garter, a small pub once located on the London Road in Tunbridge Wells.

The sordid chain of events that apparently led to Makepeace's disappearance and death in September 1966 began when he made "untoward advances" toward Mrs. Doyle at the pub and during subsequent liaisons at other locations in and around Tunbridge Wells. Mr. Doyle, a suspicious man by nature, apparently hired Mr. Horace Rampling, a private inquiry agent based in Sevenoaks, Kent, to shadow Mr. Makepeace and Mrs. Doyle. Mr. Rampling evidently provided Mr. Doyle with several photographs depicting questionable behavior on or about September 21, 1966.

On the evening of the same day, Mr. Doyle confronted Mr. Makepeace in The Horse and Garter and threatened his life. Albert "Big Hands" McGuire, the pub's landlord, a retired professional fighter, was able to intervene and prevent violence at that time.

Mr. Makepeace disappeared a few days after this confrontation. Soon thereafter, Mr. and Mrs. Doyle relocated to Glasgow, Scotland, adopted assumed names, and became greengrocers. Mr. Doyle died in 1995, Mrs. Doyle three years later.

Born in 1910 in Winchester, Etienne Makepeace was often called "England's Tea Sage," a moniker he earned in the early

1960s. He is the author of many articles on tea and lectured frequently on the subject, often at the Royal Tunbridge Wells Tea Museum. Makepeace, a bachelor, has one surviving relative, his sister, Mrs. Mathilde Makepeace O'Shaughnessy of Billingshurst, Kent.

RENOWNED ANTIQUITIES COLLECTION ACQUIRED

The Royal Tunbridge Wells Tea Museum has reportedly purchased the Hawker Collection of Antiquities from the heirs of Dame Elspeth Hawker, who died last October in what the police have labeled suspicious circumstances. The fabled Hawker Collection, originally assembled by Commodore Desmond Hawker, perhaps the richest of the nineteenth-century tea merchants, includes more than 2,000 paintings, maps, artifacts, and objects d'art, all related to tea. The collection has been on display at the Royal Tunbridge Wells Tea Museum for the past forty years, on loan from the Hawker family.

"We made the decision to purchase the collection," says Nigel Owen, the museum's director, "to ensure that our institution will remain one of the leading tea museums in the world." Dr. Felicity Adams, the museum's chief curator, adds, "The Hawker Antiquities Collection is absolutely one of a kind. By purchasing the collection, we have secured an important cornerstone of Britain's tea heritage—a treasure trove of artworks and artifacts that can now be enjoyed by the public in perpetuity."

Barrington Bleasdale, Esq., the Hawker family's solicitor, reported that the current generation of Hawkers expressed great delight in knowing that the collection—always a source of great pride to the family—has at last found a permanent home. The family apparently also plans to sell Lion's Peak, the Tunbridge Wells estate on Pembury Road, designed by famed nineteenth-century architect Decimus Burton.

Neither the museum nor Mr. Bleasdale would provide the details of the purchase transactions. However, outside sources say the Hawker Collection of Antiquities is estimated to be worth upwards of fifty million pounds—possibly more, had valuable pieces been sold individually to collectors.

New Lecturer at Royal Tunbridge Wells Tea Museum

The Royal Tunbridge Wells Tea Museum announces that Nikolai Melnikov, a self-taught expert on Asian teas, will be giving a lecture entitled "The Teas Russia Loves" on Friday, March 2 at 2:00 p.m. in the museum's Grand Hall.

Mr. Melnikov, now a British citizen and a resident of Frant, East Sussex, was born and raised in the former Soviet Union, and served in several diplomatic posts, including a stint at the Soviet Embassy in London during the mid-1960s. "Few Britons realize it," Melnikov says, "but Russians consume more tons of tea each year than the English do. Tea truly is one of Russia's national drinks."

When asked how he developed his expertise, Mr. Melnikov replied, "I had unusual opportunities to read and write about tea during my younger years. The information that flowed through my typewriter stayed with me."

Mr. Melnikov has recently become the third volunteer docent at the museum. His lecture is free and open to the public.

ELIZABETHAN FICTION GURUS TO MEET
AT LOCAL TEA MUSEUM

Professor Laurence Garrett, of the University of Kent, has announced that the Kent Chapter of the Society of Elizabethan Fiction will hold its upcoming one-day conference, "The Elizabethans Invented the Romance Novel," on February 26 at the Royal Tunbridge Wells Tea Museum. Persons interested in attending the conference should apply to Professor Garrett.

ROYAL TUNBRIDGE WELLS TEA MUSEUM POSTPONES
ITS ETIENNE MAKEPEACE EXHIBIT

The Royal Tunbridge Wells Tea Museum has announced that it will postpone its previously announced plan to create an exhibit devoted to the life and work of Etienne Makepeace, England's so-called "Tea Sage." The exhibit was to be located in a new gallery, being constructed in vacant space on the museum's second floor, that will highlight the lives and careers of "unusual characters" who played important roles in the history of tea in Great Britain.

Dr. Felicity Adams, the museum's chief curator, explained that, "We decided to 'table' the idea of a Makepeace exhibit because our research into his life has produced confusing results, to say the least. On the one hand, millions of Britons consider Makepeace a unique individual who encouraged countless people to become interested in fine teas. They admire and respect Makepeace for the positive things he did as England's Tea Sage. For example, he was a successful lecturer (not an easy thing to achieve!) and a famed radio personality who managed to 'connect' with his audience and build a large following on the BBC.

"On the other hand, an equal number of people point to the recent disclosures about how and why Makepeace died, argue that he lacked moral principles and integrity, and believe that honoring him with a museum exhibit would be inappropriate.

"At the end of the day, we found it impossible to plan an exhibit in the near term that would tell the Etienne Makepeace story honestly and completely. Perhaps some day in the years to come, we will acquire more information about the Tea Sage's motives and be able to move ahead."

Dr. Adams adds, "It is wise to learn from the past, but foolish to allow the past to dominate our future."

ABOUT THE AUTHORS

Ron Benrey is a highly experienced writer who has written more than a thousand bylined magazine articles, six published books on technical topics, and scores of major speeches for the CEOs of Fortune 100 companies. He holds a bachelor's degree from the Massachusetts Institute of Technology, a master's degree in management from Rensselaer Polytechnic Institute, and a juris doctor from the Duquesne University School of Law.

A native of Royal Tunbridge Wells in Kent, England, Janet Benrey has experience as a successful entrepreneur, a professional photographer, and an executive recruiter. Over the years, Janet has written magazine articles for consumer, business, and special interest publications before working in books. Janet earned her degree in communication (magna cum laude) from the University of Pittsburgh. Together, they are the authors of three books in the Pippa Hunnechurch series, including *Little White Lies* and *The Second Mile*. Ron and Janet love to sail as much as they love to write, and they make their home in Maryland.

If you enjoyed
THE *F*INAL *C*RUMPET
check out the latest by Wanda L. Dyson

abduction

Karen Matthews's worst nightmare has become reality—her baby is gone. When the police call psychic Zoe Shefford to locate the child, Detective JJ Johnson sees the complicated case growing into something truly frightening. Will Zoe and JJ be able to decipher the truth from all the deception before the kidnapper strikes again?
ISBN 1-59310-666-1

obsession

Zoe Shefford and Josiah Johnson team up again to track a serial killer targeting beautiful young coeds. Can they rely on God to stop the serial killer?
ISBN 1-59310-245-3

intimidation

FBI Special Agent Donnie Bevere's wife has been a pawn in a complex game of power, greed, and international terrorism. He must rely on the only people he knows he can trust—Dectective JJ Johnson and private investigator Zoe Shefford—as his wife's life hangs in the balance.
ISBN 1-59310-244-5

Available wherever books are sold.
Or order from:
Barbour Publishing, Inc.
P.O. Box 721
Uhrichsville, Ohio 44683
www.barbourbooks.com

You may order by mail for $9.97 and add $2.00 to your order for shipping.
Prices subject to change without notice.

If you enjoyed

THE *Final* Crumpet

then read

Dead as a Scone

by Ron and Janet Benrey